STORM SHELTER

A DELTA STEVENS MYSTERY

WITHDRAWN

Linda Kay Silva

Other books by Linda Kay Silva:

Taken By Storm
Tory's Tuesday

STORM SHELTER
A DELTA STEVENS MYSTERY

Linda Kay Silva

Cover Design by Hummingbird Graphics
Book Design and Typesetting by Paradigm Publishing

Printed in the United States on acid-free paper
First Edition

Library of Congress Catalog Card Number: 92-063129
ISBN 0-9628595-8-3

DEDICATED TO:

GINA—My best friend, my soulmate, my love. Of all the places I've ever been, you are where I want to be. Now and forever, I want to laugh the hours away and spend the rest of my life doing the HND with you! Thank you, Princess, for being who you are and loving me for who I am. We make a great team.

IN MEMORY OF:

My Grandfather, JOHN HENRY JONES—Who told me I could be anything I wanted to be and made me believe it. If only Papa could see me now.

VERY SPECIAL THANKS TO:

J.P. and GINNY—Whose Costa Rican dreams are just moments away. When the four of us laugh together, nothing else really matters.

CHRISSY—For 16 years of the greatest friendship in the world. Believing in each other is what we're all about. You're the best!

My cousins, KEV, KATE, KRIS, and OTIS—What an incredible gene pool we share. If I haven't told you before, I love you.

BARB—For your wisdom, your guidance, and your understanding of what it takes to get through tough times.

TERESA—For accepting the two of us, and for caring enough to send for Mrs. Prindable!

My "boys"—YERGO, HARRY, ADAM, DEVIN, and COTE—You know the true meaning and value of loyalty and friendship. You guys are, quite simply, the best men in the world! I'll never forget you.

My "girls"—AMANDA, SHIREEN, SARAH, ZOE, CLAUDIA, WICHTER, DANIELLE, CARLA, TOBIN, and ALLISON—Don't ever stop fighting for what you believe in. You are the future.

JACKIE and RUSH—For your encouragement and support. What great pals you are.

KATHI and GINGER—For running a class act and making us feel welcome. Thank you for your wonderful show of support.

DEANNA and BRENDA—For having a vision and including me in it. This is quite a ride!

1

Locking the last cabinet, Ben Friedman filched a small bottle of Quaaludes as he slipped the keys into the pocket of his oversized lab jacket. He'd always considered it one of the few "perks" of being a pharmacist. After all, there was little excitement in mixing potions for runny-nosed children and grumpy adults. What harm was there in skimming a little for personal enjoyment? At least he wasn't selling Valium on the side to neurotic housewives who had nothing better to do than feel sorry for themselves. He wasn't about to play a part in that. The Quaaludes were for his own use.

Lifting his hand out of his pocket, Ben turned out the lights and started for the back door when he heard an odd thumping sound. Reaching again for the lightswitch, he jumped back as he saw a silhouette hovering ominously behind the unopened inventory sitting behind the counter.

"Who's there?" Ben asked, his voice quivering in the semi-darkness of the lab. Its echo came back at him like a slap in the face.

As the room burst into a wave of bright, fluorescent light, the silhouette transformed into a small, angular man wearing a black turtleneck sweater, black trousers, and a black seaman's cap.

"Th-the money's already in the vault," Ben stuttered, backing away from the silent intruder. Something glistened in the man's hand, and Ben could see the sharp edges biting the light.

Still, the dark ghost did not move.

"I'll give you anything you want," Ben begged, backing into one of the glass cabinets. In the harsh light of the room, which seemed to illuminate everything except the intruder, Ben saw two ice-blue eyes glaring at him. They reminded him of shark's eyes—unmoving and murderous.

"Anything. Really," Ben continued, unable to take his eyes off of those lifeless ones staring back at him.

Finally, the specter stepped forward, eyes riveted like two half-penny nails to Ben's, as if attempting to hypnotize him. As the intruder's right hand slowly raised the blade in the air, the demon spoke.

"Anything?"

Ben nodded quickly. The slow, even warmth of his fear spread down his legs, creating a wet spot against his brown pants. "Anything."

The intruder raised the gleaming knife to shoulder height before coming to a halt. The cold, hard eyes were now framed by questioning eyebrows as he pointed the knife's sharp tip directly at Ben.

"Even retribution?"

Arms and legs trembling, Ben attempted a verbal reply, but he could only nod up and down, up and down.

"Good. Then place your keys on the counter and you may leave."

"M-my keys?"

"The keys to this cabinet." The trespasser's voice was cold and devoid of emotion.

Reaching into his pocket, Ben slowly withdrew the keys and quickly set them on the glass cabinet with a "tink." The sharp, watchful eyes frightened him almost as much as the blade hanging in the air like a guillotine.

Without touching the keys, the specter looked at them, smiled, and then nodded, as if he was having a conversation with himself.

"Go."

Ben lurched for the back door. Before his trembling fingers could reach the shiny knob, a flash of brilliance erupted from the hilt of the knife as it plunged deep between his shoulder blades and out his chest. Staring at the blade protruding from his chest, Ben tried to grab it, cutting his hand as he vainly tried to pull it out. He felt no pain now, only a slow numbing sensation he often felt when doing drugs. As he gasped and gurgled, Ben slid down, leaving a bloody trail oozing down the white door. Rolling over on his side, Ben tried to focus on the hazy face of death leering over him. Had he ever seen this man before? Ben wondered, his head now swimming like that time in high school when he first got drunk. With his life slowly trickling out of him, staining the white lab coat bright red, Ben Friedman uttered the last word he would ever speak.

"Why?"

As Ben's head hit the floor, the killer swiped the keys off the counter without making a sound.

"You weren't listening, were you?" he replied, staring down at the dead man. "Retribution, my friend. Good old everyday, garden-variety revenge."

2

Sighing loudly, Delta squinted into the night staring
blankly back at her.

"What's with the heavy sighs? That's the fifth one in
as many minutes," Jan said, as she slowed the patrol car
through an intersection.

Delta turned to her partner and smiled. Although she
and Jan had only been partners a little over six months,
Jan already read her well.

"Is it Megan again?"

Delta looked down at her hands folded in her lap. While
she and Jan had very distinct styles and backgrounds, they
jelled immediately. The way Jan handled herself when they
first met made Delta warm up to her quickly. Delta remembered it as if it happened yesterday.

"I'm sure you did your homework on me," Jan had said
the first night she hopped into the patrol car. Jan had to
hop because she was so short, and this made Delta grin.

"Maybe."

"Well, I've done the same," Jan said, adjusting her
seat belt. "I don't usually beat around the bush, so excuse
me if I seem a little blunt."

Delta bristled, and waited for the "I know you're a
dyke and if you touch me, I'll kill you" routine. There
seemed to be two genres of female cops: the very gay, and
the very straight— few were in between. Many straight
female cops wouldn't have a thing to do with their lesbian
colleagues, and vice versa. Delta hoped that this woman
wasn't one of those who looked upon her lesbian counter-
part with disdain.

Delta's left eyebrow rose as she waited for her new
partner to cast aspersions. "And?"

"And it's no secret that the guys think you're a lesbian." It wasn't an accusation as much as a simple statement. "It makes no difference to me who you sleep with
or what you do on your own time. My main concern is that

you and I get home to our families, whoever they may be, at the end of every shift."

"Then it won't bother you to be in a car with a lesbian for ten hours a night?"

Jan laughed. "Only if you don't use deodorant."

And that was the end of that.

Now staring at Jan's profile, Delta felt pleased. True to her word, Jan neither judged nor condemned Delta's lifestyle nor choice of lovers.

"Yeah, it's Megan," Delta said, settling back into the seat, and gazing out the window into the dark of the night. People of the night reminded her of vampires and other night-crawlers who carefully pick their way through the endless alleyways and deserted parking lots. To Delta, the earth held two coexisting realities: one of the day, where business and industry boomed and people functioned like parts of an enormous clock, and one of the night, where shadows cast irregular dimensions on homeless souls who roamed aimlessly through the darkness. For the night creatures, time was of little import and the major industry was one of either staying alive or finding personal enjoyment.

It was the personal enjoyment industry that Megan had been a part of. Her life had consisted of lying on her back and collecting money from men who paid for a service most men got for free. Only recently had Megan quit her "night" job for a position in the bookstore, at the university, where she was finishing up her business degree. For that, Delta was very grateful. The thought of Megan turning tricks nauseated her, not to mention the dangers of being a prostitute. But Megan had left that life, and the night people with it, far behind.

"How was Mark's game yesterday?" Delta asked, changing the subject.

"He had two hits and stole a base. . ."

Delta waited for the "but." Mark was one of those little boys who possessed more heart than talent.

"But he made two errors at second."

Delta nodded thoughtfully. Right from the start, she had liked Jan's kids. They were well-behaved, respectful, and loved sports. Delta even had gone to a few Little League games and actually enjoyed herself. It was at the first game that Delta's understanding of and respect for Jan, the mother, grew.

They were sitting in the stands with the other mothers, while Jan's husband Dennis was coaching first and her oldest boy, Mark, was playing second. Mariah, who was eight, was climbing one of the larger trees overhanging the creek, and Justin stood in front of them, his two little arms covered to the elbows in mud, showing his mother the frogs he had caught.

Jan didn't miss a thing; she somehow managed to admire the frogs, tell Mariah to stop acting like a monkey, and clap when Mark fielded a ground ball cleanly—while ignoring what some other mother was saying about *her* son never getting a chance to play. Delta was surprised that being a good mother and being a good cop took many of the same skills.

"I'm afraid Mark's a little too preoccupied to be an infielder, but Dennis won't see it," Jan explained, driving down one of the more well-lit areas of their beat.

"I told you. His glove is too big, that's all. Dennis should get him a smaller glove if he wants him to be an infielder. Second basemen always have smaller gloves."

Jan nodded. "Think Dennis would know if I slipped Mark a new one?"

Delta laughed. Jan was always playing games with her husband. Fooling each other seemed to keep their twelve-year marriage fresh and lively. Once, when Dennis made Jan's lunch, he included a trick hard-boiled egg that couldn't be peeled. Delta laughed until her sides ached when Jan cut the egg open, only to find the damn thing was made of rubber.

The radio suddenly jumped to life. "S1012, what's your 20?"

Delta picked up the mike and cleared her throat before answering. "This is S1012. We're heading south on Steinbeck."

"S1012, 10-25 to 1515 Stein Way. The Leather and Lace bar."

The call was a back-up to a popular biker bar well-known for its violent patrons and "accidental" stabbings. Delta requested information about the conditions at the scene. "Could you 10-13 us on that one?" she asked calmly, as Jan drove them up Steinbeck.

"S1012, we have a 418 with a possible 10-31 involved. Be advised, T1418 and S1020 are at the scene."

Switching on the lights, Delta jotted the info on her notepad. They would be arriving as the third back-up unit at a bar where some customers were fighting; and one possibly had an arrest record. It was vital to know as much about a scene as possible prior to becoming a party of it. If one of the fighters had an arrest record, the police would need to approach the situation more cautiously.

Someone with an arrest record was often more desperate than someone who had drunk a little too much and was just acting up. An ex-con not wanting to go back to jail could become extremely hostile in an instant. After all, they *knew* where they would be going and would do what it took not to be sent back.

As they pulled into the jammed parking lot, Delta picked up the mike and notified dispatch that they had arrived. Before she could hang up the mike, Jan was out the door and standing with four other patrolmen. Standing next to the men made Jan appear like a midget, as her five-foot-three frame was overshadowed by their bulkiness. Jan's petite build often made people underestimate her. But Delta had seen Jan in action and knew she was every bit as capable of tossing a large man to the ground as were those four male cops. The thought made Delta proud.

Striding up to the officers, Delta's own five-nine build was a match for all but one of the men, who towered well over six-four. "Whatcha got?" Delta asked, eyeing a biker who had just slunk from the bar.

"Buncha fuckin' dirtbags can't even drink in peace," one of the cops answered.

"They oughtta shut this dive down," came Officer Johnson's baritone voice. "We bust our humps on this place a couple of times a week. I'm sick of it."

Delta glanced over at Hank "Downtown" Brown, one of the meanest cops she'd ever met. He had a reputation for fast hands, swift batons, and a quick temper. He was so nicknamed because he was always threatening to take suspects downtown if they weren't cooperative. Although she had never worked with him as a partner, she'd seen him in action more times than she cared to count.

"Let's just kick some ass and get the hell out of here," came Brown's infamous line. He settled everything as if he were some outlaw sheriff in the wild west.

"Bartender says there are about twenty of them inside, all spoiling for a fight."

Brown looked around the group. "That evens up the odds."

Delta and Jan exchanged glances that did not go unnoticed by Brown's partner, Highbaugh. Delta had gone to the Academy with Highbaugh and he turned out to be a good cop. She couldn't imagine how he could stand to be Brown's partner.

"You two can stay outside if you'd like," Highbaugh offered.

Delta resisted the urge to crack him over the head. Even with her incredible arrest record, she was amazed at how many of "the guys" still treated her like a woman first, a colleague second. While she used to get angry, now Delta only shook her head at their profound ignorance and wondered if things would ever really change.

"No thanks," she answered, shaking her head. "Someone has to go in there and make sure you guys remember which side you're on."

Delta glanced at the front door as the four male cops donned black leather gloves. Because of the A.I.D.S. scare, most cops wore black leather gloves as part of their uniform. But these cops wore gloves for one reason: so there would be no marks on their knuckles should they be investigated for misuse of authority. Since the Rodney King beating, cops everywhere were sensitive to the cry of police brutality. These four were sensitive only about getting caught. Delta had no use for cops with the "bust their heads open" mentality, but clearly, the city was still hiring them. A year and a half ago, when Delta had hunted down the murderous cops who had killed her first partner, Delta wore her own reputation like a badge. Relentlessly, she had pursued the cops responsible for the death of Miles Brookman, the only man she had ever truly trusted. Maybe the only man she had ever loved. This fact was known by most of the law enforcement personnel within a hundred miles of River Valley—and the fact that Delta Stevens was one cop you didn't mess with. Her loyalties and her integrity ran deep enough for her to take on more than most people could ever dream of handling.

"Let's do it," Downtown Brown said.

Jan looked at Delta and shrugged. "You ever get the feeling they forget the protect part of the 'protect and serve' motto?"

Grinning, Delta hiked up her utility belt and followed the men into the bar. Once inside, Delta realized that the entire fracas, if there was one, had ended. The only residue from the fight, if there had been one, was two heavy-set, bearded bikers arm wrestling with great vigor surrounded by an enthusiastic crowd.

"Damn. We're too late," Brown cursed, eyeing the crowd.

Delta walked up beside him and patted his shoulder. "It's okay, Hank. I'm sure you'll get another call tonight that will give you a reason to bash someone's head in."

"Funny, Stevens. Just 'cause you like everything nice and tidy on that snoozer of a beat of yours doesn't mean the rest of us want to die of boredom, too. I go where the action is."

Delta's right eyebrow shot up in a cynical curve. "And if there isn't any, you make some of your own?"

Brown huffed at her and started to turn away, when something caught his eye.

"Hey, Glen," he called, motioning to his partner. "Is that what I think it is?"

Delta looked where Brown was pointing and saw what had caught his attention. Underneath the huge arm of one of the arm wrestlers was a butterfly knife, so named because it looks like a butterfly when it is properly opened. They were popular knives among the biker crowd because they were easy to conceal. They were also as illegal as hell. She knew more cops who had been cut by butterflies than by any other blade.

"Come on, Hank, don't make a big issue of it. Just confiscate it and leave him alone," Delta said, hoping to divert an unnecessary confrontation. "We don't need to start what we came here to prevent."

Hank turned and smiled at Delta. He was a towering monster of a man and used every inch of his stature to intimidate others. Delta, however, didn't intimidate easily. Brown sneered, "Watch a real pro, Stevens."

Before Delta could stop him, Downtown sauntered over to the two large men, pulled out his baton and slammed it down hard on the table. Everyone in the bar stared at Brown and the two arm wrestlers. Glancing over at Jan, Delta shrugged. He had initiated contact with the men; there was no turning back now.

Slowly, the two arm wrestlers released each other's hand. "You ain't got no beef with us," the wrestler with the ZZ Top beard growled.

Delta took a step closer to the scene and wondered why Highbaugh wasn't joining him.

"Del?" came Jan's small voice from behind her.

Turning back to Jan, Delta shook her head. "We can't just walk away, Jan. Someone needs to save him from himself." Delta spotted Highbaugh across the room, but he only shrugged.

"Then," Jan replied, "End it here, so we don't wind up carting half these people to the hospital."

Nodding, Delta turned from Jan and moved slowly toward the table. If she moved in too quickly, the arm wrestlers might feel outnumbered and become aggressive. She cursed Brown for putting her and everyone else in this precarious position. With the knife still on the table, and everyone waiting for someone to make a move, Delta's muscles tensed.

"You guys know you're not supposed to be carrying these knives," Brown said, as he placed his foot on the chair and leaned on his knee. "Says so right in the parole booklet." Brown touched the knife with the tip of his baton and grinned.

Maneuvering to the opposite side of the gathering crowd, Delta did not take her eyes from the knife. Why in the hell was he just letting it sit there? Pick the damn thing up!

As if reading her mind, the hairier biker lunged for the knife just as Brown sent his baton crashing onto the biker's knuckles. As the bear of a man let out a cry of pain, he swiped the knife off the table with his other hand, while pushing Brown's baton out of the way with the damaged hand.

One second faster, three beers earlier, and he might have reached Downtown's throat. Instead, the biker pitched forward, surprised by the baton blow Jan had struck against his back and kidney area. Still clutching the knife, the biker went down on one knee and grabbed his lower back with his free hand. Still huffing and puffing, he rose to his feet and reeled around, only to find himself staring down the barrel of Delta's .357 magnum.

"Drop it!" Delta ordered, pressing her finger lightly on the trigger.

Dropping the knife with a clatter on the hardwood floor, the biker fell back to one knee and grabbed his back again, finally experiencing the full force of Jan's blow through his beer-soaked nervous system.

Suddenly, the instigator of this commotion found his voice again. "I oughtta bust open your stupid skull, you fucking dumbshit!" Brown yelled, raising his baton.

With very little movement, but enough so everyone in the bar could see it, Delta turned her revolver at Brown, who stopped his baton in mid-air.

"Don't," Delta threatened, glaring at him.

The bar was now ten degrees warmer and filled with emotional electricity.

"Put your baton away and go back to work," Delta ordered, keeping an eye on the downed biker. "There's nothing more for us to do here, Brown, so leave it be."

Highbaugh stood next to Brown, who lowered his baton to his side. Brown's expression was a cross between disbelief and profound anger. "You're making a big mistake, Stevens."

Lowering her weapon, Delta shrugged. "Why don't you boys move along now. Jan and I will handle these guys."

Highbaugh grabbed Brown's arm and helped move his reluctant body toward the front door. "Someday, Stevens," Brown yelled when he reached the front door, "you're gonna have to learn to lighten up and be one of us!"

Delta shook her head as she bent down to pick up the knife. "Brown, if being one of you means acting the way you just did, then I'd rather be a meter maid." Watching them walk out of the door, Delta holstered her weapon and motioned for the biker to stand up.

"You pack a mean punch, little lady," the biker said, grinning a toothless smile at Jan as he rubbed his bleeding hand.

Looking at the knife, Delta inspected it more closely. It didn't look like any butterfly knife she had ever seen. This appeared older, as if it might be an antique.

"Nice knife, huh?" the biker said.

Delta nodded. "Nice enough to go to jail for?"

"Ah, man, can'tcha gimme a break?"

Delta looked up from the knife. "I already have." Examining the knife again, Delta was sure it was an antique. "What are you carrying a knife like this around for, anyway? It looks like an antique. I thought bikers kept Bowie knives in business."

The biker resumed smiling. "Got one of those, too."

"I'm quite sure you do. So answer the question." The smile disappeared as quickly as it appeared. There were three things men on the street would boast endlessly about: their cars, their weapons, and their sex tools. They were usually pretty honest about the first two.

"It is. I ain't ever seen one like it either."

"Just the same, they're illegal and I'm going to have to take it in."

The biker nodded.

"But that's all I'm taking. If I have to come back here tonight, I'm coming with a paddy wagon and plenty of 'cuffs. You understand?"

"Yes, ma'am. And thanks, man. Thanks a lot."

Looking over at Jan, who was motioning to her that they should get going, Delta asked, "You need medical attention for your back or anything? I mean, I wouldn't want you to sue me a week from now because of back problems."

He shrugged her off. "Nah. But you can tell that little piece of rat shit that just left that if I ever have the chance of meetin' him in a dark alley, he's gonna need more than that baton to keep me from twisting his neck like a fuckin' turkey."

Smiling, Delta stared out the door. "I'll be sure and tell him."

In the car, Jan shook her head and started to fill out a Quik-Form about the incident. "You amaze me," she said. "That guy could have torn your fool head off."

Delta started the car and drove a few blocks before replying. "The real danger in that bar wasn't those bikers, and you know it."

Jan nodded. "That's another reason why you amaze me so. After all you've been through, you're still able to work with morons like Brown."

Delta looked out the window at the moon. "Grudges are a waste of energy, Jan. I learned that one from my grandmother a long time ago. Young cops fly out of the Academy, ready to right the world of all its wrongs. When they find out it doesn't quite happen that way, they get a little hard-headed."

Jan's eyebrows raised in question. "And Downtown Brown? Is he, too, just hard-headed?"

"Him?" Delta grinned, thinking back to him standing there like John Wayne on rope soap. "No. He's just a dick with a big stick, that's all."

"That's all?"

Delta grinned at her. "Isn't that enough?"

3

It was 1:45 when they received their last call. "S1012, we have a possible 603 at 91 North Hemingway."

Jan picked up the mike and answered that they were less than two minutes away.

Flipping on the lights, but no siren, Delta whipped a U-turn and barreled down 15th Street. Delta hated prowler calls. Inevitably they painfully would remind her of the steep darkness of the inside of the warehouse, where she had tried to escape from a man sent to murder her. A man whose light she snuffed out with two shotgun blasts and that still woke her up at night. The same asshole who had blown Miles's head off a lifetime ago. Since then, Delta regarded 603s as dangerous as "possible shots fired" or "officer down" calls.

As they drove up, Delta remembered that 91 North Hemingway was a tiny drugstore called Troy's. It was a regular drugstore with signs in the window announcing that it was going out of business. Like so many small businesses, Troy's had been unable to keep up with the larger franchises.

As they pulled into the darkened parking lot, Delta noticed that the orange neon "Closed" sign was lit, but the interior lights were on and pouring out into the barren parking lot.

Delta reached over and pulled the shotgun free from its stand. The shotgun had saved her life once, and every time she grabbed its cold barrel, she remembered the blast that propelled her assassin away from her that night in the warehouse. Since then, the shotgun had become her best friend.

"Call for back-up," Delta whispered.

After issuing their back-up request, Jan and Delta slowly and quietly made their way to the back door of the drugstore, which flapped open like a flag in a strong breeze. The call was no longer a "simple" prowler call, but a possible burglary-in-progress, and Jan quietly relayed this information back to dispatch.

Unlatching the safety on the shotgun, Delta motioned for Jan to go in as the low shot. Delta would be over her with the shotgun. Jan nodded and pulled her sidearm from her holster. Unlike Delta, who carried the powerful .357 magnum, Jan carried a 9-millimeter automatic, newly adopted by the department. Most officers liked the automatics because they could squeeze off more rounds than the revolvers. Delta carried a 9-millimeter weapon while off-duty, but she liked the solid feel of the .357 and the way it kicked. She felt that the .357 required more thought when shooting, thus lowering the possibility of injuring innocent people. With the automatic, the rounds were shot so rapidly, that once the trigger was squeezed, you were committed.

Still, she favored the shotgun.

Jan carefully propped the door open with a brick before entering the room, her automatic sweeping the room. In her effort to see beyond her, Jan nearly stumbled on the dead body lying in the entrance.

"Shit!" Jan gasped, crouching behind the corpse for cover.

"Dead?" Delta asked, shotgun resting on her left shoulder and finger poised to stroke the trigger.

Jan looked down at the open eyes, felt for a pulse, and then nodded. "Let's see if our killer is still hanging around."

Five minutes later, after a thorough search turned up no suspect, Delta went to the car and called for Homicide and the coroner before returning to find Jan staring down at the corpse. Real death didn't look like it did in the movies. Corpses often looked like wax mannequins or large ventriloquist dolls.

For a moment, Delta gazed down at the open eyes and wondered why it was that some people died with their eyes open and some with their eyes closed. Was there something voluntarily happening with the nervous system that prompted most victims of murder to die with their eyes open. The thought brought goosebumps to Delta's arms.

"What are you staring at?" Delta asked Jan, who was now squatting and looking intently at the knife protruding from the victim's back.

"Get a load of the handle on that knife."

Delta knelt next to Jan, as she listened for sirens in the background which would announce the arrival of the homicide unit and entourage.

Bending over the body for a better look, Delta studied the knife hilt, which was about six inches long and bejeweled with red, green and blue stones. The design on the metal blade appeared antiquated, perhaps from another country. And the double-snake design gave it a distinctly ancient flavor. Besides the beauty of the handle, Delta noted that the knife had been driven so hard into the back of the dead man that none of the blade was showing; the hilt rested squarely against the blood-soaked lab jacket of the victim. Delta wondered if the victim had seen the knife coming. Had he known he was about to die? Was he trying to escape the brutal death awaiting him? Did he look into the face of his murderer before he died? Was that why his eyes were still open? Shrugging off her questions, Delta turned to Jan and sighed.

"Whoever did this is awfully strong," Delta remarked, staring at the gleaming handle.

"Or awfully angry."

Delta didn't seem to hear this. Instead, she examined the hilt more closely. In the Academy, she had taken a couple of courses on weapons, and this particular knife wasn't what it initially appeared.

"It's a dagger," she stated.

"You suppose those stones are real?"

"Hard to tell." Rising, Delta was careful to avoid touching or stepping on anything that might be evidence. "I doubt it. Our murderer would probably have taken it with him if it was worth anything."

"You think this is a burglar caught in the act?" Jan asked, looking around at the apparently untouched goods in the store.

"Hardly. Look. The keys are in the drug cabinet and there isn't one bottle knocked over."

Jan joined Delta at the counter. "Whoa. Whoever did this could have cleaned the place out and made a few thousand bucks on street sales."

"Precisely my point. They didn't."

Jan nodded slowly. "Motive?" Jan had worked with Delta long enough to know of her penchant for a good murder mystery.

"Too early to call," Delta mused, studying the corpse, the dagger, and the pill cabinet. On the wall above the back counter, were pictures of the store's employees. Delta didn't need to look twice to know which picture was of the dead man. "That poor guy came awfully close to getting away, didn't he?"

Jan shuddered. The blood had coagulated and was already beginning to emit the stench of death. "Just what we need. Another murder in our fair city. Any more of these and the D.A. is gonna have somebody for lunch."

Delta grinned. "Well, it's not going to be us."

In the near distance, Delta heard the approaching sirens turn the corner and roar into the parking lot. She could tell by the squeal of the tires which Homicide detective had been assigned to the case, and she cringed at the thought.

"Those detectives. Don't they ever sleep? How in the hell did they get here before back-up?"

"You already said it. The D.A. is getting tired of people being murdered with nary a suspect to pin it on. She's been running those homicide boys overtime. If they don't come up with someone fast, she may just bust them down to dog catcher."

Delta nodded, remembering last night's muster when the Sarge had said re-election time was coming up and the D.A. needed a suspect for the two unsolved murders in the past three months. Delta hated the politics of law enforcement. She wanted cops to catch the killers because that's what they were paid to do, not because the District Attorney needed a solid case to try. Still, D.A. Alexandria Pendleton had been good to the cops in River Valley and if nailing a suspect would insure her a second term, Delta was all for it. It was Alexandria Pendleton who put Miles's murderers behind bars for a long, long time.

Still looking at the corpse, Delta averted her eyes from the pool of dull red blood. "Wonder why the killer let him get so close to escaping?"

Jan shrugged. "Maybe he knew the guy."

"Maybe. Or maybe our man is just a real sicko."

Jan shook her head. "Aren't they all?"

"Who? Men or murderers?"

Jan shrugged. "Aren't they usually the same?"

"Why, my little partner, I do believe I just heard a sexist comment coming from the old married one." Delta winked, but she could see that the smell of blood was nauseating Jan.

"I'm just sick of the whole murder scene thing."

Delta nodded and knelt down for one last look at the dagger before Forensics showed up and confiscated it. "I may be way off here, Jan, but something in my gut is telling me that what we have here is more than just a single murder."

"Well, do us both a favor and keep your ideas to yourself. The last time you offered to help Detective Leonard, he nearly had you suspended. Let this one go, Del."

Delta withdrew her notepad from her pocket and quickly drew a sketch of the hilt. She knew Forensics would have plenty of pictures of the hilt by the time they were through with it, but that didn't guarantee she would ever be allowed to see them.

Glancing at Delta sketching, Jan shook her head. "Delta . . ."

"I know what I'm doing, Jan. Trust me. Something tells me we're going to see this guy's handiwork more than just once."

Jan groaned. "And something tells me that we've just entered the game."

Delta grinned. "Bingo."

4

The stench of blood and death still lingering in her nasal passages, Delta plopped down on the chair next to Connie, a striking Mexican woman, who was navigating a little, dwarf-like creature through a maze on her computer. Once the elf was safe atop a giant toadstool, Connie turned and greeted Delta with a flawless smile.

"Hi, Con," Delta said softly. "You and Eddie winning?"

"Eddie" was the name Connie had given her computer years ago.

Connie grinned widely as she answered, "Do ducks pooh in the water?"

Delta forced a grin. "Luckily, I wouldn't know."

The constrained grin did not go unnoticed. Turning the monitor off, Connie reached over and laid her hand on Delta's knee. "You okay?"

Delta glanced sideways toward the women's bathroom to signal that she needed privacy. What she was going to say wasn't for general consumption.

Once in the bathroom, Delta paced over to the far wall. She had waited all night to talk to Connie about her fears of failing at her relationship—not that she wasn't comfortable talking to Jan, but Connie really understood her relationship with Megan. Connie had been there since its onset and well knew the hurdles Delta and Megan had faced and surmounted.

Connie folded her arms and waited. "I know that look. You're still worrying about Megan, aren't you?"

Turning to face Connie fully, Delta nodded. Connie Rivera was her best friend. They had been through the best and worst of law enforcement together. Without Connie's masterful computer genius and her incredibly analytical insight, Delta might not have brought Miles's killers to justice. Without Connie's wisdom and compassion, Delta would have foundered in the days after the trial. She spent hour after hour searching for some meaning to all of the death and destruction which tore a jagged gash through her spirit, like a tornado in a cornfield. Connie had been her island in the midst of tumultuous waters, when Delta struggled with the love she had for a woman who walked on the other side of the law. It was Connie whom Delta turned to when she needed a dose of common sense or a warm hug. And right now Delta needed both.

Jamming her hands in her pockets, Delta exhaled loudly. "It hasn't been a year yet and already things seem to be souring. There's so much about this job she doesn't understand, and there's so much about the changes in her life that I don't understand."

Connie smiled warmly. "Being a cop's lover is a hell of a lot harder than either of us could ever really know. Ask Gina. She worries so, and I'm not even out on the street. Give Megan some time to get used to the fact that you risk your life every night out there."

"A year isn't enough?"

"Maybe for you. Don't put her on your timeline."

Delta thought about this before responding. "I just want her to understand why I love what I do. I don't think she gets it."

"Can you blame her? Not many people understand why someone would want to risk their lives for people they don't even know. And, considering her own checkered past, she's going to need some time to adjust. Don't rush her, for God's sake. She's the best thing that's happened to you in years."

Delta studied her nails. "She is, isn't she?"

"Yes, and she's trying to understand why you spend twelve hours a day at this crazy job."

Delta broke into a grin. "It is crazy, isn't it?"

Connie nodded and absent-mindedly started to braid her long black hair over her shoulder. "Very crazy. And now that she isn't in the middle of any craziness herself, she might not understand why you want to be. But, Del, she loves you, not your job."

"Yes, she does."

"Then, stop your moping around and go tell her how much you love and appreciate her. Damn it, Del, you have to bend here a little, too. You're so used to getting your own way that, when someone else has their own opinion and ways of doing things, you make them fish or cut bait. Lighten up on her a little, will you?"

Delta looked down into Connie's dark brown eyes. Connie Rivera was the only person in the world who could be so candid with Delta without worrying about pissing her off.

"Con, I don't know what I'd do without you."

"You'll get my bill."

Delta laid her hand on Connie's shoulder. "You're worth every penny, my friend."

Connie's eyes warmed. "All I know is that it's obvious that you two adore each other. Don't let your job stand in the way of your happiness, Del. You can have both, but you have to be willing to compromise as well."

"Are you saying I don't?"

Connie shook her head and smiled. "Not unless you absolutely have to. You're the most stubborn woman I know, Delta Stevens. If you want this one to work, you're going to have to bend."

Delta heaved a loud sigh. She wasn't used to bending. She was used to calling the shots in both her personal and professional life. Patience came seldom and compromise was something other people did. "I'll try. But we both know that flexibility isn't one of my character strengths."

"Don't I know it." Opening the door, Connie walked back to her desk and pulled the disk from Eddie before turning the computer off. "If you're serious about making your relationship work, you'll dig deeper into yourself to find a little compromise. Megan deserves that much, Del, and you know it."

Picking her keys up off the desk, Delta knocked a small black case onto the floor. She had seen plenty of these cases around Connie's house, but Connie seldom left them on her desk for any of her "superiors" to see.

"Not another game," Delta mocked, tossing it back on the table. "You must spend a fortune on these things."

Connie picked the case up and looked carefully at it. "Not this one. It came in the mail for me this morning."

Delta took it from Connie's hands and inspected it. "I can't believe you still play these silly things." In college, Connie had been a whiz at beating people in computer simulation adventure games. Connie had graduated from M.I.T., or "The Institute," as alumni liked to call it, and was exceptional at anything computer-related. When computers started to infiltrate police departments around the country, law enforcement officials were suddenly faced with their own ignorance about computer operations. Many P.D.'s were desperate to hire qualified people who could manage, control, and understand the intricacies of computer operations. Connie was one of those people. She knew how to enter computers which were off-limits to everyone except the FBI and the Justice Department. She could make a computer do everything except wash windows, thus making her a most valuable resource on River Valley's department.

But when work was slow for her, she would pop in a computer simulation game and play when no one was looking. Not that anyone ever really checked on her. Most of the captains didn't really know what she did. All they knew was that they went to her whenever they needed information from some file. Unfortunately for Connie, there were few games that challenged her extreme intelligence, but she played everything in hopes of finding something to keep her entertained for a few hours, while she waited for an assignment.

Laying the case down, Delta shook her head. "That's odd. No label or manufacturer or anything."

Connie glanced casually at it and shrugged. "One of the guys probably sent it to me. Remember when Bear sent me that game that I didn't know was pornographic until I walked into the dungeon?"

Delta nodded and smiled, remembering how embarrassed Connie was when the guys gathered around her computer. "Well, good luck in your simulated fight for truth and justice." Grabbing her windbreaker off the peg, Delta jammed her arms in. "You going home?"

Connie nodded. "Soon. I just need to get passed this one creature and I'll be on my way."

Delta shook her head. "I hear those games are addicting."

"And I hear your mother calling you to come home. Let me know how it goes with you and Meg, okay? You know, she's my favorite of all the women you've seen since I've known you."

Delta smiled down at Connie. Although nearing forty, Connie could easily pass for being in her mid-twenties. Her long black hair hanging down around her lower back accentuated her Latina heritage and gave her a Native American appearance. Her skin, carmel in color and void of any imperfections, was warm and inviting. But the feature which was so alluring, so hard to resist, was her flashing smile. Connie could sell the Brooklyn bridge with that smile. She could also talk Delta into just about anything with her playful grin and dancing eyes.

Zipping her jacket up, Delta headed for the door. "I thought you always had a thing for my little girlfriend."

"I do. She's a good woman, and as Goddess knows, she's good for you. You need someone who won't let you walk all over her."

"I thought you were on my side?"

"I am. That doesn't mean I have to agree with you when you're acting like a boob. Go talk to her. Tell her how you're feeling. And for Pete's sake, stop feeling like you have to be in control of every situation."

"I don't do . . ."

"Oh, yes, my friend, you do. And it would be ill-advised for you to argue this case unless you want me to point out all the times your controlling behavior munched your relationships. Now get out of here, so I can get Link back to the Crystal Palace of Lanzarr."

Delta chuckled. "Munched?"

"Like a dragon eating my little dwarf here. Do yourself a favor, Storm, and bend. I promise, it will only hurt a little."

Picking her truck key from the rest of the keys on her ring, Delta nodded. "10-4. Thanks."

"Now go, before Link gets swallowed up by some menace and I have to start over."

Delta just shook her head. "You and those damned games. I'll never understand it."

Connie shrugged as her hands moved the joystick to help Link avoid a slimy creature rising from the bog. "Mental gymnastics, Del, that's all. Now go home. Directly home." Turning from the computer, Connie frowned. "And whatever happened on your beat tonight, you better just leave here. I know you better than you think, Storm, and I know you handled something tonight that's bugging the shit out of you."

Delta opened her mouth to respond, but Connie held up her hand. "Not now. You deal with your relationship now and leave the job here."

Delta nodded and waved goodbye to Connie before she pushed open the glass doors. Excited about spending a few quiet and loving moments with her lover, Delta pushed back the images of a jeweled dagger, a dead pharmacist, and a sick murderer skulking around her beat.

5

When Delta entered the bedroom, her heart fluttered. She often got those "honeymoon" goosebumps when she saw Megan. The connection they shared ran deeper than simple physical lust; Delta loved Megan Osbourne on a level she had never experienced before. And now, seeing Megan sitting primly at her vanity, brushing out her lengthy blonde hair, Delta felt the familiar and welcome pangs of love. It was a love born from a time in her life more painful than any Delta had ever encountered.

It was a little more than a year ago that Delta was in the middle of an emotionally exhausting murder investigation in which Megan played a vital role. It was with Megan's help that Delta and Connie had been able to unlock the mystery of the brutal murder of her partner and friend, Miles Brookman. Delta and Megan were drawn to each other almost immediately, and once they made peace with their opposing professions, they fell into bed and into love. Shortly after the trial, Megan quit prostituting and opted, for the first time in her adult life, for a life on the right side of the law.

Leaning into the room from the doorway, Delta smiled. "Busy?"

Looking over her shoulder, Megan smiled back and laid her brush down. Her smile displayed even rows of perfect white teeth surrounded by lips so pink they needed no make-up. But it wasn't her sensuous mouth that captivated Delta's attention all those months ago—it was her incredible, electric blue eyes that flashed brilliantly whenever they looked into Delta's. Those eyes expressed more than her beautiful mouth ever could. And when they gazed into Delta's eyes, they lit up and glimmered like nothing Delta had ever seen.

They were shining at Delta right now.

"Never too busy for you, my love."

Delta slowly closed the door and leaned against it. Even in the dim light of the room, Megan was the most beautiful woman she had ever met. But it wasn't just her physical being that exuded beauty and grace; there was a warmth and compassion about her that emanated beauty of the richest depth. Megan was an incredible woman, not just in physical appearance, but inwardly as well.

"Can we talk?" Delta asked.

Megan cocked her head and her hair fell over one shoulder. "I was hoping we could."

"I don't want to fight," Delta said, not moving from her place at the door.

Rising, Megan floated over to her as if walking on wind. "Neither do I."

"I've been an ass about this whole thing."

Taking Delta's hands in hers, Megan's smile widened. "Yes, you have. But then, we all have our moments, don't we?"

Delta nodded.

"But you're in luck. Today, there happens to be a sale on forgiveness for people who are having their moments."

Delta sighed. "I'm glad. My moment seems to have extended itself some." Delta looked up into Megan's eyes and saw the same love and concern she'd seen nearly a year ago. Megan was one of the few women Delta knew who actually towered over her. Standing over six feet in her stocking feet, Megan was all legs. And when she wore pumps, which was almost always, she stood at an imposing six-three.

Delta had fallen in love with Megan before she was aware of it, so embroiled was Delta in finding Miles's murderer. When they found themselves drawn to each other, it opened a whole different side of the world for each of them, worlds in which both were just now beginning to struggle. And while their careers had been on opposing ends of the justice spectrum, neither was willing to give up the love they had found.

"Meg, are we okay?"

Stepping up to Delta, Megan placed her arms across her shoulders and pulled her closer. Delta could smell her Opium perfume—the same scent Megan had worn when they first met.

"God, Del, I hope so. You can be such an impossibly stubborn fool sometimes."

Delta bowed her head. "I know. But that's what you love about me."

Megan stifled a grin. "Sometimes, it is. But I worry when you try to stop all the crime personally."

Pulling back enough to see Megan's face, Delta inhaled slowly. "And you think that's what I do?"

Megan shrugged. "That's how it feels sometimes. You get so involved in your work that you forget we exist. You go away from me, from us, and I don't know how to reach you."

Delta knew exactly what Megan meant. Sometimes, the job preyed so heavily on her mind, Delta could think of nothing else. "I want us to last, Meg. I want us to be the couple that younger lesbians look at and ask us how we do it. I want forever. You know that, don't you?"

Megan's eyes softened with the tone of her voice. "Yes, I do. But honey, you also want to save the world from itself. I guess . . . I just thought that we would be enough for you, and now, I'm not sure." Megan let go of Delta and walked over to the window and opened it. Sounds from the city flooded in and she had to close it again. "And, frankly, that scares the shit out of me."

The pain in Megan's voice ran hotly through Delta's heart. She'd had this conversation with every lover she'd been with since she became a cop, and the problems were always the same: she spent too much time doing what she loved and not enough time with the ones she loved. She had hoped she would be different with Megan. She had hoped, by some miracle, that she had changed enough to put her relationship first. Clearly, she had not.

"I don't know how to change, Meg. I honestly don't know what to do to make things any better. I thought I was giving our relationship everything I had, and BOOM, you tell me I'm not. I honestly don't know how to give a relationship my best energy."

Megan smiled sadly. "I know. And if I weren't so crazy about you, I would have walked out the door a long time ago. I need you to be here, to be present with me in our relationship. You can't put a relationship on autopilot when your job demands it and come back expecting us not to have crashed."

"Have we crashed?" Delta asked, the words jumping off her lips.

Megan shook her head. "Not yet. But if you keep devoting more time and energy to your career, we may. I can't hold our relationship together by myself."

Fear grabbed Delta by the throat. "I don't want to lose you, Meg."

"Then don't. That choice is up to you. I know how much your job means to you, but damn it, Delta, sometimes you just have to stop being a cop. Sometimes, you need to just be Delta Stevens, Megan's lover. I'd even take just plain old Delta Stevens."

Curling up in Megan's arms, Delta felt very small. "Maybe that's what I'm afraid of. Maybe I don't know who that is anymore."

Megan kissed the top of Delta's head and hugged her tightly. "Well, my love, I think it's time you found out. Put the badge away when you come home and give your mind a rest. Focus on us, on our love, and see where that takes you. Let our relationship be number one for awhile."

Burying her face in Megan's hair, Delta sighed. It seemed such an easy request. Why had it been so hard in the past to put love first and the job second? And why hadn't she learned from her past mistakes?

"I'll try harder to do that, Meg. Trust that I will."

Megan pulled away and stroked Delta's cheek with the back of her hand. "Oh, Delta Stevens, trust you to what? Trust that you'll jump in front of a speeding bullet to save some street person? Trust that you'll push the speed limit when responding to a domestic quarrel? Trust that you'll come home and forget about the abused child you held, or the dying man's last words? That's a tall order from someone who cares about your job as much as you do."

Delta nodded. Yes, it was. Megan knew her well enough to know that Delta might stop thinking about her job, but she never truly would stop living it. She cared about what happened to the people on her beat. Sometimes, that caring took over her whole life.

But her life was different now. Now, Megan loved her in spite of her flaws and weaknesses, and Delta wasn't willing to give that up.

"I don't deny that it is a tall order, but damn it, Megan, why can't I have both? Why can't I be a good cop and have the love of my life, too?"

"You can, it's just going to take a little work. All I'm saying, sweetheart, is that relationships take a lot of work, and both people must be willing to work hard at keeping it together."

"I'm used to hard work," Delta replied. The fear receded for the time being, leaving her feeling a little stronger.

"Well, this might prove to be even harder than police work, Delta Stevens, because relationships don't come with manuals, proper procedures, or guarantees. It's going to take more patience and understanding than either of us has ever given before. I mean, let's face it, we're coming at this from two completely different angles. If we stop communicating, we're finished. Through. Kaput."

"All right, I get the picture. Just tell me that we're still on firm ground."

Megan kissed Delta. "Still firm, my love. It isn't time for a major panic, but we do need to get back on parallel paths."

"We can do that," Delta said, kissing Megan lightly on the cheek. Megan's rational approach to life was another facet that so attracted Delta to her in the first place. "I love you so much, Megan Osbourne."

"And I," Megan replied, kissing Delta tenderly, "am crazy about you."

"Then, we're okay?"

Megan grinned. "Count on it."

6

A low, threatening growl filled the still night air like an ominous warning. Chained to the two-by-four securely bolted next to a rack of gloves was 120 pounds of broad-chested, mean-looking Doberman, baring teeth in a vicious snarl. Ever so slowly, the massive beast rose to its feet, while emitting menacing warnings. Its beady eyes locked onto the intruder's as it bared even more fangs and lowered its pointed head.

Before the dog could leap, a large piece of meat flew out of the darkness and landed with a splat at the feet of the animal, who sniffed at it before devouring it in two large bites. As it licked its chops, the dog began wavering back and forth like a drunk on the street. In less than a minute, it salivated profusely, then wobbled over into the corner and slumped down on its side. As the dog labored to breathe, it whined a moment and then suffered a body-shaking convulsion. It shuddered once more before gasping its last breath as it laid its head down and died.

Thirty seconds later, the intruder stepped over the dog's bulk and peered closely at the vast assortment of guns and knives enclosed in a "burglar proof" case. The case was wired to an alarm by a thin, translucent wire running the length of the glass.

Turning from the case, the dark-clad intruder crept through the shop until he came to an imposing set of armor, standing watch in the corner opposite the dead Doberman. As a beam of moonlight bounced off the knight, the intruder stood, mesmerized by the ancient beauty and strength of a long-forgotten warrior.

Shifting ever so slightly, as if afraid to awaken the sleeping Titan, the thief's hand moved to touch the long, double-bladed ax held in the left glove of the knight. Running his fingers up the handle to the blade, like a man running his fingers along his mistress's leg, the thief smiled at the sharpness of a blade few knights ever truly mastered.

In an instant, without making a sound, the intruder lifted the ax from the gauntlet and held the ax in both hands. For a moment, the intruder stared at it, as if doing so might magically transform him to a time when men were chivalrous and women were nothing. Ah, those must have been the days.

Rubbing the blade lightly with his fingertips, amazed by the biting sharpness of an ancient relic of man's bloodier history, he quickly withdrew a cut finger from the blade and gently stuck his finger in his mouth to suck the blood. He smiled at the knowledge that the blade could still hurt—even maim.

Hoisting the ax over his shoulder, the thief stepped over the dog once more and headed for the window. In the far distance of the dark night, sirens blasted through the air, warning of their approach.

Turning to the dog, the thief nodded. "Sorry old boy. Must have it."

Hearing the sirens round the corner, the intruder looked at his prize and smiled before scrambling out the window. The game was afoot, and they didn't even know it yet.

7

Jumping in the driver's side of the patrol car, Delta held out the report she'd been reading.

"What is it?" Jan asked.

"It's the detective's report about the pharmacist's murder a few days ago."

"Yuck. Why would you want to read that thing?" Jan screwed up her face and pushed the report away from her. "I've got this good book I've been rea—"

"Funny." Opening the report, Delta ran her finger down the page until she came to the note she was looking for. "It's a bizarre case."

"Most murder cases are."

Delta shook her head. "This one feels different. There are some strange things that just don't add up."

"Like the fact that we're not sure the perp took anything?"

Delta nodded. "Not that we know of. I believe the killer came after something specific and I think he got it." Delta looked down at the report, which had various areas highlighted in yellow.

"What makes you so sure?"

Flicking on her spotlamp as they cruised in a neighborhood where the streetlights had all been broken, Delta inhaled slowly. "You noticed how perfectly neat every drug cabinet was? He didn't even rummage around looking for drugs, nor did he just swipe whatever drugs could be found for a quick street sale. I think he knew what he wanted before he got there."

"What about the pharmacy inventory?"

Delta shook her head. "It isn't finished yet. But I'd bet my truck that there's a certain drug missing from those cabinets."

"So, are you leaning toward a failed burglary?"

Delta studied the report before answering. "This wasn't a random killing. I don't believe that a burg got caught and had to kill Friedman."

"So maybe the motive was murder."

"Don't you think the perp would have at least tried to make it look like a robbery? And if the motive was murder, why in the drugstore? The murderer could have waited outside, instead of risking the confines of the store. Remember how dark the parking lot was?"

Jan nodded.

"The killer could have waited, killed Friedman in the darkness of the parking lot, and been long gone before anyone ever knew. Instead, the murderer chose to kill him in the light of the drugstore. It doesn't make sense."

"Most murders don't, Del."

Delta acted like she didn't hear her. "And why did he leave the dagger? A relic like that is a pretty big clue. This guy didn't stab Friedman with a butcher knife. He killed him with an antique; and a valuable one at that."

Jan turned and stared at Delta. "What's with you?"

Closing the report, Delta shrugged and looked out the window. Catching crooks was something she was extremely good at, and she prided herself on the length and breadth of her arrest record. As a young girl, she dreamt of arresting bad guys and being a hero. The first time her grandfather bought her a shiny toy badge from Safeway, Delta was hooked. She wanted a real one when she grew up, and as soon as she finished college, she went straight into the Police Academy.

She had never regretted it.

"It's the mystery of it all, Jan. Don't you want to know why Ben Friedman was killed?"

"Sure, but let the detectives earn their keep. It's our job to try to prevent crimes. When we can't, it's the dicks' turn. Give it a rest."

Delta did not turn her eyes from the road. "Resting" wasn't something Delta Stevens did very well. Ever since she took this beat, she felt a duty, an obligation, to the people on it. If there was some kind of crazed maniac going around murdering people, it was up to her to help stop him. She couldn't simply hand over the case to the detectives and then go about her merry way. She had to do something. It was what made her Delta Stevens.

"Del? What's going on in that head of yours?"

"Nothing. It's just that Homicide has their hands full with those two murders earlier this month. It won't hurt if I just think about the evidence, right?"

Jan laughed. "Right. And I should apply to be the Queen of England."

Delta turned toward her. "What's that supposed to mean?"

"It means you never mind your own business. Everyone's business on our beat is your business, Del. The only real question is whose business are you minding this case for?"

Delta turned away, her fierce loyalty to the District Attorney who put Miles's murderers away was worn on her sleeve like expensive cufflinks.

"Ah, now we get to the bare bones of the matter. I know who you're covering for now. I can't believe it took me this long to figure out."

Delta looked away from Jan. "I don't know what you're talking about." But Delta knew they both knew what, and who, they were talking about.

"The media is having her for breakfast, lunch, and dinner over the unsolved murders in this city, and District Attorney Pendleton is desperately in need of a suspect."

Delta shrugged. "So?"

"So, it's re-election time, and wouldn't it be nice if you could hand a suspect over to her? How close am I?"

"Pretty close." Delta said it so quietly, Jan barely heard her.

"Excuse me? Did I hear you say 'pretty close?' How about giving full credit where it's due? I'm on the mark, aren't I?"

Delta inhaled a resigned sigh. When she and Alexandria Pendleton first met, they weren't exactly on the same side. Alexandria needed a clear case in order to convict the cops who were running a drug ring that had killed two officers, and Delta handed her one. Well . . . it wasn't spit-and-polished clean, but it was enough for Alexandria to go on. Alexandria had gone for the maximum sentence and got it. In Delta's book, Alexandria Pendleton was a heroine.

"Look, if I can help Alex out, then I will. Besides, this last murder is our business now. It happened on our beat, and we're involved in it whether or not we want to be."

"Involved? Interesting choice of words."

Delta grinned. "You know what I mean."

"Why, Delta Stevens, if I didn't know you were so crazy in love with Megan, I'd think you have a crush on our renowned District Attorney."

Delta felt her face flush hot. "Don't be stupid. I owe her a big favor, that's all. I believe in paybacks."

"I remember."

"You may remember, Jan, but you can't possibly know the debt I feel for the way she put those scum away. She asked for the max, and she got it. Not only did she get it, but she kept me out of it as much as possible. I put my career on the line to find Miles's killers and she made sure I still wore a badge when the trial was all over. I owe her for that."

"I just don't like how you act when you feel you 'owe' someone. From what I understand, she did her job well when she prosecuted those cops. But Del, that's what the good citizens pay her to do. She didn't really do anything out of the ordinary."

Thinking back to the warehouse, where she was supposed to have been killed, Delta shivered. Not Jan, not Alex, not anyone except Connie, Megan, and Gina knew to what extent her involvement was in setting the dirty cops up to take the fall. Alexandria didn't just do her job, she had done it exceedingly well. For that, Delta would be eternally grateful.

Before Delta could respond to Jan's comment, the radio interrupted.

"S1012, we have an S-100 at 137 South Pope Street. What's your 20?"

Jan replied that they were one minute away from the address given and that they'd take the call.

An S-100 meant that a silent alarm had gone off, and there was the possibility of catching a burglary in progress. It also meant that a back-up unit had been dispatched as well. The call, while not entirely devoid of danger, usually meant that the units arrived after the damage had been done. It was rare that cops walked into a burglary-in-progress and actually caught someone.

Delta turned the interior lights on while Jan rifled through the personal address book she always carried with her. Glancing over at the tiny notebook, Delta shook her head. Jan was the only cop Delta ever worked with who carried around the names and type of stores on their beat. Each entry was listed alphabetically and cross-referenced by street and street number. It was a pretty comprehensive guide to the merchants they frequently dealt with. Jan used it as a means of better preparation whenever they rolled up to an address. She would flip through her book and announce the name and type of business before getting out of the car. Knowing her routine by heart, Delta slowed down and waited for Jan's pronouncement.

"It's that little hunting and sporting goods store called Omega's."

Delta winced. It wasn't the safest place to catch a thief. "Oh, great. Just what we need: to face a perp who is better armed than us."

Jan smiled. "Aren't they all? Geez, just the other day, Hayward had to take out a thirteen-year-old who was carrying."

"I heard. Is the kid going to make it?"

Jan nodded. "Until the next time, I suppose."

Delta knew the fears Jan carried with her, having children growing up in such a hostile and exceedingly violent society. Jan had been in tears when trying to explain to her children why that truck driver had been beaten up on television during the Rodney King riots when he hadn't done anything. Her kids did not understand.

It was times like those that Delta did not envy motherhood.

Turning her attention to the call at hand, Delta grabbed both her baton and her flashlight.

"If there's someone in there, Del, let's take him out early. I don't like the idea of being in a gunshop with some whacko."

"Got it."

Pulling into an alley a half a block away from Omega's, Delta and Jan hopped out of the car. When Delta came around to Jan's side, Jan handed her the shotgun.

"A gal's best friend," Delta whispered, turning her radio on low.

As they approached the darkened building, Delta heard a clattering sound from around the corner. Kneeling down, Delta swung the shotgun around the damp brick edge and sighted a shadow running away from the back entrance of Omega's.

"Damn!" she cursed, handing the shotgun to Jan. "I'll go." And in an instant, Delta was off, her thirty-six inch stride propelling her toward the shadow bolting away from her.

"Police!" Delta yelled, knowing that it made absolutely no difference to the retreating thief. The law prohibited cops from shooting at a fleeing felon. Only cops in movies could pull out their weapons and blast a hole in the back of some sleazy crook. Real life law enforcement was vastly different than what the public saw on television. She either had to catch him or forget it. As he scaled the six-foot alley wall leading to the main boulevard, Delta knew she would probably have to forget it. Once in the thick of things, he would blend right in.

And then, quite suddenly, he stopped when he reached the top of the wall, turned toward her, and threw a shiny, metallic object at Delta. Then he clambering over the top and out of sight.

"Son of a bitch!" Delta muttered, barely catching a glimpse of metal before diving behind a trashbin.

Pulling her revolver, Delta sped around the bin, aiming her .357 at the top of the wall, but he was gone. She hadn't even heard him land on the other side.

"Gone. Damn it!" Reholstering her sidearm, Delta pulled her radio from its case and gave what description she could of her would-be assailant and the direction she thought he headed. Pulling her flashlight off her belt, Delta searched for the object the perp had thrown at her.

As the light swept in front of her, the object glistened beneath the rays from the heavy six-cell flashlight. Raising the light to eye level, the object shone brightly against the dull, splintered side of the fence surrounding the trash cans. Mesmerized by the gleam, Delta stepped closer for a better look.

"I'll be damned," she said, eyeing the six-pointed Chinese star stuck in the wood. It was a very sharp, very impressive-looking weapon used by martial arts experts in the Orient. Delta hadn't seen one since her Academy days.

Taking a handkerchief from her back pocket, Delta wrapped it around the star and tugged hard, pulling the star from its cutting grip on the aged wood.

She then entered the back door of the shop. The lights were on and Jan was taking notes from a man in stocking feet and bare chest. The man was kneeling down, stroking the dead Doberman, and shaking his head every now and then as he answered questions.

Jan stopped taking notes long enough to fill Delta in on what she'd heard so far. "He lives a few blocks away and has an audible hook-up to the alarm. Apparently, he'd been robbed a couple of times before he got the alarm and the dog.

Delta nodded, feeling her heart bang heavily against her chest as the adrenaline coursed through her veins like she'd overdosed on caffeine. It had been awhile since someone on the street had attacked her, yet the feeling was always the same.

"Anyway," Jan continued, "When he got here, he found the back window open and the dog dead. He doesn't think anything was stolen but won't be sure until he does a final inventory."

Squatting down next to him, Delta touched the dog's ear. "A pet?"

The man shook his head. "Not really. Still, you spend ten, maybe twelve, hours a day with an animal, I guess you kind of start caring more than you know. I hope whatever killed him didn't hurt him any. I'd hate to think he suffered."

Delta studied the man. A Marine tattoo on his right arm and a possible shrapnel cut across his left brow suggested to Delta he was a veteran of some war, probably Vietnam.

"Sure was a beautiful dog," Delta remarked as she stood and leaned against a sign announcing a 50% clearance sale.

"Yes, he was." The man rose, pulling his sagging pants with him. "What kind of a creep comes into a store, kills a dog and leaves without taking anything? I mean, all of my antique swords are still in the case, none of the more expensive knives are missing. I've got some valuable stuff in here, and it doesn't look like he took a thing."

Delta and Jan exchanged glances.

"Maybe he didn't have time," Jan offered.

Delta looked at Jan out of the corner of her eye. Turning to the owner, Delta showed him the Chinese star. "You sell these?"

Looking at the star, the shopkeeper shook his head. "No way. They're illegal, and I run a clean business."

Delta smiled. "I'm sure you do, Mr. . . . "

"Ein. Matt Ein."

"Well, Mr. Ein, I'm sure you run a legit business, but can you tell me where I would be able to purchase one of these?"

Bringing Delta's hand closer to his face, he studied the star. "Kids usually purchase stars from martial arts and mercenary magazines."

Delta caught the hesitation in his voice. "But?"

Matt Ein shook his head. "But this sure isn't one of them."

"What do you mean?"

"Officer, that there is a real Ninja star, not one of those toys sold in those magazines. It's an antique of sorts; you know, the ones the ancient Ninjas used to have. You can tell by the carved dragon emblem in the middle."

Delta looked more closely at the star. She hadn't noticed the dragon emblem on the other side of the star.

"Del?" Jan glanced at the star. "Where'd you—"

"He threw it at me," Delta answered. "A real Ninja star, eh?"

Matt Ein nodded and pushed some stray hairs away from his face. "It sure is. Lucky for you the guy throwing it wasn't a real Ninja. Legend has it they were flawless."

Delta nodded. "A good thing he wasn't." Delta carefully wrapped the star in the handkerchief. "There seems to be a lot of antique weapons floating around the streets these days. Have you recently sold a dagger with gemstones on the handle?"

Matt Ein shook his head. "I don't sell antique daggers, but I do collect them. If you have a picture, I might be able to place it for you."

Delta nodded and watched as Jan wrote this information in her notepad. "Mr. Ein, are you sure nothing was taken from the store?"

"I've looked through every case, and they're locked tight. Even the crossbows, which I don't keep locked up, are all there."

"Thank you. If you don't mind, Officer Bowers will want to ask you a few more questions."

As the mobile crime unit, or "dust-busters" as Delta referred to them, arrived to take prints, Jan pulled Delta aside.

"He threw that at you?"

"Yeah. Pretty ballsy, don't you think? Rose up like a damned cobra and flung it at me. And let me tell you, that would have smarted like hell."

"I'll say. Those tips look like little razors."

"And I'll bet they cut like them, too." Turning from Jan, Delta glanced over at a beautiful suit of armor standing regally in the corner. One arm lay quietly at the side, while the other was bent at the elbow palm up.

"Great armor you have here, Mr. Ein," Delta tossed the words over her shoulder, not taking her eyes off of the shiny relic. She loved knights and chivalry and tales of King Arthur. A teacher in junior high school turned her on to Medieval lore. It was one of her good memories of her prepubescent days tangled in the web of her memory.

"Twelfth or thirteenth century?" she asked, feeling Matt Ein move beside her.

Drawing his hand up to his mouth, Matt Ein did not respond.

"Mr. Ein?"

Eyes wide, Matt Ein stared at the armor, transfixed. "He stole my ax. That bastard stole my ax."

Delta looked over at Jan, who shrugged. "The knight was holding an ax?"

Slowly removing his hand from his mouth, Matt Ein shook his head, still staring at the armor. "Not just any ax. It was a double-bladed ax—a gift from my grandfather to go with the armor." Plopping down in front of the armor, Mr. Ein laid his face in his hands and shook his head. "Anything. He could have swiped anything but the ax."

Delta knelt beside him and laid her hand on his shoulder. Empathy whirled through her as she thought about the silver I.D. bracelet her grandfather had given to her and how she felt when she thought she had lost it. There was something special about gifts from grandfathers.

"You'll get your ax back, Mr. Ein. Sooner or later, a relic like that will show up. Don't you worry."

"I hope so. I took care of that ax as if the knight might use it any moment. I sharpened it when I first got it and I polished it once a week."

"I know how you feel. We'll do everything we can to get it back." Turning to leave, Delta said a few words to the dust-busters dusting the glass cases. Then, she jumped back into the driver's seat of the patrol car and waited for Jan to finish with her notes before starting the car. "A jeweled dagger, a Ninja star, and an ancient ax—two lives taken, no money missing, and no motive. Curiouser and curiouser."

Jan raised her head from her report. "You think this is related to the murder of the druggist?"

Delta shrugged. "Hard to tell, but there are some commonalities we can't ignore."

Jan lightly touched Delta on the knee. "No, there are some commonalities that *you* can't ignore. Face it, Del. You're hooked."

Delta smiled. Yes, she was. "The report said that the dagger was inspected by a weapons expert who believes it came from some island near Greece."

"And?"

"And now we have an ax ripped off."

"So, our weirdo is into creative weaponry. Why did he murder the pharmacist? And why did he leave such an obvious clue as the dagger?"

Delta shook her head. She only had a few pieces of the puzzle, and Jan was jumping way ahead of the game. "I'm not sure. Not yet."

"Maybe you're not sure, but by the look and feel of it, you have your heart set on finding out. But I'm curious. If he threw the star at you, where is the ax?"

Delta opened her mouth to answer, but then stopped. Yes, where was the ax? The burglar didn't have it with him when she was chasing him, yet it had been stolen. Was he coming back for something else when she caught him? Had he stashed the blade someplace else? Maybe he had an accomplice. As usual in police work, there were way more questions than answers.

A new crackle erupted from the radio. "S1012, we have a 5150 at 717 Emerson. See the man."

Jan acknowledged the "nutcase on the loose" call and said they would be on their way shortly.

"Just what we need. Another fruitcake," Jan said.

But Delta barely heard her. Delta wasn't thinking about the 5150 or the man they were going to meet at the scene. She focused instead, on an ancient dagger, a murdered pharmacist, a dead dog, a stolen ax, and a Ninja star.

8

When she came through the back door of the station, Delta was not surprised to find Connie at the controls of her new computer game. The weeknight's calls were tedious and slow compared to weekends, and Connie already finished the work she had been assigned hours ago. On nights like these, when Connie was finished perusing the inactive files for any leads or updates, when she was through gathering information for any number of detectives who would require her help, when she stopped inputting data from the day's events, she would pull out a game and wait until someone needed her services.

Connie called it staying sharp. Delta called it playing.

Connie said, "Hi," as Delta approached but did not remove her eyes from the monitor.

"Hi yourself." Sitting next to Connie, Delta watched her maneuver a dwarf with long black hair around a castle. "Con, you've been playing these dumb games so long, they're even beginning to look like you."

Connie smiled. "Isn't that the truth. She does kind of look like me, doesn't she? Only, I have bigger breasts."

Delta shook her head and decided to leave that one alone. "Graphics are better and better these days, aren't they?" Delta asked, observing Connie's dwarf dodging the wicked-looking ghosts and green goblins. The graphics were some of the best she'd ever seen. Leaning closer, Delta noticed tiny beads of sweat on Connie's upper lip. She had seen Connie play hundreds of these games in the past, but never had Connie been this absorbed.

Delta watched quietly as Connie instructed the dwarf to do things such as stab, read, kick, jump, and assorted commands that moved the character at Connie's whim. It was fascinating to see the screen transform from one scene to the next as the dwarf made her way through the Land of the Night. Finally, when the little warrior was killed in the Land of the Night, Connie flicked off the screen, shaking her head in frustration.

"Tough game?" asked Delta.

Connie wiped her lip with the back of her hand. "Really hard. I've never played one this sophisticated." Still staring at the blank monitor, Connie flipped her hair over her shoulder and turned to fully face Delta. "Maybe I'm losing my touch."

Delta smiled. "That, I'll never believe." Reaching into her bag, Delta carefully pulled out the star, still wrapped in her handkerchief, and set it on the table. With her thumb and index finger, she cautiously unwrapped it. "What can you tell me about this?"

Connie leaned over for a closer look, but did not touch it. "It's one of the weapons popularized by the ancient Ninja assassins."

"Assassins?"

Connie nodded, and Delta could tell her wheels were spinning.

"Ninjas were an elite group of warriors who purportedly could steal through the night without being heard. There are scads of Ninja tales throughout the Orient. Many of those center on the superstition that they can move through walls without anyone hearing. Excellent folk material. Where did you get it?"

"It was thrown at me."

"Tonight?"

"Yep."

"Did it get you?"

Delta shook her head. "Fortunately not."

Connie rubbed her chin. "Did it stick when it landed?"

Delta nodded. "Half-way in."

"Straight in?"

"Straight in."

Connie studied the star for a moment. When Connie was training for her black belt in karate, she had also studied the weapons used by the Masters in the Orient. Delta knew Connie's mind was retrieving data just as a computer might.

"These take some real skill to master," Connie finally announced. "They're not easy to throw. Whoever tossed it is likely highly trained in martial arts. Too many cops underestimate the powers of the martial artist. But anyone who can throw one of these with accuracy is just as dangerous as someone with a gun."

"You're telling me." Delta looked at Connie as she studied the star more carefully. Delta had once scoffed at the power of the martial arts expert, until she saw Connie take down the largest men in the department in a martial arts demonstration. After that, Delta became a believer in the power of self-defense.

"Con, would a martial arts expert also know how to wield a double-bladed ax?"

Connie's eyebrows shot up in question. "Don't tell me someone threw one of those at you, too."

"Very funny. One was ripped off from a sporting goods store tonight by the same guy that chucked that little gem at my head."

"If a martial artist was well-versed in ancient weaponry, and many of them are, then yes, I imagine he could."

Delta sighed loudly. "I don't need a crackpot, would-be Ninja warrior running loose on my beat."

"Oh, he's not a Ninja," Connie remarked. "If he was, he would have split your skull open. Unless, of course, it was just a warning shot."

"Great."

"What are you going to do with it?"

"I suppose I should turn it over to the detectives and let them figure out what it all means."

Connie stared at Delta. "Why do I get the feeling that that's exactly what you *aren't* going to do?"

This brought a sly grin to Delta's face. "You can be so cynical sometimes."

"And you can be such a bullshitter. Do your job, Del, and go home. Remember what's causing friction between you and Megan? Go home and let someone else unravel this mystery."

"What about you?" Delta jerked her head toward the lifeless monitor.

"I just need to try one more time before I go home. I'm almost to the next level."

"Uh-huh. Just as I thought." Standing to leave, Delta patted Connie on the shoulder. "Don't let the dragons swallow your little fairy princess. Or whatever." Carefully picking up the sharp star, Delta headed for the door.

"Del?"

Turning back, Delta waited. "Yeah?"

"Let it go. Focus on your personal life right now."

"Right, chief." Pushing through the heavy glass doors, Delta looked at the star one last time. An alarm was ringing like a church bell deep within her.

Something told her she hadn't seen the last of the mysterious assassin.

9

"Did you turn the star over to Burglary?" Jan asked at the start of their shift.

Delta did not take her eyes away from the alley she'd been staring down.

"Yes."

"Delta?"

"Shit, Jan, why doesn't anyone trust me on this?"

"You know damn well why. That look in your eye says you're taking all of this a little too personally. Did you really turn that star over?"

"Yes, damn it, I did. The dicks weren't overly enthused by the whole thing. And Burglary and Homicide don't communicate enough to figure out that the guy who used the dagger might be the same guy that threw the star at me."

"That's because those guys don't make the quantum leaps you do. You have absolutely no proof that these cases are remotely related."

"It doesn't take a rocket scientist to figure it out though, does it?"

Jan shook her head. "You're impossible. You'll think whatever your crazy little head wants to think. When you get this way, there's no talking you out of it."

Delta pushed back her seat and didn't bother to respond to Jan's correct analysis of her character. She hated the thought of her beat being infested with some whacked out burglar or murderer or Ninja wanna-be or whatever the hell he was. While her beat was one of the roughest in the city, Delta took pride in her close rapport with the merchants and people on the street. High visibility and her knowledge of the streets were aimed at keeping gutter mongrels to a minimum. If there was some nutcase running around with ancient weapons and breaking into people's shops, it was her business, even if she wasn't a detective. That's what made her such a good cop.

She cared.

She cared that someone was killing people and animals and attacking her in the process. She cared that the people who paid her salary were being victimized by this night stalker. What no one understood about Delta was that she really, truly cared about the safety of the people who lived and worked on her beat. And if some crazy asshole was threatening that safety, it was up to her to stop him.

What she found so odd was that the crimes had been committed in such close proximity. The pharmacy and the knife shop were less than five blocks apart. Whoever this guy was, he didn't think anything about the risk involved in striking so soon after the last crime and in the same neighborhood. And he obviously didn't know the greater risk of attacking the cop whose job it was to protect that neighborhood and the people in it. That was Delta's best advantage; he underestimated her.

They cruised along for another fifteen minutes in relative silence, until Delta spied a teenager sauntering down the street with his hands in his pockets.

"Pull over in back of that kid," Delta said, pointing to a tall, thin Mexican youth.

But before Delta was out of the car, the boy, seemingly with eyes in the back of his head, sprinted away.

"Damn it!" Delta yelled, taking off after him.

As Delta chased him down the sidewalk and through a crowd waiting in line for the last showing at the movie theater, Jan swung the patrol car ahead to cut him off.

"Julio, damn it, it's me! Officer Stevens!"

Just before jamming across the street, the kid came to a sudden halt and slowly turned around. "Whyn't chu say so, man? You scared the shit right outta me."

Chest heaving as she reached him, Delta took a moment to catch her breath in front of the smiling eyes of the teenager. "¿Qué pasa, Julio?"

The boy shrugged. His jacket was emblazoned with his gang's colors, and they seemed to dance as he moved. "Not much." Julio turned toward the wall and laid his hands and feet spread-eagle, as if he were going to be searched.

"You got eyes in the back of your head, amigo?" Delta asked, always amazed at Julio's street savvy.

Julio turned to her, still keeping his hands on the wall, and grinned a charming smile ornamented by a silver cap on his front tooth. "Call it a sick sense, man." His face, though pock-marked, was soft and dark. He did not look like a boy who belonged to one of the toughest Latino gangs in the city.

Moving up to him, Delta pretended to search him. It would be certain death if one of his brother gang members saw him talking to a cop, so he acted like he was being busted.

"Whatcha need now?" Julio asked, turning back to face the wall.

Delta had saved Julio's girl one night from what would have been a horrible gang rape by rival members of another gang. In his own quiet way, Julio offered to be Delta's eyes and ears about anything non-gang related. This wasn't the first time she asked for his help, and she doubted it would be the last.

"I need to know what you've heard about a martial arts expert prowling around my beat. You know the stuff—judo, karate, tae kwon do, shit like that." Turning Julio completely around, Delta knew why he had run—he was stoned.

"You talkin' 'bout the dude that left an eight-inch knife in Friedman's back?" Even stoned, Julio was a great source. "Word has it there's a new man in town who doesn't want to be fucked with."

"What's he after?" Delta pulled her notepad from her pocket and pretended to be writing him up.

Julio shrugged and stuck his hands in his pockets again. "Dunno. The line says he ain't no gang member or nothin'. Just works solo."

"Import?"

"Don't think so. Things have been pretty cool lately. 'Sides, you know us, man. We do our own. No one 'round here brings in guys to do the dirty shit unless it's big. Ain't nothin' big happenin'."

Delta nodded. "Is that all?"

"All I know. No one's seen him, though. We only heard of him." Julio wiped the glaze from his lips. "He piss you off, eh, Stevens?"

Delta looked away. "I don't like killers in our neighborhood, do you?"

For a moment, Julio said nothing. "If I catch word a anythin' else, I'll letcha know."

"You do that." Tearing off a piece of paper, Delta handed it to him and walked away. "You do that, Julio." Turning back around, Delta pointed her finger at him. "And lay off the dope, will you? It'll only fry your brain cells."

She turned back to the patrol car and heard him mutter something about it being too late for that.

"What was that all about?" Jan asked, as Delta sat back down.

"Just hunting and pecking, that's all." Delta looked at her nails in feigned disinterest.

"Delta Stevens."

Without looking at Jan, Delta shrugged. "Do me a favor and swing by Megan's for a minute."

"More pecking?"

Delta tried to hide the tiny grin on her face. "More pecking."

10

Megan swung the door open and grinned. "Hi there, handsome. What are you doing here looking so sexy in your uniform?" Sidling up to Delta and nuzzling her neck, Megan hugged her tightly. "You know how women in uniform drive me crazy."

"Women? Plural?"

Megan smiled. "Singular. Make that particular."

Delta nodded. "That's better." Gently prying Megan's arms off from around her neck, Delta kissed her lightly on the mouth. "Isn't that one of the main reasons we became involved?"

"That, and the fact that you're great in bed."

Delta blushed and then peered over her shoulder to make sure Jan couldn't possibly hear them.

"So, to what do I owe this honor, Officer Stevens?" Megan's eyes twinkled as she held her hands out to be handcuffed.

"This is business, I'm afraid."

Megan lowered her hands and feigned a frown. "Business? Darn. I was hoping this was a social call."

"I wish it was."

"How silly of me to think that you would do something as spontaneous as drive over here to flirt with me."

"Maybe some other time."

"Mmmm. I'd like that. You know what they say." Megan pulled Delta closer and nibbled on her ear. "Variety is the spice of life."

With chills running down her spine and goosebumps popping up on her arms, Delta slowly pulled away. "You drive me crazy. You know that, don't you?"

Megan's eyes sparkled. "I hope so. Now, what is it you need, Officer Stevens?"

"Meg, I need you to tap some of your old sources for me."

"How old?"

"I need to know who the new man is in town. He's a martial arts expert, or he may even be a weapons enthusiast. I think he's pulled two jobs so far, all on my beat."

Megan nodded, the color slightly leaving her face. "Very dangerous?"

"Extremely. He's already killed once. Something tells me he'll do it again."

"And you want me to see if any of my street buddies know anything."

"You know I wouldn't ask if it wasn't really important."

"I'll see what I can do, but I don't have much to go on."

"I know. We don't have much. Only that he has a predilection for ancient or antique weaponry. It's possible he may try to pawn off an ax that he ripped off. Try your pal—what's that pawnbroker's name?"

"Carl Locodo?"

"Yeah, he's the one."

"We're looking for the creep who threw that star at you, aren't we?"

Delta nodded. "Yep. I think he's the one who killed the guy in the drug store."

"I'll see what I can do. Carl owes me a favor or two. I'll see if he can check out the other pawn shops around the city as well."

"Great. I really appreciate it, hon. Right now, we're pretty much stumped."

Megan stepped up to Delta and ran her hand along the inside of her uniform top. "You know I'd love nothing more than to help." Bowing her head, Megan sighed. "It's weird that you should come by tonight."

"Weird? Why?"

"After our talk the other night, I felt like all I had done was point the finger at you, blaming you for our rough spots."

Delta waited, threading her fingers through Megan's and holding Megan's hand against her chest.

"Then I realized that some of my blame-laying was misplaced. All this time, I've believed that you were spending too much time and energy on your job. I don't hate what you do, Delta, I . . ."

"What is it, Baby?"

Shrugging, Megan shook her head. "I can't believe I'm saying this, Del, but I think I'm jealous."

"Jealous? Of Jan?"

"No, silly, of your job. When the four of us were working to bring Miles's killers in, it was the most exciting thing I've ever done in my life. Since then, I've just gone to school and work, with nothing really interesting to grab my attention."

"Thanks."

"You know what I mean. Delta, I understand why you love your job so much. Really, I do. Maybe I'm a little envious that it's so much more exciting than what I'm doing now. I mean, didn't it ever occur to you that there was a definite danger in being a prostitute?"

"I never really thought of it that way."

"Well, there was. And I enjoyed knowing it was risky. Then, I got involved with you and Miles's murder case, and there was even more excitement than hooking."

"Are you saying you're bored?"

Megan shook her head. "Not with you. Not with my life. I just want you to know that I'm a little envious of the excitement and the thrill your job brings you. Delta, I love you more than anything in the world. I wouldn't ever want you to stop being a cop, if that's what you want. But part of my problem with our relationship is *me*. I'm not saying that you don't still need to work on making our relationship first; I just need to come to terms with the fact that my life just isn't as exciting as yours."

Delta released Megan's hand and took hold of Megan's face between both of her hands. "Is that why I saw that law book laying on the floor the other night?"

Megan nodded and smiled shyly. "I'm thinking about changing my major."

"From business to law?"

"What do you think?"

Pulling Megan to her, Delta kissed her tenderly on the lips. "I think you'd be a great lawyer."

"Really?"

"Really."

"Do you understand that I didn't mean to put all the blame on you."

Checking her watch, Delta nodded. "I'm not perfect, Meg. And most of what you were saying was right. Can we finish this conversation later? I really need to follow up on a few things before the shift ends."

Megan nodded and ran her hand through Delta's hair. "I love you so much, Delta Stevens. I'll be waiting up with bells on. Nothing else. Just bells."

Delta grinned. "I thought you wanted to finish talking."

"Oh, we will. But when that's done . . . I'll leave the rest to your imagination. Now get out of here before I throw myself at your feet and beg you to stay."

Taking one step out the door, Delta turned and smiled. "Really?"

Megan's grin instantly transformed into a warm smile. "Really. Delta Stevens, when will you ever get it through that thick head of yours that I love you?"

Delta shrugged. "Sometimes, I don't feel like I deserve it."

"Sometimes, you don't. Now get going before Jan falls asleep."

"I love you."

"I know."

11

"You're not going to let this one go, are you?" Jan asked, starting the engine.

Delta shook her head. "No, Jan, I'm not."

"Because of the D.A. or because he tried to take you out?"

"Maybe both. Maybe neither." Delta stared out the window. Sometimes it felt like the women in her life were always questioning—always demanding reasons why she did the things she did. After college, Sandy, her ex-lover, never let up on why she would "throw away a college education" to work with street scum. Delta believed that becoming a cop was the beginning of the end for their relationship. And even when Delta tried to explain why she wanted to be a cop, Sandy didn't listen or care. Delta had spent her entire childhood reading comics and dreaming about being somebody's heroine. She wanted very much to be an X-Man or a member of the Fantastic Four—to be so brave and courageous and take chances no one else would. Few knew of Delta's past penchant for comics. Delta's love of the comic book heroine "Storm" was one of the reasons Connie had nick-named her "Storm." That, and the fact that Delta always stormed into situations when she was a rookie. In fact, she was still like that young, energetic woman who proudly donned badge number 182.

"Delta?"

"Huh?"

"You okay? You want to take a break or something?"

Delta looked at Jan and sighed. "Jan, something inside tells me I have to stop this guy. There's more to this than the murders. I don't know what it is, but my gut instinct is screaming at me to dig harder and deeper than I already am."

"How much harder can you dig, Del? You've tapped into most of your reliable street sources. What more is there for you to do besides work yourself to death? And look where that's already gotten you."

Delta studied Jan's profile. For Jan, the job was just that: a job. One which was ten hours long, and she left it behind when she hung up her badge and nine-millimeter. For Delta, it extended well into the hours of her personal life. She could not leave behind in her locker the details she had witnessed during the night, nor could she easily forget about the victims and suspects and great lines of people who tramped through her life every night. They became a part of her psyche, some adding to her worries, some not, and either way, Delta wasn't capable of letting go completely. These people—their pain, their losses— were all a part of Delta's life. And though she often wished she could be like Jan and leave it all behind, she wasn't capable of doing that; it just wasn't in Delta's chemistry to turn away and not look back. Being involved was what she did best. If she could only learn how to successfully balance both her career and her relationship, she'd be one of the happiest people in the world.

"I know that, Jan, but I can't let go." Delta listened to herself say this and then shook her head. "No, wait a minute. It's not that I can't let go of it. It won't let go of me."

"What does that mean?"

"It means, this creep has his hooks in me and isn't letting go. It's almost like I'm being reeled in. It's weird. That's the only way I can explain it."

"That *is* weird. Well, if he's reeling you in, then I feel sorry for him. He's got a hold of a much bigger fish than he could possibly bargain for."

As they cruised along the darkened streets like a tiger shark in the belly of the darkest ocean, Delta began scribbling notes on her pad and tried to hum an upbeat tune.

"Is Dennis getting ready for the big race?" Delta asked, as they rolled up to a stoplight.

"As usual, he and the guys have this betting pool going. They bet on each other—you know, who's going to lose the most, who's going to luck out, that sort of thing."

Delta shook her head. Men were only boys in big bodies. "The ponies have never been kind to your husband."

Jan nodded. "Isn't that the truth. He's tried a thousand different systems, and none of them have worked."

Delta chuckled. "Remember when his system was to bet on the horses that peed just before going into the starting gates?"

Their laughter was interrupted by the radio announcing they had a "possible shots fired" call. It was one of the worst calls a beat cop could get. There might be a gun involved, there might be a crime in progress, and there might already have been a crime committed. A 216 could be an extremely dangerous situation. Or it might not.

The call was a lot like being a little pregnant or sort of blind; it left a cop with more questions than answers, and answers were a cop's greatest allies.

Jan flipped open her book and ran her finger down the list of addresses. "It's the Oakwood Apartment Complex."

"Let's hit it!" Delta said, turning on both sirens and the lights. In less than a minute and a half, they pulled into an alley paralleling Hemingway Street.

"The car lot?" Jan yelled, as Delta killed the ear-piercing sirens.

"Yes." Car lots made for good cover when driving up to a 216 because they offered plenty of hiding areas should there be an ambush. Delta had seen a fellow officer go down once because he parked right on the street when responding to a PSF call. He hadn't even gotten completely out of the car when he took two bullets in his leg and one in his abdomen. Since then, Delta always made sure she parked where there was sufficient cover.

Slipping between two Gremlins, Delta motioned for Jan to look at the side door of the apartment building, which stood wide open. There were no lights on the inside, only a very dim exterior bulb, shining nakedly against the peeling paint. From her place behind the Gremlins, Delta spoke into her radio and asked for the E.T.A. of back-up. The answer was one minute.

When back-up arrived, Delta sent them to the other side of the apartment building, issuing orders on what and what not to do. Ever since she shot her would-be assassin in a warehouse, Delta became the expert in searching and maintaining a perimeter around build-ings. Every officer in the city knew of her success against an armed man in a dark warehouse, and her victory was legendary.

Delta motioned for Jan to cover her while she ap-proached the open door. Entering dark buildings was a greater threat than almost anything else a cop could face. Delta didn't know if someone was inside, waiting to shoot her. She didn't know if there was another crime going down and she was just about to walk into the middle of it. She basically knew zero about the situation.

What she did know was that someone had called the police because they believe they heard shots being fired. Shots fired plus an open door leading into a dark building meant trouble.

When Delta reached the door, Jan slid in behind her, taking the low point as she had done at the pharmacy. As Jan and Delta criss-crossed through the interior hallway, Delta flicked on the lights. So far, she didn't see anyone. Next, they came to a sparsely furnished dining room area that had a card table for a dining table. There were papers and a fast food bag strewn across it. Looking around the corner of the dining room, Delta saw a man lying half in and half out of the kitchen. God, how she hoped this man wasn't dead.

Cautiously moving into the kitchen, Delta inhaled deeply and held her breath as she looked down at the pool of blood already coagulating underneath the man. Delta leaned back against the wall and tried to control her gag reflex by inhaling slowly through her mouth.

No matter how many times she looked death in the face, she could never get used to it. Feeling Jan touch her elbow, Delta turned and shook her head. They needed to finish the search of the house before they tended to the victim. Delta shook off her chills and continued with her inspection until she was sure there was no one else in the apartment.

"Dead?" she asked Jan, knowing the answer, but wanting to make sure.

"Very."

Delta stared down at the lifeless body and shook her head sadly. "Did you make the call?"

Jan nodded as she stepped around the body. "They're on their way."

In another half hour, the homicide unit rolled up and eased to a stop before Detective Russ Leonard stepped from the unmarked car.

Sergeant Leonard looked like Danny DeVito, only taller. He combed what was left of his hair across his wildly receding hairline. He wore his too baggy slacks up practically around his thick neck. As he glanced across the room, much like a rat looking for food, Leonard wiped his nose the length of his sleeve.

"Oh, God," Delta moaned. "Not him. Anyone but him."

Jan looked out the door to see who Delta was talking about. "Leonard? He's a good dick."

Delta sighed as she leaned up against the kitchen counter, careful not to touch anything with her hands. "I know."

"So, what's the problem?"

"Problems. Make that plural. When I was in the Academy, Leonard gave a lecture on crime scene protection. At the time, he smoked these awful cigars. Well, when we investigated a mock crime scene, I pointed out that his cigar ash could be misleading if he smoked around the crime scene. I thought my point was brilliant. He thought I was being a smart ass."

"What did he do?"

"He took off my cap and ground his cigar out in it."

"You're kidding."

"Then he stuck it back on my head."

Jan chuckled. "Don't tell me you're still mad."

Delta waved her off. "Have you ever worked with the guy?"

"No."

"Then save your guffaws until later. Once you work with him, you'll know exactly what I'm talking about."

"Stevie!" Leonard exclaimed, as if they were the best of friends.

Delta cringed. Two of her ex-lovers called her Stevie. It was sort of cute from them. Coming out of Leonard's fat mouth, it sounded obscene.

"Jesus Christ, Stevie, can't you keep a tighter rein on the crackpots on your turf? This is the third one in just over a week. You spendin' too much time at Winchell's Donut Shop or what?"

Delta turned to Jan, who rolled her eyes and stepped back into the dining room.

"Don't be an ass, Leonard. A man has died here. Show a little respect, will you?"

Leonard stared down at the corpse. "They seem to be droppin' like the proverbial flies, Stevie. What's up with that?"

Delta winced at one of Leonard's many mispronunciations. Shooting a look over to Leonard's partner, Chuck Connell, Delta shook her head. Connell was the nicer of the two, but he spent most of his time playing audience to Leonard's "picture this" scenarios whenever he was reconstructing a scene. In a way, Delta felt sorry for Connell. He had to act like he actually liked Leonard.

Delta, however, did not. It wasn't just that Leonard had made a fool of her in the Academy that fueled her dislike for him. He was one of the biggest chauvinist pigs she'd ever met. Once, at a Christmas party, Leonard had had a little too much scotch and entertained a group of men with his distorted view of female detectives and police officers. When Delta heard his comment about women cops being physically weaker than male cops, she walked over to him, plucked his cigar from his mouth, and dropped it in his scotch glass.

"Care to test that theory, Detective?" she had said, towering over him. Had it not been for Connie's quick action to pull Delta from the group, Russ Leonard would have found out the hard way just how wrong he was.

"Leonard, they're people who are dying, not flies. Try to remember that before you open your mouth."

"Touchy, touchy. Who pissed in your Cheerios this a.m.?"

Delta shook her head and walked away. "Jackass," she mumbled to herself, walking over to the crime scene tech, who was dusting a glass for prints. "Coming up with anything, Manny?" Manny Espinosa was one of the best techies Delta had ever met. He was thorough, precise, and knew his stuff.

"Not much. Looks like he bought it from someone he knew. Two glasses with alcohol. This one here is full, probably the killer's. He was smart enough not to pick it up."

Delta nodded. "Keep up the good work, Manny." Delta walked back over to the corpse to find Leonard kneeling over it. "Don't be sore, Stevie," Leonard said. "I was only jokin'."

Delta didn't respond. Instead, she wrote notes on her notepad about the layout of the apartment and the arrangement of the body.

"Looks like your psycho has struck again," Leonard said, rising and looking up at Delta.

Delta towered over the stump of a man. "I don't think so."

This brought a chuckle from Leonard. "Oh, you don't?"

"Nope. What you have here, Leonard, is another murder. Period. I don't think it has anything to do with the guy that chucked that star at me over at Omega's."

"Sounds like you're lucky he didn't give you a new part in your hair." Leonard put the tip of his pencil to his tongue and jotted down a few notes. "But fear not, Stevie, because I'm gonna get him for you."

Delta watched, as Manny stepped over to the body. "You done here, Sarge?"

Leonard waved a hand at him, and Manny started taking pictures of the victim.

"Yeah, Stevie, you just leave it up to me and my men. We'll bring this bastard to his knees before long."

Delta shook her head. "Not if you insist on connecting this murder to the other."

Leonard sniffed and stopped writing. "Oh? Jeez, Stevie, if I would have known it was amateur detective night, I would have worn my best suit."

Connell faked a chuckle.

"I may not have a badge that says I'm a detective, Leonard, but I know evidence when I see it, and this evidence doesn't point toward my man."

Folding his arms, Leonard looked amused. "And tell me, Agatha Stevens, just what clues, what hard evidence lies before us that supports your half-baked theory?"

One of the things that made Leonard a good detective was that he looked for hard evidence that was nearly irrefutable in court. He would search until he found that one link, that one tie that would connect a suspect to the scene of the crime.

"Take a good look around you, Leonard. My perp has a thing for ancient weaponry. We've already established that as one of his M.O.'s."

Leonard's thick eyebrows shot up. "Been reading our reports, have you?"

Delta shrugged the question off. "It's not important. What is important is the fact that this guy had his head blown off with a large-calibre handgun at point-blank range; that's not something our walking anachronism is likely to use."

A wicked grin slid across Leonard's face. "How can you be so sure, Stevie? The M.O. is still the same. This sicko is killing for pleasure. Just because he decided to use a gun makes no difference. Don't overlook the obvious."

"And don't underestimate your opponent, Leonard. Whoever killed this man did so out of anger and vengeance. To put a gun in someone's face and pull the trigger takes a great deal of hostility."

"Yeah? So? Our psycho is one angry shitbag. Don't get caught up in all that ancient weaponry crap, Stevie. Look, I'll tell you one thing about his psychological profile, and that's that this guy likes to kill. He's enjoying the game. Maybe he really enjoyed blowing this guy's face off."

Delta didn't think so. If the guy that threw the star at her was enjoying the game, what pleasure would he receive from simply pulling the trigger? It simply didn't fit.

Leonard walked over to Delta and reached up to put an arm around her. "You're trying to attach a thinking personality to this kook. You'll never make detective thinking like that. You have to look at the evidence you've been given, Stevie. You can't work on just hunches alone, and that's all you have here, a hunch. Trust me. Until I learn otherwise, this killer is the same guy who offed that pharmacist. Period."

Delta shrugged. "If you link this killing to the others, I guarantee it's going to take longer to find both murderers."

"Place a wager on that thought, Stevie?"

Delta shook Leonard's outstretched hand. "What'll it be?"

A sly smile spread across Leonard's face. "Your Mickey Mantel card for my Don Drysdale."

Delta shook her head. In the Academy, Leonard had overheard her conversation with one of the guys about her collection of baseball cards. He had approached her about buying her Mantel card then, but she had flatly refused. This time she said, "No way. My Mantel for your Mays and Rose cards."

Leonard thought about it for a minute. "You're on." Squeezing Delta's hand in his, Leonard grinned widely. "I've been wanting that Mantel card ever since I heard you had one. This one is going to be a sweet victory."

Delta smiled. "Not if you continue the investigation the way you're going. Kiss your Mays and Rose cards goodbye, Leonard." Turning away, Delta said her goodbyes to the crime unit and joined Jan out by the patrol car.

"Okay, I see your point. He's a bit on the gross side, but I don't think that's why you dislike him so much."

Delta cast Jan a questioning look. "No? Then why?"

Jan grinned. "You can't stand him because he's got a crush on you."

"A crush? You've got to be kidding." Delta pretended to gag.

"Delta, don't you see how he looks at you? How he has a little pet name for you? He even took a chance and put his stubby little arm around you. I'm telling you, Leonard has the hots for you."

Delta shuddered at the thought. "What a disgusting thought."

"Maybe, but it's true. Trust me. As a straight woman, I can safely tell you that Detective Russ Leonard has a crush on you."

"Well, he just better keep his crushes to himself." Starting the engine, Delta made a mental note to have Connie get the rest of the psych profile Leonard referred to in the apartment.

"Del?"

"Yeah?"

"You sounded awfully sure of your theory in there. Is there something you need to tell me?"

Delta tried pushing the feelings in her gut away, but they lingered like a bad odor. There was something about this case that seemed to have a mysterious hold on her. Her intuition sounded various alarms, and she had the oddest feeling that the killer was watching them, sizing up every move they made. It felt as if someone was standing behind her, testing her, seeing how she reacted.

"It's just a gut thing. I can't really explain. About the only thing I know with any assurance is that someone who throws Chinese stars at pursuing cops wouldn't be so unimaginative as to use a handgun. Our perp has a different motive."

"So you think this murder is totally unrelated to the one at Troy's?"

Delta nodded. "There wasn't a wallet on our corpse back there. He was having, or attempting to have, a drink with someone prior to being shot. I'm willing to bet he knew his killer. I don't believe Friedman knew his killer. Friedman was stabbed, that guy back there was shot. Serial killers, if that's what we have, tend to use the same method when killing."

"That's pretty slim evidence."

"I know. But for now, it's the best I can do."

"Well, you'll never convince Leonard unless you have—"

"Cold, hard facts. I know."

"And since you don't, I wish you'd let it rest. We've got enough to worry about without you chasing ghosts."

Chasing ghosts? Delta felt as if she was chasing shadows—shadows that were looming over her like clouds covering the moon. No, there was something more to this case than anyone knew.

But Leonard was right about one thing.

Hunches weren't enough. If Delta was going to get this psycho off her beat, she'd have to have evidence—she'd have to put the pieces together and catch him before he killed again.

Because one thing she was sure of.

He would kill again.

12

When the shift was over, Delta sauntered over to Connie's desk and plopped down next to her as she had done practically every work night for the last three years.

"Did you get them?"

Connie nodded.

"Excellent. You got everything?"

"Well, not exactly. There's a lock on one of the files that keeps me from downloading the data, but girl, do I have some interesting information for you."

Delta scooted closer. She so loved when Connie got the goods. "Go on."

Turning the monitor off, Connie faced Delta. "The dog was poisoned by some chemical compound unfamiliar to the coroner or the M.E. According to the report, the tech guys spent eight hours searching through medical journals trying to find out just what it was."

"And?"

"And the coroner couldn't place it because it's an extremely old compound not listed in any modern journals."

Delta knew where this was heading.

"The compound found was a substance and a mixture used well before the Middle Ages by alchemists."

"No kidding?"

"The compound took awhile longer to unravel because of the interaction of the chemicals together. Once the coroner separated them, he looked into possible origins of the compound."

"And he came up with chemicals used a long time ago."

"Yep."

Delta's eyes lit up. "Excellent!"

"Hold your camels, *ma amie*, that's not all. The report lists the dagger as an artifact from the fifth or sixth century. They had some experts take a look at it. Apparently, it's from an island off the Greek coast, and, get this, the gems on the handle are real."

"No way."

"Scout's honor."

"You were kicked out of the scouts."

"Okay, blood oath and you can have my firstborn. Our murderer left behind jewels worth over a hundred thousand dollars."

Delta leaned back and shook her head. "You're telling me he left a dagger worth a hundred thousand dollars in the back of a dead man?"

"Yep."

"Whoa. Why wouldn't he take it?"

Connie shrugged. "I've been thinking about it all night. I think he wants us to know about his little penchant for old things. Maybe he's trying to throw us off track. Perhaps he has things on his mind other than murder or money."

Delta nodded. "Well, money certainly isn't a motive or even an issue if he left something that valuable. Assuming, of course, he was aware of its value."

"True. And I doubt the perp would have left something that valuable in the back of someone he hated. That doesn't fit the profiles."

"Right. So, if money isn't the motive, then what?"

"What do we have left? Love, revenge, passionate outbreaks, things of that nature. Something more emotional than physical.

Delta rubbed her hands together. "Excellent! Damn, you're good."

Connie grinned. "Well, that's what Gina says. I'm having Eddie check past unsolveds to see if there are any other weird murders where ancient weaponry was used. It may prove nothing, but it's worth a try."

Delta patted Connie on the back. "Good work. And the psych profile?"

"Should have it for you by later this morning."

Delta rose and clapped her hands together. "All right! Con, I owe you."

"Yes, you do. Megan called and said she enjoyed the visit and wants you not to tarry on your way home. She mentioned something about 'just bells'." A sly grin crept across Connie's face.

"Say no more."

With that, Delta headed out the door.

13

Delta answered the phone on the first ring. "Did you get it?"

"It took some doing, but Eddie and I were able to slip in the back door of the system. When will cops ever learn how to lock computer files?"

"Would it make any difference to you?" Delta poured herself a cup of coffee and picked up the note Megan left for her. "Hang on a minute, Con. I'm reading a note from Megan." Reading the little love letter Megan slipped under her coffee mug made Delta warm inside. Last night had been a wonderful evening for them. When she got home, Megan was indeed wearing only bells that she had bought at Sarah's Bare Necessities. Just the thought of Megan playing with the little tasseled bells on her nipples aroused Delta. Finishing the note, Delta sighed. If only their relationship could always be so good.

"Have a nice night?" Connie asked.

"Remember 'just bells'?"

"Mmm. Sounds like it was better than good."

Delta grinned. "Bingo. Now, what have *you* got for me?"

"Nothing quite as enticing, I can assure you, but it's pretty interesting stuff. Got a pen ready?"

Delta picked up the purple pen Megan had written the note with. "Shoot."

"I just had enough time to get the highlights, so if this appears brief, you know why. There's more, but I figured you'd want only the major details."

"Right."

"The psych report indicates that we're dealing with a very insecure man of about forty years old. He has had some abuse in his life, possibly from his father or someone else in his family. He may have been in love with his mother or someone who he highly respected and felt demasculinized by that woman."

Delta sipped her coffee. "God, however do they come up with this shit?" Delta wrote the word 'emotion' on the paper and circled it. "Go ahead."

"He has an IQ of around 130 or 140, and has attended college. He isn't from around here but knows someone who is and may be staying with them. He is an only child, probably molested little girls when he was younger or tortured small animals."

"And what kind of underwear does he wear?" Delta quipped.

"Briefs. Anyway, they say it's possible our guy's a martial arts instructor or may even be from the Orient. He's single, has few friends, and is well-traveled."

"And why is he killing and stealing weird things?"

"The shrinks think he's trying to punish someone, and this is his way of acting out his superiority complex. According to them, he'll continue on his little crime spree until he's caught."

"Oh, don't give me that 'he wants to get caught' line. They say that about everybody."

"On the contrary, Del. According to them, he *doesn't* want to be caught. He wants to be superior. The report says he is angry enough to both stab someone and shoot someone in the face. The report also says he is possibly impotent. Maiming makes him feel more powerful and secure. The crimes are his way of excelling. Weird, huh?"

"Very." Delta looked at her pad and circled a few more words. "So Leonard will be checking out all of the martial arts studios."

"Most likely."

"But he's not from around here. That lead's a dead end."

"He'll check it anyway."

"What's your best guess on how to approach it?"

"The weapons. I'll bet they're not that hard to track down. The problem lies in whether or not he's purchased them here in the States or abroad."

"Anything else?"

"That's about it for now. We'll just have to see what Leonard and his men come up with."

Delta finished her coffee and set the mug in the sink. "Why does that worry me?"

"Because he's taking a different angle than we are. And Del, that's not a bad idea. The more bases we all cover, the better."

"You really think so?"

"Why not? Let him dig for his clues. We can take or leave those that don't apply to our theories and then see who comes up the winner. Leonard isn't going to jump to any conclusions, Delta. You know that."

"Maybe not, but the psych report supports Leonard's theory that the two murders are related." Delta sighed. "That's why I hate those damned things. Sometimes they just go in circles."

"And sometimes they're right on the money. Take it for what it's worth. Like Gina said, psychiatry isn't an exact science, so don't expect that from psych reports."

"I know, I know. I guess I just wanted the report to support our idea that the murders aren't related, that's all."

"Why the vested interest?"

"He's attacked me, killed a dog and murdered someone on my beat. If he's declaring war, for whatever twisted reason, then I think we should answer back, don't you?"

"You bet. If there's someone out there who has no compunction about attacking a cop, then everyone needs to be more alert. Let Leonard do his thing, Del, and we'll do ours." Connie leaned away from the phone and yelled at one of the dogs. "On a more pleasant topic, were those your bells I heard ringing in the night?"

Delta smiled. "You're a pig."

"Are things better, then?"

The thought of Megan's firm, naked body lying on top of the turquoise satin sheets made Delta's smile grow. "They're not any worse."

"You didn't answer the question."

Delta doodled for a moment before answering. "You know, Con, we love each other and we're attracted to each other, but times like last night are so few and far between."

"Because?"

"I spend too much time at work, and her life is opening up in directions she never knew existed. We're not connecting on any level except physically."

"But what did that physical experience say to your heart?"

"That we're in love. That we want to be together, that—"

"Then, hang with it, Del. Stop trying to find immediate answers. Let Megan experience what she needs to experience without you getting paranoid and scared."

"What about the other side of the problem? She thinks I work too much."

"You do."

"So, I should stop working so hard?"

Connie chuckled. "You'll do that only if you stop breathing. No, Delta, don't do what doesn't feel good or right for you, either. It's that transitional stage you're in. Everyone goes through it. You just have to learn how to ride the bumps."

Delta thought about this for a minute. "This bump feels more like a mountain."

"They always do. Listen, give yourself a break. Just make sure you keep the lines of communication open and talk your feelings through with her."

They did talk much last night. As a matter of fact, talking was the last thing on Delta's mind. "I'll give it my best shot. The idea of losing Megan just scares me so much."

"And you know what you do when you're scared?"

"What?"

"You throw yourself into your work."

"Like I'm doing now?"

"Bingo. Why don't you two come over for dinner tonight and be a little sociable? It might do you both a world of good."

"Sounds good."

"Until then, stop thinking about this murder case and try relaxing your brains for awhile. I swear to God, Delta Stevens, you're as type-A as they get."

Delta grinned. "Is that from another psych profile?"

"Might as well be. We'll see you around six, okay?"

"Six, it is. Oh, and thanks for the info."

After Delta hung up, she re-read Megan's note. Life, it seemed, was just one huge puzzle. If she could find the missing pieces to the murders, she could solve the case and save others from dying. If she could fit the pieces of her job and her relationship together, she could save herself and Megan from any more heartache.

Oh, if only it were that easy.

14

Megan danced into the kitchen, bearing a plastic baggy full of chicken parts. Her long, blonde hair, knotted in a French braid down her back, bounced freely behind her.

"Aren't you in a fine mood," Connie noted, planting a kiss on Megan's cheek before returning to peeling potatoes.

"Why of course! You're looking at a gal who scored the highest grade in her boring econ class." Megan twirled around once more and held her face out for Gina to kiss the other cheek.

"That's fantastic!" Gina cried, taking the baggy from her and giving her a hug. "Our genius."

"Let's celebrate." Opening the refrigerator, Connie pulled out two bottles of champagne.

"You knew," Megan said, throwing a suspicious look toward Delta, as she came through the front door bearing a bag of groceries. "Delta Stevens, you told!"

"I couldn't help it," Delta said. "I'm so proud of you, I had to share it with somebody."

Megan took the bag from Delta, set it on the counter, and laced her arms around Delta's neck. Megan was the only woman Delta had ever been with who could put her arms completely around her neck without having to step on tip toe. "You're such a sweetheart. Thank you."

Pulling chilled glasses out of the freezer, Connie stepped out the door and onto the patio, where she popped one of the corks and tossed it for Cagney, her large Doberman, to chase after.

"Someone else is in an awfully good mood," Delta noted, watching Connie carefully pour the champagne into the long, fluted glasses. "What's up with her? You guys have a good day together?"

Gina shook her head as she emptied the chicken out into a bowl. "I wish. No, my little angel is in such a fine mood because she finally got beyond the first level of that damned computer game. You should see her. She's hooked."

"It doesn't usually take her this long to finish, let alone get beyond the first stage, or level, or whatever-the-hell she calls it." Delta winked at Connie through the sliding glass door.

"I know. That's why she's feeling a bit triumphant." Rummaging through the grocery bag, Gina pulled out barbecue sauce and popped open the lid. "She spent the better part of the afternoon at that damned computer."

"I suppose it's better that she chase after warlocks and goblins than other women," Megan offered.

Gina shrugged. "Maybe. I don't suppose another woman would be able to keep her up as long as that game has. She didn't come to bed until almost ten this morning."

Delta peered through the glass door as Connie tossed the second cork for Cagney to chase. "I have to admit, Gina, that I haven't seen her so involved in one of those silly games as she is with this one."

"Maybe we could send her to Adventure Games Anonymous," Megan offered. "You know, 'Hi. My name is Connie, and I'm addicted to computer games.'"

Delta grinned. "I wouldn't worry too much about it. Connie needs her own little world."

Gina sighed heavily as she slapped barbecue sauce on the chicken. "It doesn't usually bother me, but I've never seen a game get to her like this one. At one point, she slammed her fist on the desk and yelled at the monitor. It's frustrating the hell out of her."

"Good. Look at it this way: it'll keep her honest. We certainly don't want her thinking she's a genius." Delta winked at Gina, who smiled weakly at her and said, "I don't know, Del. It feels as if there's more to it."

"Well, you would know. Five years is a long time to spend with a computer dork." As everyone laughed, Delta looked up from the cutting board and studied Gina's face. Delta always thought Gina was a handsome woman, and as she approached forty, her temples were the only part of her hair that was graying. Gina used to say she got ten gray hairs for every patient she failed to help. The gray gave her a distinguished appearance, and Delta always hoped that she would age as gracefully as Gina had.

"Want me to talk to her?"

The sliding glass door opened, and Connie leaned in the doorway. "You guys coming or not? I can't drink all of this delicious champagne by myself." Connie entered the house and placed her hands on her hips. "Okay, what's going on here? No, wait," she said, holding a hand up to stop them. "Don't tell me. You guys are talking about me spending too much time on the computer, aren't you? I can tell by the look on my lovely gal's face." Sidling up to Gina, Connie nuzzled her neck.

"I was just mentioning how frustrated it's made you," Gina explained.

"You do seem to be a bit . . . entranced." Delta looked over at the computer screen, which was on pause. The monitor displayed outstanding graphics that appeared almost three-dimensional. The still picture on the screen looked like an opening to a cave, and there were large green trees and shrubs all about. It could have been a snapshot, the graphics were so advanced. "Did you just now stop playing?"

Connie nodded. "About two minutes before you got here. I left it on because I wanted to show you."

Delta glanced helplessly at Gina, who merely shrugged.

"Del, this is one of the toughest games I've ever played. Last night, there was this beast with about fifty heads. It had the body of a dog and the heads of snakes. I had to find a way to kill it before I could get to the next level. Before I knew it, it was eight in the morning, and I was still battling away."

Her interest piqued, Delta started for the computer. "So, how'd you do it?"

"Oh, no," Megan groaned, "not you, too." Taking Gina's arm, Megan headed for the porch.

In a flash, Connie was in front of Eddie II with a joystick poised in her hand. She reminded Delta of a little kid showing her best friend all of the toys she got for Christmas. "Here. You try."

Delta took the joystick. After Connie released the pause button, Delta maneuvered the dwarf to a position where she could strike with the sword. As soon as the blade went through one of the heads of the beast, the dwarf was killed by a different head.

"What happened?" Delta asked.

Connie grinned. "That's what I wanted to know. I stayed up all night trying to stab the right head."

"And did you?"

Before Connie could reply, Gina and Megan entered the room and swiftly pulled their partners away from the computer.

"This is family night, remember? Quality time, remember? No shop talk and absolutely no computers!"

For the remainder of the dinner, talk centered around a variety of issues, none of which had to do with police work or computer games.

Around ten o'clock, Delta and Megan decided it was time to go home.

"Next week's family night is at Megan's, right?"

Megan nodded. "I've reserved the hot tub, so bring your suits. Or don't. It's all up to you. I thought we could play dirty password among the bubbles."

Gina grinned, as she slipped her hand through Connie's. "Sounds like fun."

"Absolutely decadent," Connie mused. "See you tomorrow night, Del."

"You bet." Delta hooked her arm through Megan's and started down the walk. Before they were to the car, Delta stopped and turned back toward the door, where Gina and Connie stood arm-in-arm.

"Hey, Connie, how exactly did you kill that beast?"

Connie smiled a knowing grin—a grin that said she had hooked Delta into the mysteries of the game.

"I poisoned it."

15

"S1012, we have a 187 at 2121 Wharton Ave. See the lady."

Delta and Jan exchanged glances. Another murder so soon after the last?

"This is S1012. Please 10-13." Jan asked dispatch to advise them of the condition of the scene.

"S1012, you have a 219, suspect fled scene. Owner will meet you at front gate. Copy?"

Delta glanced at Jan, who spoke calmly into the mike. "Dispatch, is that a two-one-niner?" Jan asked.

"10-4."

"Multiple victims?"

"Negative."

"10-4. Who's back-up?"

"S1011 and R1921 will back-up and establish perimeter. Copy?"

"S1012, we copy. S1011, what's your 20?" Jan asked, wanting to know where S1011 was and how long it would take them to arrive. S1011 immediately answered. "This is S1011. We're four away. We have a 213 we're just clearing. Over."

"10-4."

Suddenly, dispatch came back on. "S1012, the woman specifically requested a female officer."

Jan smiled into the mike. "Then you requested the right unit, didn't you?"

As the patrol unit zipped through the maze of streets, Jan cleared her throat and stared out the window. "You think it's him, don't you?"

Delta nodded, her stomach quietly convulsing. Since the call was a stabbing, it already fit his M.O. "It wouldn't surprise me."

"Could be gang-related."

Delta nodded. "Perhaps."

As they walked into the large, immaculate grounds of a Spanish-style home set far off the streets, a near hysterical woman in her mid-50s jumped out from behind a limousine parked in the circular driveway. Frantically waving her arms in the air, and mascara running down her post-facelift cheeks, her eyes were wide with terror.

In the floodlights that brightened the entire front yard, Delta noticed a tall, rather husky man in his 30s leaning against the limo. When he saw Delta, he stood up straight and removed his hands from his pockets. He didn't say a word but pointed to the woman, who was racing around the yard, grabbing her head and her chest and crying "Ohmygod, ohmygod, he's . . . he's . . . "

Immediately, Jan moved over to the woman and tried to calm her, while keeping a wary eye on the man by the limo. As soon as Jan touched the woman's arm, she sat down on the grass and sobbed.

"I'll take her into the house and try to calm her down, Del," Jan said, helping the woman up from the lawn.

Delta radioed they had arrived before slowly approaching the man.

"I'm Jordan Martin," the man said in a deep baritone. "I'm a neighbor."

Delta quickly sized him up. For all of his apparent macho nonchalance, the man appeared quite shaken and was trying to hide it, but Delta knew the signs. His face had a pallor to it, and the heavy line of perspiration dotting his upper lip indicated the nervousness he was feeling.

"Can I see some ID?" Delta asked, not taking her eyes off his hands.

Jordan Martin reached into his back pocket and pulled out an old brown leather billfold. As he handed Delta his driver's license, he told her that he lived behind the old house.

"I came running as soon as I heard Mrs. Griffin scream. My wife will tell you as much."

Keeping one eye trained on Mr. Martin, Delta looked at his driver's license and saw that he was, in fact, Jordan Martin who resided in the house behind the property. This didn't, by any stretch of the imagination, make him innocent in her eyes. It simply meant he was who he said he was.

Handing his license back, Delta's surveyed the property. "Where's the body?"

Jordan's head jerked backwards. "The other side of the car. Hope you haven't had dinner recently. It's a pretty gruesome sight."

"Well, Mr. Martin, my partner and I would appreciate it if you would have a seat on the porch over there until we can take a look around and ask you a few questions."

"I'm not in any trouble, am I?"

Delta straightened up to her full height. He was taller than her by a few inches. "That depends. You just stay there while I take a look around." Delta watched as Jordan lumbered over to the porch and sat down. She then rounded the front bumper of the black limo.

As she came around the driver's side of the bumper, Delta first saw two shiny black shoes lying heel up. For a moment, the universal clock rewound itself to that split second in time when she came around the bumper of her patrol car to find Miles's bullet-ridden body bleeding on the pavement.

So intense was the memory, so deep was the wound, that Delta had to steady herself against the limo before continuing.

What she saw when she came to the front of the limo brought the sour taste of bile to her throat. Lying face down on the pavement, with his head split in two from the back, was someone dressed in a chauffeur's uniform. His head looked like two halves of a watermelon, as bits of gray matter slowly oozed down either side. The grotesque nature of his gaping wound wasn't the sole reason vomit threatened to escape Delta's stomach. The slimy brains glistening under the porch lights seemed almost surreal, and the amount of blood was too vast to comprehend. What was hardest for her to focus on was that his arms had no hands.

His handless arms ended at a puddle of quickly congealing blood and were outstretched, as if he had tried to crawl away from his assailant.

"Oh shit," Delta muttered, moving to the front of the limo and wiping her mouth with her handkerchief.

"Pretty nasty stuff, huh?" came Jordan's deep voice from the porch.

Trying to keep her stomach from flying out of her mouth, Delta inhaled slowly and deeply before walking over to question Mr. Martin, who, as she soon discovered, neither heard nor saw anything. He had simply come running to the older woman's screams.

When Jan and Mrs. Griffin came back from the house, Delta was covering the body with a sheet from the back of her unit.

"Del, she says she'd like to stay out here with you and Mr. Martin, if you don't mind."

Delta looked over at the petrified older woman. "No problem. Mr. Martin, would you mind sitting on the other side of the porch from Mrs. Griffin until the detectives arrive? They're going to need separate statements from both of you."

"Why can't I talk to you ladies?" Mrs. Griffin asked, eyes wide with terror. She reminded Delta of a fawn in the middle of the road about to be hit.

"Don't you worry about a thing, Mrs. Griffin. My partner and I are just going to make sure that none of the evidence is destroyed."

Mrs. Griffin rubbed her eyes. "Evidence? What's happening to the world?" Shuffling over to one of the porch chairs, Mrs. Griffin sat down.

"Did she say anything that could help?" Delta asked Jan.

Jan's eyes narrowed. "Poor thing. She kept babbling something about hands. What have we got here anyway?"

"We've got a body with a head split like a dropped coconut and no hands."

"No what?"

"No hands. Cut off and gone."

"Oh God. Someone killed him and then cut his hands off?"

"Or vice versa. I just want to get a good look around before Leonard and his men get here and move us out."

"Gotcha. I'll take care of Mrs. Griffin." Jan reached up and lightly touched Delta's face. "Are you okay? You're looking a little pale."

"If I can keep my burrito down, I should be okay. I don't suggest taking a look."

"Don't worry, I won't. Unlike you, I don't have much interest in the macabre." With that, Jan whisked off to start taking Mrs. Griffin's statement.

When she was alone, Delta held in a breath and forced herself to squat down and take a closer look at the handless arms. The smell of death clung to her clothes and hair like cigarette smoke in a bar.

Leaning over, careful not to touch the body, Delta studied the pavement beneath the wrists and saw divot marks. There was only one mark on either side of the wrist, which meant that it only took one huge hack to sever the hand from the wrist. Whoever had done this was extremely strong and using a weapon that was both heavy and sharp. Examining the marks on the pavement, Delta saw that the ends of the divots were slightly shallower than the middle. Noting this in her notebook, Delta rose. It appeared as if the hands had been cut off by a weapon with curved edges.

Tucking her handkerchief back in her pocket, Delta exhaled loudly. There was little doubt in her mind as to who had committed this bizarre and brutal act. She knew, by the unique manner of the attack, as well as the strength of the blows, who was responsible for this. She also knew she was damn tired of people on her beat losing their lives to some deranged psychopath.

Scanning the area, Delta wondered if he was out there now, watching . . . waiting for his next move. Closing her eyes, Delta listened to herself for a brief instant. She did not feel his ugly and insidious presence; all she felt was the spark of a rage slowly kindling beneath the surface of her exterior. Inhaling slowly, Delta uncapped her pencil and outlined the entire murder scene in her notebook. The spark had now ignited, and Delta felt the slow burn of anger and determination erupt inside her. There was one thing Delta Stevens didn't do very well and that was to be on the losing side of anything.

And this was one game she had every intention of winning.

16

Even though District Attorney Alexandria Pendleton made it clear that they needed a suspect, Leonard had not handed one over to her. Delta knew it was because he insisted on linking the shooting murder to the other murders. If he persisted in his line of thinking, the shooting homicide would throw him so far off track, he might never find his way back. In the meantime, people were dying, and it was quite possible that two murderers were on the loose. The thought made Delta's stomach queasy. Before entering the station, Delta popped two Rolaids into her mouth and chewed them quickly before heading to the bathroom to splash water on her face. When she looked up from the sink, she saw Connie's reflection in the mirror.

"Bad night?" Connie asked, holding a towel out to Delta.

Pressing it gently to her face, Delta breathed deeply into the towel and tried not to think about her burning stomach or searing shoulders.

Sighing a painful sigh, Delta looked out from the towel. "Did you hear?"

Connie reached up and wiped a drop of water off Delta's cheek. "I heard there was another murder, but didn't get many details. They've had me combing the files for information on the shooting."

Delta reached back and rubbed her own neck. "It was bad, Con. Really awful stuff."

Connie took Delta's hand and motioned for her to sit on the bench. Standing behind her, Connie gently rubbed Delta's neck and shoulders as she had done on so many nights like these.

"You're really tight. It must have been horrible."

Delta closed her eyes and concentrated on Connie's fingers kneading her neck.

"Grotesque would be an understatement. Try macabre. Whoever this piece of shit is, he is seriously twisted. I'm sick and tired of him prowling around my beat murdering people. He's definitely without con-science."

Connie nodded. "The worst kind of killer."

Delta turned to face her. "Yeah, but most killers don't maim their victims. Most killers don't chop the hands off their victims. Most killers don't . . ."

Suddenly, Connie went white. Backing up, she leaned against the lockers and shook her head as if she was dizzy.

"Con? You okay?" Delta was up in an instant and standing by her side. "Do you need some water or some-thing?"

Without saying a word, Connie simply waved her off.

"I know it's gross," Delta continued, "I'm sorry if—"

"It's not . . . that," Connie forced out.

"Well, speak to me. Say something. You're scaring the crap out of me."

Slowly moving over to the bench, Connie sat down and wiped her face with the towel. Delta had nursed Connie through plenty of nights of illness, but she'd never seen her quite so shaken by a crime.

"Slowly, Del, and without missing any details, tell me what you saw tonight."

"Are you sure?"

Connie nodded slowly. "Positive. What happened out there tonight?"

Delta told her about arriving at the house, seeing the chauffeur with his head split open and how the chauffeur was also missing his hands. Connie listened very careful-ly until Delta was through.

"Did you find them?" Connie asked. Her voice was so quiet, it was barely above a whisper.

"The hands?"

Connie nodded.

"Nope. Connie, what's the matter?"

"Oh my God," Connie said, bringing her hand to her mouth.

Leaning down next to her, Delta patted her shoulder and waited for Connie to get a hold of herself. Something about this story had rocked Connie, and Delta knew her well enough to know she'd explain at her own time.

Slowly licking her lips, Connie stared down at her hands and into the damp towel. She swallowed hard before she was finally able to ask Delta, "He . . . he chopped them off with the ax, didn't he?"

Delta nodded.

Connie's eyes did not blink. She did not look at anything but the towel, and she did not move. Her chest accelerated its heaving motion, and Delta watched as her pupils grew smaller and smaller.

"Con?"

"You said that he killed the chauffeur."

Delta nodded again.

"The chauffeur was wearing the usual black chauffeur's uniform, wasn't he?"

This time, Delta's eyebrows knitted into a frown. Connie's reaction was really beginning to frighten her. "Yes, he was. I don't know why he went after the chauffeur and not Mrs. Griffin, but—"

"I do."

Delta caught her breath and waited.

Connie looked up from the towel and locked eyes with Delta. Her pupils were so small now, they blended with the deep brown of her eyes. "Con, you're really scaring me. Tell me what's going on? What's the matter with you?"

Connie's eyes riveted to Delta's. "I know why the perp killed the chauffeur."

Squatting next to Connie, Delta barely breathed. "You do?"

Eyes still locked to Delta's, Connie breathed in through her nose. "Hang with me on this one, Kimo, because it's so far out there, even you might have a hard time believing it."

"If you believe it, that's good enough for me."

Rising slowly, as if she was just recovering from being drunk, Connie paced over to the sink and got a drink of water. After throwing the Dixie cup into the trash, Connie inhaled and started explaining.

"Try to follow me on this, Del, without asking any questions, okay?"

"You got it." Folding her arms across her chest, Delta waited.

"Remember the other day, when I told you how I killed that fifty-headed beast in the computer game I've been playing?"

Delta cocked her head in question, trying to link up this far-reaching non sequitur with the horrible death of the chauffeur. She had expected a curve, but this was more of a spit ball, and Delta could only nod.

"Well, do you?" Connie's voice ranged between anxious and desperate.

"I remember." Delta thought back to that evening. "You said you poisoned him."

Connie nodded. "In these adventure games, when you successfully pass an obstacle, you get something for your success. Sometimes, it's a weapon, or a magic spell, or even a map. But it's always something you need in order to conquer the next level. Are you with me so far?"

Delta nodded, unsure if she followed at all.

"Do you know what it was that I got for killing that beast?"

Shrugging, Delta had no idea where Connie was going with this.

"Del . . ." Connie put her hand on Delta's shoulder and stared intently into her eyes. "I was awarded an ax. A double-bladed ax."

Delta's eyes narrowed. "An ax? Could be a coincidence."

Connie shook her head. "No, Del. I was awarded the same kind of ax that was stolen from Omega's."

Delta walked over to the sink and got herself a cup of water. "A double-bladed ax?"

"Yep. And do you know what I had to do with that ax?" Connie didn't wait for an answer. "I had to cut off the demon's hands in order to get my next prize."

Delta stood straight and peered into Connie's face. "And what prize was that?"

Connie exhaled loudly. "Gloves."

"Gloves?"

Connie nodded. "Gloves much like those worn by the chauffeur. You've seen the kind. They're short at the wrist like the gloves cowboys wear."

Delta mulled this over. What was Connie suggesting here? "You cut off his hands in order to get the gloves?

God, Con, don't you think this could just be a freaky coincidence?"

"With the singular exception of the shooting death, which you yourself said you don't believe is related, that game completely parallels your killer's every move thus far."

Delta swallowed hard. "Even the first death?"

Again, Connie nodded. "My dwarf started out with what I thought was a sword. But since she's a dwarf, the length of the sword deceived me. All along, she was carrying . . ." Connie paused here for emphasis, "a dagger."

Delta shook her head like a boxer who had just received a staggering blow. "Go on."

"When I figured out that I couldn't kill the fifty-headed beast with my dagger, I went back to the first level to see what I had missed. You can always go backwards in these games, but never forward unless you have all the right things."

"And?"

"And I missed the fact that the necromancer—"

"Necromancer?"

"Yeah. You know, an ancient druid who often mixed potions?"

Delta nodded. "Oh yeah. Like Merlin?"

Connie nodded energetically. "A necromancer could speak to the dead as well as mix roots and plants for potions. They often acted like modern-day pharmacists."

Delta nodded slowly, the picture becoming clearer to her. "Ah. Our first victim, Ben Friedman."

"Exactly. Earlier in the game, the necromancer gave me directions and I thought that was all he was good for. It never occurred to me to kill him. But later on, when nothing I did could get me to the next level, I went back and stabbed him. Then I took his bag full of potions and elixirs."

Delta cocked her head. "Potions?"

"More like poisons. The necromancer knew what was needed to kill certain animals." Connie waited for understanding to register on Delta's face.

"What you're telling me is that someone is playing a game on us?"

"Not *on* us, Del, *with* us."

Backing away, Delta walked over to the sink and splashed more cold water on her face. "You mean this whole thing is being orchestrated?"

"I'd bet a year's salary on it. When the fifty-headed beast died, Dori, my warrior-dwarf, picked up a battle ax."

"So, if the necromancer was the pharmacist—"

"And the beast, the Doberman—"

"And the ax was used to kill the chauffeur," Delta sat down heavily, "then we're up against one fucked-up sicko."

"Not quite, Del. We're up against a highly intelligent psychopath."

Delta let all of this information sink in before responding. "So the bottom line is you're playing a game created by a killer, who is acting it out. Is that it?"

Connie nodded.

"Is there any way possible for us to find out who created the game? I mean, there must be something, some kind of clue."

"There must be. Almost every program has what's known as a back door. It's kind of like a secret code that enables you to enter the belly of the game. If I can unlock the back door, it's possible we might find out who made it and why."

"There wasn't a label or anything on the disk?"

"Nothing. That's why I played it before all the others. I wasn't even sure it was a game until I put it in Eddie. When I saw how outstanding the graphics were, I decided to try it out." Connie paced across the room."I did think it strange that someone would send me a game without any instructions or even a note."

Running her hand through her wavy hair, Delta sighed. "So, there's some wacko out there who has sent you a game that he is re-enacting out on the streets."

"I'm afraid so. What we don't know is if he is leading the game or following it. That's where he has us. So far, I'm a few steps behind."

Weary, brain-tired, sick to her stomach, and emotionally exhausted, Delta bowed her head and rubbed the back of her sore neck. "Who on earth could think up such a thing? And more importantly, why?"

Moving over to the door, Connie shrugged. "Someone with an extraordinary mixture of intellect and insanity."

Delta rose and joined Connie at the door. "Miles once told me there were only four reasons why people murder: money, revenge, passion, and silence. Which is it for our psychopath?"

Connie shrugged again. "I'd rule out money."

"Why?"

"Did you get a good look at that dagger? It was valued over one-hundred thousand dollars. If our killer was after money, he had an entire pharmacy full of drugs that had a street value of thousands of dollars. No, I'd rule out money."

Delta nodded. "Yeah, if he wanted money, he would have gone after Mrs. Griffin. She's loaded."

"Right."

"And silence?"

"If he wanted to silence someone, he'd probably do it so that the body was never found. You have to keep in mind, we're probably not dealing with your everyday murderer. I believe he left the dagger in Friedman's body as a clue. Whoever he is, he's a game player, Delta. It's the game he's enjoying, not the murders themselves."

"Then it's revenge or passion."

"Or both."

Inhaling deeply, Delta held Connie's hand. "Can you get in this back door?"

"I'll give it my best. Even if I do, that doesn't guarantee we'll have any more answers than we have now."

Delta looked past Connie's shoulder and saw herself in the mirror. A killer on the loose was a frightening thing, but one who was playing games with the cops was beyond Delta's comprehension.

"Con?"

"Yeah?"

"I want him. And I want us to do whatever we have to do to get him."

"I know, Del, I know."

17

Gina set a pot of coffee and some sandwiches on the table, before throwing an afghan over a sleeping Megan. "Let me get this straight—the actions of the game are happening on the street?"

Connie and Delta nodded in unison. "Someone knows I play these adventure games, and he made sure I received that disk."

Gina sat down and rested her chin in her hand. "That would presuppose that the killer knows you. Swell."

Connie reached over and set her hand down on top of Gina's free hand. They had been together so long they were like bookends, with volumes of stories about their life together tucked neatly in between.

"I sure feel safe now," Gina said sarcastically, scooting closer to Connie.

Connie wrapped her arms around Gina. "More than likely the killer knows me, yes. It would be too much of a coincidence to think otherwise."

"So, what does that mean?"

"It means he's done his homework. It means he is aware of just how far along in the game I am."

"It means," Delta added, "That it's someone we know."

"Are you talking about another cop?"

Connie shrugged. "Maybe. Wouldn't be the first time." Connie shot a knowing look over to Delta.

"So, what now?" Fear was almost tangible as the words came out of Gina's mouth.

"Well, it isn't time to panic or make irrational decisions," Connie answered. "What we have to do is start the game over to make sure I haven't missed any vital clues."

Delta nodded. "We have to retrace the murders and see what the correlation is between them and the game. This disk may be our only shot at catching the perp."

"So, we have to move backwards in order to move forward."

Connie nodded and moved over to her computer desk. Flipping various buttons on, Connie waited for the game's introduction to appear before pausing the game. "I've taken a good look at the disk, and this is a home job made by someone using very advanced equipment. There are no labels, no copyright numbers, no nothing. The perp was very careful to leave out any identifying marks."

"Yet, it was sent to you at work." Gina walked over to the desk and pulled a chair over next to Connie.

"I'm afraid so."

"Got any ideas?" Grabbing Connie's hand, Gina held it in her lap.

"I don't want to rule anyone out, but it's highly unlikely it's any of our guys at the station."

"What makes you so sure?"

Connie grinned. "If any of them were half as good at computers as I am, I'd know. We would all know. It took a remarkable computer talent to be able to put together this kind of program with the graphics he's installed. We're not dealing with someone who dabbles with computers. This is someone who really knows his stuff."

"But we're still not ruling anyone out," Delta stated. She'd been burned once by her brothers in blue. She would never let that happen again.

"No, we're not. What we are going to do is make sure I haven't missed anything in the game, and then try to see if there's a back door." Connie fluffed up her back pillow and released the pause button. "We'll have to take turns manipulating Dori around, because my eyes get tired and my wrists start to ache. So just watch for the next hour or so and see how the game is played. Gina, you'll take down all of the words and instructions on the screen so we can refer back to them."

"What do you want me to do, Con?"

"Watch carefully, Delta. People's lives may depend on how well you understand the game."

When the music and introduction to the game came on, Delta read the title out loud. "*Death on S.U.P. Mylo.* Odd title."

"Odd character."

"Here's the rest of the intro. 'A sinister force has taken over the palace of Sabine. Young Dori was outside the palace walls when the city was besieged by the great and powerful Dark Lord. The Dark Lord wants to rule the almighty city of S.U.P. Mylo, but the forces of the Dark Lord demand the shedding of innocent blood before he can set foot at the bottom of the Great Mountain and claim his prize.

" 'You are Dori—young and wise warrior, who was out practicing with the blade your father left you, when the Dark Lord and his minions captured the palace and the city of Sabine. Only you can save the Sabines from the wrath of the evil Dark Lord. But first, you must enter into deadly combat against the wild and vicious creatures inhabiting the forest around the foothills of the Great Mountain. Once you are successful, you will then have to face the final challenge—the evil powers of the Dark Lord himself. Only if you defeat him will the sacrifice of innocent lives cease and the world be restored to normal.

" 'To defeat the Dark Lord, you must cautiously use every skill at your disposal, both mental and physical. You may find allies along the path, but *beware!* Only a champion of outstanding worth can battle the Dark Lord. If you succeed in defeating the Dark Lord, the Dark Force surrounding the city will be lifted. If you fail, all of Sabine will be destroyed by the Dark Lord's unforgiving wrath, and you will have sacrificed your life in vain. Choose your champion well. Good luck.' "

Delta studied the words carefully before they disappeared from the screen. The twinge in her stomach was much like the one she felt when she thought someone was watching her investigation of the chauffeur's death. Could these two forces of reality and fantasy be so intricately related?

"Got it all," Gina said, as she employed her shorthand so that later she could transcribe the information.

In the quiet of the evening, Delta watched in awe as Connie maneuvered little Dori from one peril to the next, swiftly hacking any creatures coming toward her and jumping over lesser threats.

"You're really good," Delta murmured, watching the ease with which Dori escaped potentially hazardous situations.

Half an hour later, they were facing the fifty-headed beast, and Connie finally leaned back in the chair and watched as Dori tricked the beast into eating the poison.

"So far, so good."

Delta nodded and watched Gina jot down notes. Delta wondered what she'd have said two weeks ago if someone had told her that she'd be involved in a computer game and that her involvement might save lives.

With the battle ax in little Dori's hands, Connie started moving her toward the door.

Suddenly, Delta bolted upright. "Wait!"

"What?"

Images of an alley, a trash can, a man in black, a shiny object humming as it whirled past her ear swam freely in the forefront of her mind's eye. But it wasn't what she was seeing that was important—it was what she wasn't seeing. The killer hadn't been carrying the ax when she chased after him.

"The ax!" Delta announced.

"What about it?"

"He didn't have it when I was chasing him in the alley."

"Are you sure?"

Delta nodded. "How else could he have thrown that star at me? Yes, I'm positive he didn't have it."

Connie paused the game, and the music stopped as well. "Then what happened to it?"

Delta thought back to the details of that call. "He came through the front door because that's what set the alarms ringing. But he exited out the side window and into the alley. I don't know where he put the ax, but it wasn't in the store when we arrived, and he didn't have it in his hands."

"Maybe he hid it and came for it later. Or maybe he came back for something else." Restarting the game, Connie made Dori shove the ax through a different opening than the one Dori used as an entrance. "I didn't even look to see if there was another way out."

"How about that little porthole thing right there?" Gina asked, pointing to the screen with her pencil.

As Dori neared the opening, the screen suddenly changed, and Dori was standing in a darkened tunnel. "Bingo," Connie said, smiling.

"Bingo?"

Connie nodded. "I haven't been here before. This may be where some clues are hidden."

Delta leaned against the back of the chair. "This is frightening. So far, the game mimics my every move."

Connie stopped maneuvering Dori and stared at Delta. "My God, Del, that might be it. Maybe you're the key to this whole thing."

"Well, let's go and see where she takes us!" Gina said.

As Dori moved down to the end of the tunnel, she came to a group of what appeared to be cardboard boxes stacked a little higher than she.

"Maybe this is it."

Connie licked her lips, but said nothing.

For the next fifteen minutes, Connie had Dori stomp, kick, hit, pounce, rip, open, and sit on the boxes, all to no avail.

Delta exhaled her disappointment. Just when they thought they were getting somewhere. "Damn. I thought we had something."

"We do," Connie offered, staring at the monitor. "We just don't know what it is yet."

Hearing the spring of the couch move, Delta swung around in her chair to gaze at Megan, who was rising from the couch. Delta greeted her with open arms and kissed her sleep-crinkled cheek. "Did we wake you, hon?"

Megan cast Delta one of her killer smiles. "Oh, no. Stomp 'em! Chop 'em up! and other assorted commands actually added to my sleeping enjoyment." Megan bent down and kissed the top of Delta's head. "I thought I was dreaming about a rodeo or something."

Delta blushed. "Sorry."

"Don't be. I have an eight o'clock class anyway." Leaning over to see the monitor, Megan squinted to get a better look. "How are you faring against the evil forces of the world?"

"Not great."

"What exactly were you trying to kick, hit, and bite?"

Connie leaned back in her chair and rubbed her eyes. "Just a bunch of boxes. Dumb, old boxes, and we're stumped. There's got to be a clue here somewhere."

"Well, hang in there, good and wise forces," Megan winked at Connie, who grinned. "I'm sure you'll get it. I think I'm going to pop in and take a shower, if you don't mind."

As Megan moved down the hall, she offered one last line over her shoulder. "If I were playing that game, I'd try reading the box. You know, maybe it's UPS or Fed Ex or something. I don't know. Gina, will you help me find something in your closet I can wear in place of this wrinkled shirt?"

As Gina rose, Delta and Connie stared at each other. Then, ever so slowly, as if they were afraid it might not be the answer they were looking for, Connie typed in R-E-A-D. She glanced over at Delta and grinned before pressing the return button. "She might have something, you know."

"Press the damn thing."

Hitting the return key, the monitor went completely blank, as if someone had turned the computer off. For a long, pregnant pause, nothing showed up on the screen.

Finally, the monitor started to change. Six barely distinguishable words came into view on the screen. Like the Cheshire cat in *Alice in Wonderland,* the six white words gradually appeared against the blue backdrop of the computer. Like separate little ghosts, they seemed to hover until they finally stood out against the stark contrast.

Six little words, and each one brought chills up and down Delta's spine.

Six words.

"HELLO CONSUELA—LONG TIME NO SEE."

18

Delta held her breath. Connie cursed beneath hers. Together they stared at the six words as the second row of words formed on the screen. The monitor, now back to its regular color, read:

"You remember me now, don't you? Sure you do! Who else is masterful enough to create such a complex and successful plan? Who else could test the powers of your own intellect so thoroughly? Who else, but that scrawny little propeller-head you and your buddies humiliated all those years ago at M.I.T., remember? Ah, how I wish I could see the look on your face at this moment."

Connie inhaled and stood up so quickly she knocked over her chair. "Not you."

Delta grabbed her hand to keep her from leaving. "Who? Who is it?"

Connie swallowed, eyes still glued to the screen. "His name was . . . is . . . Elson Zuckerman."

"And you knew him from college?"

Connie nodded. "Elson was a . . . well . . . we called him a scrawny little propeller-head at school."

"And that sent him over the edge? Come on, Connie. Don't tell me people are being hacked up because someone called him names."

Connie slightly shook her head. "No. It wasn't just that."

"Then, what? What could be so bad that he'd go off the deep end and start killing people?"

Connie sat back down and quickly tied her thick hair into a knot. "God, it's been years." Her voice sounded far away.

"If you don't tell me what the hell is going on here, I'm going to scream. Who is this guy?"

Looking up at Delta, Connie shook her head sadly. "Elson Zuckerman was a bitter little man who had it in for me at M.I.T."

"*You* had an enemy in college? I thought you were one of the most popular students on campus."

Connie sighed. "I was. At the Institute, I was at the top of my class."

"Naturally."

Connie faked a grin. "And the second guy on the totem pole was always Elson. The other guys got used to me being at the top, but Elson never could. He wanted to be first in our class so badly, he did everything except sleep with the professors. I'd never met anyone with such a horrendous ego in my life."

"Was he mad because you were a woman?"

Connie shrugged. "I guess. There weren't too many Latina women in college back in the seventies, let alone a woman at a predominantly male school perched at the top rung. I guess he thought the position was reserved for him. He used to make reference to the fact that I was cheating him from his rightful place. Whenever he said stupid stuff like that in front of the guys, they'd be all over him. I mean, they would even give him wedgies. Can you imagine? Being in college and guys are still giving you wedgies?"

Delta smiled, remembering the many times she'd pulled her brother's underwear so far up, he practically sang soprano. What an odd tradition, she thought. Must have been painful. "Guy sounds like a class A jerk."

"It wasn't all his fault. His dad was a physicist, and his mom was another scientist of some sort. They had high expectations of him. Too high. I think it drove him to the edge."

Delta nodded. She remembered how frightened some of her friends would get whenever they would bring a "C" home. "Still, Con, the man's a psycho, and you're trying to tell me it's because his underwear was pulled over his head?"

Connie shook her head sadly. "God, I haven't thought about this in years. Our final project was for each of us to design and implement a program that would sell to an outside software company. I designed one of the first desk-top publishing packages with inter-office phone link-ups."

"And Elson?"

"He created what he spent his entire life doing—a simulated adventure game."

"The guys used to tease him about playing the games as a way of not dealing with reality. He would just swear at them and continue playing. He was very, very good."

"And?"

"Well, the night before the presentation, the guys got a hold of his disk and they added a bunch of porno scenes to it. You could have rammed a Mack truck through the professor's gaping mouth when a naked woman walked onto the screen and started to fondle Elson's hero."

Delta suppressed a smile. It sounded no more harmful than some of her college pranks. "So, what happened?"

"Elson bolted out of the room. It was a week before we saw him again. He walked right into class and confronted me. He said he knew I was trying to keep him from usurping his place at the head of the class. He said I was trying to humiliate him and that, someday, I would pay the price. He was so angry, it was the only time I had ever been afraid of him."

Delta could only shake her head. "Wow. What a wacko."

"It wasn't his fault, really. His parents had set him up to play the victim. You know, the kid that was always picked on, even in grammar school?"

"Yeah."

"That was Elson. His parents convinced themselves and him that he was the brightest kid around. Once he started extolling his intellect, people would torment the poor guy. And believe me, he was tormented."

"What happened after he confronted you?"

Connie shrugged. "It was our senior year. I never saw him again."

"He just disappeared?"

"Yep. Gone without a trace. He left M.I.T. and never returned. He didn't even leave a forwarding address."

"All because of an ill-conceived joke? Didn't anyone try to find out where he went?"

"I tried. The only thing I found out was that he withdrew from the last semester and moved out of the dorms."

"Still, one rotten joke shouldn't push someone to murder."

Connie stood up and walked away from the table. "It wasn't just one, Del. Elson was the goat for a lot of people's jokes. And I, well, I was a crazy young girl hanging around crazy guys who would do anything for a laugh. We never meant to hurt him."

Delta sensed there was more and folded her arms across her chest and waited.

"Me and the guys knew he had finally scored a date with this freshman he'd been talking about for months. Around the guys he'd pull up his pants and tell them how he was going to have his way with this girl. Well, as luck would have it, she went out with him. While he was out with her, we rigged a loudspeaker from his bedroom to the roof overlooking the main quad where everyone hung out."

Delta squirmed in her seat. "That's brutal."

"Pretty rotten, huh? But that wasn't the worst of it."

"There's more?"

Connie nodded, her eyes welling up with tears. "He . . . he couldn't get it up. I . . . can't begin to imagine the utter humiliation he must have felt. Everyone knew. I mean, *everyone* was out in the quad that night. We had violated every possible human right imaginable. When I look back on it now, I am so ashamed." Connie bowed her head and sighed.

"God, Con, we've all pulled regrettable stunts in college. That's where we go to make our mistakes. Up until then, we make our parents' mistakes. Don't be so hard on yourself."

Connie inhaled slowly, her sadness still evident around her eyes. "How could we have been so cruel? It's not like we hated him or anything. He just got on our nerves with all of that 'I am the smartest of you all' talk. I swear, we must have heard that once a day, and that really burned the guys. They would have done anything to pop the veins in his face."

"Still, you didn't make him a nutcase just by picking on him."

"I know that. But now, with people dying at his hands, I can't help but feel responsible."

Delta turned back to the screen. "Look. There's more."

The screen suddenly scrolled down and more writing appeared. "Yes, Consuela, I am quite sure you remember. I told you long ago that I would return. Did you think I had forgotten all of the pain and anguish you caused me? Did you think I could forget your cruelty and humiliating jokes? Did you truly believe you had escaped my wrath? Not likely. I've spent a lifetime planning our little reunion. You do remember the last words I ever said to you, do you not? I believe I warned you that I would be back, and . . . well . . . here I am. I do so hope you enjoy it. Alas, the "boys," as you used to endearingly call them, did not fare as well in their part of the game. But you . . . you were always the brightest of that pathetic lot. You and your ideas and opinions, always stealing center stage.

" 'But now, the stage is mine. And the script is the challenge to discover just how brilliant you really are.' "

"What does that mean?" Delta asked, jotting the words down on Gina's steno pad. "You don't think . . ."

" 'They were disposed of so quickly and easily, it wasn't even enjoyable. But then, they never were as "gifted" as you, my dear. Isn't that what all the professors thought about you? You were always the one who could do no wrong, even when you publicly destroyed me that mortifying night. You, the one who got a scholarship because someone had heard about the scams you and your brothers used to pull to get money. A cheap carnival trick, and you had them all falling down before you.

" 'Pathetic. You never paid for the painful experiences you caused me. Retribution is at hand, Consuela. I am going to right the scales of justice. I am going to prove, once and for all, that I am, and always have been, your intellectual superior. I am going to show you and the rest of the world my intellectual and computer mastery over you and your over-rated intelligence. As you humiliated me, so too will I embarrass you by committing crimes right under your nose that you will be unable to stop. Oh, the "boys," that disgusting group of hormonal retards, are long gone. It's just you and me now. How cozy. Just as it should have been so long ago.' "

Delta quivered from the chills. "What a wacko. This guy's really sick."

The monitor changed to a new paragraph. " 'I tracked you down and spent months designing this program especially for you. Every minute detail was researched and carefully planned. Oh, it took some doing, but it's impeccable. You see, I intend to pit my superior genius to your feeble brain, and the stakes . . . well, let's just say they're considerable.

" 'As you may have figured out already, everything that happens in this game will happen somewhere along the beat of your dear *compadre*, Delta Stevens.

" 'Surprised? Don't be. I know *everything* about the life you lead here in River Valley. I've done my homework well. Because she is touted as one of the best cops in the city, I believe she will suit you well as your warrior against the dangers she'll soon encounter.

" 'But I digress. First, you must solve each level in order to prevent a death of someone on Officer Stevens' beat. Your job is to try to get far enough ahead to find out where I'll strike next so you can prevent me from killing again. If you don't catch me before the final level, then a tragedy of great proportion will befall you and your little city.' "

"What does he mean?" Delta asked, frantically scribbling the note down on the pad.

No sooner had she asked the question, than the screen transformed from words to a picture of a high-rise. As they watched the building get more detailed, it suddenly exploded into a fiery mass before the screen went blank.

Connie placed her hands over her mouth. "God, no," Connie whispered through her hand. "This can't be."

" 'Make no mistake about it, Consuela, I'll play the game with or without you. I will continue moving through the city, preying on the helpless innocents unless you and your warrior find a way to stop me. The final level will be the destruction of one of the largest hotels in the city. You will have to live with the knowledge that your cruelty, your lack of humanity toward me caused the deaths of hundreds of people who did nothing to you. After that, I shall come for you for the final *pas de deux*. But for now, it's time. The game, as Sherlock Holmes was fond of saying, is afoot. Adieu and good luck.' "

Connie steadied herself as the screen slowly faded.

"What a fucking psycho," Delta said, hitting the side of the monitor.

Connie slowly shook her head. "Not just a psycho, Del. He's an intellectual giant. Don't ever forget that. He's been making these games well before anyone even thought about them. He's brilliant at it."

Delta slowly rose and stretched. "So what? Can't you do it? Can't you beat him?"

Connie looked away from Delta's probing eyes. "I don't know."

Delta gently touched Connie's chin and turned her so they were facing each other. "Look, you've played every available game on the market. You've had people from Silicon Valley send you games to test for bugs. You're brilliant at solving puzzles. Of course you can do it."

Connie's eyes suddenly teared up. "This is different, Del. This time people's lives are at stake. And you don't know . . . I've played his simulations before."

"And?"

Connie turned. "And I never won."

Delta took her into her arms and stroked her back. "But you're not playing this game alone."

Connie backed away and wiped her eyes. "We'll need help on this."

"You've got it. Whatever you need, we'll get it."

Connie nodded, already deep in thought. "We'll have to get as much of Leonard's information as possible."

"Done."

"We should call in some major think-tanks for this."

"Done."

"We may need Leonard's assistance."

"Leonard? Are you serious? Can you imagine him standing still long enough to even listen to our story? He'll die laughing before he gives us any information."

"We need his help, Del. I can't stay up twenty-four hours a day playing the game. Besides, we don't have all of the reports. The more data we have, the better our chances will be."

As much as she didn't want to, Delta saw her point. "What else?"

"We'll need to get big scrolls of butcher paper, so we can map where we've been and make a map of your beat."

"Good. And we'll get a bunch of different colored markers, too."

Connie nodded once. "We'll have to write down everything we do. We have to look at everything as if it had a potential clue. Nothing can escape our grasp. Nothing."

"What's our first step?" Delta asked, rising from her chair.

Connie glanced over at the phone. For a moment, the air in the room felt as if the temperature had just dropped twenty degrees.

"I'm going to find out just what happened to the boys from M.I.T."

19

Shortly after nine, Gina pushed open the door with her knee, her hands full of butcher paper. "I'm back," she said, setting the rolls down.

Delta was busy mapping the streets of her beat when Gina walked in.

"Where's Connie?" Gina asked, grabbing one of the rolls before it fell on the floor.

Delta looked up from her drawing. "Out for a walk."

Gina sat across from Delta and folded her hands on the table. "What happened?"

The room was so quiet, it seemed to be listening as well. "She found out what happened to the guys from M.I.T."

Gina bowed her head, afraid to hear, afraid not to. "Dead?" The word seemed to hang in the air as if it were a stage prop held by a thin wire.

Delta nodded. "All of them. Dead."

Gina slowly raised her head. "How?"

Laying her thick marker down, Delta exhaled and ran her hands through her hair. "One died of an overdose of cocaine, one was hit by a hit-and-run driver, and one apparently committed suicide."

"Apparently?"

Delta shrugged. "Hung himself. No note. Nothing."

"Were there any others?"

"One other. Douglas Rowe. No one seems to know where he is. Con thinks he's wearing cement booties or is in a thousand Ziplock baggies. Evidently, Elson hated him the most. He never had a nice thing to say about anyone. Even Con said she had a hard time with him."

"And she thinks Elson murdered them all?"

Delta nodded. "I'm afraid so. This Elson creep is one fast worker. He was able to murder four men living all across the United States in less than two weeks. One lived in New York, one in Lubbock, Texas, one in Boston, and Doug lives, lived, whatever, in Tallahassee."

Gina rested her head on the table. "And now he's after my lover."

Delta stood and walked over to Gina. During their years of friendship together, Delta had never seen a more devoted, more supportive partner than Gina. She never seemed to get upset about the long hours Connie put in and she was always there to lend a hand, personally or professionally, when they needed it. She was a great friend to Delta and Megan, and a wonderfully giving partner to Connie.

"He's not going to get her. I promise you, Gina. I'll die before I let some whacked-out psycho even come close to Connie. He may be calling the shots for now, but he's playing on my turf. That, my friend, is to our distinct advantage." Taking Gina's hands in hers, Delta spoke softly. "I swear to you, Gina, I won't let anything happen to her. He's messing with the wrong women, and I'll blow his brains out if I have to. No harm will come to Connie, if I have anything to say about it—and I do."

Gina swallowed back the tears and nodded. "You forget. I've seen you and Con in action. Whoever this Elson is, he's grabbed a tiger by the tail."

"Two tigers." Delta smiled.

Gina forced a grin. "She's your best friend and my lover. If you can't keep her from harm, no one can. But I have a bad feeling about giving that disk to Leonard. If we give up that disk, we might be giving Connie's life up as well. I'd rather we try than have someone else try and fail. I couldn't live with myself knowing we gave up the only chance we had to catch him."

"We need help on this, Gina. You've heard Connie say so yourself."

"I know. But Leonard? I've heard both your opinions on the man. Isn't there any way around him? Can't we bypass the system just this once?"

Delta inhaled slowly and shook her head. "Not this time. I'm not going to do anything to put Connie's life and the lives of others in danger. The least we can do is see if Leonard will be of any help. And we can't find that out until we at least talk to him."

"Fine. Talk to him all you want, but please don't give up that disk."

Suddenly, the back door swung open, and Connie walked in. The tear streaks on her face and her red eyes were tell-tale signs of her emotional state.

"Delta's right, hon," Connie answered, striding over to the fireplace. "People's lives are at stake here, and I don't know if I can figure this out on my own."

Gina rose and put her arms around Connie. "Baby, are you okay? You look exhausted."

Connie shrugged. "I don't have much choice but to be okay. We have a lot of work ahead of us. I've given it a lot of thought, and I think we have to ask for help. We can't afford to go out on a limb by ourselves with so many lives involved. The amount of time it might take to move the game forward before we stop him is enormous. It may take more than what the four of us can do."

Delta rose. "You sure you want to give up the disk?"

Connie looked into Delta's eyes and Delta saw eyes reflecting the pain and loss of the people roaming around in the alleys of her memory. "I'm not sure of anything anymore. It's like living a nightmare, and I don't know how to wake up. I, I can't believe anyone could be so vindictive, so vengeful. And for what? Stupid college pranks?" Connie sat down heavily on the couch and held her head in her hands. "They were good men, and now they're gone. Gone because they teased someone who never let go of his anger, who never forgave them their childishness."

Delta knelt in front of Connie. "You can't blame yourself, Con. He's twisted and he's killing again; people who don't even know him; people who did nothing to him."

Connie looked up, her face haggard from the stress and sadness. "That's why we have to get help. It would be different, Delta, if he took me one-on-one. But to go out and kill people who never did him any harm . . . We can't afford any mistakes. We have to see what Leonard can tell us."

Delta reached out and took one of Connie's hands. It was clammy and cold. "Then we'll play it your way. It's your call, Con." Delta cast a quick glance over at Gina, who turned away. "If that's how you want to do it, then the case is closed. We'll take the disk to Leonard and see if he's willing to work with us."

Connie looked at her with red-rimmed eyes and nodded. "Thank you. I think I need to lie down and take a nap. The news about the boys was . . ." Connie stopped and shook her head sadly before standing up. "I still can't believe it."

Watching Connie move slowly down the hall, Delta hurt for her. She knew too well the numb feelings of losing a loved one. It was a pain almost worse than death because it seared her soul like a branding iron, scarring her for life. And there was no medication, no miracle drug that easily healed that kind of deep pain. Only time.

And unfortunately for them, time was the one luxury they did not have.

20

"You're joking, right?" Leonard picked his teeth with a ballpoint pen and rose from behind his shabby wooden desk. "You're standin' there telling me that if we figure out some dumb game the killer sent you, we'll be able to catch him?"

Connie nodded.

Delta didn't. The heat of the office seemed aimed directly at them, as a tiny bead of sweat rolled down Delta's spine. She knew this wouldn't go over well with a man who founded his reputation on the concrete. There was a running joke in the department that Leonard would I.D. his own mother on the street if he ever stopped her. Leonard was scrupulous in his efforts to find tangible, plausible, and irrefutable evidence no matter what kind of case he was on. If he couldn't touch it or bring it to court, he tossed it out.

Not that this was a bad trait. It just wasn't conducive to an open mind. And Delta needed him to open his mind. The disk, the story, the whole case rested on what Leonard called a game. It was simply too abstract for a man with concrete underwear to grasp.

Leonard looked intently at Connie, his beady eyes staring hard at her. "So, you think he wants to get caught? Is that it? Psychologically speaking, the bastard is doing this so we can catch him, right?" Sarcasm dripped off Leonard's tongue.

Connie shook her head. "You weren't listening."

"Well, I'm listening now."

"I wouldn't categorize him with all of your other nutcase profiles. The man is brilliant. He's also vindictive and psychotic. This has nothing to do with his desires to get caught. It has to do with revenge and the lengths he'll go to ensure that retribution."

Leonard nodded and pulled half a cigar out of his pocket and stuck it between his teeth. "Somethin' about proving he's smarter than you, isn't that what you said?"

Delta twitched. Leonard was mocking them now.

Connie sucked her breath in through her teeth and continued. "That's part of it, yes. Detective, this man is not a run-of-the-mill murderer. You will never catch him if you box him with the others. He's bright. He's scrupulous to details, and he doesn't care who he kills."

Leonard took the cigar from his mouth and studied it. "Excuse me if I have a hard time swallowing the fact that this kook is carving people up because of some college pranks done to him over twenty years ago."

"Stranger cases have happened," Connie pressed. "Don't turn away because it's not found in the textbooks. Look at Ted Bundy! He was brilliantly insane. This is one time, Leonard, when you have to stray from the books and try something different."

Leonard chuckled. "Different? Yeah, I'd say that was a good word. And you want me to put some men on this . . . bizarre game?"

Delta felt her muscles tighten. For a second, she saw herself grabbing him by the throat and shaking him.

"Not just that, Sergeant. We need men to know what you know. We need to work together on this. If you could at least take a look at the game and see some of the parallels that have transpired, maybe you'd see that we have to work together to stop him."

"Together." Leonard's voice was void of emotion.

"Yes, together. If we knew the evidence you've collected, it might help us in areas of the game where we're stumped. And if you knew where we were going and what we were doing in the game, we might be able to lead you right to him."

Delta nodded. "Think of it this way, Leonard. We may have what you need to bring in a suspect."

Leonard ran his hand across his stubbly chin. "I know that the D.A. is getting uptight for clues, Stevie, but not even she is going to buy this. We've got nothing here but supposition, and it's strange supposition at that. Sorry, ladies, but as desperate as our D.A. is for a suspect, even she would wonder if you two have been sniffing bottles of white out."

Connie leaned over the desk, her neck veins bulging. "It's the best lead you've got or are going to get. You and your men could use a clue right about now because I know for a fact that you've got nothing. Zip. Zero. *Nada.*"

Leonard stiffened. "You don't know that. We're on top of it."

"Oh yes, I do. I know you've come up empty-handed. I've gotten my hands on just a few of your reports and right now, you're chasing your own ass."

"Those reports are under lock and key, Rivera." Leonard glanced over to Delta and frowned. "Oh, yes. I forgot. Departmental rules and regulations don't seem to apply to you two."

Delta took a step forward. She had had enough. "Listen, you son-of-a—"

Connie grabbed Delta's arm and squeezed tightly. "Look, Detective, people out there are being killed every third night. So far, they've been whacked with some kind of weapon that was stolen from the last crime. There are certain patterns he's established if you'll only detour from your manual and take a look at them. What you need is something to help you on your way, and I'm offering it to you. Because right now, you're spinning in circles."

Delta grit her teeth and stared darts through him. Somehow, she did not feel they were even in the same ballpark. "Admit it, Leonard. You've got nothing."

Connie joined in. "And you know it. The D.A. wants a suspect and all you've got is a bunch of paperwork. Right now, Detective, you're just farting in the wind."

Leonard leaned back in his chair and studied them. "You think so?"

Connie nodded.

Leonard clasped his hands behind his head and said smugly, "I shouldn't tell you this, but we have some very solid leads on the shooting."

Delta pushed past Connie and towered over the desk. "And I've told you that murder is unrelated. Are you so pigheaded you can't see that?"

Leonard smiled. "And I've told you, Stevie, that you've shown me absolutely no proof of that. Look, ladies, I'd love to sit here and trade 'what ifs' with you, but I have work to do. I'm not an unreasonable man, Delta. You know that. You have a theory and I've heard it. Why don't you leave the disk, and I'll take a look at it."

Delta did not budge from her looming stance over the desk. She wanted to reach across the desk and pull his intestines out through his mouth. When she heard Connie rustling around in her purse for the disk, Delta whipped around and stared questioningly at her.

Connie looked into Delta's face, but said nothing. Pulling the disk from her purse, Connie sighed. "It's copy protected."

"So?"

"So there's an internal mechanism that will destroy the files if you try to copy it. I imagine the device is Elson's own design. He's taken precautions to make sure it can't be duplicated. That would defeat the purpose of the game."

"Which is him against you."

Connie shrugged. "That's an over-simplification, but close enough, so be careful." Placing the disk on the desk, Connie averted her eyes from Delta's penetrating gaze. "Lose it, and we're screwed."

Delta felt all of her energy drain away. Had Connie lost her senses? Tossing that disk on the table was like tossing her life away. Every muscle in Delta's body cried out for her to take the disk and run, but she had to trust that Connie knew what she was doing.

Leonard looked at Delta as if he knew she was biting her tongue. "I'll see that it gets some attention from Krispel. You know him, don't you, Rivera?"

Connie nodded. "He's usually swamped with work, but he's a good guy. Maybe he'll come up with something."

Rising, Leonard stuck his hand out and shook Connie's. "I know I sound like a tightass sometimes, Rivera, but it's my job to question every detail. You can rest assured that I'll do my best to see if there is really anything to it." Leonard turned to Delta and grinned. "Contrary to your opinion, Stevie, I do follow up on every lead, no matter how bizarre. If this is a righteous lead, it'll get the consideration it deserves."

Delta grabbed his hand and pulled him to within inches of her face. "The only consideration I'm concerned with is Connie's life. If anything happens to her because of your department's dragging its feet, I'll be coming after you personally."

Leonard's grin widened. "I believe that you would. Trust me, Stevie. I'll do what I can, within reason."

"Well, reason this . . . ," Delta continued. But Connie took her by the arm and pulled her away from the desk. "Thank you, Sergeant," Connie said, pushing Delta through the door. "I'll expect to hear from you soon."

When the door closed behind them, and they were down the hallway a bit, Delta turned on Connie.

"Are you crazy or *loco* or something? Did you hit your head in your sleep? How in hell could you just give away the only strand between you and Elson? Now we have nothing! Damn it, Con, I've never questioned decision-making before, but did you honestly believe he was going to do anything with that disk?"

"No."

Delta stopped walking. "No? No? Then what in the hell are you thinking? Delta waved her hand in front of Connie's face. "Hello, hello, is anyone home?"

Connie smiled. "Yes."

"Then why did you give it to him?" Delta's voice rose, and several secretaries peeked out from behind their computers.

Connie looked hard at Delta for a moment, before a slow, tiny grin played around the corner of her lips. "I didn't."

Delta frowned. "You didn't."

"Nope."

"But I saw—"

"You saw me toss a game disk on his desk."

"A disk?"

Connie nodded. "It wasn't our disk. God, Del, did you really think I would put my life on the line by giving our resident gumshoe the only real lead we have?"

"Well . . . "

"Oh, come on, Storm. You know me better than that. I needed to feel him out first. But you were right. Leonard is of no use to us right now until we have some solid leads for him. He's only willing to help if it's a give-and-take situation. I gave him the disk, and I'll take his data whether he wants me to or not. He's a good detective, Del, but he's of no use to us until he accepts what we're offering him."

Delta let a huge sigh release from her lungs. "You had me going, that's for sure. Man, for a minute there, I thought you'd lost your mind."

Connie's smile deepened and her eyes softened. "That's certainly possible, you know. The way I see it, we did what we're supposed to do: we informed him of additional information. But now that that's done, I'll make a few calls to friends of mine who are a little better at this than I am and see if we can't get a little more help on the computer end of things."

"Well, we've faced worse odds."

Connie nodded. "Indeed, we have."

"But we still need what Leonard has."

Connie grinned. "Yes, we do. And since we couldn't get it going through proper channels, well . . . let's just say that it's time to warm Eddie and to call in a few markers. Believe me, there are more than a handful of investigators who owe me a favor or two."

"Thank god for favors." Opening the door for Connie, Delta asked, "There's one more thing I'm curious about."

"What's that?"

"Farting in the wind?"

Against the early morning sky, both women threw their heads back and laughed.

21

The butcher paper was taped to the den walls, and different colored felt pens lay strewn across the table. Delta unfolded a map of her beat and continued enlarging it on her drawing. Gina had just walked in and poured a stack of library books on the floor, while Connie taught Megan how to play the game and move Dori from place to place. Tension hung ominously in the room like smoke from a burnt roast.

"No clue goes unnoticed, and nothing in the game is ever trivial," Connie pointed out as Dori turned a rock over to reveal a key to the next level. "You must check everything out, no matter how stupid it may seem. That may mean talking to trees, eating rocks, or setting houses on fire. You have to think like Elson . . . this is a fantasy. Anything goes."

Megan nodded. "Got it." Suddenly, Megan reached over and paused the game. "Do you really think he expects you to work on this day and night?"

Connie shook her head. "No. So far, his pattern has been to strike every third night. I think he means to give me some respite. He wants to beat me at my best. The win wouldn't taste as good to him if he didn't give me my best shot."

Gina moved over to Connie and hugged her from behind. "He sounds so insane."

Connie nodded. " 'There is no genius without a mixture of madness.' Seneca, I think. You know, Jack the Ripper, who was never caught, had an incredible intellect."

"Frightening," Megan murmured, looking over at Delta for reassurance.

"And unpredictable," Delta said from the kitchen.

"Exactly."

"So, now what?"

Connie turned in Gina's arms and hugged her. "We start at the beginning once more and take notes on everything. Delta will map out each level and see how it pertains to her beat. Meg will write down every name, every street, every beast, everything that appears in writing. Then, you and Gina will hit the books and research everything you find. If you come up with a Jones Street, you comb through every source we have until we find whether or not it has any significance."

Delta and Megan nodded and glanced over at the growing pile of books on the floor. They had every almanac, every desk reference, every major dictionary ever printed. There was a complete set of encyclopedias, books on mythology, genealogy, history, biblical literature, and the like. Megan and Gina had been at the library all morning checking out the necessary material. The job of research appeared an impossible task.

"Don't worry, Megan. It only appears insurmountable. You'll get the hang of it. I've played his games before, and he's a master at hiding clues right in front of your face. At least, that's how he did it in college."

"And my job is to write down every action Dori makes in order for something to happen," Megan stated.

Connie nodded. "Right. Like when Dori read the boxes. You'd write 'Read box, discovered Elson note,' so if we have to go back, we'll remember what we've done."

All three women nodded as they received their assignments.

"But Con, if we have to start at the beginning, won't we waste time?"

Connie shook her head. "The way these games work has to do with the order in which you accomplish a set of goals. In other words, I couldn't kill the fifty-headed beast until I acquired what was needed. The computer knows the sequence of events and can only move forward when those events are done in the right order. I wasn't cautious going through the first time because I didn't know what was at stake. I might have missed some important clues."

A sick streak pierced Delta's stomach. On the street, she knew the parameters to work by, as well as how her capabilities fit into those parameters. But this, this was altogether different than anything she'd been trained for. She felt like a blind person trapped in a maze.

"What do we do when we discover who his next target is?" Megan asked, uncapping a pen.

Connie's eyes narrowed. "We set him up."
Delta nodded. "And then we take him out."

22

Jan was speechless.

Only when they had stopped for dinner did Jan put her thoughts to words.

"Delta, I think you're looking for trouble if you go at this on your own. Especially if you've already spoken to Leonard about it. Or have you forgotten the warning given to you after the trial?"

Delta bowed her head and moved her food around her plate with her fork. How could she forget? She'd received not one, but two warnings after the trial of Miles's murderers; both were the same: "Follow departmental rules from here on out, or you're gone."

"Warning or not, Connie's in trouble. What would you do if she were *your* best friend?"

Jan took an apple out of her brown sack and took a small bite. "I'd go over Leonard's head only *after* I gave him a chance to run with it on his own."

"That would take too much time. While he was busy checking and re-checking, people would be murdered as Elson goes on his merry game-playing. You know how departmental bureaucracy is."

"Yes, and I also know you aren't one who goes through proper channels if you think there's a faster route."

This brought a grin to Delta's face. She couldn't deny shirking departmental rules, especially if she felt those rules hampered her from getting the job done. "I get results. And I'm not about to chance it with Connie involved. We got away with the disk swap once. I'm not going to get on my knees and beg for someone's help. As far as I'm concerned, we did what was required. The rest is moot."

"You slipped him a phony disk. I don't call that 'doing what was required.' I call that faking procedure. I don't imagine that will go over very well once it's discovered."

Moving her tomato off her salad and to the side, Delta looked up at Jan. "If I can't keep my best friend from harm, then this job really won't be worth a damned thing to me anyway."

Jan took another bite out of her apple but said nothing.

"And I'll understand if you—"

"Don't even say what I think you're about to say, Delta Stevens. We've been partners long enough for you to know that I would never bail out on you, even if I thought you were out of line. I understand that sometimes you have to do what you have to do and to hell with the system. I'll do whatever I can, short of losing my job."

Delta grinned warmly at Jan. She had certainly lucked into getting a partner like Jan. Delta was more than surprised when she realized they had paired her up with another woman. Many departments still did not pair two women together because of some archaic idea that they wouldn't be as safe or as intimidating. Delta often wondered if they paired her with Jan because they thought another woman might tone her down a bit.

Well, if so, it was a nice idea.

In theory only, of course.

Looking at Jan, Delta nodded. "Thanks. I wasn't sure you'd understand."

"Don't get me wrong. I won't let you put our lives in danger, Del, but I sure won't let anyone stop us from investigating murders happening on our beat. The last murder stayed with me all night. He's sick, Del, and I want him off our beat just as much as you do. And if he's after Connie, then it's no holds barred. So, count me in."

Delta reached over and patted Jan's hand before checking the beeper worn on her belt.

Jan watched Delta's hand move to the beeper. "Is that for Connie?"

Delta nodded. "In case she comes up with something while we're out here. I want her to be able to reach me."

"God, she thinks of everything. That woman is a genius."

Delta smiled. "Let's hope so, Jan. Her life depends on that."

23

Pulling out of a park popular with the drug dealers, they received a call.

"S1012, you have a possible 240 in progress in the parking lot of 31109 West Twelfth Street. Copy?"

"This is S1012; we copy. How many involved?"

"S1012, no number given. Call came from a payphone."

Delta turned the lights on and looked over at Jan, who reached for her flashlight. They were seconds away from the parking lot of a bar where they were called. Delta didn't look forward to intercepting a fight tonight. Some night, she wished onlookers would just let the guys beat each other senseless. After all, when was the last time any cop got a 240 with two women involved? Shaking her head, Delta pulled her baton out and sighed.

As they drove up, Delta saw one man pummelling another on the ground. When they stopped, Delta was frozen by the image in front of her. The man hitting the other man was wearing black gloves.

"Jan, wait! He's wearing gloves."

Before Jan could answer, Delta's feet were on the pavement and running. This time, Delta said to herself as the suspect tossed the beaten man to the ground and ran away, the little bastard wasn't going to get away.

Winding her way through the parking lot, Delta knew he was heading for the cyclone fence surrounding the car lot next to the bar. If he made that fence, she would lose him.

"Damn it!" she yelled, as he leapt onto the fence. Even petty hoods knew that few cops would risk tearing their hundred-and-twenty dollar wool pants climbing after them. Besides, climbing a fence with close to fifteen extra pounds of gear was no easy task even if one wasn't wearing wool pants.

Inhaling deeply, Delta pushed with all of her might and made one desperate lunge for him before he could get to the top of the fence.

"Lemme go!" the perp cried, as Delta grabbed one sneakered foot. "I didn't do nothin', man."

Delta ripped him down off of the fence and wrestled him to the ground. Wiry and full of fire, he fought and elbowed and clawed until he saw Delta pull her baton. As she raised her baton to come crashing down across the top of his skull, Delta realized he was just a kid. Her slight hesitation gave him just enough time to buck her off. In the next blink, he scrambled to his feet and was making his way across the grass when she chased him again and came crashing down on him, full-force, and got him in a full-Nelson headlock.

"Lemme go!" the kid yelled.

Holding him up off his feet, Delta whirled him around once before slamming him face first into the hood of a parked car.

"Police brutality, man! I ain't done nothin'!"

Grabbing him by the hair, Delta forced him to the ground and slapped the handcuffs on him. Then she grabbed him by the collar and yanked him to his feet. "Beating somebody up isn't 'nothing,' you little punk."

Unexpectedly, a huge smile lit up the boy's face. "I dunno whatcher talkin' about, man."

Jerking him along by his shirt, Delta soon had him back in the parking lot of the bar. As soon as they rounded the corner, she sensed that something was wrong; something was terribly unfamiliar. Jan was leaning against the front of the patrol car with the trunk wide open and the victim nowhere in sight.

"Uh, Delta . . ."

Delta looked around. "Where is he? What happened?"

Jan motioned with her head to the back of the car. "In the trunk."

Cocking her head in question, Delta pushed the kid over to Jan. "Stay here, punk," she growled, pushing him to the car. "Jan, what do you mean, he's in the trunk?"

The boy snickered.

"See for yourself."

Peering into the trunk, Delta heard the boy break into near-hysterical laughter. In the trunk was a mannequin dressed like a man. For a moment, Delta said nothing.

She just stood there, looking perplexed at the stiff figure laying with painted eyes staring blankly at her.

Whirling around, Delta grabbed the laughing boy by the shirt and rammed him up against the car.

"What in the fuck is this about?" She screamed into his face. The laughter ceased immediately.

"Look, I ain't done nothin' illegal. This dude offered me a hundred bucks to put these gloves on and pretend to beat up that stupid doll. It was a hundred bucks, man."

Delta did not release her iron grip. Inside, her heart raced, her adrenaline pumped, and her lungs heaved. She felt like the seams of her patience were ripping apart. "What guy?"

"I dunno, man. He was wearing a hat and dark glasses. I didn't ask him no questions, man; I just took the gloves and the dough and split."

Delta rammed him harder against the car. Every muscle in her body was in fighting mode, and her right hand kept opening and closing as if she were pumping her own blood pressure. "What else did he say, goddamnit?"

"He, he said for me to tell the lady cop . . . let me see . . ."

"Think, damn you!"

"Del . . ." Jan's voice cut through the night.

If Delta heard Jan, she gave no indication. "What else did he say?"

"He said to be more, more imaginative than that. Yeah, that's it. That's what he said."

"Is that all?" Delta had lifted the youth off the ground and held him pinned to the car with one arm. The seam inside was slowly tearing.

"Yeah, man, I swear! It was a hundred bucks, man. Easy cash."

The seam tore completely open. She wanted to bash Elson's face in and she was beginning to take it out on this trembling boy. She wanted to hit something so the fear and frustration building inside her would be released. She wanted to shake this boy until she could know everything that passed between him and Elson. She wanted . . .

"Del, let him go."

She did not hear. In the far recesses of her mind, Delta saw herself holding Elson off the ground. He was pleading for his life in one instant and laughing at her the next.

"Let him down, Del." Jan reached out and touched Delta's arm.

Looking over at Jan as if seeing her for the first time, Delta stared blankly.

"Put him down."

Pulled from her trance, Delta looked from Jan to the scared boy to Jan and back to the boy, who tried grinning.

"Oh," Delta said, slowly lowering him to his feet. "Yeah, sure." Releasing him, Delta turned to Jan, who still had her hand on Delta's arm.

"You okay?"

Delta nodded, feeling her anger subside. Pinching the bridge of her nose, Delta quietly asked Jan, "Take care of him, will you?"

Jan gently squeezed Delta's arm and silently moved over to take care of the boy, who appeared relieved to have the smaller, quieter cop take over.

After Jan I.D.'d the boy, she took the driver's seat and watched as Delta slowly climbed in.

"You sure you're okay? That didn't look so swell to me."

Delta turned from her thoughts and nodded. "He's toying with us. That bastard set us up. It's as if he's watching us."

Jan turned the car left onto Tennyson. "That's a pretty scary thought."

"Yep. He knows our every move before we do."

Jan shook her head. "That's not all, Del. He *made* us move. Like pawns on a chessboard, he moved us with that little charade. He's in charge and he knows it."

Delta nodded. "The message for us isn't to be more creative. He's letting us know it's his game and he's in control." Delta pulled some change from her pocket. "Pull over so I can let Connie know of his latest ploy."

"Maybe it will give her something to go on."

"Maybe. And maybe it will scare the shit out of her." Delta glanced over at Jan, who looked more serious than she ever remembered her looking. "Until Connie can come up with something, we're playing this hand blind. We can't make a move until she figures that damn game out. God, how I hate this."

Jan nodded. "I know. Until then, we just ride it out and do the rest of our job, okay? We can't let it get to us."

Nodding, Delta stared out the window. It was already getting to her; that was evident by the way she handled the boy. From now on, she would have to be cool and show more control. From now on, she would allow him to move her until she could find her way to the other side of the chessboard. And when she did, she would trade up for a queen.

Then, they would play by her rules.

24

Moments after they I.D.'d the boy, Delta's beeper went off. "Pull over Jan. I just got a buzz from Connie." Jumping to a payphone, Delta called Connie at her desk. "It's me. Whatcha got?"

"It's a good thing we started over. We were way off."

"How so?"

"I've been fighting this one-horned creature I walked away from the first time I played."

"You mean a unicorn?" Delta watched a prostitute cross the street to an awaiting car.

"I don't think so. This thing is ugly. I mean, it's hairy and huge and doesn't look a thing like a unicorn. It's gross. Anyway, I've done everything I can, but I can't beat it using the gloves. I don't think he intends on beating his next victim to death. I'm not even sure he plans on using the gloves as a weapon."

"Because?"

"Elson wouldn't need gloves to beat someone to death. He has a black belt in karate. He could kill a man without even using his hands."

"Great."

"Don't worry on that end. I could kick the shit out of him even with his black belt. How's your night so far?"

Delta replayed the parking lot scene for Connie.

"So he really is watching us."

Delta nodded. "Yep. Appears that way. Not only is he watching us, he's got us going out to calls."

"Don't be surprised if you find a bug in your truck or on any of your equipment. Elson is an electronics whiz, and it wouldn't be difficult at all for him to be patched right in to your radio."

"That's a comforting thought." Delta peered around the corner of the phone booth and got the chills thinking about him watching her now.

"He knows we've started on the disk for real. His little stunt tonight was just to let us know that he knows."

Delta squinted into the darkness. She had been trying to shake the gut feelings bubbling like a witch's cauldron inside her. Emotions lingered, thoughts paused, images flashed through her like she was viewing two different movie screens. "Con, I get these strange vibes whenever I think he's near. It's as if, as if I can sense his evil, his insanity. It's scary."

"I'm sure it is. You've always been an extremely empathic individual, Del. Maybe you tune in on some strange level."

"Well, I wish I didn't. It's invasive." Delta inhaled slowly and waved to Jan, who was motioning for her to hurry up. "Con, what baffles me is the fact that this guy has so much to offer, yet he would rather ruin lives for some sort of vengeance."

"That's why he's so menacing, Del. He's willing to throw everything else aside in order to prove the one thing he couldn't prove twenty years ago. There's a lot of anger inside Elson Zuckerman, Delta, and that rage makes him very, very dangerous."

"Dangerous is an understatement. He sees us, hears us, manipulates us, and we don't even know where he is. I feel like we're looking for a certain flea in a room full of dogs."

"Don't go getting all negative on me, Storm. We've uncovered a few more clues tonight. That's why I beeped."

Delta watched a man walking his dog down the street. Until Connie's college pictures of him came from the Institute, everyone on the street was Elson Zuckerman. "I'm listening."

"Okay, so far, he's only hit while you're on duty."

"As far as we know, yes."

"His pattern is to strike every third day, and he's only covered five blocks of your beat."

"Give the man credit. He's done his homework."

"Yes, he has. Enough to include you in nearly every facet of the game. I move Dori on the screen, and you move in real life. It's as if you're his creation personified."

"Well, we're going to have to find a way to use that to our advantage, won't we?"

"Exactly. You've got one more hour left of your shift. I'll be surprised if he kills tonight. Another pattern of his is to strike between ten and one. You know, he's such a head case, he's probably into the 'witching hour' and all that crap."

Delta checked her watch. "It's one-fifteen now."

"Looks like he's giving you the night off."

"Good. Are we doing an all-nighter tonight?"

"I've been pounding down the coffee."

"Great. I'll meet you at your place around four-thirty."

"You bringing Megan?"

Delta thought about this a moment. "She's at her place tonight. I'll stop by and see if she wants to come out and play. But I'll tell you, these exams are really tiring her out."

"Maybe we should postpone it then. You two need to spend some time together."

"Right. Your life is at stake and you want me to go home and try to make my relationship work. Sorry, pal, that's not how it works. Megan understands."

"Does she?"

"She'll be fine." Delta hesitated a moment before asking the question that had been preying on her mind all night long. "You don't think he'd hurt them, do you?"

There was a discernible pause before Connie answered. "Megan and Gina?"

Delta swallowed hard. Just the thought nauseated her. "Yeah. You don't think . . ."

"I really don't know. I've thought and thought about it, but I haven't a clue how distorted he is or might get."

"Maybe we should get them out of here. You know, send them on a little vacation somewhere."

"Sure. You try to move Gina from here, and she'll rip your arms off and suck the blood from your body. Not a chance. She's made it perfectly clear she's not going anywhere without me. Believe me, Del, I already tried. She's not budging."

"Understandable. Who can blame her?"

"No one. So you go see Megan before hauling your tired ass over here, or I'm not letting you in."

"I have a key."

"I have two big dogs."

"They're pussycats."

"I'll change the locks."

"I'll climb in through the window." Delta grinned. It felt good hearing Connie be herself.

"Fine. Have it your way. But when she dumps you like a road apple, you're not staying with us. This inn is full."

"She isn't going to dump me."

"She will, if you don't start paying some attention to her."

Delta threw her hands up, and the phone dropped from her ear and clanged against the phone booth. "Sorry. I dropped the phone."

"Are you sorry enough to go see her?"

"Yes! For crying out loud, you don't have to fcrce me!"

Jan honked. Delta ignored her. "Did you get a hold of your computer pal in Arizona?"

"He's in Europe. I have a few other calls out, but summer is an impossible time to get in touch with people. Consider us on our own for the time being."

Delta had anticipated as much. It wouldn't be the first time they faced hostile and uneven odds. "Well, I'll be over after awhile. Save some java for me. In the meantime, take a break. Give your head a rest. We'll pick up the pace when I get to your house."

Connie sighed heavily into the phone. "You're something, you know that?"

"Yeah, and when we figure out just what, then we'll all know. See you later."

Backing out of the phone booth, Delta slowly inhaled and looked up at the clear night sky. She felt like a time bomb with a sizzling fuse. She would have to do the one thing she was worst at; she would have to be patient. She would have to remind herself that every step she took, every corner she turned, brought her closer to the man-monster behind the wheel of this sick and twisted ride. She must remain patient, even though every tick of the clock brought them nearer to another level, nearer to another death. She would play his dangerous game and move like some mortal being steered by an insane god. Maybe that's what irked her the most; he was using her. The bastard was watching her and pushing her to places of his own design. Delta knew she had no other choice but to do as he dictated. He was calling the shots and she hated him for it. She didn't like being used. She didn't like him thinking he could push her this way and that.

Ah, but when the tide turned and the time was right; when the second hand paused between the strokes and the final grain of sand suspended in the air, the soliloquy would be hers. Because, although he was capable of moving her like some puppet on a string, what he did not know was the strength of Delta's character and her commitment to those she loved. What he could not possibly know was the grit and determination that sewed Delta's soul together and weaved through her the strength of hundreds of women.

And that, Delta thought, as she moved toward the patrol car, would be his ruin.

25

When Delta finally let herself into Megan's peach-and mint-colored apartment, she wasn't the least bit surprised to find Megan asleep with an accounting book across her lap. At her feet lay a thick law book open face down. Bending down to pick up the law book, Delta smiled and shook her head. She never realized just how important college was to Megan. At first, she took business courses, believing that was her forte. Then, she took one criminal justice course and fell in love with law; not just the law she witnessed being a part of Delta's life, but courtroom law. The kind of law criminal lawyers study. Megan had been bitten, and Delta was beginning to understand what was going on in her head. Sitting on the edge of the couch, Delta lightly touched Megan's cheek with her fingertips.

She was the most incredible woman Delta had ever loved. Unlike anyone Delta knew, Megan had picked her life out of the gutter and was polishing it to a brilliant shine. She demanded more than life had previously given her and was carving out a life for herself in college.

Yet, where was Delta in all of this?

Looking down at the woman she loved resting peacefully, Delta slowly traced Megan's thick eyebrow with her fingertip. Delta had to admit she'd neglected her relationship as soon as it got on stable ground; a pattern she had developed early on in her relationship career. It was the biggest criticism her ex-lovers had about her.

And it was true.

Somehow, she expected Megan to work on her own changing life and keep the relationship strong as well. Feeling her eyes start to water, Delta inhaled deeply and swallowed back the tears. How was it she was the best partner in the world when she was wearing a badge, but when that badge came off, she expected her personal life relationship to function on auto-pilot? Connie was right; Delta would lose this precious gift if she didn't start participating as an equal member of the partnership.

The problem was she didn't really know how to do it. She could give her career 110%, but she hadn't ever really given that to a living, breathing being.

Tracing Megan's face with her index finger, Delta bent over and gently kissed her cheek. If there was anyone who could help Delta love better, if there was anyone who could show her what it meant to give something besides her job everything she had, it was this woman right here.

Slowly taking her hand out from under the pillow, Megan made little sleepy noises. "What time is it?" Wrapping her arm around Delta, she stretched.

"Four-fifteen."

Megan opened one eye. "You look beat."

"I am."

Stretching the length of the couch, Megan's pink nightgown hung precariously off one shoulder. "How did it go tonight?"

"Do you mean my beat or the game?"

Sitting up, Megan took Delta's hand in hers and kissed the back of it. "Both."

"Connie's been working on the game all night. I'm on my way over to help her out, but I wanted to stop by and see you first." Delta did not let go of Megan's hand.

Moving closer, so there was no space between them, Megan reached over and ran her fingers through Delta's hair. "What's the matter, baby?"

Delta closed her eyes and concentrated on Megan's fingers in her hair. Megan knew her better than any lover ever had. She read right through Delta's tough facades and knew when Delta needed to be held or stroked.

God, she loved Megan.

"Del? Talk to me."

Slowly opening her eyes, Delta leaned over and kissed Megan's lips. It was a soft kiss, the kind that said 'I don't know what I'd do without you.' The kind that shuts out the rest of the world so that all she felt was the warmth spreading from her lips to the rest of her body.

"Megan, I love you." Delta breathed, as their lips barely moved apart. "I love you more than I've ever loved anyone."

Megan smiled and caressed Delta's cheek with the back of her hand. "I know you do."

"Do you? Do you know that I do care about the things you're learning in school? Do you know that I am so very proud of you for your excellence in class?"

Megan nodded and held both of Delta's hands. "Yes, I do."

"But I don't say it enough."

"No, you don't," Megan softly concurred.

Delta bowed her head. "And that scares me."

"It scares me, too."

Shifting her weight so she could fully face Megan but still hold hands, Delta sighed. "I'm not the best partner in the world. I'm realizing that more and more."

Megan started to reply but shook her head. "Go on."

"I get wrapped up in my work and expect you to do all of the maintenance on the relationship. It's not fair, I know, but I don't know how else to be. Ever since I became a cop, I haven't been able to give anything else the kind of energy I give my job."

Megan squeezed Delta's hand. "Able and willing are different, my love. The Storm I know is able to do anything her will desires. What hurts sometimes is I don't know how much you *want* to give to me—to us."

"I don't want to lose you." Delta's voice was so quiet, Megan barely heard her. "But I don't know how to keep you, either."

Pulling Delta to her, Megan wrapped her arms around her and gently rocked her. "Oh, Delta. My brave, strong cop. I love you so very much." Rocking Delta in her arms, Megan lightly kissed her neck. "You've just taken the first step towards keeping me."

"Really? God, Megan, sometimes I get so scared." Pulling back so she could see Megan's face, Delta's felt small. "Have you ever felt like you never really learned how to love someone? Like you keep trying to do what's right, but you make the same stupid mistakes all the time?"

Megan grinned a warm smile. "More times than you'd know."

"It scares me because I do so many things so well, but I feel like a beginner when it comes to making a relationship work. No matter what I do, I always get comfortable with the relationship and I stop working on it. I don't know how to fix that."

"Well, sweetheart, you have the first ingredient, and that's caring enough to want to make it work. As long as we both talk and learn and fight to make it work, we'll be okay."

"I want to be better than okay. I want, no, I need to know that I am 50% of the relationship. Right now," Delta pulled Megan back to her, "I feel like I'm about 10%."

Kissing Delta's cheek, Megan held her tightly. "Sometimes, you are."

"But you deserve the best."

"Yes, I do."

Delta pulled back once more. "I want to be the best. I want to be your last. I just don't know how to be that; how to get there."

Kissing both of Delta's hands, Megan took Delta's face in her hands and looked long and hard into her eyes. "*We* get there by working together. Delta, being too comfortable in a relationship usually means someone has stopped working or growing. You wouldn't stop working or growing on the job, would you?"

Delta shook her head. "If I did, I might wind up dead." Then it hit her. "Oh. That's what will happen to our relationship."

Megan nodded. "Are you willing to let that happen?"

Delta shook her head. "I'll do anything to keep that from happening, Meg. But talk hasn't helped me before. We can talk and talk and talk, and I'll end up going back to coasting if we don't find a way to get this relationship maintenance stuff through my thick head."

Megan lightly touched Delta's cheek. Her eyes were so loving and filled with understanding, Delta thought she might cry. "Del, I know this might be hard to hear, and you don't have to answer me right now, but will you go to counseling with me?"

Delta hesitated for a moment. "Counseling?" She had always thought counseling was a fad; something rich housewives made up to have something to do. Sandy, her latest ex, had shelves filled with self-help manuals and did everything but read them aloud to Delta.

Then, Delta wasn't interested enough to know what it was Sandy was trying to say.

But now, she was.

"Counseling. Honey, you're a wonderful woman trapped behind that damned badge. If the badge always comes first, we won't make it. Counseling will just help us sort through some of the feelings and fears we both have about the role that badge plays in both our lives. Maybe if we understand that, we can help you be the partner you want to be."

Inhaling deeply, Delta nodded, her face still in Megan's hands. There wasn't a question. She would do whatever Megan wanted her to do, and if seeing a shrink would help, so be it. "I'll do it. I'll do whatever it takes to learn how to love you better. Best."

"My love," Megan whispered, bringing Delta's mouth to hers. "You already love me better than anyone ever has."

"But it isn't good enough. Not for me, anyway."

"Shh. It will be." Megan's lips barely touched Delta's in a kiss searing with emotional energy. "Together, Delta, you and I can face anything. Trust me. Counseling will only make us stronger."

"I do trust you."

"Good. Because I know how hard it is for you to agree to counseling. I wouldn't have offered it if I didn't think it would help."

Holding her tightly, Delta whispered, "I love you, Megan."

"I love you, too, my scared little Storm. Don't you worry about a thing. We're going to be just fine."

"That's better than okay."

Megan's smile deepened as she lay on the couch and pulled Delta down next to her. "Yes, sweety, it is. Will you lie with me awhile before you go?"

Delta glanced over at the clock. She was already late. "Connie . . ."

"Already called and told me to keep you here until school. You're mine for the morning."

Laying her head down on Megan's chest, Delta sighed and clung to her like a soft raft. "She takes good care of me."

"Yes, she does. But it's my turn now."

Listening to the slow, steady tempo of Megan's heart, Delta's muscles relaxed as Megan stroked her hair and kissed the top of her head. As her arms and eyelids got heavier and heavier, Delta forgot all about a man named Elson and a bizarre murder case. The only thing she cared about at that moment was hearing the rhythmic beating of a heart she loved more than anything else in the world.

26

"Any progress on the game front?" Jan asked as she started the engine.

"Not much. Connie and I worked all afternoon trying to figure out what to do with those damned gloves, but we're stumped."

"How frustrating."

"And exhausting. Knowing that every minute brings us closer to another murder drives Connie like nothing I've ever seen. She subsists on coffee and nerves alone."

Jan cut her eyes at Delta. "And how are you?"

Delta shrugged. "Scared. Angry. There are a lot of weird emotions tumbling around inside. According to our info, he'll strike again tonight between ten and one. We spent the last two days mapping, playing, and researching, and still, we don't have a clue."

Jan blew a hard breath out of her mouth. "Great. We know he's out there, he's coming, and he's going to hurt someone, and there's not a damned thing we can do about it."

Delta nodded. "It's not for lack of trying."

"What's the hold-up? With a brain like Connie, I would have thought you'd have it by now. I mean, the game can't be that hard, can it?"

"The problem is, we don't have a key. You know, all those dumb games have one thing that tips the scales in the player's favor. There's something that ties the game together but we just haven't found it. Connie's exhausted and I . . . well, if I never see another computer, it will be too soon for me."

"That bad, huh?"

Delta nodded. "That bad. If we don't break a major clue soon, I don't know if anyone will be able to stop him."

"Leonard has nothing?"

"Nothing we can use. As long as he insists on tying Elson's crimes with the shooting, he's lost in a cornfield. We can count him out for awhile. For now, it's just the five of us and Eddie."

As the night wore on, Delta's senses got keener. She was like an owl in the dark; she could see things in an alley a hundred feet away that most people would miss right under their noses. She could distinguish between a man, a hooker, a crossdresser, and a pimp without looking twice, and she practically knew by the smell when a street hood was carrying a piece. There was a draw, a sense that allowed her to creep through the night, like a cat on a fence, through a hostile and frightened city. She relied on her intuition, her gut feelings that told her when danger was present, or when she was close to her quarry. It had never failed her yet, and she always listened to it.

Like now.

It was ringing like a boxer's bell.

"Jan, stop!"

Jan slammed on the brakes without question. "What?"

Delta shined her spotlight at the base of a huge bronze statue of a cowboy standing with a lariat in his hands. "I, I don't know." Something deep inside her was trying to push its way through.

Jan waited.

As the spotlight waved across the massive statue, Delta stared at it. There was nothing unusual about the statue, but for some reason, it drew her attention. She'd seen it a thousand times, yet she'd never really looked at it.

Why was she looking at it now?

"Del?"

Delta did not answer. There was something picking at her subconscious, but it was, as of yet, unformed. Try as she might, she couldn't bring it to her consciousness. But it was there. She knew it. She could feel it.

Ever since Elson's cold, metallic eyes had first targeted her, she felt a bizarre sort of energy from him. It wasn't that she felt watched, but she felt . . . hunted. Yes, that was it, it was as if he were hunting her. Like a snake slithering through the grass, he was watching her and waiting for the moment to strike.

Delta finally turned from the cowboy and faced Jan. There was something about the damned thing that was pulling at her, trying to get her to see something beyond her vision. Closing her eyes, Delta opened her mind and allowed her thoughts to bump into each other, hoping they might jar some idea, some picture loose in her mind.

It was like having something on the tip of her tongue, and then forgetting it; the more she thought about it, the harder it was to retrieve. Instead, she just stopped thinking about it and let her mind find it itself. There was something Connie said about cowboys, but she couldn't remember what it was or why it was important. Was it Connie who said it, or Megan? Maybe they both did. But what was it, and was it of any importance?

Next, Delta saw herself with her father when she was a kid. They used to walk down to a small corral around the corner of their house and watch the local riders jump and barrel race. Her dad would lift her up to the fence and they would sit and bake in the sun, as the gleaming horses kicked up the red clay dirt beneath leather-clad riders.

Delta loved those days. The days before the good and the bad found their way into her heart. The days when corruption and evil happened only in cartoons. She always rooted for the local rider who rode the black horse, and wore the shiny black chaps and expensive leather boots. That horse would sweat so much, it looked glossy, like someone had painted it with varethane.

And the rider. What a rider she was. She could maneuver her horse around those barrels as easily as a race car driver races around a track. She would give her horse one swift kick to start it in motion, and then, with reins firmly grasped in her left hand, her right hand would . . .

Her right hand.

"That's it!"

"What?"

"Pull over. I think I have it. Let me check with Connie and I'll be right back." Jumping from the car, Delta raced over to a payphone and dropped some coins into the phone and waited for Connie to answer.

"Con, it's me. I think I've got it." Delta's chest heaved with excitement. "We've been taking the wrong approach here. We've been trying to beat that one-horned beast."

"Of course we are. That's the point."

"Is the game on?"

"Yes. Been working all morning, and it feels like I'm never going to break through to the next level. If I didn't love Eddie so much, I'd put my fist through his monitor."

"Well, hang on, because I may have our answer." Delta could hear Connie typing away at the keyboard. "Is Dori wearing the gloves?"

"She's done everything but eat them. And to be perfectly honest, she's tried that as well."

"Hear me out on this, will you? We've been approaching the game from Elson's standpoint. So far, we've tried killing everything we run into. That's not our way, that's *his* way."

"Yes, but it's *his* game."

"True. But does he want us to think like him or think like us?" Delta waited for an answer and heard Connie breathing into the phone.

"Tell me what you're thinking, Storm."

"What if the gloves were used like a cowboy uses gloves? You know, to rope, to catch calves, to—"

"To ride? Not a bad idea, Del. It's worth a shot."

Delta held her breath while she listened to Connie pounding the keys. Looking at her watch, Delta cringed. It was 9:30. "Con?"

"I know, I know. It's almost ten. I'll give it everything I have. I've got to get close to it first. You go back to work, and I'll beep you the moment I have anything."

"Great. I'll be waiting." Delta heard her own heart pounding in her ears as she hung the phone up. It was a long shot, but then long shots were her standard operating procedures.

"Well?" Jan asked when Delta returned to the car.

Delta folded her long legs into the passenger seat. "For some reason, that statue caught my attention. I thought back to when I was a little girl, and I used to watch the barrel racers. I remembered the gloves the riders wore, so I thought—"

"Maybe that's what the chauffeur's gloves were for?"

Delta nodded. "We've been trying to kill it. I guess that's what these computer games are all about. Anyway, Connie mentioned something about cowboys the other day, so when I saw the statue, it triggered a memory of mine. Instead of trying to kill the beast, I thought maybe we should try to ride it."

Jan cocked her head in question. "Ride it? What kind of animal is it?"

"It's a big, hairy, four-legged animal with a horn coming out of the middle of its head. You should see it. It's horrible looking. Looks kind of like a buffalo."

Suddenly, Delta felt her pager vibrate, and she jumped back out of the car to make the call.

"Yeah?"

"You were right." Connie's voice was filled with excitement. "I've managed to get Dori to mount it. And you know what? It really isn't a beast at all."

"What is it?"

"A unicorn."

"A unicorn? Excuse me a minute, Connie. You may be the brain in the family, but even I know that unicorns are beautiful white horses with a golden horn. That beast couldn't possibly be—"

"But it is! Megan did the research and found out that your description is how modern man views unicorns. The ancients envisioned them much differently. They saw them as having the head of a horse, a lion's tail, stag's legs, and sometimes being quite hairy. It was believed to have been very ferocious and catchable only by putting a virgin before it."

"So? What happened when you rode it?"

"I didn't say I rode it. I said I got on it. As soon as I did, the screen changed."

"Another level?"

"I wish. Another challenge." Connie sighed heavily. "Every time Dori tried to make it go somewhere, she fell off. But we're on the right track. I'm sure of it."

"What should I be looking for?"

"Can't say. How about low-flying Ninja weapons?"

Delta winced. "Not funny. I wish I could do more. I feel so helpless out here."

"Helpless? Del, you got us on the unicorn. You're doing more than your fair share. Right now, it's my turn. You just be careful out there."

"Always." Waiting to hear the dial tone, Delta bowed her head against the glass. A unicorn, a rider with gloves, and still they had nothing to go on. It was all so maddening. What was worse was feeling him skulking around in the shadows of the night. She could smell his gruesome presence as surely as one smelled a broken sewer line. He was out there, watching, waiting, and getting ready to make his next move.

And they were not ready.

27

Six blocks away, the luminescent lights pierced through the darkness and glowed as moonlight glows off a sleeping pond. From the distance, amid the blaring car horns and screeching tires, loud booming voices and thunderous noises could be heard across the cityscape.

"Damn."

Delta opened her tired eyes. "What?"

"I promised Mariah that I'd take her to the carnival before it ended."

Delta sat up and glanced out the window at the crowd of people streaming away from the light show that exploded above the dark city. Delta hated when carnivals came into town because so many riff-raff came with it or were attracted to it. While Delta personally loved carnies, she had to admit that crime went up when one came to town.

"So, when does it end?"

"Tonight. Tonight's the last night. Shoot."

Delta felt for Jan. She couldn't imagine how hard it must be to work full-time and keep track of family activities of three children and a husband. It was all Delta could do to remember to feed the cats. "You were only taking Mariah?"

"Yeah. It was supposed to be our monthly mother-daughter thing. Originally, when she brought it up, I was glad she wanted to go and not the boys. They love all those rides where your stomach is forced out of your mouth and you don't regain your equilibrium for a week. Mariah's idea of a wild ride is the merry-go-round. Thank God for small favors."

Delta nodded, implying she understood, when she really didn't. She loved wild rides. "Too bad you missed it."

"Yeah, well, maybe next time. Their schedule is pretty regular."

"Think she'll notice?"

Jan smiled. "Unfortunately, yes. Just the other day, Samantha, her best friend, was telling her how much fun she and her family had there. When Mariah found out there was a dragon on the merry-go-round, she went wild."

Delta remembered Mariah's collection of dragons. "She still collecting dragons? I figured she'd grown out of it."

Jan turned and stared at Delta. "You did, did you? And just when, exactly, are you going to stop collecting X-Men comics?"

Delta grinned sheepishly and turned away. The lights from the carnival cascaded across the sky like an eerie rainbow. The closer they got, the more sounds and smells lifted themselves to her senses. As her mind rambled about, a picture of a dragon jumped to the front of her brain, sending that spark to her intuition. She remembered Dori slashing her way through some dragons on the way to their current level. Dragons seemed to be the up-and-coming creature of the 21st century. Everyone had them; from crystal shops to toy stores, even Hallmark Cards had a special dragon card line.

"Dragons, eh?"

Jan turned again, her eyes narrowing. "What's going on in that head of yours?"

Shrugging, Delta picked up the mike and announced they had a disturbance at the carnival, but would not yet need assistance.

"Damn it, Stevens! One minute we're talking dragons, and the next we're going to the carnival. What's brewing in that brain of yours?"

As the car slowed to a stop, Delta waited for Jan to face her. "It's one of my hunches. Something in my gut is telling me to pay attention."

"Pay attention to what?"

"I'm not sure. Connie said that she fell off the unicorn every time she tried to ride it somewhere, but that she can sit on it. Where's one of the best places to find a stationary unicorn?"

Jan reached for her baton. "On a merry-go-round."

Delta looked at her watch; it was 10:15. Elson was already fifteen minutes into the killing hours.

"Delta, you don't really think he would do anything at a carnival, do you?"

Gazing out into the crowd, Delta shrugged. "Frankly, Jan, I think this S.O.B. is crazy enough to try anything."

28

Rolling her window further down, Delta smelled the scent of buttered popcorn as it wafted into the car. Her gut was ringing loudly, waving red flags to her brain. There was danger here, that much she was sure of. Whether or not it was Elson, she did not know.

Leaning out the window, Delta asked a mime which way to the merry-go-round. The mime grinned, tipped his hat, and pointed north.

"Of all the people who could have given us directions, and you ask a mime?"

Delta ignored the remark and peered through the crowd ahead of them. There were two yellow poles limiting all but emergency vehicles, and a high school couple sat atop one of them. The young girl admired the stuffed teddy she'd won for her boyfriend.

"Let's go," Delta said, jumping from the car as it rolled to a stop. In an instant, she and Jan were out of the car and threading their way through the thickening crowd. Delta looked over at Jan and saw her slip her baton into the holder.

"You won't need that," Delta said coldly.

"And why not?"

Without breaking stride, Delta answered, "Because if he's in here, I'm taking him out."

"Del, this isn't the Wild West. We can't just—"

Suddenly, Delta stopped. "No, Jan, it isn't. It's sometime in the distant past, and I'm chasing after dragons and following the paths of dwarves. Don't tell me I can't whack him. He's after my best friend, Jan, my best friend. Someone who was there for me when my life was in danger."

"What are you going to do?"

"He's harassed her and is following me all over town. I'm going to call Connie first to see if she has anything for me. Then, if I get to him before he gets to me, he's finished. The end. I'm taking that sick piece of shit out for good." Turning away, Delta made her way to the

information booth, showed her badge, and then phoned
Connie to apprise her of the situation.

When Delta hung up, she turned back to find Jan
standing with her hands on her hips. "Damn you, Delta.
Sometimes you forget who's on your side."

"Look, Jan, I'm sorry if I come off like a maniac, but
I'm a little pressed for time. I think he's here and there's
no time to lose."

"No, Delta, *we're* a little pressed for time. You're not
working alone, you know. I'm your partner. I want to help
Connie as much as you do. But I can't if you won't let me."

"I'm sorry, Jan."

"Stop being sorry, Delta, and just tell me what I can
do to help."

"Get us to the merry-go-round."

Jan smiled. "It's easy for a shrimp like me to get
through these crowds. So, pay attention and watch a
master at work." Pushing through the crowd, Jan nearly
lost Delta on the first turn.

The air, which had smelled of popcorn earlier, now
hung heavily with the odor of sweaty bodies, stale hot
dogs, and sticky cotton candy. The odors lingered and
mixed together, creating a stifling effect that was hard to
breathe in.

The noise was incredible as well, and the clanging
and grinding gears sounded like an out-of-tune orchestra.
Children were screaming from being dropped off the edge
of one ride or "looped-de-looped" on another. Bells rang,
shots from the arcade popped, and the constant hum of
motors was the background music tying it all together.

About a hundred yards away, at the far end of the
carnival strip, Delta saw the merry-go-round, and she
could hear the pipe organ accompaniment grinding like
a rusting clock. Delta was experiencing sensory overload
in every way imagineable. Perhaps, she thought, that
was the ultimate appeal for children. Like a drug, the
carnival sights, smells, sounds, and experiences overdosed her senses. All, that is, except for the one she lived
by.

Her gut.

And right now, amid the beeping, buzzing, humming,
grinding, and screaming sounds that clattered about her

eardrums, Delta sensed his presence. She felt him watching her as they slowly pushed through the crowd and made their way to the spinning ride. Wherever he was and whatever he was doing, he knew she was there.

And he was waiting.

"He's here," Delta said to Jan, as they were about fifty yards from the merry-go-round.

"How do you know?"

"I can feel him. There's something evil, something profane about him that makes me know he's here. It's in my gut. I can't really explain it, but I know he's here."

"You've felt this before, haven't you?"

Delta nodded, eyes trying to see through the crowd. "And it hasn't been wrong yet."

Jan stopped and grabbed Delta's arm. "Plan?"

"Let's take either side and try to pinch him to the west. Keep him away from the bulk of the crowd. You call back-up on your way over to the other side and have them set a net around the carnival. With any luck, maybe we can run him into a snare."

"Del, if we set a net and you're wrong—"

"I'm not wrong. Trust me on this, Jan. He's here and he knows we are, too."

Jan looked at Delta and nodded. "You're sure."

"I'm positive. I'd bet my life on it."

Before they could take two more steps, Delta froze. They were now close enough to discern the people on the merry-go-round and the mounts they were riding. As the crowd parted and Delta got a clear view of the merry-go-round, every nerve in her body tingled.

First, an alligator, several horses, and a toad circled by. Up and down, up and down, the animals came and went. Then, she saw it. The gold horn first, as it rounded the corner behind the dragon. As soon as the horn was in sight, Delta felt everything slow way, way down, as she waited for the rest of the mythical creature to round the corner as well.

But it wasn't the animal that caught her attention next. No, it was a black gloved hand wrapped around the brass pole running up the center of the unicorn's neck. The left glove was firmly grasping the pole, but the right glove was waving in the air in animated conversation.

Before Delta could see anything else, the rump of the unicorn disappeared.

"That's him!" Delta yelled, pulling her .357 from its holster. Still keeping her eyes trained on the merry-go-round, Delta waited for the gold horn to come back around.

The crowd, seeing Delta whip her gun out, scattered in every direction, as others turned to see what it was that had this cop's attention.

As the beast and the rider rode up and down before them for a second time, Delta's peripheral vision took over, enabling her to see the whole picture. When she did, her blood ran cold and a gasp stuck in the middle of her throat. For the first time, Delta saw the reason his right hand was gesticulating wildly; he was having a conversation with a little girl who was riding the hippo next to him.

"Oh my God," Jan murmured, pulling out her radio.

But Delta did not hear her. Already, Delta was frantically making her way to the merry-go-round. If Jan was behind her, she did not know, and she did not feel she had a second to lose in finding out.

The fourth time Elson circled around, he was closer to the little girl but was looking out into the sea of people moving away from the rampaging cop wielding a gun. When Delta finally pushed beyond the edge of the crowd, she looked up in time to see a slow, vicious grin slime across his face like a slug as his eyes locked onto hers. Those eyes, for that fraction of a second, were taunting, ridiculing eyes—the eyes of a madman, of one who enjoyed the pain he was causing; one who, for all of his purported genius, could not be reasoned with. The man with those eyes had stared at her once before, when he turned and threw a star at her. She would never forget the rage and insanity of those eyes, and even now, they held the same look about them.

As he and his mount disappeared, Delta pulled the reins of her frantic emotions, and both they and she skidded to an abrupt halt. As she stopped, Jan rammed into the back of her.

"What are you doing?" Jan asked, as Delta lowered to one knee and aimed her .357 toward the merry-go-round.

"I'm gonna blast his ass off that horse."

Jan grabbed Delta's shoulder. "No you're not! You don't even know if that's him."

Delta felt the drops of sweat form on her lip. "It's him. Believe me, Jan, I know what I'm doing." Taking aim, Delta regripped her revolver.

"Delta, don't. That's a tough shot, and you know it."

Delta did not respond. Too many people had died already because of this maniac. If it was up to her, this psycho would never kill again.

And right now, it *was* up to her.

Holding the revolver with two hands, Delta raised it a little and ignored the shouts coming from the anxious crowd. Many people lay flat on the ground, while others watched, mesmerized by the action.

But Delta neither saw nor heard any of it. She concentrated on aiming at the spot where the unicorn horn first came around the bend. Next to her, Jan was warning Delta about something, but she really wasn't listening. If there was any voice she heard, it was Miles's, and he was saying, "Sometimes, when a life is on the line, the only rules that exist are those in our own hearts."

In her heart, Delta felt she was doing the right thing. Maybe it was the only thing, but to her, it felt right.

As the merry-go-round ground in its eternal pattern, Delta held her breath and gently placed her finger on the trigger. Waiting for what seemed like an eternity, the golden horn finally came bouncing up and down around the bend. Only then was Delta's worst fears realized.

Both Elson and the little girl had vanished.

29

"No!" Delta cried, jamming her weapon back in her holster and running through the crowd. "Stop this thing!" she commanded the elderly controller, who looked like he'd seen far too many carnivals.

Even before it slowed, Delta jumped on, as frightened children clung to parents or brothers and sisters. Jan moved to the far side of the merry-go-round from which Elson and the little girl exited.

Racing past various creatures and horses, Delta made her way to the empty unicorn coming to a slow stop.

Nothing.

Both the hippo and the unicorn were riderless, as were other creatures which had been dismounted when the riders saw Delta hop onto the ride.

"Damn it!" Delta yelled as she ran to where Jan was. Jan was speaking loudly into the radio and giving directions and orders to back-up.

"See anything?" Delta asked, as her beeper suddenly vibrated. Glancing down at the little red light flashing intermittently, Delta returned her attention to Jan's answer.

Shaking her head, Jan grabbed three teenage boys who had been cramming popcorn into their mouths. "They did."

Delta looked down at the boys. "Did you see a man wearing black gloves jump off this with a little girl?"

All three boys nodded in unison.

"Which way did he go?"

"That way," the larger boy said, pointing in the direction of the big rides. "He wanted for something?" The short, pock-faced one asked.

Turning to Jan, Delta waited for her to finish on the radio before telling her to take the straight path down the middle of the midway.

"Meet me at the ferris wheel."

Jan nodded. "And you?"

"I have to call Connie. She may have our only lead. We'll never find him in here without one."

"Del?"

"Yeah?"

"I'm sorry. I should have let you—"

"Don't worry about it. Let's just find her."

At the emergency booth located across from the merry-go-round, Delta dialed Connie's number. She answered it on half a ring.

"Delta, you've got to find him. He's crazier than I thought. He's, he's going to kill a little girl or someone little. I think it's a little girl. You've got to find—"

"He's already got her."

A small, bird-like sound escaped Connie's mouth. "God, no."

"What can you tell me, Con. We're at a carnival with hundreds of people and any number of ways for him to escape. You've got to give me something to go on."

The line was silent. Delta waited for what felt like hours for some response. "Connie?"

Again, that sharp, sorrowful sound crossed the lines. "I . . . I don't have . . ."

"Come on, Consuela! Get a grip here. I need you. Now is not the time to fold on us. A child's life is at stake."

"I'm trying."

"Where in the hell did he go?" Delta pressed the phone tightly to her ear to see if she could hear Connie at the keyboard, but the carnival noise was much too loud. "Damn it, Connie, where are you?"

"Okay, okay." Delta heard Connie draw in a big breath. "Okay. After Dori sat on the unicorn, I had her just sit there and pet it. You know, try to make friends with it or something."

"And?"

"And a little girl came out of the bushes and started talking to Dori."

"Can you speed it up, here, Con, I'm in a hurry."

"The little girl, obviously a virgin, hopped on the back of the unicorn, and it started to flap its wings like it was going to fly. Instead, a large vulture swooped onto the screen and took them both to this city in the clouds."

Delta nodded, her eyes already scanning the carnival for anything remotely resembling a bird. "What next?"

"I don't know. The bird dropped them off on a cloud, and I haven't been able to figure out what to do. God, Delta, not a little girl?"

"Is that all?" Delta knew Connie was weakening every second, and she needed her to stay strong and coherent. They couldn't afford for her to collapse now. Not now. "Connie, give me your best guess."

The line was silent again. It was several seconds before Connie said anything again. "I'd say go to the highest rides. Look for anything that has to do with hawks or eagles or clouds. Anything that might resemble a bird would be good."

"Got it. If you get anything . . ."

"I'll beep you right away. Del, if only I could find a key. If I knew what the pattern was, we could at least have an edge."

"Keep looking. I've gotta go." Delta started to hang the phone up but heard Connie's voice.

"Del?"

"Yeah?"

"You have to find her. I don't know what I'd do if he—"

"We're doing everything we can."

"There's one more thing."

"What's that?"

"When you find him, kill him. Do it for me."

Delta said nothing and hung the receiver up. She had never heard Connie speak like that before—Connie, who put spiders outside and never even owned a fly swatter; Connie, who bought hundreds of dollars of rain forest each year. The woman who valued life above anything else wanted him dead. Already, he was affecting her life. Already, he had tainted her spirit with his vengeful game. *That* was why he grinned that sadistic smile. He was winning—and he knew it.

Standing and looking at the ferris wheel, Delta shook her head. It was also too easy to trap him up there, and he would not be taken so easily.

Glancing around, Delta saw the lights and heard the noises of eight or nine other rides and knew she would stop them all if she had to.

Running over to the ferris wheel, Delta met Jan, who was standing with the operator and waiting for each seat to come to a stop at the bottom of the platform.

"This isn't it!" Delta yelled above the carny music. "Too obvious. He's taken her somewhere where he can get away. Look for bird symbols or clouds or something."

Jan nodded and turned to say something to the conductor, who stroked his chin as he thought about whatever she had said.

Delta studied the midway. The first three rides were ground rides, so she crossed them off her list. The fourth ride was the teacups, and that didn't fit. But there was something about the fifth ride that caught her attention. The chairs took the riders up in the air and swirled them around and then rocked them in a mock thundershower before disappearing back into the darkened tent where the ride both began and ended. The ride was called the "Goliath Cirrus."

"Cirrus," Delta mumbled. "Cirrus." A classroom flickered across her memory track; a classroom with a professor she had only once, to fulfill a requirement. He was lecturing about cumulus and . . .

"Cirrus! Cirrus is a type of cloud! He's taken her in there!" Sprinting across the midway, with Jan following close behind, Delta ran to the front of the "Goliath Cirrus" ride.

"This is it! I'm sure of it!" Delta yelled above the noise. "He's here." Delta ran over to the young, zit-faced controller and ordered him to stop the ride. "Did a man and a little blonde girl just go in there?"

The apathetic controller yawned and stretched. "I get lots of people on this ride. I don't pay much atten—"

Reaching across the controls, Delta yanked him to his feet. "Listen, asshole, this man had black leather gloves on. Did you see him or not?"

Nodding quickly, the controller stammered, "Yeah. Yeah, I remember seeing that dude. Cute little girl."

"Have they come out yet?"

"I, I don't think so."

Delta's pager went off again, as she thrust the lanky teenager back into his chair. "I said stop this goddamned thing now!"

Flipping a switch, the kid backed off and held his hands up, as if he were being arrested. "Sorry."

Jan hopped on the first car that came by. "Del, I'll go through. I'll drive him toward you. You meet the cars as they exit."

"Did you call back-up?"

"On their way. Go on."

Delta turned back to the controller. "No one else goes in there, you understand?"

The boy nodded.

"You send the chairs out to me slowly one at a time."

"Slowly," he repeated, as if he wasn't sure he heard her.

"Is there another way out?"

The teenager shook his head and then nodded. "Yeah, but only the engineers and tech crew know about it."

Watching Jan disappear through the two cloud-covered curtains, Delta felt her beeper again.

"Remember," she admonished the controller, as she withdrew her .357. "Send the chairs through slowly." Leaping over the railing, Delta waited at the mouth of the dark tunnel and signalled for the controller to begin. The first carriage slowly pierced through the darkness and pushed open the double doors, which had a tornado painted across them. Inside, two teenagers, oblivious to the fact that the ride had started again, were making out. When they looked up and saw Delta pointing her gun in their direction, the girl screamed, and the boy wiped his mouth. With a jerk of her head, Delta sent them flying out of the car and scurrying for safer ground.

As the next car made its approach, Delta's stomach tightened.

This was it.

She could feel it.

The next car was empty, as was the third. Delta slowly licked her lips and tasted blood. In anxious anticipation, she'd bitten her lower lip.

When the fourth car passed her, Delta felt the reverberation once more and tried to ignore it.

"Come on, you bastard," Delta growled, watching the fifth car emerge. At first, she thought it was empty. But as she peered closer, she could see the sole of a shoe protruding from the bottom of the car.

"Stop!" Delta yelled, jumping over the railing. In an instant, Delta was in the car.

As it slowed to a stop, Delta looked down and saw the still body of the little girl lying on the floor of the car. For a second, Delta thought she saw her move, and reached down to gently lift her from the floor. When Delta touched her arm, she realized the little girl's body was limp.

"No," Delta murmured, kneeling on the floor of the carriage. The girl's hair was in disarray, and her dress was mangled and slightly torn. When Delta turned her around to see if she was breathing, two empty eyes stared back at her, as the head flopped awkwardly to one side.

"No," Delta moaned, setting the tiny body on the seat of the carriage and feeling the small-boned wrist for a pulse she knew was not there. Already, there was a certain discoloration in her neck, face and lips, and it was difficult for Delta to look at the dark, unmoving, lifeless eyes of the little girl she had failed to save.

Failed to save.

This was a failure worse than any she had ever imagined. She had been given a chance at stopping him and this was the consequence of her inability to do so. Inside, rage grabbed at Delta, replacing the sadness in her spirit. She could handle white-hot anger. It was the sorrow of seeing a tiny body broken by a madman that shook her most.

"Del? Did you find som . . ." Jan pushed through the tornado doors and stared down at the still body. "Oh, no." Reholstering her gun, Jan barked orders to the controller before doing the same into her radio. When she turned back around, Delta was kneeling over the girl, trying to resuscitate her.

"Del," Jan said, touching her on the shoulder. "Del, it won't do any good. Her neck looks broken."

Moving away, Delta looked down at the crooked neck and slumping head. She was dead. Her life energy had been snuffed out by a man she probably didn't know. Inhaling deeply and forcing her angry tears back, Delta shook her head.

He had crossed that line and killed a child.

In Delta's mind, Elson Zuckerman had just signed his own death certificate.

"Del?" Jan whispered, helping her to her feet.

"Fucking bastard," Delta said, feeling her hands and legs tremble. "Fucking crazy bastard." Reaching a shaking hand out, Delta closed the little girl's eyes. She was so young, so innocent. She had done nothing but talk to a man she did not know was evil. Feeling her insides split like stitches busting, Delta fought to control her rising rage. She needed to keep her head. She needed to control the emotions running like the carnival roller coaster over the landscape of her being. He had won this round. Delta swore it would be his last.

Jan bent over and twisted the girl's hair around her finger as she studied the lifeless face. The child looked like she could be Mariah's age.

"Homicide and ambulance are on their way." Squeezing Delta's shoulder, Jan glanced at Delta's belt where her pager hung. The red light was flickering. "Del, your pager. You need to answer Connie's call."

Still staring at the broken body, Delta barely heard Jan. He had killed her, just like that. He had her little neck in his hands and snapped it like a pencil, and for what? How could he be so cruel and so full of hate that he could destroy a life that had never even touched his? A life that had so much living to do, yet he snuffed it out like it meant nothing. How could such a base individual continue living?

"Delta Stevens, did you hear me?"

Delta shook her head and looked questioningly at Jan. "What?"

"Your beeper. It's been going off for awhile now. Why don't you call Connie, and I'll meet the guys out front. We've cordoned off the streets, and Leonard is on his way. I'll wait here. You go call Connie."

Glancing down at her beeper, Delta nodded. "I'll be right over there."

As Delta's trembling fingers dialed the phone, she heard the sirens in the distance. They were coming to the aid of a child who could no longer be helped. Pushing away the image of the little blonde girl being zipped up in a black body bag, Delta shivered. This was happening too fast. Things were spinning out of control, and if she didn't get a grip on him soon, many more people would end up like the little girl. With her ear pressed hard against the phone, Delta heard Connie pick up the phone before it could finish one ring.

"Con?" Delta said, her voice weary and worn. How was she supposed to tell Connie that he had murdered a child?

"Please, Storm. Please tell me he didn't . . ."

Inhaling deeply, Delta squeezed her eyes closed. There was no easy way to tell her. "I'm afraid—"

"Don't say it. Don't you dare say it."

"He . . ." Delta couldn't bring herself to say it.

"Did he . . . did he break her neck?"

Even with her eyes slammed shut, a teardrop managed to force its way through. "Yes." Delta heard a muffled sob emit through the phone lines.

"Is she—"

"Yes."

"And he?"

"I don't know. He disappeared. It's possible he may still be in the carnival, but who knows? The Sarge has everyone on it, and Leonard's on his way." Delta wiped her eyes. "Con, I am so sorry."

No response.

"I did everything I could."

"I'm sure you did."

"What now?" Every ounce of energy drained from Delta.

"Take care of business there. I can't help you out tonight. He won, again. He wants to hurt me, and he has. More than anyone could ever imagine."

Delta waited for more. She knew by the sound of Connie's voice that she was crying. "Con, there's nothing you could have done. You're giving it your best. No one could ask for more."

"I, I know. But a little girl, Del. A little girl?"

"He's sick, Connie. He's a twisted prick who doesn't care who gets in his way."

"Not even a child."

"No, hon, not even a child." Delta watched as Leonard's men drove through the emergency entrance. "Connie, what was he after?"

"Was she wearing a ribbon in her hair?"

"I don't remember, why?"

Inhaling a shaky breath, Connie answered, "In the game, a vulture swooped down on Dori and the little girl and picked the girl up in its talons."

Delta thought how fitting it was that Elson should portray himself as a vulture.

"Dori wasn't able to catch the girl when he dropped her, but the vulture held a piece of rope or . . . oh Delta, what have I done?"

"Don't start blaming yourself, Connie. He was crazy before college, crazy in college and he's a fucking lunatic now. No one can make someone insane. You know that."

"But maybe I did. Maybe that's what he's trying to do to me: make me crazy."

"Well, he won't. I won't let him. And before this is all over, I'll see him dead. Just don't start blaming yourself."

"That's what Gina's been saying all night."

"Well, listen to her. She's the pro when it comes to head cases and she knows what she's talking about." Delta looked over at the crime scene and saw Leonard coming toward her. "Look, I gotta go, honey. Leonard's on his way over. Maybe now, he'll listen to reason."

"Reason? If you can find an ounce of reason for all of this, then let me know. If he'll listen, Del, have him check out whether or not she was wearing a ribbon when she left the house. It's important."

"Will do. And you hang in there, okay? We're going to get him. It may take time, but he'll pay."

"I hope so, Del. I really do. I'd love nothing more than the chance to meet that bastard one-on-one."

"Not if I can help it. Take a breather, and I'll see you when I get in." Hanging up the phone, Delta made her way over to the crime scene, where Leonard met her half-way.

"Stevie," Leonard yelled as he approached her. "Damn it, you knew something and didn't let me in on it. Shame, shame. You know better than that."

"It was a lucky guess, Leonard."

Chomping on his cigar, Leonard shook his head. "Maybe I oughtta look into that game you gave me after all. Seems you know when crimes are going to happen before anyone else. Either that, or you've got a crystal ball hidden somewheres."

Delta shrugged, resisting the urge to knock his cigar down his throat. "I'm just a good cop, Leonard, that's all. I follow my gut and it lead me here."

Moving away from Leonard, Delta inhaled a few deep breaths and watched as Jan walked over holding a soda. "You okay?" Delta asked, noticing for the first time, how pale Jan had become. Suddenly, Delta realized how difficult it must be for Jan to see a child her daughter's age lying in a crumpled heap. How close to home this crime must have hit.

"Jan?"

"I'm okay. I just need to call home, that's all. Let me know if I can help out here." Handing Delta the soda, Jan walked back over to use the phone.

As the crime unit snapped photos, took measurements and dusted for prints, Delta surveyed the area just beyond the midway.

With all the noise, flashing lights, and smells of the carnival pervading her senses, Delta felt it as surely as if he had reached out with a gloved hand and touched her.

He was watching.

Watching and waiting.

30

Delta was not the least bit surprised when she received a call the next day from Detective Leonard. Everyone from the Police Chief to the District Attorney would be on Leonard's case for a suspect, and Delta knew he was as empty-handed as a street bum. Before the carnival murder, they were pressing Leonard for a suspect, and they got one when they arrested a local man for the shooting death. But now, with that man in custody and another murder on their hands, the tide had turned.

Tides always turned when a child was the victim. Even the press, which had shown only a passing interest in the other murders, was digging for a better story. The heat was on, and it was burning Leonard's ass.

Opening the door to his office, Delta found him pouring over reports, chomping on his unlit cigar and running his hand over the bald spot on his head. His clothes looked like they'd been slept in, and his face had aged overnight.

Leonard glanced up at Delta and gestured toward the chair across from his desk. "Sit down, Stevie." His tone was more weary than commanding. It had clearly been an extra long night for him.

Rubbing his red eyes, Leonard took the cigar from his mouth and pushed himself away from the stacks of paper on his desk. "Stevie, would you like to tell me just what the hell is going on down on your beat?"

Delta fixed her eyes on him. He was desperate for a suspect. Probably got his ass chewed on for not having one sooner. "What would you like to know?"

Leonard leaned across the desk and attempted a snarl. "Damn it, Stevens, don't play games with me."

Delta wondered at his choice of words, but let it go. It would do her no good to press his overly sensitive buttons at this point.

"Stevens, I've got one witness who claims you knew this asshole was wearing gloves. I've got dozens of witnesses who saw you and Bowers moving toward the merry-go-round with your guns drawn just prior to his abducting the girl. I have a ferris wheel operator who heard you say something about 'it' being too obvious. I have a teenager who nearly shit his pants when you grabbed him and barked at him to shut the damn ride off. Do I have to go on?"

Delta leaned back in the chair. She had to give it to him—Leonard and his men had been thorough in an area with too many wanna-be witnesses, where the noise level was nearly impossible, and the real witnesses a little buzzed off beer. "Leonard, I don't know why it's so hard for you to accept, but we're on the same side. Although there are times when I wish we weren't, the fact remains. Just what is it you want me to tell you?"

"The truth, damn it! You and Rivera came here babbling some horseshit story about a computer game, you're only seconds behind every murder, you have information you're very clearly withholding, and I'm totally in the dark. The suspect I was holding for the first whack is out, and I feel like I'm left stuffing the bag. What the hell is going on?"

Delta rose slowly and walked over to the bookcase. "You have the disk, why don't you tell me?" Delta tossed out a red herring. "You still have the disk, don't you?"

Leonard's face dropped.

"Don't tell me—"

"Misplaced is all."

"Then, I can't help you." Delta leaned over the back of the chair. "You blew me and Connie off like a couple of amateurs; like we go around inventing stories just so we can play detective. And now that you're backed up against a hot stove and your ass is on fire, you want our help. We offered our help right from the start and you chumped us, Detective. What on earth makes you think I'm going to put myself in that position again?"

Leonard shrugged, his body language shouting defeat. "I'm sorry, Stevie, if I made you feel that way. But you gotta admit—your story was a little way out there. If I jumped at leads like that all the time, I'd never solve a case. Cut me some slack here, will you? I need your help."

Delta's left eyebrow rose. "Are you asking for my help?"

"I'm asking for your cooperation. I need a perp. Pendleton is all over my case, the media is making my department look like the keystone cops, and I've got nothing but a bunch of bodies lyin' on cement slabs in the morgue; one of which is a little girl. I know you don't care for me much, Stevie, so do it for her."

Delta tried not to look taken aback. Had Russ Leonard actually shown a human emotion to her? Impossible. "What do you want to know?"

"Then, you do know something."

Delta shook her head. "I didn't say that."

Leonard sighed heavily. "You know a hell of a lot more than you've shared with me. Don't make me play hardball, here, Delta, because I will if I have to."

"I don't know what it is you think I can do for you. I gave you a pretty accurate description of Elson with the Identikit. You had the disk and lost it. There's not much else to work with."

"Bullshit. First off, it'll be a cold day in hell before anyone convinces me there's a disk that Rivera can't copy. She's a whiz, Stevie. You two have that game, and I'd bet a month's salary on it."

Delta shrugged. "Maybe."

"I mean, how else is it that you're always so close every time that motherfucker hits?"

"I get feelings."

Leonard chuckled. "I've heard about cops like you, Stevie; cops who have a sixth sense. In all my life, I only saw two cops who really had it; one is my retired partner, and the other was Miles Brookman. You've inherited that trait from him, Stevie. I can see it in your eyes."

Delta shrugged again. "But feelings aren't hard, concrete evidence, Leonard. I'm surprised you believe in them."

"Oh, I believe in them, when they lead me to hard, concrete evidence. Yours may be able to do that. Because whatever is going on down there, you got bit. Something's under your skin, Stevie, and I want to know what it is."

Delta shrugged. "It's my beat and my people who are dying, Leonard. Why don't you give a little first? After all, can't we both give and take a little here without compromising either of our positions?"

"You're not giving me much of a choice, are you?"

Delta shook her head. "I did, and you blew it." Folding her arms across her chest, Delta waited.

Leonard leaned on the desk and looked intently at Delta. "He's clever, Stevie, whoever he is."

"Yes, he is. Very much so."

"There's a pattern to his killings."

"Yes, there is. I know all of this. Tell me something I don't know."

Leonard shoved himself away from the table and stood at the window. For a moment, he held his hands behind his back and rocked back and forth on the balls of his feet. "Her name was Helen Carver," he said quietly. "She was only eight."

A ball of sorrow rose in her throat as Helen's cherubic little face hovered before her, her hollow, empty eyes gazing into nowhere. It was a picture Delta would see for the rest of her life.

"Can you give me the files to the other murders?"

"You know I can't do that. You may not give a rat's patoot about regs, but I do. I'm not even supposed to release Helen's name, but I know Rivera would find out eventually. Now, you give."

Delta crossed her legs. So far, he hadn't given her anything she couldn't have gotten herself. "What would you like to know?"

"How did you know it was him on the merry-go-round?"

"He was wearing gloves."

Leonard started to note this but stopped. "Gloves? You knew it was our man because he was wearing gloves?"

Delta nodded. "He cut off the chauffeur's hands to get the gloves so he could use them when he broke Helen's neck. You see, all of the murders are intricately linked together. The disk, Leonard, is our only real hope."

Leonard nodded, as he jotted this information down.

"I can even tell you how the next one will be committed."

Leonard glanced up from his notes and frowned. "Excuse me?"

"You're right. We do have a copy of the disk and we've been playing the game for some time."

"I knew it."

"Yeah, but what you don't know is that once we get ahead of Elson in the game, we should be able to head him off at the next murder. As long as we trail in the game, people will die."

Leonard's eyebrows rose. "You can tell me how the next murder is going to happen?"

"We think so."

"How?"

"Was Helen wearing a ribbon in her hair when she left the house? It wasn't anywhere on her or in the Goliath Cirrus after we found her."

Leonard shuffled through the reports. "A ribbon?"

"Yes, Leonard. I assume you asked the mother what Helen was wearing when she left the house."

"Connell was in charge of that. I'll have to check his report."

Delta shook her head. "You do that. And while you're waiting for your concrete evidence, here's some not-so-hard data. Each murder is directly linked to the one before and the one after. It's the domino theory. These games require certain tasks to be completed before you can move on to the next level or challenge."

Leonard was quickly scribbling this information in his notes.

"He killed the pharmacist to get the poison to poison the dog to get the ax to kill the chauffeur to cut off the hands to get the gloves to break her neck and get the ribbon to strangle the next victim on his list."

Leonard laid his face in his hands and shook his head. "And this is the house that Elson built."

Delta shrugged. "That's about it."

"Damn it, Stevie, this is less than proof. What you're giving me here is pure speculation. I can't take any of this to the D.A. She'd laugh me right outta court."

"Maybe. But until we work together on this, you're going nowhere. You won't even make it to court."

Leonard shoved his reports aside and leaned across the desk. "I wish I could give you more, Stevie, but right now, I can't. You know how it goes with child homicides.

If I give you any more information on her than I already have, I'm putting my job on the line."

Delta nodded. "I understand." Moving toward the door, Delta gripped the tarnished knob. "And Elson is putting the life of my best friend on the line. It's no competition. If I have to choose, I'll always choose someone's life over my career."

"What does that mean?"

The corners of Delta's mouth turned up slightly. "It means that this is a no holds barred contest, and the rules no longer apply to me. You stick to your regs, Leonard. I'll take the low road and we'll see who stops Zuckerman first."

Leonard slowly rose. "I didn't hear that."

"Good."

Leonard moved slowly out from behind his desk. "You be careful, Stevie. The lines you cross could cost you more than your job. He's one twisted fuck. Messing with him might cost you your life."

Delta shrugged. "But then, that's what we get paid the big bucks to do, isn't it, Russ? To put our asses on the line."

As Delta pulled the door open, Leonard stopped her. "Stevie, I want him as bad as you do. You gotta know that. We just have different approaches to the same problem. You do what you need to do. If there's anything I can kick over to you, I will. Just know that I want that bastard and I want him now."

Turning, hand still poised on the knob, Delta nodded. "Thanks. You know, that's the first time you and I have agreed on anything." Walking out the door and down the hall, Delta smiled.

Maybe there was hope for Mr. Hard Evidence after all.

31

When Delta returned to Connie's, she wasn't surprised to find Connie working on the game. Gina was asleep on the couch, and Megan was studying the now massive charts, graphs, and maps lying in the middle of the floor.

"He wanted to pick your brain, didn't he?" came Connie's voice from the table.

Delta nodded. "He's desperate. Alexandria is pressing him for a perp and they had to release the only suspect they had."

"Couldn't tie him into the shooting, eh?" Connie said over her shoulder.

Delta shook her head. "Guess not. He didn't elaborate too much on it. He was really bummin'."

"Had he even looked at the disk?"

Delta slipped her arms out of her windbreaker. "No. It's been 'misplaced'."

Connie did not move from the computer. Dori was in a swamp, jumping from various floating objects in an attempt to get to the other side. Sometimes, the objects were alligators, and they would eat her if she landed on them, and Connie would have to start again from the edge of the swamp.

"I'm not surprised. He probably threw it away the second we walked out the door." As an alligator rose and grabbed Dori, Connie slammed the joystick back down on the table. "I hate this part!"

Delta shook her head and bent over to kiss Megan before walking over and giving Connie a hug. "Need a break?"

Connie shook her head, but Delta saw Megan out of the corner of her eye. She was nodding.

"Con, let me take over for a bit."

"But—"

"No 'buts.' Go rest for a bit, and I'll call you when I get her out of the swamp."

Pausing the game, Connie looked at the grandmother clock standing in the corner. "It's already nine?"

"Go rest, and take Gina with you."

Stretching, Connie rose slowly. "You'll wake me as soon as you get her out?"

"I promise." Watching Connie and a sleepy Gina trudge down the hall, Delta turned to find Megan staring at her.

"After you left this morning, Del, she broke down. Cried for almost an hour. That little girl's death was more than she could take."

Delta nodded as she grabbed the controls. "Her name was Helen. She was eight."

"God, Del, what kind of a madman are we dealing with?"

"One beyond help. One who needs a bullet between the eyes."

"Well, he's getting to her. If tearing her up inside was one of his goals, it's working. Helen's death hit Connie hard."

"She's blaming herself, isn't she?"

"I'm afraid so." Megan got off the floor and walked over to hug Delta's neck. For a long, quiet moment, the two embraced, blocking out the pain of the real world and reconnecting their spirits in a hug that meant more than just a simple show of affection.

"I'm scared for you both," Megan said quietly. "Very scared."

Delta did not let her go. "Because he's getting to us?"

Megan nodded, burying her face in the back of Delta's hair. "Because he's very, very sick. If he could do that to a little girl, what would he do to you or Connie? His hatred of her must run very deep."

"Deep enough to pull his insanity to the surface."

"Aren't you scared?"

Delta nodded, pulling Megan closer. "Shitless. I'm afraid for the people on my beat. I'm afraid of what he's doing to Connie, and I'm scared to death we aren't going to solve this damn game before he follows through with his greatest threat."

"You've faced worse odds before and come out on top."

Turning in Megan's arms, Delta stared down into Megan's electric blue eyes and nodded. "That's about the only thing that keeps me going. That, and you. You've been very understanding about all of this. We haven't had much alone time lately."

Megan smiled warmly and kissed Delta's nose. "She's my friend, too. She was there when you needed her most and offered her home to me when I was a complete stranger. God only knows if you'd be alive if it wasn't for her. She's been a good friend to you—to us."

Delta winced at the thought of what might have happened to her during the investigation of Miles's death if Connie hadn't worked with her.

"Yes, she has. Does it bother you that we haven't had any time to work on our relationship? That we haven't had any personal time at all? I mean, you mentioned therapy, yet—"

"We will. We'll make it a priority right after we get Connie out of this. Delta, don't you know that I just want to be with you? Whatever you need from me, whether it's to help map stuff or just stand by and be understanding, you have. I want to be in on this until the very end."

"And until then? What do you do about that big bag of fear you carry around?"

"Fear is something I've learned to live with since we've been together."

Delta's left eyebrow rose. "Oh? You've learned to live with it, have you?"

Shrugging, Megan pulled away and sat in Delta's lap. "I try hard. It isn't easy to always wonder where you are and if you're okay. It isn't easy wondering if you're coming home in one piece. It's even harder to know that you'll do whatever has to be done to save someone whose name you don't even know. That fear eats me up sometimes."

"And now? Now we have some sick piece of shit out to kill our best friend. What do you do with that fear now?"

"Well, to be honest, since I'm involved in it with you, the fear isn't overwhelming. That's not to say I'm not frightened, because I am. At least now, I know what you're looking for and where you're going with this case.

Sometimes, understanding why you love this job so much helps me understand you."

Delta leaned back a little so she could see all of Megan's face. "Really?"

"Delta, when I see you in action, when I see the passion you have for your job and for the people on your beat, I want to be a part of that passion. I need to be a part of that. When I'm not, it feels like your job is a mistress and that I'm waiting for you to return from her."

Kissing Megan softly at first and then letting her lips linger against Megan's, Delta sighed. "You're an incredible woman, my love. Sometimes, I don't realize how punishing this job is on you—on us. And then, when I do, it slaps me across the face, and I get scared I'm going to lose you." Looking deep into eyes that could swallow her whole, Delta suddenly felt very little. "I'm not, am I?"

Megan smiled. "God, I hope not. I'd hate to think I'm putting in all this time just to be single again. Delta Stevens, you just don't get it, do you? I love you. I love being a part of your life. And right now, if your life centers around keeping the one person you love most safe from harm, then so be it."

"Wait a minute. Love most? I don't think . . ."

Megan put her fingers gently over Delta's mouth. "Shh. There's one thing I've known about you right from the very start, my love, and that's that you can live without food, you can live without sleep, but you can't live without Connie."

"That's cra—"

"Hush. It is not. You wouldn't know what to do without her, and vice versa. It's okay. I've never been jealous of the love you two share, and I never will."

Hugging Megan tightly, Delta inhaled her perfume in through her nose. "I love you more than anything. You know that, don't you?"

"You better. Because I'm the best thing that's ever happened to you, my rough and tough little copper." Megan kissed Delta warmly on the lips.

"Mmm. Yes, you are. And I'd like nothing more than to show you just how much you mean to me, but we need to get back to work."

Hopping off Delta's lap, Megan scooped up some of the pieces of butcher paper. "I've been a busy bee. Want to look?"

Delta took one of the pieces from her and studied it for a moment. "Whew. There's a lot of stuff here."

"That's the problem. There's so much damn information, I don't even know where to begin." Taping the piece of butcher paper to the mantel, Megan stepped back and studied it. The bevelled mirror above the fireplace reflected her lithe figure, and she smiled into the mirror at Delta. "Today, Gina and I decided we should tape all of these to the walls, so the information is all here in front of us. Here." Bending over, Megan picked up the second sheet and handed it to Delta. "Hang that one up across from here."

Delta took the sheet and shook her head at all of the facts and figures scribbled across it. "You've been very thorough."

"Connie's a slave driver. She wants everything recorded, so we just did what she said."

Delta nodded. "I just wish we had a head start. I'm getting so fucking tired of being half a step behind. Just once, I'd like to see where we're going before we get there."

Megan squatted down and picked up the next pieces to be hung. Moving across from the fireplace, Megan taped the butcher paper to the wall. Watching the woman she loved move with such grace and beauty, Delta paced over to her and took her in her arms.

"Have I told you lately how beautiful you are?" Delta asked, swinging Megan around. As she did, Delta's eyes caught their reflection in the mirror. But it wasn't their reflection that jumped out of the clear plate glass and into the living room, it was something else.

"Megan, look!" Spinning Megan around, Delta pointed excitedly to the mirror, but Megan didn't notice whatever Delta was pointing at.

"What, honey? What is it?"

"Don't you see? Look harder." Moving Megan just to the left, Delta ran over to the fireplace, gesticulating at the reflection of the butcher paper.

The game is called 'Death on S.U.P. Mylo,' right? In the mirror, 'SUPMYLO' is 'OLYMPUS' spelled backwards."

Megan's eyes grew wide. "I'll be damned, you're right! This might be the key we've been looking for!"

A sudden rush of adrenaline pumped through Delta's veins, lifting her beyond her exhaustion, beyond her despair, and even beyond the fear. Finally, after three deaths, they had the key to the game; they finally had the clue they'd been looking for.

Megan glanced down the hall. "We should wake her, don't you think?"

"And tell her what? That we have the real title of the game?"

Megan shook her head. "Oh, we have much more than that, my love. What we have is the glue that binds this whole game together."

"And that is?"

"Olympus, Delta. As in Mount Olympus. You know, where the immortal gods of ancient Greece lived. Elson's main reference is the ancient Greeks."

Delta thought back to the dagger and the unicorn and the title of the game. "You're right. We've got it," she said, trying to maintain her excitement.

Megan smiled. "Damn straight, we do."

"And now, that son-of-a-bitch better watch his step, because it's only a matter of time before we're breathing hot and heavy on his heels."

Megan nodded, and then turned to all the charts she'd made. "Yeah, but how much time?"

Delta sighed and ran her hand through her hair. "I only wish we knew."

32

"So, when Delta discovered the anagram of Supmylo and Olympus, we put some of the other facts together and realized right away that Elson was working from a mythological premise."

Connie nodded vigorously, her hands wrapped around a steaming cup of coffee. "Go on."

As if on stage, Megan gracefully swept across the room to the first piece of paper with the now-known title scrawled over the original title.

"While Del worked to get Dori across the swamp, I went through every level's worth of notes and circled everything that had any semblance to Greece or Greek mythology. I'm sure I've missed some, but I'm pulling books on Greek mythology from the campus library this afternoon."

Connie studied the largest piece of paper and saw only a few key words circled. "Without a key like this, we would have been chasing our own tails for a long time."

Delta and Megan nodded.

"Take level one, for example." Megan floated over to the table for a matching yellow pen before returning to the paper. "We know that Elson used a dagger of Greek origin to kill Friedman. Just like Homicide, we focused on the nature of the weapons he used instead of looking at the whole picture."

Gina stood up for a better look. "So, he intentionally used bizarre means to kill in order to throw us off?"

Connie joined them at the paper. "Elson had everyone scratching their heads over his choice of weapons. But the weapons are both clues and distractions at the same time."

Megan nodded. "Right."

Connie stared down at the paper. "Christ, he's good."

Megan tapped the butcher paper with her pen. "What we also haven't paid attention to are the collective names of the people he's attacked or the places he's shown up."

Flipping the cap of the yellow marker onto the floor, Megan recircled a few names.

"The name of the drugstore—"

"Troy's," Connie murmured, her eyes lighting up. "The ancient city of Greece."

"Where," Megan continued, "if we're slightly up on our Greek mythology, we would know that was where Helen of Troy was from."

"The name of the little girl." Delta's voice was so soft, it was barely audible. "Leonard shared that piece with me this morning."

Connie shook her head as she loomed over the paper. "Elson must have sought this little girl out some time ago to be able to have her there when he needed her."

Delta nodded, trying to suppress her awe at the incredible planning his sick scheme took. "He did seem to be speaking with her as if they knew each other. I mean, she didn't appear frightened."

"And wouldn't you, as an eight-year-old girl, have been a little afraid of a creepy-looking little man wearing black gloves?"

All three women nodded.

"He's done his homework on this, Del," Connie said, shaking her head. "God knows how long he's been in River Valley making all of this come together."

"Yeah, but he also left us a crib sheet." Delta turned back to Megan, who waited patiently to go on.

"The hunting shop where he stole the ax is called Omega, which is Greek for last."

Connie stared harder at the paper. "He knew when the carnival would be in town, the names of the victims and shops, and has every last detail worked out."

Delta laid her arm across Connie's shoulder. "He's put a great deal of time and energy to prove he's smarter than you."

Connie nodded and pointed to the paper. "Go on, Megan. My knowledge of Greek mythology is rather weak."

Delta's eyebrows shot up as if asking a question independently of her mouth.

"Elson and I were in the same English class when we were freshmen," Connie explained. "I bombed completely on the Greek portion of the class, a memory he has obviously held onto." Connie stared at her hands. "He outscored me on every major exam and used to rub it in my face. I remember the rest of the class hating him because he was so mean about it." Looking back up, Connie wiped a tear away. "Go on, *amiga*. Let's hear the rest."

Megan inhaled slowly. "The chauffeur's murder stumped us for a moment because we were focusing on the primary and not the secondary. We highlighted the victim of the violence and not the person who discovered it. Only when Delta pulled up her copy of the report did it all make sense."

"Who *did* discover the body?" Connie asked.

Megan held up a hand. "Not so fast. The chauffeur's name was Ted Daniels; there's nothing mythological about that name in any way. But I searched through your reference collection anyway."

"And you found?"

"Nothing."

Megan turned to Delta and gave her the floor.

"You see, Con, the chauffeur worked for a Mrs. Elaine Griffin. A gryphon, spelled g-r-y-p-h-o-n, is a mythological creature with the body of a lion, eagle's wings, and a beak."

Connie shook her head. "That's reaching, Del, don't you think?"

Delta shook her head. "I thought so, too. But Megan pulled out a dictionary of Classical, Biblical and Literary Allusions, and it says that gryphons were fond of gold and were known to hoard it in their dens. Mrs. Griffin is loaded."

Connie nodded and looked at the paper where Megan had jotted down notes on Mrs. Griffin. "Incredible. What else?"

"That's it so far. We've centered on the big ticket items for now, and I don't know how Delta feels, but my mind is like oatmeal. I think we could all use a break."

"A mythological premise?" Connie said to herself. "I should have known he'd choose an area he knew I was weak in." Then to the group, "You might have just saved my life. Thank you so much."

Taking the marker from Megan, Connie made a larger circle around the title. "Now that we know the name of the game we're playing, we have his point of reference. We're going to need everything we can find on Greek mythology, extensive historical and present-day maps of Greece, and an easy reference history book. We'll also need a map of Delta and Jan's beat with the names of all the shops and stores."

Delta raised her hand as if she were in class. "I've got that last bit covered. Jan has all that information in a little black book. We'll insert that info onto the map I've drawn and highlight anything remotely Greek."

A slow smile spread across Connie's face. "Great. Things are finally going our way. We needed a break and you two just handed us one."

Delta walked over and hugged Connie. Renewed hope flowed through Delta as Megan and Gina joined them in their hug. They finally had the information needed to move ahead of him. Now, all it took was scrupulous attention to details in the game and they had him.

"So, what now, Chief?" Delta asked, touching foreheads with Connie.

"Now, our work begins in earnest." Connie looked over at Eddie and sighed. "Let's get through the next level and see just what kind of clues we can pick up now that we know the premise of the game."

"And then?" Delta asked, slowly pulling away so she could see Connie's eyes more clearly.

Connie's eyes narrowed and the room stilled. They all seemed to know what she was about to say even before she said it.

"Then, we finish it."

33

Megan's job in the game was the third level—the carnival. For hours, she combed through books and maps of ancient places and names, trying to locate the slightest clue that might send them that half a step forward. More than once, she called Professor Rosenbaum at the university for his expertise on Greek and Roman mythology. He proved to be an invaluable resource and offered to come over and assist should they need his help.

Jan had come over to lend her help by giving them her little black book, and Delta was pouring through the little black binder noting every store, restaurant, merchant, and car dealership whose name had anything to do with Greece. And with every minute that slipped through the hourglass, Delta felt the pressure mounting. Every second of every minute brought Elson closer to another kill, closer to the spilling of more blood. Already, it was three in the afternoon, and all they had done was uncover Greek names and places. Then, they backtracked on the last three crimes to fit the names into the Greek formula. The work was tedious and tiresome, and the few steps forward they did take seemed minuscule.

Glancing over at Connie, who was busy maneuvering the joystick, Delta wondered just how much longer Connie could hold up. Already, the lines on her face seemed deeper, and the luster and brilliance of her eyes were clouded in a fearful haze. Connie was driven for answers, fighting for her life and those Elson had already targeted in the preceding days or weeks it had taken him to plan his scheme. Suddenly, Delta shuddered. How many weeks, even months, had he been in River Valley devising his strategy? How mad must he really be to hunt those whose names fit into his twisted game? The profundity of his hatred ran so deep, he was threatening to pull them all into it; for surely, Delta hated him enough to know that she would kill him if they ever met.

Looking about the room, Delta saw three exhausted women functioning on willpower and grim determination alone. None of them could guess how many levels there were or just how many people Elson would kill on his way to revenge. When would the next level be the last level before his victim, his target, became Connie?

Stretching out her long frame, Delta leaned over and kissed Megan on the head. "How're you doing?"

Leaning against Delta's legs, Megan stretched also. "You know, I've been sitting here piecing this third level together, but there's something that just keeps poking at me."

"And that is?"

Slapping the green marker in her palm, Megan pointed to the butcher paper. "He's had everything planned down to the final detail so far, right? He knew the ride they would go on, he knew there was a unicorn on the merry-go-round, and he even had a little girl named Helen as a victim."

Connie pushed the pause button and turned to listen. "Go on."

"Well, it's so pat. He's been so precise. Don't you think he cut that last murder a little close?"

Delta looked at the paper but didn't see where Megan was going with this. "I don't get your point."

"Honey, he killed her on the last day of the carnival. He almost missed it." Megan waited a moment before continuing. "The whole computer game angle would have been ruined if he'd have missed killing Helen. Don't you think it's a little risky to wait until the last night of the carnival to kill her?"

Connie and Delta exchanged glances. For a moment, no one said anything, but all eyes were locked on the long piece of butcher paper on the floor.

"Too risky, for a man with his intellect. Luck and coincidence have no place in this game for him. He had to have planned to go on the final night of the carnival. There's so little margin for error in the game and he'd never cut it that close."

Delta considered Megan's words. She was right. There had to be a reason why he waited until the closing night. Grabbing the cellular phone, Delta dialed information. "Can I have the number to Troy's pharmacy, please?" Delta quickly jotted the number down before turning to explain. "The last day of any carnival is like the closing night of a play. It's a big deal and easy to plan for. Meg is right. He had to have known it was the last night. I want to see if Troy's was having a special or if there's any significance to that night at Troy's."

Connie was off her seat in a second and joined Delta at the phone. "Damn. How could I have forgotten the element of time?"

"We've been working on so many other angles, it's no wonder that one slipped by."

"We can't afford any 'slips,' Storm."

Delta grinned. "I know." Waiting for someone to answer at Troy's, Delta drummed her fingers impatiently. "God, it's taking them forever."

When the phone finally picked up, Delta heard: "The number you have dialed is no longer in service . . ."

Staring at the phone, Delta handed it to Connie, who listened to the repeated message.

"What in the hell?"

In one long step, Delta reached for the black binder and flipped through it.

"What are you looking for?" Gina asked.

"I'm not sure yet." Dialing the second number, Delta pushed the top of her mechanical pencil and pressed the sharp tip to the paper, as she listened on the phone. "Uh-huh. That's great. I have a question for you, if you don't mind. Did Troy's go out of business? They did. Do you remember exactly when that was? Uh-huh." Delta waited a moment and then wrote the date down. "Thank you so much. Oh no, there's no trouble. I just needed a prescription refilled, that's all." Turning to Connie, Delta handed her the date. "Look at the date."

Connie took the paper and stared at it. "It's the night of the first murder."

"He was killed on the last business day."

Suddenly, Gina was on her feet. "Omega!"

All three women turned to her.

"That's the answer! That's the clue you're looking for! Omega is the last letter of the Greek alphabet. He's killing people on the last day of something."

Connie looked at the date again. "The last day of the carnival, the last day Troy's was open. Of course! For

Elson's scheme to work, he had to plan his attacks well in advance. He can't afford random killing because it might not fit into the game."

Delta's heart picked up a beat. "Yes! So, Elson wasn't cutting it close. He's had everything prearranged."

Connie ran over to the large plastic Coke bottle filled with change and dumped it on the floor. "And the most important arrangement he had to make was the time element. He had to know where and when he would strike in order for the game's pieces to fall into place!" Scooping up handfuls of change, Connie turned to Gina and dumped them in front of her. "Honey, buy every newspaper published in the city. We'll go through them and find everything that's ending or going out of business."

Delta reached over and squeezed Connie's hand. The two women grinned hopefully at each other. "This is major clue number 2. One more strike, and he's out."

"Let's hope so, because we haven't much time."

As Gina grabbed the change and headed out the door, Delta peeked at her watch.

No, there wasn't much time. In less than seven hours, he would hit the streets again, stalking some innocent individual who had done nothing wrong except fit into his psychopathic plan of revenge. In seven hours, he would brutally take the life of someone she was sworn to serve and protect.

In seven hours, she would come face to face with Elson Zuckerman.

34

Jan scrutinized Delta before shaking her head. "Wait a minute. Could you run that by me once more?"

Delta nodded. "After we figured out the timing of the murders, we went through all the papers and cut out anything that had a final engagement or showing or sale or whatever. While Megan and Gina did that, Connie kept playing the game. All night, she had Dori pushing these boulders out of the road. But the only place she could push them was straight down the narrow path she was on. Connie figured that the boulders might be the equivalent to bowling balls."

"So, of the three bowling alleys on our beat, you came up with Dino's? How come? The only Dino I know of is the Flintstones' pet dinosaur."

Delta grinned. "Not this one. Megan did some excellent research that showed Deino, spelled D-e-i-n-o was one of the immortal Gorgon sisters. According to Greek legend, the Gorgons were these three ugly sisters who had to share one eye and a tooth between them."

"Rough life."

"Do you want to hear this or not?"

"I'm all ears."

"The Gorgons' job was to protect the nymphs who guard this pair of winged sandals."

"You mean the ones the F.T.D. Florist wears?"

Delta hit her forehead with the palm of her hand. "God, Jan, you and your kids watch too much T.V."

"Well, are those the sandals or not?"

"Yes, they are."

Jan shook her head. "Now that's all well and good, but I don't think old Dino named his bowling alley after some toothless witch."

"Of course he didn't. But Elson doesn't care about the origin of the name. He's been over every inch of our beat. He can turn practically anything into a Greek myth if it's close enough. And he had to stretch for Dino's because Deino is only occasionally mentioned by writers as the third sister. Megan cross-referenced everything she had until she came up with Deino spelled with an 'E'."

Jan nodded. "I guess if he didn't care about the spelling of gryphon, he wouldn't much care about the spelling of Dino's."

Delta nodded. "Exactly. He was also banking on us not being able to pull up the reference on a little-known mythological figure. Fortunately, Megan and her professor have made great strides together. He helped point us in the right direction."

Jan sighed. "God, Del, what planning this must have taken."

"Yep. We figure he's been mapping this out and plotting for a few months."

Jan nodded. "He'd have to have. It's all so linked together."

"And in doing so, he's created a pattern in the killings that enables us to play along. Every twist and turn in the game has been intricately planned on the street beforehand. He has a routine that he *has* to follow in order for the game to parallel his actions."

"And part of that routine is that he'll strike again tonight?"

Delta nodded. "All of the pieces are finally fitting together." As she rolled into the parking lot of the bowling alley, Delta pointed to the sign below the flashing blue Dino's sign. "See Dino's sign?"

Jan read it aloud. "Last night for co-ed leagues. So?"

"So, every time he's murdered, it's been someplace where it was the last day of something. It was the last day of the carnival, and the last open day of Troy's pharmacy. "We called Matt Ein at Omega's and found out that the ax was stolen on the last day of sign-ups for a big game hunt in Africa. I don't think this is a coincidence."

Jan shook her head. "Hardly. But what about the chauffeur? How does he fit into this scenario?"

Delta leaned back in the seat. "That one was a little tougher for Elson. Mrs. Griffin's statement said she was called by a man wanting to donate a large sum of money to the A.I.D.S. foundation, of which she's the chairwoman. She saw this man, collected what later turned out to be a bogus check, and returned home. One minute later, the chauffeur was dead and she was left wondering why.

"That makes two of us."

"What Connie thinks is that Elson didn't know where she lived, so he had to find a way to follow her. He must have scoped her out a long time ago. I'm telling you, Jan, he's been in River Valley a long, long time and has really done his legwork. He found out where Mrs. Griffin lived and he killed her chauffeur just like that."

"But how does that killing fit into the time scheme?"

Delta licked her lips before answering. "That one was almost so obvious, we missed it. "The chauffeur bought it on the last day of the month."

Jan whistled and shook her head. "Your brain cells must be on overload."

"Way beyond. I'm exhausted. Everyone's just about on empty at this point. If we don't get a major break in this case soon, I don't know how much longer we can continue at this pace."

Jan glanced back up at the sign. "So, today's the last day for the co-ed league and that fits into his pattern. Now, what is it he's after?"

"Since Dino's and her sisters' job was to protect the winged shoes, Connie thinks bowling shoes fit into the game plan quite well."

"Shoes? The man is going to murder tonight for a pair of shoes?"

Delta nodded sadly. "Pathetic, huh? Dori pushed the boulder into the lair of one of the gorgons. One of the mortal Gorgon sisters was named Medusa."

Jan's eyes lit up. "Medusa! Now I remember. My kids and I saw that Harry Hamlin movie a long time ago. What was it called? *Clash of the Titans*, I think. Medusa is that woman with snakes for hair."

Delta smiled. "Yep. She had hair of snakes, tusks for teeth, claws, and wings."

"She didn't look like that in the movie. I mean, she was ugly and everything, but I don't remember any wings."

Delta simply shook her head. "We're talking Greek mythology here, Jan, not Hollywood."

"Oh, sorry. Go on. How did Dori finally kill Medusa?"

"The myth has it that looking at Medusa's eyes turns people into stone. Perseus, the hero of the story, had to sneak up on her and kill her from behind. Dori did the same and strangled Medusa with a golden rope we'd won earlier in the game."

"Ah. Helen's ribbon."

"Exactly."

"Then what?"

Shrugging, Delta played with her baton. "That's as far as Connie's gotten. We killed the gorgon, but the winged shoes never appeared. We think we might have missed something along the way."

Jan nodded and reached across to touch Delta's hand. "How's Connie holding up?"

"Barely hanging in there."

"I can't imagine what this must be doing to her. Day in and day out of playing some morbid computer game? It would drive me nuts."

Delta nodded. "Maybe tonight will be the last of it."

Jan eyed Delta suspiciously. "I don't like the way you say that."

Delta shrugged. "What can I say?"

"You plan on taking him out, don't you? No, don't answer. I don't want to hear it if it's true. You know how I feel about that, Del."

Delta stared out the window. "He's toying with the people I love most, he's snapped a little girl's neck, and he's terrorizing people who are counting on us to keep them from harm. And what will the courts give him when we catch him? A free ride to the loony bin for a couple of years. He's already beaten the system, and he knows it! They won't send him to the chair, and he won't get a life sentence like he deserves because his defense will be that he's played so many of these games he can't distinguish fantasy from reality. Remember the Dan White Twinkie defense? We'll bust our humps to haul him in, and those idiot judges will send him to some fancy medical facility until Elson decides it's safe to act sane again. Don't tell me you can't see that."

"Of course I can see that. But that doesn't make you his judge and jury."

"No? You saw what he's done to those people. You watched as they lifted Helen's body onto the gurney. Suppose she was one of yours? Suppose they decided—"

"Stop. You can't rationalize just blowing him away, Delta. You just said our job is to protect people. Well, hard as it may be to believe, that includes people like him. Our job is to catch him—alive, if possible—and let the justice system do their job. If he's a threat, a real threat, then we take him out like we would anyone else who was threatening harm to someone. But don't appoint yourself executioner out of some skewed sense of loyalty. That's not your responsibility."

"No, but it's my duty."

"You're not a killer, Delta Stevens. I know what you've had to do in the past, but you're not a murderer. If you go after him, you're no different than he is."

Delta shook her head. "I disagree. He's a cold-blooded killer who is after my best friend. If I get to him before he gets to us, you know I'll take him down. My mind was made up long ago. Period. End of story."

"I won't be a part of an execution, Del."

"I understand that. You can walk away if you need to, but I'm going to do what I think needs to be done." Delta stared out the window and watched a group of teenagers walk into Dino's. "I'm getting that feeling again." Reaching for the mike, Delta was stopped by Jan's firm grip.

"Del, I know how important it is for you to stop this bastard, but don't do anything you won't be able to live with afterwards."

Delta nodded, not taking her eyes off the glass doors to the bowling alley. "Trust me, Jan. I won't."

"Promise me."

"I promise. Can we get a move on now? I've got some crazy feelings going on in my gut." Pressing the button down on the mike, Delta told dispatch they were at Dino's and to await a call for back-up.

"Come on," Delta said, getting out of the car. As they headed to the back entrance which led to an alley, Delta saw that the door was propped open by a Coke bottle.

"I don't like the looks of this," Delta whispered. Looking hard at the beam of light shining through the six-inch opening the bottle allowed, Delta's interior alarm rang loudly.

He was in there.

She knew it. She could feel it. And she hated him for it.

It was the same sensation that haunted her at the carnival. There was an evil essence that permeated the very air around them whenever he was near. It created a thickness, a sort of invisible cloud that passed through her, touching off the intricate alarm system she lived by.

"Want to split up?" Jan asked, reading Delta's mind. "You take the front, I'll stay here and let you run him out to me."

Delta nodded. "We'll make it look like a routine check, so we don't scare everyone. Call for back-up just in case."

Jan nodded and did so. "And Del?"

"Yeah?"

"Be careful."

Scooting around the corner, Delta thought of Miles. Weren't those her last words to him?

Nodding to herself, Delta shuddered and pushed open the glass doors.

35

Walking into the bowling alley, Delta's nose was immediately accosted by cigarette smoke. Young and old alike had cigarettes hanging from their mouths, and it didn't matter if they were bowling or playing video games.

Bells from the games filled the air and mingled with the crashing of bowling balls creating an eerie cacophony. A thin blue haze of smoke hovered like storm clouds, as overweight bowlers puffed madly between frames. As her eyes moved like an eagle's in search of prey, Delta felt him watching her. Like the haze of smoke, his dark presence loomed.

Yes, he was there, and he knew she was as well. She was not foolish enough to think that her presence would make a difference to him. It probably turned him on. Maybe that's what this was truly about; he was finally living the games he'd spent a lifetime playing.

Delta shrugged off the revulsion she felt just from thinking about him. Yes, he had planned very, very well for his revenge. Even if he was caught, what jury wouldn't think him insane as he prowled about killing people like some ancient warrior? He had already manipulated the system to his favor. He could exact his revenge and pay the very small price of a few years in a mental institution for the criminally insane. It was a brilliant strategy.

Scanning the small crowd of midnight bowlers, Delta did not see a man who was as small-framed as Elson. If he was there, he was out of her visual range. Looking around the perimeter of the alley, Delta noted five different exits he could leave through. It was possible he had already left, but she doubted it. For this game to work for him, he had to follow through with duplicate actions or the computer aspect of the game would no longer matter. He had to complete the next level.

Pulling her radio out, Delta turned the volume up a notch. "Five-oh-nine, this is one-eight-two. What's your twenty?"

Delta waited for a response. When it didn't come, her heart pounded harder. "Five-oh-nine, this is one-eight-two, do you copy?"

Still no response.

"What in the hell?" Delta wondered if Jan might not have her radio turned on, and then remembered that Jan had called back-up with it. It was on. She just wasn't responding.

Delta swallowed back the anxiety rising within her. "Five-oh-nine, this is one-eight-two; can you read me, over?"

Nothing. The silent airwaves clutched Delta's throat. Where was she, and why wasn't she answering? Ducking into the slightly quieter video game section of the bowling alley, Delta caught her breath. One of her worst fears began clawing at her imagination. Not Jan. She had lost Miles because she hadn't pulled the shotgun out fast enough, but the thought of losing Jan . . .

Before she could complete the thought, an unfamiliar voice broke through the airwaves.

"Call off the dogs, Stevens, or she dies."

Delta glared at the radio in her hand. He had her. That mother-fucking bastard had her partner. If she could have reached through it and ripped his tongue from his mouth, she would have. Like a vice, his voice gripped her. In one panicky moment, Delta thought about screaming at him over the radio. She wanted to yell and swear and threaten to do all sorts of horrible things to him. Instead, she sucked in a deep breath and calmly ordered everyone off the frequency. She alerted all units that she had a potential hostage situation and for everyone to back off at this time.

Peering out of the video section, Delta searched the bowling alley one more time. There was no sign of him anywhere.

Suddenly, Leonard's voice came on. "Okay, Stevie, we get your message loud and clear. We do nothing until we get the signal from you."

Raising the radio to her mouth, Delta again ordered everyone off the frequency, including all higher ranking officers.

Inhaling a painfully tight breath, Delta spoke again into the radio. "Let her go, Elson." Delta's voice was cold and hard. "We have this place surrounded. Give it up."

Elson laughed into the radio on the other end. "And quit the game so soon? I think not. I'm having much-too-much fun."

Delta held her radio too tightly, her fingernails were turning white. "What do you want, Elson?" Delta looked up as she heard the sound of a helicopter hovering overhead. It surprised her that Leonard had been able to get one in the air so quickly. Was he having her tailed?

"Elson? Are you still there?"

"Of course. I was just explaining to your partner here, that I'll break her neck if she tries anything other than what I instruct. Thus far, she's been extremely cooperative. I suggest you do the same, unless you care to find her looking much like that poor child at the fair."

"I'm listening."

"There are three doors leading to the back room, where your lovely partner and I are located. One will open up right to me, and the other two do not. Choose the wrong one or fail to move quickly enough, and she dies. You have one minute to decide. Simple enough?"

Delta nodded. "It's me you want. Let her go."

"One minute, Stevens. That's all you've got."

Delta wiped the sweat from her upper lip. The smoke from the bowlers was stifling and made her light-headed. "Elson?" Delta checked her watch.

"Forty-five seconds."

"Elson, if you harm her, I'll kill you. Is *that* simple enough?"

The radio sputtered. "You're wasting precious time with your silly threats."

Looking at the three doors, Delta felt her stomach turn. He was behind one of them. He was back there, holding her partner hostage, while he continued to play his demented games.

She believed with every cop instinct she possessed that he would kill Jan. If she did nothing, he would kill her and possibly escape before they could erect a solid net around the block to contain him. If she chose wrong, she was sentencing Jan to death. Again, he had the upper hand. Again, he was calling all the shots. And again, he held another life in the palm of his hand. As much as Delta hated every fiber in his body, she had to admit that he was good.

But she was better.

Moving toward the middle door, Delta's mind raced through the story Megan had read to her about the gorgons. They were blind, had snakes for hair, could turn people to stone, and they protected the nymphs who cared for the prized winged sandals. There were so many details; so many things to remember. Connie believed the winged sandals were Dori's next prize. She needed those shoes.

Shoes.

That was it! Bowling shoes. Delta shuddered. Her partner's life hinged on a pair of bowling shoes. Running the length of the bowling alley, Delta grabbed the attendant standing at the bowling balls.

"The shoes! Which door are the bowling shoes behind?"

"The one on the far right. Is there a problem?"

Looking at her watch, Delta saw that she had only ten seconds left.

Wiping the sweat from her palm, Delta drew her sidearm and ignored the cries coming from the frightened bowlers who watched her run across five lanes and stopping when she reached the door on the right. With her right hand, she carefully wrapped her fingers around the knob and gently tried to turn it.

It didn't budge.

Backing up a step, Delta braced herself and kicked the door in. As it crashed open against a shoe rack, she knelt on one knee, her .357 magnum aimed immediately at the two people sitting on the floor in front of her. Heart racing, temples pounding, Delta poised the revolver at Elson Zuckerman, whose head was slightly behind Jan's. He had Jan in a headlock, so that most of his face was shielded. Jan's hands were locked onto his arm that was squeezing her neck and turning her face red. Jan's gun was still in the holster and her baton on the floor. Whatever had happened between them had happened so fast, Jan did not have the time to pull her gun.

"Good choice," Elson said calmly. "You impress me, Officer Stevens. Thus far, you have managed to come in contact with me twice. That's two more times than I would have believed possible. You do make a fabulous warrior."

Delta steadied her breathing as she caught the right side of his face through her sights. "Let her go." Delta stiffened her trigger finger, so that the slightest movement would send a round through his right eye.

If only she had a clear shot . . .

"Don't even think about it, Officer Stevens. You saw what I did to little Helen. I can do the same to your partner. By the time you pulled that trigger, she'd be a dead woman. Surely, you don't doubt that I can, or would?"

No, Delta didn't doubt it. Not for a second. "What do you want?"

A slight, malevolent grin slid across his face. "Oh, I got what I came for, and he didn't even fight."

Delta stole a glance over his shoulder and saw a young man lying on the ground with a yellow ribbon around his neck. He was in his stocking feet.

"I must say," Elson continued, "I am quite surprised to find that you've figured the game out. I hadn't anticipated trouble from you until level six or seven. That's a credit to you, Stevens, more than it is to Consuela. She would be nowhere without you. You are an exceptional adversary. Thank you for making this so enjoyable."

Delta looked at Jan's blue eyes and wondered why she hadn't seen them before. They were saying a million things to Delta, held a million fears—that she might never see her children again; that she might not have the chance to say goodbye to Dennis; that she might not even live to see tomorrow. Her eyes reflected the same kind of fear a deer's does just before being hit by a car.

But Delta's eyes spoke right back to her. Delta eyed her strongly. She had lost one partner already. She wasn't about to lose another. Not now, and not to this fucking maniac.

That much she was sure of.

"Cut the horseshit, Elson. Let her go, and maybe I won't kill you."

The smile slithered wider. "Oh, I like that. Would you forfeit your partner's life to save that of your dear friend? The one who delights in belittling people? You would exchange one good life for a tainted one? What an added twist! Delta, you have truly made this one of the most enjoyable experiences of my life."

Jan's eyes were watering now, either from the pressure on her neck, fear, or both.

"Maybe." Delta knew that squeezing a round off so close to Jan's head was a great risk at best. If the shot wasn't clear, she couldn't chance hitting Jan with an errant shot. She needed just a little more room.

"Oh, and maybe not." Elson's smile grew. "I see that Consuela has chosen her champion well. I've done a great deal of research on you, my friend. I know that you don't play by the rules. That's why you and Consuela make such an admirable team; you have opposing personalities. You are the rebel who breaks the rules, and she is as consistent as the sun coming up. Well, rule bender, let's see, what's that one cop rule about never giving your weapon up? Didn't some poor slob buy the farm with his own gun somewhere in an onion field some time ago? Yes, I do believe I read that book. Why not make this interesting, Storm, and put your weapon down?"

"Because I'm not insane like you."

Elson's smile dropped a little. "Be true to your rebellious nature. Put the gun down, and I swear, I'll spare her life. I give you my word as a gentleman."

Delta shook her head. "Kiss my ass."

The smile did not waver. "You don't think I'll do it, do you?" Elson tightened his grip on Jan's neck.

"On the contrary. I'm sure you will. I've already written her off as dead, you crazy fuck. I've seen what a 'gentleman' you can be. My only concern now is that my partner doesn't go to her grave alone." Delta steadied her aim on the top right portion of his skull. She just needed one clear shot.

"You're bluffing." The smile faded a bit.

"Am I?" Delta cocked the trigger—an act done only by cops on T.V.

The smile completely vanished. "You're killing her by not putting your gun down. You understand that, don't you?"

Delta shrugged, keeping her eye trained on his face. "Maybe. That's a chance I'm willing to take." Delta looked into Jan's eyes and saw the imperceptible acknowledgment of what Delta was about to try.

Suddenly, Elson stood, jerking Jan to her feet. Backing toward a stairway Delta hadn't noticed before, he regained his composure. "I believe you would, Stevens. I believe you would stop at nothing to protect the life of that bitch, Consuela."

Delta inhaled, ready to stroke the trigger. "It's no contest, Elson. Connie's my best friend. Bowers is just my partner, and a shitty one at that."

Cranking his hold on Jan, Elson stepped closer to the stairs. "I'm a fraction of an inch away from breaking your partner's neck. I'll give you one more chance to put your gun down and save her life. Her life is in your hands. It's that easy."

"Not a chance. If she dies, you die. That's even easier." Beads of sweat rolled down Delta's back as she trained the gun on his forehead. She didn't doubt that he'd snap Jan's neck, regardless of what Delta did. Delta saw no other alternative but to take him out before he could harm Jan. Inhaling slowly, Delta readied herself for her final aim.

"Do it," Jan uttered through clenched teeth. "Kill the fucker."

Before Delta could squeeze off a round, Elson tossed Jan at Delta before flinging a Chinese star at Delta's thigh. Delta's gun exploded and the two women crashed to the floor as Elson scrambled up the wooden stairway.

"Shit, shit, shit!" Delta yelled, grabbing her right thigh as she fell against a shelf stacked with bowling shoes. Clutching her gun, Delta rolled to her side and tried vainly to get up, but the intense pain from the points embedded deep into her flesh brought her back to the floor.

"Jan?" Delta asked, seeing Jan slowly rise from the ground. "Are you hit?"

Shaking her head, Jan gasped for air. "No." Grabbing her radio off the floor Jan announced, "This is S1012. Suspect fled to the roof of the building. Description: five-foot-six, one-thirty-five, brown hair, short levi jacket, blue jeans, white tennis shoes. He is armed and very dangerous." Jan inhaled another breath to continue. "We also have a 187 and an officer down. Repeat, officer down; request an ambulance."

Delta sat on the floor, holding her throbbing thigh in both hands. Blood soaked through her pants and began dripping slowly to the concrete floor beneath her. She did not hear the response from the radio, concentrating instead on not passing out.

"Go after him!" Delta growled, as a hot streak of pain seared through her leg.

Jan was at her side in an instant. "No way, pal. I'm staying here with you." Jan set her radio down and knelt next to Delta. "If he's on the roof, he's ours." Glancing at the blood-covered star, Jan gulped in some air. "Want me to pull it out?"

Delta nodded. "Do it fast."

"The doctor will yell at us."

"Who gives a shit? I'm bleeding to death."

Grabbing the star, Jan turned her face away and yanked it free from Delta's leg, sending a short spurt of blood across the room.

"Son-of-a-bitch!" Delta cried, holding her head in her hands. "God, that hurts."

Taking a towel off the rack, Jan applied direct pressure to stem the bleeding. "How's that?"

Leaning back against the shoe rack, Delta sighed. "Better." Placing her hand over Jan's, Delta helped put pressure on her leg. "Damn that asshole and his fucking stars. I should have blown his head off." Feeling the throb bang her head like a drum, Delta felt weak. "How are you?" she asked, squeezing Jan's hands beneath hers.

"Honestly?"

"Uh-huh." Her world slowly started spinning, and Delta knew it was simply a matter of time.

"I think I shit my pants."

Delta smiled and nodded, glad that Jan had stayed with her. "When you thought he was really going to break your neck?"

"No. When I thought you were really going to send a bullet whizzing past my ear." Jan pressed harder as the towel turned a bright red.

Delta shrugged and watched as the blood dripped off the towel. "Too close to call."

"You weren't bluffing, were you?"

"Nope. I was sure he'd kill you first, just out of the meanness of it. I could never live with myself if I just stood there and watched him snap your neck." The walls seemed to breath in and out with Delta, and her head was beginning to float off her shoulders.

"You really think he would have?"

Delta nodded. "Killed you? Yep. Even if it was just to make a point. The guy's a control freak. He wants us to think he's got this whole damn thing under his thumb."

"Does he?"

Delta grinned a drunken grin. She was sure the walls were moving. Or maybe she was. It was getting harder and harder to tell. "Not anymore."

"Well, thanks for keeping me alive. For a minute there . . ."

"Wasn't even close." Jan's face was becoming fuzzy, and Delta knew it wouldn't be too long before she passed out.

"Maybe not, but I'll be sure to have my kids and my husband thank you anyway."

"Hey, that's what we're about." Taking a deeper, slower breath, Delta was almost ready to let herself succumb to the waves of nausea rolling over her. "Did he say anything to you while you were in here with him? I mean, why did he do this? Why you?"

"Don't you get it by now? The asshole admires you. I think he likes you."

Delta shook her head but wasn't sure if it moved. She didn't quite feel like she was in her body anymore, as grayness and unconsciousness pounded against the shores of her mind. Any moment now, her world would fade to black.

"No . . . I don't . . . get it." In the dismal blackness that enveloped her, Delta heard Jan's last words.

"He said he wanted to meet the woman brave enough to track down and face a man as dangerous and as brilliant as he is. He said you were the last of the true champions, or something to that effect. Can you believe it? The guy thinks you're great."

Delta could not answer. As the last particle of consciousness gave way to the dark reality of unconsciousness, Delta focused her last bit of energy on Jan's face and whispered, "And I was just kidding about you being a shitty partner."

"No kidding."

Slumping against Jan's shoulder, Delta exhaled her final conscious breath. "No kidding."

36

As the last stitch was sewn into her leg, Delta winced. The star managed to cut a five-inch gash in her thigh that was one inch deep. Even with the pain medication, her leg throbbed like she was in the bass section of a stereo speaker.

In the far corner of the room Jan sat filling out report forms and glancing over every now and then to see if Delta was all right.

"That's about it," Dr. Leslie Weeks said, tying up the last bit of thread. "I know I'm wasting my breath on you, Delta, but I do need to warn you that because of the location of the stitches, you should stay off your feet for a few days to let it heal. Give yourself a day or two for it to mend. It's pretty deep, and you'll risk infection if you push too hard. I'm going to cut you loose for a few days, all right?"

Delta's immediate reaction was one of displeasure. Then she realized that being off work might actually give her more time to hunt Elson down. Maybe there was a silver lining on that star Elson embedded in her.

Dr. Weeks winked at Delta. "I can imagine the trouble you'll get yourself into if you're not working."

Delta smiled. She had always liked Leslie. Ever since she stitched Delta up after a riot broke out, she made sure she always came back to Dr. Weeks.

"I'll be back to check up on you in a bit. For now, lay your head back and rest a minute. You're done fighting crime for the night."

Delta grinned. "Thanks, doc. You do good work."

Dr. Weeks smiled a near perfect smile. "Wait till the department gets my bill."

Leaning her head back, Delta closed her eyes and fought the desire to scratch her stitches. She remembered the first time she got stitches; she was five, and she ran under a garage door that had a bolt sticking out. The bolt caught her square on top of the head, but she just kept running. If she remembered correctly, they were playing kick-the-can, or something similar. As she thought back to the second time she got stitches, Delta barely heard the door open and someone sitting down on the chair beside her.

"Had a rough night, eh, Stevie?"

Slowly opening her eyes, Delta looked up at the ceiling and not at Leonard. "What do you want, Leonard?"

"How are you feeling?"

Delta lowered her eyes and squinted at him. For all of his rough edges, Russ Leonard really did care. "Like someone tried to make a shishkabob out of me. Did you get him?"

Leonard averted his eyes as he shook his head. "The bastard had a fucking helicopter waiting for him. He just grabbed a hold of this rope and away he went."

Delta remembered hearing the chopper blades shortly before seeing Elson. "A helicopter?"

"Can you believe it? Dropped a line, he grabbed it, and away he went. We couldn't shoot at it and have it crash on the streets below."

"So, he got away."

Leonard nodded. "I'm tellin' ya, Stevie, I'm gettin' really tired of this shitbag."

"You and me both, Russ."

Leonard scooted the chair closer. "Then work with me, Stevie. Give me everything you have on this guy."

Delta closed her eyes and leaned her head back. Her leg was on fire.

"Come on, Stevie. You know the kind of trouble I could get you in for withholding evidence in a case like this."

As the pain travelled up her leg, Delta shook her head. "I've got nothing to tell. We have a psycho loose."

"Bullshit."

Jan rose from the chair. "Sergeant, Delta is telling you the truth."

Leonard looked at Jan and shook his head. "I figured you for smarter than falling for Stevie's bag of tricks, Bowers. She's snowed you, too, and look where it almost got you. Laying on a slab next to Helen."

Delta jerked her eyes open and her head forward and immediately regretted doing so. "Back off, Leonard. You had your chance to work with me and you fumbled. Leave us alone."

Leonard shook his head. "Can't back off now. Everyone from the Chief to dispatch wants to know how it is that you and this Elson guy referred to each other by name. You have a lot of questions to answer when you leave here, Stevie."

This revelation hit Delta hard. She had forgotten that piece. Of course everyone would be wanting answers by now. It was clear to everyone that this case had developed into something more than a serial killer. Downtown would want to know just what that development was.

"Can you explain that to me, Stevie? Because in a few minutes, the big bosses are gonna be breathing on your ass so hard, you'll think you're in a hurricane."

Delta looked at him and grinned. "Lucky guess?"

Leonard snorted. "The way I see it, maybe you've had more than one contact with our nutcase."

"And maybe you should have listened a little harder, Leonard. The way I see it, we came to you with evidence, and you shooed us away like we were some wet-eared rookies. Try explaining that to the Chief."

"Don't fuck with me, Stevens. This is a homicide case you're messing with. Right now, you're standing in the way. You may be getting closer to the perp who's pulling the jobs, but you sure as hell ain't preventing these deaths from happening. It's time to stop playing amateur detective and give me everything you have. And, in case you're the least bit confused, this isn't a request."

This made Delta laugh. "Leonard, if the Chief and the Captain really wanted to know how Elson and I knew each other's names, they'd be in here right now. Don't bullshit me. You started with nothing, you have nothing, and you'll finish the fourth quarter with nothing. I needed your help and came to you ready to deal. Maybe if you would have compromised a little, my partner's life wouldn't have been threatened tonight. So don't go telling me what you're going to do to me, Leonard, because you're full of shit."

Leonard was suddenly on his feet. "Now look here, Stevens—"

Before he could say another word, Jan was right in his face. "Back off, Leonard. Back way off."

Leonard sneered at her. "Don't go looking for trouble, Bowers."

"And don't you even think about harassing the cop who saved my life tonight."

"She's the reason your life was in danger in the first place."

"That shows just how little you know about this case, Leonard." Jan stood on tiptoe so she could be in his face.

"I know enough."

Jan's voice rose to a level Delta had never heard. "Delta is one hell of a cop, and you know it. If she wasn't, I'd be on a slab in the morgue right about now. She's closer to Elson than you'll ever be by scratching your balls and waiting for a clue to walk through the door. Connie and Delta came to you, and you burned them. You turned them away because what they had to offer wasn't concrete enough. Well, take a good long look at that star over there, and you tell me if that's concrete enough."

"That's where you're mistaken—"

"Right or wrong has nothing to do with it. I'm alive because Delta knew which door to pick. I'm alive because she was able to bluff him into going for the stairs, instead of killing me. I'm alive, you narrow-minded, pig-headed man, because for the past two weeks, she's done nothing but eat, sleep and drink this case. He's in her head. You can't force that kind of knowledge out. You have to possess it yourself. Delta owns it, so just back the fuck off."

Leonard backed away from Jan and sneered hard at Delta. "You're both nuts. I'll have both your badges before this thing is over, hero or not. This isn't your own personal case, Stevens. As usual, you're breaking all of the rules the rest of us swore to uphold. And those you don't break, you make up. Well, I swear, this time it's gonna cost you. This time you've crossed the wrong guy. You get in the way of my investigation again, and I will have your badges." Turning on his heels, Leonard stalked out of the room.

Stunned, Delta stared, slack-jawed, at Jan. "Is that how you discipline the children?"

Jan stomped across the room and looked out the tiny window in the door. "Oh, he's just an arrogant asshole."

"Well, thanks."

Jan walked back over to the bed and slid her hand on top of Delta's. "No. Thank you. When Dennis heard the call on our police monitor at home, he said he sat down and prayed. When I called to tell him I was all right, he cried. Right then and there. I've never heard him cry like that. He said he didn't know how to thank you."

Delta bowed her head a little. "Leonard was right on one point. You wouldn't have been in trouble if it wasn't for me. I shouldn't have put you in that position in the first place."

"Not true. We went after a perp. A perp, Delta, who strangled a young man in a bowling alley. Don't blame yourself, Del. It won't do us any good."

Delta shrugged. "I didn't mean what I said, you know, about you being a crummy partner."

Jan grinned. "The word was 'shitty,' and I know. I'm your partner, Del. For better or worse, we went into that situation together and came out together. *That's* what we're all about."

Suddenly, the door burst open again, and a tall, shapely, red-headed woman strode through the door with Leonard in tow.

The moment Delta saw her, a smile slipped easily across her face. The emerald green eyes with a hint of gray and the intense gaze were features Delta started admiring long ago. District Attorney Alexandria Pendleton was one of the most striking women Delta had ever met. It wasn't enough that her beauty stopped people in the street, but her poise and her presence were larger than life. Her confidence, her strong sense of self entered the courtroom before she did, and Delta thought that was what made her such a damn good prosecutor. She had gone for, and received, the maximum sentence for Miles's murderers; a gift Delta held most dear.

When their eyes met, Delta noticed a slight curl to Alexandria's lips. They had worked closely together during the trial, and Delta admired the work ethic of the city's first female District Attorney. Alexandria Pendleton was thorough, swift, efficient, and uncompromising. She dug deep and left no stone unturned. Delta wondered what stone she was turning over now.

Taking her jacket off, Alexandria turned and nodded to Delta. "I see you've gotten yourself into another tight spot, Officer Stevens."

Sitting up, Delta looked into the eyes sparkling back at her. These were not the eyes of a woman who was coming to tell her to cough up her information to Leonard. Instantly, Delta relaxed. "I suppose one could look at it that way." Delta did not want to notice Leonard standing at the door. "It's good to see you again, counselor."

Alexandria grinned slightly and motioned for Leonard to step in. "I was going to call a meeting tomorrow morning, but since the Chief and everyone else's mother has called me about tonight's incident at the bowling alley, I thought it best we discuss matters now."

Delta's left eyebrow rose. "Matters?"

Alexandria reached into her eelskin briefcase and removed a familiar-looking file and laid it next to Delta's good leg. "There seems to be a great deal of action going on in your beat."

Delta had seen this look before. Alexandria was setting her pieces in order. "You could say that." Eyeing Leonard carefully, Delta saw that he was smirking. Had he called her in?

"It's been brought to my attention that you seem to have exceptional knowledge about our serial killer. Is this true?"

Delta cringed inside at the term 'serial killer.' This implied he was just randomly killing people, and that was far from the truth.

"Delta?" Alexandria prodded. "Be straight with me here."

Delta looked back into Alexandria's eyes. "Yes, it's true."

"And I understand you even know who the man is who's committing these crimes?" Alexandria had her courtroom voice on now.

Suddenly, Jan was at Delta's side. "We know now, Ms. Pendleton. I've already given my I.D. to Jonesy, and the Identikit's being copied as we speak."

Alexandria smiled at Jan. "Good. But that's not what I asked." Turning back to Delta, Alexandria's eyes narrowed. "Delta?"

Delta studied Leonard for a moment. How could he risk her telling Alexandria that they had tried to include Homicide, but that he didn't listen? Perhaps she had misjudged Leonard a bit. He was willing to take the heat just to get Elson off the streets. He appeared willing to accept the consequences of his narrow-mindedness; a fact Delta admired.

"Yes, I do."

Alexandria frowned. "How close are you to catching him?"

This caught Delta by surprise. "Very. Inches. We just need a little more time."

Nodding, Alexandria weighed her next question. "What about now? Now that you're out of commission?"

"I don't have to be."

"I think you do."

Delta looked deep into Alexandria's eyes. They were telling her more than her words conveyed.

"It might be best for all of us if you took the time and used it wisely, don't you think?"

Delta suppressed a grin. "I suppose so."

Leonard seemed to erupt from behind Alexandria. "Now wait just a minute, I thought—"

Whirling around, Alexandria towered over him. "If you don't mind, Detective, I would like to speak with Officer Stevens alone."

"But you can't—"

"Oh yes, I can. Your department has failed to come up with a suspect; a fact the public is painfully aware of, as am I. When I'm through here, I would like your explanation on how it is that Officer Stevens seems to know more about your case than you do. Until then, please excuse us."

His face turning pinker by the second, Leonard glanced helplessly at Delta before walking out the door, his fate now in her hands.

Alexandria waited a moment before returning her penetrating eyes on Delta. "I can imagine how you know so much, Delta, but right now that's not my greatest concern. What matters most is that you're close to catching him."

"We are. Inches. Seconds. We're right behind him."

"When will you be in front of him?"

"With the time off, it could be in the next three days."

Putting her hair back in a ponytail and then letting it go again, Alexandria paced across the room. "I don't think I'm making myself clear here. Can you stop him before he kills again?"

Delta thought about this for a moment before nodding. "I think so. We almost had him at the bowling alley."

Alexandria glanced over at Jan. "From what I understand of tonight's events, he almost had you."

"It was my fault," Jan explained. "I should have closed the back door when I entered the bowling alley, and I didn't. He faked me out, and I went for it."

"I see." Back to Delta, Alexandria rubbed her hands together. "What does he want?"

"He's matching wits with Connie and guts with me. It's a long story, Alex."

"Give me a thumbnail sketch."

Delta told her everything except giving the disk to Leonard. When she finished, she watched as the color slowly came back to Alexandria's face.

"And what will he do if we intervene?"

"The game will be over, and he'll blow up one of the larger buildings in the city. That's why we didn't come forward with any of this. There's more at stake here than whether or not Connie and I went through the proper channels. He's calling the shots. We're just playing along until we can gain the advantage."

"And you think he'll really make good on his threat?"

"He has so far."

Alexandria pondered this for a moment.

"Alex, this has nothing to do with ego or my dislike of Leonard or anything else. He will either play this game to the end with Connie, or hundreds of innocent people will be blown to bits."

Alexandria moved over and sat next to Delta. "And you think he could do it?"

Delta nodded. "He's brilliant. I wouldn't doubt that he already has one of the buildings rigged and ready to blow if anyone gets in his way. He wants to take Connie on, and Connie only."

"What about you? How do you figure into all of this?"

"I'm just the pawn she moves, that's all."

This brought a tiny grin to Alexandria's lips. "You're more like a knight, don't you think?"

Delta shrugged. "Hopefully, if we make the right moves, I'll soon be queen. But we can't if you take this away from us and give it to Leonard. You'll be sentencing a lot of people to their deaths. Alex, every day, every hour, Connie gets closer. We're that far from catching him." Delta held her thumb and index finger a centimeter apart.

Rising, Alexandria paced over to the window and ran her hand through her hair. "Let's be frank here, shall we? The public and the media are hounding me for a suspect. If I can get one before re-election, I'll be a shoe-in. Re-election as a woman will be tough if I can't reel a suspect in before voting time."

"So, what are you proposing?"

"What I'm proposing is this: it's clear that Detective Leonard and his people are aware that you have information you've withheld. So, I have to insist you give him all of the information you have on this Elson character. That will let Leonard get an APB out on him and help him do his job."

Inhaling deeply, Delta nodded. "Then what?"

"Then, you and your entourage have seventy-two hours to bag him before he kills again. Use whatever resources you need, do whatever has to be done, but stop him. I'll keep Leonard off your backs for seventy-two hours, but if you lose him, or he murders again, we'll have to turn the whole enchilada over to Leonard."

Delta looked over to Jan, who was nodding. "Seventy-two hours?"

Alexandria nodded and closed her briefcase. "That's the best I can do. I need a suspect, Delta."

"We'll take it." Reaching her hand out, Delta shook the D.A.'s strong grip.

"I'm counting on you, Delta Stevens. I'm sure I don't need to tell you my butt is on the line here. Don't let me down."

Delta shook her head. "Not a chance. I owe you already."

"Just stop him, Delta. That's payment enough." As Alexandria started toward the door, she turned with her hand on the knob. "Seventy-two hours, my friend. Good luck."

Delta saluted. "There's more at stake for me than your election, Alex."

"I know."

"Then do you also know that I'll give it everything I've got?"

Alexandria smiled wearily. "That's precisely what I'm counting on."

37

Stars were flying everywhere, and Delta was hopping about like a cowboy being told to dance. A large-faced balloon hovered over her, its mouth wide with sickening laughter erupting from it. On the roof of a building, Connie stood with a machine gun, a la Bonnie Parker style, trying to gun down the hysterical balloon.

"Delta, wake up!"

Opening her eyes, Delta found Connie shaking her shoulders. "What? What is it?"

"I think we've got him!"

"What?" Sitting up too fast, Delta grabbed her throbbing leg.

"Megan and I have been combing through these myth books, and I think we've pinpointed his next victim."

Delta grinned over at Megan, who just walked through the bedroom door. "Sleep well?"

Delta shook her head, remembering the balloon. "Nightmares."

"You've been a little feverish," Megan said, gently sitting on the corner of the couch. "The doctor said you might for a while."

Delta carefully leaned over and kissed Megan's cheek. Megan had been a trooper at the hospital, acting brave and strong until they were alone. Only then did Megan burst into tears as the fear of losing Delta raised its ugly head.

"How are you?" Delta asked, lightly touching Megan's cheek.

"Exhausted. Worried sick about you, my little love."

"I'll be fine. It was merely a flesh wound." Delta glanced over and winked at Connie, who frowned.

"Not funny, Storm. That bastard nearly killed Jan and maimed you. He'd better hope like hell I don't catch him before you do, because if I do . . ."

"Easy, Chief," Delta said, holding up her hand. "He didn't succeed, did he?"

"No." Connie's face was a mask of bitterness. "But he came awfully close. Too close. Next time, let's see how he enjoys facing me."

Delta shook her head. "Isn't going to happen, Con. We need you to keep your head together. My job is the streets. Yours is here with Gina, Megan and Eddie."

"For now."

Delta looked over at Megan, who shrugged. "Tell her, Connie."

"Yeah, what got you so fired up in the first place?"

"I think we finally have a breakthrough."

"Yeah? Tell me."

Connie picked up one of her notepads before answering. "Elson had to kill a gorgon to get the shoes, right?"

"Right."

"In the myth, when Medusa—the one with snakes for hair—was killed, Pegasus was born."

"That winged horse was made by that ugly broad?"

Connie smiled. "Sort of. See, Poseidon, god of the sea, was Medusa's lover before she became the horrid picture we know today. According to the legend, Poseidon gave mankind the horse as a gift. So, when a pregnant Medusa had her head cut off, Pegasus sprung from her head."

Delta nodded, turning it all over in her mind. "And where does this information take us?"

Megan slowly rose and joined Connie at the large piece of butcher paper taped next to the computer. The entire house was wallpapered in butcher paper. "Armed with this knowledge, Dori breezed through the fifth level."

Delta's heart jumped. "You're already there?"

Connie and Megan both nodded. "And this time we weren't fooled. When we reached the battle area, both Pegasus and Poseidon were in it. Pegasus was walking around snorting, and Poseidon stood there waving his trident."

"Okay. So, now what?"

"We think they're both clues," Connie answered. "But the best part is, we're already at the next level and we still have two days to work on it before he strikes again."

Alexandria's words rang in Delta's head. "We have two days, period. If we don't find a way to stop him before he strikes again, Alex is going to have to step in and give everything we have to Leonard."

Connie shook her head. "That would be a really stupid thing for her to do."

"I know, but she doesn't have any other choice. This is Leonard's jurisdiction. As much as she may want to, she can't completely ignore procedure. We either catch him in time, or all hell breaks loose."

Slowly swinging her legs to the floor, Delta wobbly stood up and reached for Megan, who helped her over to the computer. Every step brought a jolt of pain running the length of her leg. "Okay. Let's see if I can get it. The first clue has something to do with either horses or wings, right?"

Connie smiled. "Right. And the second clue?"

Delta shook her head. "The ocean? Something to do with water?"

"Nope. More obvious."

Delta stared at the screen and watched as Poseidon waved his trident in the air.

"The trident?"

Connie nodded. "What else is shaped like a trident?"

Delta thought a moment. "The only thing I can think of is a pitchfork."

"Bingo. And where will you find both horses and pitchforks?"

"At a ranch." Delta thought for a moment and then smiled. She remembered her conversation with Jan earlier in the week. "Or at a racetrack."

"Exactly. And the Springtown Stakes are in town this weekend."

Delta clapped her hands together. "But tomorrow's Saturday. The last race won't be until Sunday."

Megan nodded. "Right. But we have to consider all of the Omega options here, right? The last race might be on Sunday, but there could be more lasts involved. I called a jockey who was a . . . personal friend of mine, and he owes me a favor or two. I'm on my way over to his place for the spreadsheets on all of the horses, jockeys, owners, et cetera, so we can see if any match up with our clues."

Delta studied the screen and tried to ignore the heat burning her leg. "Good thinking. But tell me how you did it in the game."

Connie beamed. "We strangled the gorgon and got the winged sandals. Then a new level appeared. After fighting our way past assorted bad guys, we eventually arrived at Pegasus. The key thing is that we kept the ribbon we strangled the gorgon with, and that enabled us to use it as a rein to catch Pegasus."

"So, you caught the horse. Then, what?"

"What else? We rode him. He took us to a small island, where we wandered around fighting giant lobsters and stuff until we came to Poseidon's lair."

Delta's eyebrows rose. "You're already at Poseidon's cave?"

Connie and Megan looked to each other and grinned before nodding in unison.

"Yep."

"Have you killed him yet?"

Connie shook her head. "Dori doesn't have anything that would kill a god. Remember, he's immortal. He's Zeus's brother and one of the greatest gods of Olympus. Killing him isn't like killing Medusa or the others."

"So, what do we do with him if we don't kill him?"

Megan pointed to the caricature of Poseidon on the monitor. "What else? We get the trident."

Delta looked at the screen and thought about this for a moment. "You're sure we want the trident?"

Megan nodded. "Positive. That trident can create earthquakes, rivers, and streams. It is a very powerful weapon, and we think it may be the key to getting to Mt. Olympus and possibly to the end of the game. We need it—we just don't know how to go about getting it."

Connie agreed. "The point is we *know* where he's going to strike next, so the next move is ours. If we can stop him at Springtown, who gives a shit about the trident?"

"And you're sure he'll be at the racetrack?"

Connie nodded. "I'd stake my badge on it. All we have to do is locate his next victim, and Elson is ours." Connie recapped the pen and turned the monitor off.

"What are you doing? We can't stop now!"

Squatting down in front of Delta, Megan took both hands in hers. "Honey, it's been a grueling night for all of us. You've lost blood, we've lost sleep, and we'll all lose our minds if we don't get some rest. Connie needs to sleep, honey. She can't live on coffee and No-Doz indefinitely."

Delta looked at Connie, who was nodding. "Besides, Kimo, I promised Megan we'd take a break when we got a break, and we did, so I am. *Capisce?*"

Delta knew she was outnumbered. "Okay, okay. I guess I'm not thinking straight."

"Not a problem, boss. After all you've been through the past twenty-four hours, it's no wonder. Why don't we all get some winks in and start fresh in a few hours?"

Delta conceded. "All right. If we have to."

Connie grinned and messed up Delta's already mussed hair. "You have to. How's your leg?"

Delta winced. She was trying to forget about it. "It's still there."

Connie grinned. "Good. Get some sleep." Bending over, Connie kissed the top of Delta's head. "And let's see how you feel about it when the drugs wear off."

Watching Connie amble down the hall, Delta pulled Megan to her. They hadn't been alone since Delta returned from the emergency room, holding a crutch in one arm and Jan in the other. "You've been a trooper, Megan. How are you really?"

Wrapping her arms around Delta, Megan hugged her tightly. "Honestly? I'm scared, anxious, exhausted. Seeing you hobble in here was bad, but getting a phone call from Connie saying you were in the hospital, well, I could live forever and not hear those words again."

Delta inhaled the soft scent of Megan's sweet hair and ran her fingers through its softness. Megan's body trembled slightly, as she caressed Delta's shoulders.

"I'm sorry I scared you."

"Scared me?" Megan said, gently pulling away. "I was out of my mind. The second Connie called here, I knew. I don't know how, but I did. I lived ten years waiting for her to tell me if you were alive. It was awful. No, it was worse than awful."

Delta pulled her back and held Megan against her. "I'm so sorry."

"So am I. Have you ever experienced anything like that? That horrible sensation of time standing still? Well, that's what it felt like and it sucked."

Delta could only remember one instance when time stood still for her, and that was when Miles died in her arms.

"Have you ever had to hear that your lover was attacked and sent to the emergency room?"

Delta simply bowed her head. She knew it couldn't be easy. "Not really."

"Well, that's a slice of what I went through last night. Delta, I thought I'd lost you. I thought Connie's next words were going to be that there wasn't much hope. I prayed, Delta, right then and there, that this wasn't the end."

Delta couldn't look into Megan's eyes. Delta knew if she saw the pain and anguish Megan felt, that guilt would soon follow, and Delta didn't wish to feel guilty. For Delta, guilt was something someone felt when they either had or hadn't done the right thing. Given the same set of circumstances, Delta was sure she would do the exact same thing all over, even if it meant having that star bite into her flesh. "I don't know what to say."

Megan sighed. "A part of me wishes you'd turn the badge in when this caper is over; that you'll give it up and be a bean farmer. A part of me wishes you'd be scared enough one day and decide that you like living better than saving people's lives." Megan slowly removed herself from Delta's arms. "And a part of me knows that you need that blasted badge as much as you need your heart."

Delta looked into Megan's eyes and found fear, anger, and frustration at the truth. Her face showed the strain of emotions she could not control and did not want. "I don't know what to say. It's the same conversation we keep having, isn't it?"

Megan shrugged and then nodded. "But I don't know if I have what it takes to be a cop's wife, Delta."

Megan's panic transferred to Delta. "What are you saying?"

Sitting next to Delta, Megan wiped some of her curls away from her forehead. "I'm saying we have more to work on than just you not being able to give me 100%.

Delta, I love you more than anyone in the world. My love for you runs to places in my soul that I didn't even know existed."

"But?"

Megan locked eyes with Delta and hung on. "But I don't know how many more times I can go through the kind of fear I experienced last night. I don't want to be without you, baby, but I don't know how to handle the feelings I had last night. It was awful."

Delta felt like she was holding the end of an unravelling rope. "So, what are you saying?" Delta asked again, the ball of panic rising in her throat.

"I'm saying that when this is over, you and I really need to take some time away and talk about ways of approaching our relationship. My love, as much as I hate to admit it, the honeymoon stage is over. It's time we looked at what kind of work is necessary for the long haul."

Long haul. Delta felt as if Megan had just thrown her a life jacket. "You're not planning on leaving?"

Megan grinned softly. "Leaving? I'm not a quitter, Delta Stevens. You, of all people, should know that."

"Then what *do* you want, Megan? If you're not going, what do I need to do to help you stay?"

"We have a great deal to sort out, and I want to know that you're going to put as much into that sorting as you are your job. Because if I'm doing all of the work, we'll never make it."

A ray of hope, Delta thought—a woman who was willing to show her how to work on a relationship and not simply walk into another's arms just because the honeymoon was over. "I swear, Megan, when this is wrapped up, we'll head up to the mountains and work things out. I'll do the counseling shtick if that's what you want, I'll even read a self-help book. Just show me how to keep a relationship alive after the flames die down." Grabbing Megan's hand, Delta held it to her cheek and kissed the back of it. "I swear, I just want us to work. I want to be able to keep you and still be Delta Stevens. God, is that too much to ask?"

Megan shook her head. "Only if you always put Delta Stevens before Megan and Delta."

"I'll learn how not to do that."

"Promise?"

Delta crossed her heart. "I promise."

"Because if we don't talk about how to put your badge in the back seat every now and then, there's not much hope for us. You realize that, don't you? I won't play second fiddle to your job anymore."

Delta nodded. "Fine. You won't have to."

"Does that mean you're going to pay attention to my needs as well?"

"Yes. I will. I swear I will." Wrapping her arms around Megan's waist and holding onto her as if she was a life preserver, Delta hugged her tighter than she ever had. "I love you so much. I'm sorry I scared you. I'm sorry I get so wrapped up in my wor—"

"Shh." Megan placed her fingers lightly on Delta's lips. "It's time to stop being sorry and start working on us. Maybe then, you won't have to be so sorry all the time."

Delta nodded. "I'd like that."

"Me, too. Now get up, and let me help you get to bed. You're looking really pale."

"Do I?"

Megan nodded. "Uh-huh. Jan said you bled a lot. That's a pretty deep wound you've got going there, and you're going to have to stay off it."

Delta didn't answer. She could no more stay off her leg than she could stop breathing. "Do I look as tired as I feel?"

Helping Delta to her feet, Megan nodded. "You look exhausted."

"Do I look as tired as a bean farmer might?"

"What?"

Delta grinned. "Never mind."

38

Delta stared at the list of jockeys and horses lying on the table. Italian names, cutesy names, surnames, phrase-names, Irish names, business names, ballplayers' names, a hundred different types of names appeared on the list. As Delta tried to fit any sort of Greek connotation to every name, Connie sat at Eddie and retraced Dori's steps to see if there wasn't something she missed earlier in the level. As of yet, she had not been successful in taking the trident from Poseidon.

On Delta's right, Megan was thumbing through an immense volume of Greek mythology that Professor Rosenbaum had given to her. Every now and then, she would cross a name off the list and move down to the next. Between them, there was a silent determination growing. Against Miles's murderers, the four of them made a formidable opponent. They acted like a well-oiled machine, capable of grinding to a pulp anyone who was stupid enough to get in their way. They were magic, and Delta hoped their magic would work once more.

She counted on it.

Absentmindedly rubbing her bandaged leg, Delta thought back to the moment prior to Elson tossing the star into it. His beady eyes, sparse moustache and black-rimmed glasses left an indelible imprint on her mind. A dozen questions zipped in and out of focus, as she tried to recall the moments just before he tossed the star. Should she just have killed him and risked Jan's life? What had she done wrong that she would change next time they met? What had she done right? How had he gotten his hands on Jan so quickly? And why didn't he just come after Delta?

She remembered his thin, ugly lips moving but couldn't quite recall what he had said. But there was something, wasn't there? It was a word that struck her odd when he said it, but she was too worried about Jan to file it neatly away in her short-term memory. God, what was it?

Hearing Megan sigh loudly, Delta reached over and patted her hand. It felt good to be working on a case with her. Megan seemed to really enjoy the detective aspect of police work; all the evidence and clue gathering was something she was very good at. It was the cops-and-robbers part that scared the hell out of her.

Who could blame her?

In her six years on the force, Delta had been shot at, punched, kicked, and spit on. She'd had someone throw rocks at her, someone try to kill her, and someone pull a knife on her. She'd seen death and destruction on a scale only Hollywood could reproduce, and she'd had her share of stitches. And Megan was frightened for her?

No kidding.

Glancing over at Megan, Delta smiled at her. Maybe Megan was making a great decision by choosing to try law instead of business. She'd been an excellent witness in court during Miles's case, and she was outstanding at researching information for the game. Winking at Megan, Delta couldn't help but smile wider.

"What are you staring at?" Megan asked, lowering her book.

"Nothing. I was just wondering if I would ever get the chance to call you 'counselor'."

"You can call me whatever you want, my love, but for now, do you want to hear what I've come up with?"

Delta nodded. "Shoot."

"I've looked at thirty names so far; seven have Greek potential, and ten I'm unsure of yet. Don't horse owners ever name their steeds Sally or Honey or Bess? What's wrong with good old American names?"

Delta snickered. "Those are cow names, my dear, not the names of champions." Delta paused for a moment, reflecting on her own words.

"I know that. But listen to this list so far: The Aphrodite Challenge, Bellerophon, Cassie's Love, Fortuna 500, Crystal Palace, Mont Blanc Special—need I go on? And then, there are those that are barely passable, but need to be checked anyway, like Diana. Boring, plain Diana. Still, she figures in many myths and is a possibility."

"God," Gina's voice came from the corner, where she was digging through reference books. "How would you like for someone to name a horse after you? Even if it was a fast one."

Delta ignored the last comment and pondered the list before her. It did seem insurmountable, with so many names related to Greek mythology in one way or another. They needed something to help narrow down the field. Gazing out the window, Delta thought back to the moments preceding her becoming the human target. What was it Elson had said to her before chucking that star at her? She could see his face so clearly, and even see his mouth moving, but the words escaped her.

"How many of those horses have been champions?" Connie asked, putting a little body English on her joystick to make Dori avoid Poseidon's powerful right hook.

There was that word again. Why was it she got a knee-jerk reaction every time she heard it. Closing her eyes, Delta could clearly see the word 'champion' forming on Elson's lips, but the sound never came out. Had she just imagined it?

Megan checked the sheet. "Twenty were champions last year or are presently considered champions."

Delta opened her eyes and looked around for the cane Gina had bought for her. She couldn't grasp whatever notion was cruising around in her head.

Slowly standing and lightly putting pressure on her leg, Delta moved to the window and thought about last night's "stabbing." She remembered Elson holding Jan, and both Jan and the star were propelled at her at once. He must have said something to her just before he threw it. But she knew that he tossed it and ran. Then, why could she swear he said it after he threw it? And why was it even important? It was like having a piece of corn caught in her teeth, and she couldn't get it out.

Seeing Jan's petrified face through the hazy fog of her memory, Delta quieted her mind and allowed her thoughts to flow freely. Words, pictures, images bumped into each other like strangers, and pictures from weeks ago mingled with photos of the day. Like an avalanche, the memories tumbled together into one huge blur. And out of this blur came the formation of the one idea she was trying to grab a hold of.

Champion.

"Elson didn't say it," she said under her breath. "Jan was repeating what he had said to her."

Connie and Megan turned from their work and stared at her.

Limping back over to the table and ignoring the ache in her leg, Delta pulled the piece of paper Megan was working on. "All morning, I've been trying to remember something Elson said to me that might possibly relate to the horses."

Connie quickly pushed the pause button and swung around. The creases on her face deepened every day the strain wore on. "And?"

"He said something to Jan that I thought, at the time, was an interesting choice of words. It was as if he was giving me another clue. At the time, it hit me funny, but I was losing blood and passing out and I wasn't sure I heard Jan correctly."

"So?" Connie asked, rising from her chair and stretching. "What was it?"

"He said something about me being the last of the true champions. Jan repeated his words, which is why I was having such a hard time retrieving it. I kept thinking Elson said it to me, and he didn't."

Megan grabbed the sheet and ran her finger down the length of the column. "Last champion, last champion. What do you think it means?"

Delta shrugged and studied the list. "Are we looking for the last horse who was a champion? Or the champion of the last race?"

Connie strode over and joined them. "Aren't they one and the same?"

Megan shook her head. "No. I think she means the champion of the last Springtown Stakes."

"Yes!" Connie agreed, leaning closer to the list. "The last races were—"

"Two months ago," Megan said, smiling.

"Enough time for him to fit it into the game," Connie finished for her.

Running her long, tapered nail down the list, Megan stopped at the notation of the horses who had won the last races during the Springtown Stakes. "This really narrows down the horses we have to look at." Grabbing her marker, Megan highlighted all the horses considered champions from the last races at Springtown. "This feels like the right track. Pardon the pun."

Delta examined the highlighted names. There were five or six she could have crossed off easily. But the seventh one on the list caught her attention. "Here's an interesting one. Harold's Hybris. Hybris sounds like something Greek. What's a hybris?"

Megan and Connie looked at each other and shrugged. "Let's look it up," Megan said, opening a thick reference book titled *Mythology Through the Ages*.

"Here it is," Megan announced, setting the large volume on the table. "Oh my God. This is it! *Hybris* is translated as pride, arrogance, and recklessness. According to this, it is 'being so self-assured that one celebrates victory before the battle is over.' "

Connie looked at Delta, who looked at Megan. There was a hush in the room that settled like a fine layer of dust.

"That's it," Connie said softly. "It must be. He must be talking about me."

Megan inhaled loudly. "There's more. It says hybris is when a person forgets that he's human and acts like a god or plays the role of one."

"Con, are you sure he isn't referring to himself?" Delta asked, peering over Megan's shoulder.

Connie shrugged. "I don't think so. No, Del, I'm sure he's talking about me. Is there anything else?"

Megan nodded. "Listen to this. In mythology, hybris, sometimes spelled h-u-b-r-i-s, was punished by Nemesis, a child of Night. Nemesis, who was thought of as Divine Anger, was the embodiment of Revenge and Retribution. If a person became too prosperous, Nemesis would take some of that prosperity from them."

Delta held up her hand for Megan to stop. "Wait a minute. If a person is too successful, then Nemesis would take some of what they earned away?"

Megan nodded, her eyes glued to the page. "Apparently so. It says, 'If that person boasts of his prosperity, the gods look upon that as a challenge, and that challenge is usually met.'"

"He's referring to me. He's recalling the old days when I was at the top of my class. I was successful. Clearly, he thought, and still thinks, that I was proud and arrogant of that success."

Megan looked up from the book. "So, this makes him Nemesis, doesn't it? He's appointed himself a child of the night."

"Which is why he strikes only at night," Delta added.

"And he is after Retribution and Revenge. It all fits. In the figurative and literal senses, he feels it is his duty to make me pay for my actions from long ago."

Delta shook her head. "Damn, he's way out there."

Megan closed the book. "That's all it says. What now?"

"The horse is our key. If we find that horse, we may find him." Connie sat back down at the computer and released the pause button. "Megan, would you copy the hybris information and tape it over my desk? There may be clues in there that will help me with the game."

"As good as done."

"And Del, you find out when Harold's Hybris's last race is. This time, that maniac isn't going to get away from us."

Turning to her task, Delta watched out of the corner of her eye, as Connie wielded the joystick. Never, in the five years they had known each other, had Delta ever seen her so intense. The light-hearted jokester she knew so well had been replaced by an angry, bitter woman filled with rage and hostility. In a deeper sense, Connie's lightheartedness seemed lost to the realities of brutal actions that would forever change her life. Elson hadn't hurt Connie in any physical sense, but he had certainly struck damaging blows to her spirit.

Turning to Megan, who was busily printing the hybris quote on a piece of butcher paper, Delta leaned over and kissed her. "How are you holding up?" Megan whispered.

Delta shot a glance over at Connie, who was deeply absorbed in the game. "Better than she is. I'm worried for her."

"Me, too. And I'm scared for you as well." Watching the blue of Megan's eyes shimmer, Delta felt that Connie's life wasn't the only one that would be changed after this.

"What for?"

"You have to promise me to be more careful."

Delta cocked her head as if she didn't understand.

"Oh, come on, Del. I've seen that look in your eyes before. You look at Connie, and you see her hurting—you see the changes in her character these two weeks, and there's a fire burning inside you, Storm—a fire I've seen once before when someone else you loved had been wronged."

"You know me well."

"Yes, I do. And I know that sometimes that fire carries you beyond reason. That, my love, is what scares me most about your job; it's not that I hate that you're a cop. You're a damned good cop. It's just, when you get that look, the rules of life no longer apply to you. You'll do whatever has to be done to right a wrong, regardless of the danger you may face. That's what scares me most, Del. At times like those, you forget that I need you, too. You forget that I need you safe and home in one piece. That's what I mean about putting our relationship on the back burner. I want us to come first enough that you won't take so many risks."

Delta could only stare at Megan. For the first time in her life, Delta actually got it. For the first time since she started dating, she understood just what it was that the women in her life wanted. They wanted to be first. But now that she understood, she wasn't sure what to do with it.

"Don't say anything, Del. I told you, we'll talk when this thing is over. But I just want you to think about it."

"But you're scared."

"Yes I am. That fire is a part of who you are, my love. Sometimes, I think it's what gets you up in the morning. It's also one of the things I find so alluring about you.

When you feel something, Del, you *really* feel it. Be honest with me, sweetheart. Tell me what you're feeling now."

"Scared, sad that—"

Megan shook her head. "No, honey, that's not what I meant. I mean tell me about the fire. Tell me what's burning inside your heart right this minute. Because I know it's there. I can see it in your eyes as plainly as I can see your face. Tell, me, Storm Stevens, what fire burns inside you right now."

Delta licked her lips and thought for a moment. She had never put to words what that edge felt like. While Megan saw it as fire, Delta felt it as sharpness, a gathering of strength and power for the upcoming battle. It was this fire, this edge that made her better than all the rest. There was an inner strength she felt whenever she was like this and it was better than any high she could ever imagine.

"I feel like I did in college when I was getting ready for a softball game. There's this inner preparation that happens, like my soul is donning armor and gathering weapons."

"What else? Name it for me, Delta. Help me understand where your passion comes from."

Inhaling deeply and slowly, Delta attempted to do as Megan asked. "It's a feeling that says I'll do whatever it takes to win. I'll put whatever I have to on the line to be successful." As a catcher in college, Delta had taken on a lot of women at home plate. Half a dozen times, she'd been knocked unconscious because she was not afraid to take on anyone charging her.

"At any cost?"

Delta nodded. "Yes."

Wrapping her arms around Delta, Megan held her and ran her hands through her hair. "That fire, that passion pushes you beyond yourself, beyond your safety, beyond our relationship. It is the mistress I envy when you get like this. It is the other woman who threatens to take you away from me."

Delta hugged Megan as if letting go would mean forever. "I don't know how else to be, Megan. All my life, I've lived by responding to that fire."

Megan grinned sadly. "I know. And since we've been together, I've lived hoping it won't take you away from me forever. I know that look, Delta, and I know you're going after him to kill him." Megan held up a hand to silence Delta before she could respond. "And I also know that you'll stop at nothing until you see him dead. It's the stopping at nothing part that frightens me most."

"What would you have me do, Megan?"

"Do? Oh, Delta, don't you see. It's not that I want you to *do* anything. I want you *not* to do something that might endanger you. That's all I'm asking for here, sweetheart, is that you'll think twice before putting your life in jeopardy."

Delta thought about Megan's words and shrugged. "I can't promise anything, Megan. You know how I get."

Sighing heavily, Megan lightly touched Delta's cheek. "Yes, I do. Just promise me that you'll try. That's all I'll ask for now."

Nodding, Delta took Megan in her arms. "I *can* promise you that much. I swear, Megan, I'll try to think about my . . . our life together before I take any risks. I may not be successful, but you have to believe me when I say that I'll try."

Pulling away, Megan kissed Delta's lips softly. "Thank you."

Hugging Megan again, Delta shut her eyes tightly. If only trying were as easy as loving Megan.

39

Delta hobbled to the house from the backyard, where she'd been letting her mind rest among the trees. If she never saw or heard another myth again, it would be too soon for her. The last two days had been spent getting as far in the game as their energy and time would allow, and she was beat. Her eyes ached, her leg throbbed, and her head pounded. Their seventy-two hours were rapidly dropping through the hourglass. If the answer they had come up with wasn't the right one, it was over.

Sliding the glass door open, Delta turned and smiled weakly at Connie. Forty-eight hours of watching a computer monitor put dark circles under Connie's eyes. She looked dreadful.

"I think we finally got him. If there's another solution to this level, it's beyond my reach. We've done all we can do."

"What did you finally have to do?"

Delta closed her eyes; visions of Dori fighting Poseidon passed in front of her. For the last twelve hours, every time Dori got close to Poseidon, he killed her. They tried throwing snakes, rocks, magic spells, even the shoes, but nothing hurt him, nothing distracted him. Time and time again, Poseidon raised his trident and thrust it into the tiny warrior, sending them back to the beginning of the level. And although she would never admit it, Delta had grown rather fond of the dark-haired, animated figure of Dori. On the screen, she seemed so real, so heroic in her actions, that Delta found it increasingly difficult to watch her get killed.

It wasn't until after they figured out Harold's Hybris, that they knew how to approach Poseidon—or not approach him as the case turned out.

Connie pulled up a chair next to Delta and sat down heavily. "Dori was lacking the humility of a mortal. When a person forgets they're human and acts like a god, they commit hybris."

Delta nodded. She almost resented the fact that she was beginning to understand how this game and Elson's twisted mind worked. "Right. Dori isn't a god, so she shouldn't approach him as if she were."

Gina walked in and pulled herself up on the counter. She had toned down her patient load to only a few "must sees" a day, and Connie was having an increasingly difficult time just getting her out of the house. If this case was tough on Connie, it was doubly hard on the woman who loved her. Gina seldom let Connie out of her sight now, and for the past week, had been feeding Connie her meals at the computer. Looking up, Delta saw the same tired lines forming around Gina's mouth that she saw on Connie's. If they didn't have the answer, then this was really the end. Then this became someone else's ballgame.

Looking around at her best friends, Delta wondered, for the first time in her life, if that wasn't such a bad idea.

"Hi," Gina said, bending over to kiss Connie. "How are things coming?"

"I think we're ahead of him now, honey," Connie replied with little enthusiasm.

Gina's face suddenly lit up. "That's great! How'd you do it?" Hopping off the counter, Gina sat in Connie's lap.

"We did everything we could to get by Poseidon, and then we realized we were doing the very thing Elson accused me of."

"What?"

"We were arrogant. A mortal should never try to outsmart a god. That's exactly what hybris is about."

"So, what did you do?"

"After trying everything we could think of, Megan called Professor Rosenbaum at the university and explained what we had going. When she was telling him about the shoes, he stopped and asked if the shoes were all we got from the gorgon."

Gina nodded. "It was."

"Yes, but that wasn't the only thing she had to offer."

Gina glanced over at Delta, who nodded. "I hate to use Jan's analogy, but what else does the F.T.D. Florist guy wear besides winged sandals?"

Gina's eyes lit up. "That little helmet."

"Right. But that isn't just any helmet," Connie said, twisting open a Calistoga. "It's the helmet of invisibility."

"I get it. Once Dori turned invisible, she could go get the trident."

Connie nodded. "Which she did. She put on the helmet, got on the horse, and Poseidon immediately fell asleep."

"So we nabbed the trident."

"Con, that's fantastic! Now what?"

Connie and Delta shrugged in unison. "We don't know."

Taking Connie's Calistoga from her, Gina took a drink. "You don't think he intends on stealing a horse, do you?"

Coming in from the bathroom, Megan joined them as well. "I was just thinking the same thing. Don't you think stealing a horse from the hustle and bustle of a racetrack would be nearly impossible?"

Connie and Delta looked at each other. "That's precisely why he would do it," Connie said quietly. "If we look at his current pattern, his actions have become more and more dangerous, more and more sensational. He held a cop hostage, only feet away from other cops, he's attacked Delta twice now, and he's already killed numerous people. Stealing a horse right out from under everyone's noses would be child's play after those stunts. He's getting fearless, and that could be his greatest downfall."

Delta nodded. "Being destroyed by his own hybris. What irony."

"Isn't that what happens to most brilliant criminals? He's cocky now. He's been successful in every turn. Now is when he's going to make that one fatal mistake."

Megan shook her head. "Yeah, but come on. Stealing a horse at a racetrack? Isn't that a bit like trying to hide an elephant in a pet store?"

"Actually," Gina said, handing the water back to Connie, "it would be more like trying to hide an elephant in a carnival. It's been done before. When I was a kid, there was a big news story about guys who went in and dyed a horse right there in the stall. They simply walked the now-chestnut horse out of the barn and into a waiting trailer. They got a multi-million dollar horse for free."

"But where is the murder?" Delta asked, her face a puzzle.

Connie fidgeted with her bottle. "True. We didn't have to kill anyone to get the trident. Maybe there aren't any more deaths."

"Maybe just not on this level."

"You don't think," Megan offered, rubbing the back of her own neck, "That he'd murder one of the jockeys in an effort to get closer to the stables?"

Connie thought about this a moment before answering. "He's crazy enough."

"And little enough," Delta added. "It's possible that's how he plans on getting into the stables in the first place."

"Harold's Hybris's last race is at 5:30 tomorrow." Megan said, tossing down the racing green.

"That's not the killing hours," Delta said.

"No, but now would be a good time for him to switch gears. Maybe he'll kill again, maybe he won't. It's possible he may just knock someone out, kind of like Dori did."

Megan nodded. "I agree. I think we need to be at that last race so—"

"Whoa. Wait a minute," Delta interrupted. "Who's 'we'? You're not going anywhere, my sweet. Elson is far too dangerous."

Megan stood and jammed her hands on her hips. "No? Then, who? Certainly not you."

Delta eyed her leg and then looked over at Connie.

"What do you want to do?" Connie asked, already anticipating Delta's next words.

Tracing the bandage with her finger, Delta wondered how much weight she could put on it before the stitches busted. "As much as I hate to say this, it's got to be done. Bring Leonard in. We have our best lead since we started, and I don't want to lose him because I have a bad wheel."

Connie shrugged. "We don't really have a choice, do we?"

"No. It would be suicide to put any of you out there against him. Let's call Leonard and tell him what we've got going. He needs a collar so badly, he won't give a damn how we know, so long as he comes out of it with an arrest. I'll brief him on everything we have."

Megan moved behind Delta and massaged her temples. "And what, my overworked mate, are the rest of us going to do?"

"Megan, you go back to the racetrack and find everything we'll need to know about the stables, the horse, the jockey, the exits and entrances, how many stable hands there are, et cetera. Even information about the owners will help."

"Do I, uh, use my sources?"

Delta grinned. "Short of getting on your back, do what needs to be done."

Megan clapped her hands together. "How exciting."

Delta pulled Megan to her. "It's dangerous, honey, not exciting. Remember, always, that you're dealing with a psychopath. A murdering, insane lunatic, who could cut your heart out as easily as look at you."

Megan nodded. "I know. I'll be discreet. Remember, before you met me, discretion was my middle name."

Delta grinned and realized she was holding Megan's arms too tightly. "I remember."

Connie nodded and gently motioned for Gina to get off her lap. "I'll keep at the game and try to figure out what we're supposed to do with the trident."

"Good. I'll get Leonard to arrange for a surveillance van so we can be there and follow what he and his men are up to."

Connie frowned. "You think he'll do that?"

"I won't give him any choice. If he wants the goods, he's going to have to play this our way."

Connie moved over to the computer. "I'll hook Eddie up in the van, so I can be right there should I have a break in the game."

Slowly rising, and grabbing her cane, Delta put gentle pressure on her leg. "Then I guess this is it. Any questions before we make the call to Leonard?"

Megan threw her sweatshirt over her head, and bent down to lightly kiss Delta on the mouth. "Remember what we spoke about yesterday. Don't be a hero, my love. I know how badly you want him, but you do have another life outside of him and your badge. Remember that, okay?"

Kissing Megan back, Delta felt the fire burning inside. "Roger."

"Del?" Connie said sternly. "That order goes ditto for me."

Taking the racing form from Megan, Delta nodded. "Okay, okay. I promise to try and remain an innocent bystander."

Megan ran her fingers through Delta's hair. "Somehow, my love, you and the word 'innocent' together in one sentence is hard to buy. Just stick to the promises you can keep."

"You're all so cynical," Delta said. "I swear, I'll stay on the sidelines."

Connie shook her head. "And I'll turn into a tomato at dawn. I mean it, Storm, keep your promise."

"I will. Speaking of promises, Gina, are you coming with us or do you need to see patients today?"

"I'll need to go to the office and cancel my appointments first. I had an emergency call from a fellow last night, and he sounded suicidal. I'll need to call and see if he won't mind seeing one of my associates. After that, I'm all yours."

Connie nodded. "Are you sure?"

Draping her arms across Connie's neck, Gina held her. "You're all that matters to me, my love. If I let someone down because I'm not there, I'll deal with it later. But right now, your safety is all I care about."

"I love you, Gene," Connie said, hugging her.

"And I love you, Consuela."

Glancing over at her two best friends locked in a fearful embrace, Delta grit her teeth. She would die before she let anything happen to Connie; of that, she was sure.

Promise or not.

40

With Leonard's men in place, Delta painfully limped over to the surveillance van and climbed in. Every available plainclothes cop was stationed at various vantage points across the track, and each was supplied with a computer print-out of Elson's face. Delta didn't expect the picture to be much help, since he was obviously big on disguises and make-up. Nevertheless, it was good for them to have pictures of Elson's dark black shark's eyes which no amount of make-up could hide.

"Everything's running like clockwork, Stevie. If your hunch is right, he should be walkin' right into our hands in half an hour."

Delta nodded, but said nothing. Leonard had been less than skeptical in the beginning, but when she told him she might have a bead on Elson, he sat very still until she had finished her explanation. This time, he didn't balk. Instead, Leonard immediately got on the phone and started making arrangements for the bust. Elson Zuckerman had even changed the concrete, evidence-only view of Detective Russ Leonard. It was almost scary.

Chuck Connell, Leonard's partner, shook his head. "Goes against every M.O. this guy's set up, Sarge. Everyone knows he hits between ten and one. It's not yet five, and you think he's going to show?"

Delta nodded. "He'll show all right. And don't be surprised if he's through with his standard M.O."

"How can you be so sure?"

Listening to the crackling sound of the radio as officers from various observation platforms checked in, Delta answered Chuck without looking at either man. "He's a genius, Chuck. A genius who has studied his opponents and knows that we're looking for a pattern. And just when we found one, he changed. He's brilliant. No matter how big of a scum he is, you can't take that away from him."

Leonard snorted loudly. "Sounds like you admire the guy, Stevie."

This time, Delta slowly turned around. "I would hardly call it admiration, Leonard. The man is a psycho, but I respect his intelligence. I won't ever underestimate either his intellect, or his capacity for cruelty."

Shrugging, Leonard looked at one of the television screens. They had planted a camera in the stable of Harold's Hybris. "So, where's your sidekick?"

"Jan is still on the beat."

"No, I mean Rivera. Where is she? Shouldn't she be in here with us?"

Delta shook her head. "All of this equipment disrupted her computer, so she moved everything back to her car. She's in the parking lot playing the game as we speak."

Tugging on one of his eyebrows, Leonard scowled. "I don't know how you did it, Stevie, but you sure know how to get the D.A.'s attention. She laid into me the other night at the hospital and told me to get off your back. What gives?"

Delta shrugged. "I want one thing and one thing only, and that's to keep this bastard from hurting Connie. You and the D.A. can have all of the headlines and glory you want. Just get him off the street."

Turning the volume up a notch, Leonard grinned a stained-tooth smile. "How about off the planet?"

Delta nodded. She'd like that. Glancing down at her watch, it was 5:35. The race would be over soon, if it wasn't already. Suddenly, an unexpected chill swept through her body.

He was there.

Like the other times when she felt the surge of evil emanating from his presence, she sensed him. She could feel the dark, black tentacles of his insidious nature thread their way through the crowd. He was there, lurking around the racetrack, searching, planning, setting up the pieces of the game to make his next move.

Checking her sidearm holstered under her right armpit, Delta tensed. Something wasn't right. So far, no one had seen anything out of the ordinary. There were men posted everywhere, yet not one of them called in with a location of Elson. Had something gone wrong? Had they missed a clue somewhere?

"It's almost a quarter till. Why haven't we seen him?"

"Easy, Stevie. We could be here awhile. As long as that horse is here, so are we. That is, if you're sure he won't just take any old horse."

Exhaling heavily, Delta shrugged. "Leonard, we're not even sure it's a horse he's after. But if he is, then it's Harold's Hybris. Trust me."

"And if it isn't?"

"Then he's outplayed us."

"I don't like the sounds of that."

Delta nodded. "You and me both."

▼　　　　▼　　　　▼

For more than two hours, they waited in relative silence. No one had seen him, no one had stopped anyone even looking like him. Somewhere, they had made a mistake. Delta's leg was sore from standing up every now and then to pace the floor, and her head still pounded. What had they missed? Were they so far off the track that they had wasted precious hours waiting for a crime that wasn't even going to be committed? The thought made Delta's stomach ache.

Finally, two and a half hours after the race, a somber, perplexed voice sounded over the airwaves.

"Uh, Sarge, we've got a development here that I think you ought to come check out."

Delta and Leonard looked at each other before Leonard snatched the mike off the table. "What is it?"

"I'm not sure, sir. No one is hurt or anything like that, but I think you'd better have a look. And could you bring Officer Stevens with you?"

"What's your twenty?"

"Stable 9E."

Delta checked the stable map. Stable 9E was next to Harold's Hybris.

"We're on our way."

Breathless moments later, Delta and Leonard rounded the corner of stable 9E and found the officer interviewing a stable hand who appeared to be in his early teens.

"What do you have, LaFrenz?" Leonard asked.

Officer LaFrenz pointed to the stable hand. "Him."

The teen gave a weak smile and shrugged. "Some guy paid me a hundred bucks to give this recorder to Officer Stevens. Told me that she was a lady cop and that I shouldn't give it to anyone but her. You her?"

Delta nodded, staring down at the brown paper bag the teen held. "Did you get a good look at him?"

The kid shrugged. "Like any other jockey. A little heavier than most. He's been kickin' around the stables most of the afternoon."

"Did you say jockey?"

"Yeah."

"What was he wearing?" Leonard asked, bringing his radio to his mouth.

"He was wearing a black and red uniform. Pretty cool one, too."

Leonard yelled into the mike and told his people to look for a jockey wearing black and red. "Was this the guy?" Leonard asked, pulling the picture from his pocket.

The stable hand glanced at it for a second. "Nah. This guy was bald and had a moustache."

Delta swore. "It was him, Leonard. Believe me, I know he was here."

"Where did he go after he gave this to you?"

"That way." The boy pointed to the east into the next row of stalls, prompting Leonard to notify his men to seal the area off.

"Won't do you any good," the boy said, wiping sweat off his forehead. "He gave it to me over two hours ago. Right before the last exacta race."

Delta ripped open the bag and pulled out a small tape recorder. "Damn him!"

Eyes bulging, the stable hand stepped back. "I hope I didn't do anything wrong. He told me you were a friend and that it was a birthday surprise."

Staring down at the recorder, Delta waited for Leonard to inform his men of what happened. Turning back to the boy, Delta struggled to maintain her cool. "Did he say anything else? This is very important for you to remember. It could give us some important clues."

Eyebrows knitted together, the boy thought for a moment before snapping his fingers. "Yeah, he did say something else."

"What? What else did he say?"

"He said it's almost over."

"Damn it!"

Tucking his radio in his back pocket, Leonard moved over to Delta. "We lost him, didn't we?"

Delta did not answer. Instead, she looked down at the tape recorder sitting in her palm. "Yep."

"So what's that all about?" Leonard asked, jerking his head toward the recorder.

"I don't know. But I'm sure when we listen to it, we'll find out. Damn it!"

Leonard studied the recorder for a moment. "Don't think it's an explosive, do you?"

Delta looked sideways at him. "Hardly. I'm sure he's gloating. Have your men check to see if any horse is missing and keep them on top of it until the racetrack closes. If he did take a horse, knowing which one could save someone's life."

Leonard nodded and did as Delta told. Then, he turned to her and asked, "So what now?"

Taking her radio out, Delta called Connie and told her to meet them at the van. "Now, we're going to hear just what that fucker has to say."

When they got back to the van, Connie was waiting by the door. "What's he up to now?" Connie asked, jumping into the van.

"We're about to find out. Listen." Sucking in her breath, Delta slowly pressed the play button.

"Good evening, ladies," came Elson's voice. "I suppose this comes as quite a surprise. Unfortunately, it really shouldn't be, but in all fairness, the fact that you got this far credits you with exemplary gamesmanship and fortitude, not to mention some semblance of intelligence. I trust that, thus far, I have been a formidable opponent. Boring adversaries can be so tedious, don't you think? Nonetheless, you have risen to the challenge and done quite well with it. You should give yourselves a pat on the back for getting Dori through Poseidon. Your resourcefulness deserves applause." Delta looked over at Connie, while Elson applauded on the tape.

"Ah, but I am remiss in my etiquette. How is your leg, Officer Stevens? I imagine it took a few stitches to patch

you up. But you're a tough one, and I'll bet you'll be back
on your feet in no time. You gave me no alternative, you
know. For, had I killed your partner, you no doubt would
have done the same to me. Consuela has chosen well her
entourage in life. She surrounds herself with women
more capable than she; women who can balance her
inadequacies and weaknesses; women who challenge the
various maniacal forces of society. Take a good look at the
women in her life: There's you, Officer Stevens, relentless
in your pursuit of evil in the corporeal form, and the
ever-charming Gina, who attempts to rid the mind of
impurities—"

Delta reached over and clicked the recorder off.

"Stevie?" Leonard asked, raising his eyebrows.

Turning to Connie, Delta saw all the color leave her
face. "Con?"

"Turn it on, Del."

Delta pushed play, carefully watching Connie's expression.

"Now, there's an odd profession, don't you think?
Ghostbusters of the psyche. Why, all afternoon she's been
trying to tell me there are bats in my belfry." Elson
chuckled.

Connie went completely white and had to brace herself against the table. "You fucking bastard!" she yelled
at the recorder and pounded her fist on the table. "You
son-of-a-bitch! I'll kill you with my bare hands!"

Putting her arm around Connie, Delta held her tightly before she could hurt herself or the machinery around
them.

"I'll kill him! I swear to God, I'll spend the rest of my
life tracking him down if he touches a hair on her head."

"Connie, listen to me!" Delta cried grabbing Connie's
face in her hands. Leonard took the liberty of turning the
recorder off during Connie's outburst. "Get a hold of
yourself. You've got to calm down."

"He's got her, Del. God damn it, don't stand there and
tell me to be calm!" Connie's flaming black eyes were like
two pieces of burning coal. "He-has-my-lover," she enun-
ciated without moving her jaw.

"I know that. But you've got to get a handle, here. Every second counts, Consuela. I need you to get a grip. I need you. Gina needs you."

The last line triggered the response Delta was hoping for. Inhaling deeply, Connie closed her eyes and nodded. "Okay, okay. Turn that damn thing back on. I want to hear it. All of it."

Motioning for Leonard to turn the recorder back on, Delta looped her arm across Connie's waist and pulled her closer. She could feel Connie trembling, as Leonard pushed the play button.

"Are you wondering if your cute little girlfriend is in my possession? You always did have good taste in women, Consuela. And this one is a dandy."

"If he's touched her . . ."

"I suppose you're wondering why I came and left without my prize. Well, I haven't. Not yet, anyway."

Delta looked at Connie, who glared at the recorder; her jaw was set, her eyes small and intense, as if she was ready to spring. Connie had remained intact and held together by a thread, but Delta knew it would not last. The thread was fraying every second and it was clearly all Connie could do to keep it together. Her best friend injured, her lover abducted, and her own life threatened, Connie had been as reasonable as anyone could expect her to be. But Delta could feel the tide turning. She felt the slow unleashing of energy building within her. It was only a matter of time before Connie lost it and Delta didn't know who to be more afraid for—Connie or Elson.

"You came close when you thought that stealing Harold's Hybris was my next move. I enjoyed watching all of the Keystone cops gearing up for my visit. But come now, girls, stealing a horse? That's a trifle bizarre, even for me."

"Just tell me what you want, you fucker!" Connie cried, as large drops rimmed her eyes.

"I planned on taking something, all right, but it wasn't a horse. That was too obvious, don't you think? I do, indeed, have your little precious bundle of joy with me as I speak."

There was a slight hesitation before Elson went on. "And I imagine, being as practical as you are, you'll question the validity of that statement, so I'll afford you the simple luxury of hearing her voice."

Delta pulled Connie closer and held one of her hands.

"Connie?" Gina's voice was small and barely audible.

Connie steadied herself against Delta's grip. The voice was unmistakably Gina's.

"Honey, I'm okay. He hasn't hurt me or anything. I'm sorry. I should have known."

Elson's voice came back on. "Lest you panic and believe I am not following the game, let me assure you that I am. You just aren't bright enough to pay attention to the more important clues."

Connie closed her eyes and let her tears fall onto the floor. "I'm going to kill him."

"You see," Elson continued, "Hybris is what you've always had, Consuela. You are arrogant and proud of your many accomplishments. You've become blinded by self-righteousness. If you studied your Greek history and mythology closely enough, you'd know that the agent of punishment over mortals who commit hybris was named Nemesis." Here, Elson cackled like an old crone hovering over a black pot. "Apropos, *n'est-ce pas*? And you must also be aware that Nemesis's job was to take away the property of one who has become too prosperous in the eyes of the gods. That's where you blew it today. Stealing a horse would not have been taking anything away from you, my dear. You are and always have been too high on yourself, so I, as *your* Nemesis, have taken away the thing you cherish most. And until you rid yourself of hybris, you shall never get beyond the Poseidon level.

"The game is coming to a close, and I am most definitely ahead. You must be sharper than you've ever been. Your lover's life depends on your ability to find your way past the great sea god. Because if you don't, if I am successful in my next venture, I will be forced to slit her slender throat."

Delta felt Connie's body stiffen at his words. "He's a dead man. I swear to God, if it's the last thing I ever do . . ."

"You have less than twenty-four hours to deduce the next level of play. Even if you do get beyond the Poseidon level, you must face the Laestrygonians, and you know what they're famous for. Anyway, I do wish you luck as we round the bell lap, as it were. Which door is the tiger, Consuela? Choose wrongly, and you can kiss your sweetheart goodbye. Her life rests on your ability to out-think me. Thus far, you haven't been too successful in that endeavor. Oh, I'll admit you've come close, but close only counts in hand grenades and horseshoes. Isn't that what one of your precious college boys used to always say to me after we got our exams back? Perhaps with higher stakes, you can find your way to success. Until the day we meet again, *adios, amiga.*"

Connie, Delta, Leonard, and the two other officers manning the monitors stared at the tape until it came to a stop. There were more emotions than atoms in the air, as each weighed the level of their own feelings and fought the silent battle within their spirit. For a long time, no one said a word. It was as if they were waiting for more—waiting for someone to tell them this was just a sick joke. Waiting for this miserable game to come to an end.

When the tape recorder finally clicked off, Connie swiped it up, dropped it in her pocket and turned for the door.

"Con, what are you doing?"

"You heard him. Twenty-four hours. There isn't a second to spare."

Reaching out and grabbing her just before she hit the steps, Delta pulled her back to the van, painfully feeling the pull of her stitches as she did.

Connie's eyes had pinheads for pupils. "He's fucked with me long enough. If it's a showdown he wants, then that's what he's gonna get. And whether he touches her or not, I will track him to the depths of hell to take him out myself. If I have to, I'll spend the rest of forever after that son-of-a-bitch."

"You don't have to."

"Good. Then let's get the hell out of here. Time is everything to us now."

As Connie stepped out of the van, Leonard opened his mouth to say something but stopped when Delta shook her head at him.

"Don't."

"She's not running on all four engines," he said quietly.

"Don't underestimate her, Leonard," Delta replied, stepping gingerly out of the van and taking the cane he handed down to her.

"She's not thinking clearly."

"No shit. Look, her lover's life is in danger. She won't do anything to risk that life and neither will you. You want something to do? Get one of your pals over to Gina's work," Delta paused to scribble the address and phone number down, "and see if anyone saw anything that can help us."

"I don't need you telling me how to do my job," Leonard said, snatching the piece of paper up. "I want him just as much as you do."

"If that's true, then you'll work *with* us, Leonard, no matter how bizarre our directions to you may seem. You either help, or get out of the way." Delta turned around and took one step back into the van. "And I mean it. With us, or out of the way. Those are your choices. Don't mess with us, Leonard."

"Taking this into your own hands will cost you your badge, Stevie. You know that, don't you?"

"If I let assholes like Elson terrorize the people I love, then I don't deserve the badge."

"Have it your way, but I guarantee you're on thin ice, and I can hear it cracking."

"Yeah, well, if I hear anything, then it's time to worry. In the meantime, I'll be at Connie's. Let me know if you get anything." Delta stepped out of the van and grabbed her cane.

"Stevie?"

Delta turned.

"I really am sorry. I wish it didn't have to be this way. You're risking a lot goin' after this guy on your own."

"There's no other choice." Delta hesitated a second before continuing. "You gonna report this?"

"You know I have to. But I don't see why the Captain needs to know all the perticulers, if you get my meaning."

Delta smiled. Leonard had a heart after all. "Thanks, Russ. I owe you one."

"One? Try again, Stevie."

"Okay, I owe you, period. Thanks."

"Don't thank me. I haven't done anything. You've got twenty-four hours, Stevie. After that, I'm going to have to pull rank."

Delta nodded. "After that, I won't give a shit what happens, if Gina isn't home with us."

Leonard nodded. "Good luck, Stevie. I'll keep in touch if my guys come up with anything."

"Great." Limping toward the car where Connie waited, Delta felt the chills roll up her arms and down her legs.

He had one of them.

He picked her up in broad daylight and carried her away. If he had done this to Gina, what was to prevent him from snatch—

"Get in!" Connie yelled, gunning the engine. "We've got to see if Megan's all right!"

Jumping in the van, Delta grabbed her throbbing leg as she pulled the door closed. "You don't think—"

"I think he's a crazy motherfucker, and there's no telling what he's up to."

Closing her eyes, Delta tried to get a feel for Elson. What would he do? Where would he go? In his need to show them up, what was his checkmate move?

Opening her eyes, panic ripped through Delta's chest, spearing her heart with a fear she'd never felt before.

"Blow the lights, Con. He's going after Megan, too."

41

Before the car could come to a complete stop, Delta threw the cane out the door and jumped to the ground. Ignoring the searing pain shooting up her leg to the seat of her temples, Delta was in the elevator even before Connie had parked the van.

"Use the emergency override," Connie said, running into the elevator just before the doors closed.

Wiping the sweat off her palms and from the back of her neck, Delta turned to look at Connie, who stood like an Indian in front of a nickel-and-dime store—arms crossed, legs shoulder-width apart, face frowning in anger. How much longer could Connie withstand the pressure? When would she blow? Returning her attention to her own fears and anxieties, Delta feared she might be in the same position as Connie now was.

Just how long would she, herself, be able to withstand the anger and fear of knowing Megan was being held hostage by Elson?

Delta shuddered at the thought.

She had nearly lost Megan once. She couldn't bear going through that again.

Or could she?

Finally, when the ding of the elevator sounded, Delta pushed open the slowly moving doors and started down the hall.

"If he's here . . ." Delta said, trying to formulate some kind of a game plan should they encounter Elson.

"He's mine, Storm. You leave him to me." Connie's words were hard and without emotion.

"Keep him alive, Connie. You keep him alive until we have Gina back, you hear me? She could be anywhere, and we need to know where before you go and whack him." Delta started to put her key in the lock, but the door suddenly creaked open.

"Back!" Delta whispered, dropping to her knees and pulling her gun out in one swift motion. "Stay here."

Slowly pushing the door open, Delta let her .357 Magnum lead the way.

The entry hall was dark, but dusk still filtered in through the living room window, casting an eerie, iridescent light on the dim pallor of the room.

As she rounded the corner, Delta felt movement behind her and reached back to feel Connie's slender leg. As usual, Connie didn't do as she was told and, instead, joined Delta in the near-dark apartment.

Once in the living room, Delta's eyes rapidly searched for any clues or signs that whoever left the door open might still be there.

There was nothing.

Listening to her instinct, Delta knew they were alone in the apartment. She did not fear Elson's presence, nor did she sense anyone else. Delta and Connie searched the entire apartment, from the closets to the deck, and still, they found no one. Reholstering her gun, Delta sat on the couch and rubbed her pounding temples.

"We're too late." Picking up the phone, Delta called the college bookstore at the university. If Megan wasn't there, Delta didn't know what she was going to do.

"This is Officer Stevens from the River Valley Police Department. Is Megan Osbourne in?"

"Let me check."

As Delta waited, she impatiently drummed her fingers on the counter.

"No, Officer, she hasn't come in. Does this have to do with the gentleman that came by to see her earlier?"

Delta's heart raced. "A man came by to see Megan?"

"Yes. He said he had some news about her lost cat and wanted to see her right away. I thought—

"If Megan does come in, would you please tell her that something very important has come up and that she must stay at work until I come to get her. If anyone comes to see her, tell her not to leave under any circumstance. Do you understand?"

"Yes, but, oh, wait a minute, Officer. There's a note here that says she's called in sick for the day. Said it was a family emergency."

"Thank you. Please be sure to give her the message for me." Hanging up the phone, Delta turned to find

Connie gazing out the window. "She called in sick. I'm going to try your place." Dialing Connie's phone number, Delta caught her breath when she heard a busy signal. "It's busy. Let's go." Writing Megan a quick note telling her to call the moment she walked through the door, Delta walked over and hugged Connie. "We'll find her. You have to believe that."

"I know."

Delta pulled away and locked eyes with Connie. She could tell by the look in Connie's eyes that she was losing it. "Don't you dare give up on her. Or me. I've never let you down, have I, Chief?"

Connie shook her head. "No."

"And I won't now. We haven't even begun to fight yet, Con."

"Fighting is something we know how to do. Getting a step ahead of that bastard is another story. I can't believe I didn't see it coming. How could I have been so stupid? You know, the sad part is, he's right. My arrogance led to—"

"Shut up, Connie. I won't stand here and listen to this shit. Right now, our women's lives are at stake. We don't have time to stand here berating ourselves for it. So pull yourself together." Delta watched as her words changed the beaten look Connie had in her eyes to a look of determination.

"You're right, Storm. We've got two things to do tonight: find Megan and Gina and kill Elson."

Delta headed for the door. "Then let's do it."

42

After speeding through town and blowing every red light, they came screeching to a halt in front of Connie's house. Parked out front were Megan's car and a metallic blue Porsche, which Delta didn't recognize.

"You know that car?" Delta asked Connie.

"Nope. And it would be just like Elson to drive up in a Porsche."

Drawing her gun again, Delta waited for Connie to unlock the back door. Without a second's hesitation, Delta slammed through the door and pointed her automatic at a tall gentleman wearing a tan smoking jacket. He was sitting opposite Megan, who was wearing a mixed look of surprise and outrage.

"What in the hell are you doing?" Megan asked, staring at Delta.

"God, you're here." Striding over to Megan, Delta reached out and pulled Megan to her feet and held her tightly.

"Well, of course I'm here." Wrenching herself free of Delta's vice hug, Megan blushed. "Excuse me, Dr. Rosenbaum, but we're usually not this demonstrative in front of people. You'll have to excuse my over-zealous girlfriend."

Turning toward the professor, Delta put her weapon away before shaking his hand. "Dr. Rosenbaum? The professor?"

Dr. Rosenbaum smiled and shook Delta's hand. "And you must be Delta."

Delta nodded and introduced Connie. "Please forgive us for the, uh, unconventional entrance. We thought maybe . . . well . . . we just weren't sure . . ."

"What she's trying to say, professor," Connie offered, "is that we were worried something had happened to Megan."

Megan set her pen down. "Why didn't you just call?"

"We did. The line was busy and . . ."

Megan looked intently at Connie. "What's happened? Connie, what's the matter?"

Delta blew out a heavy sigh. "Elson has Gina."

"What?" Megan sat back down, visibly shaken.

Delta sat on the couch next to her. "He took her from work. We thought—"

"That he had me?"

Delta nodded. "Your apartment was unlocked. He tried to get you at work, but you changed your schedule."

Megan stared at her hands. "I called in sick. I wanted to get Dr. Rosenbaum's help just in case the racetrack thing didn't work. I take it that it didn't." Fanning herself, Megan got up and got herself and glass of water.

"He probably stopped by here to get you, but Dr. Rosenbaum's car must have discouraged him from trying it."

"Well, I'm glad I could be of some assistance," Dr. Rosenbaum said.

Delta laid her hand on his shoulder. He was a very handsome older man, a little taller than she and sporting graying sideburns. "You've helped us more than you know."

"Well," he said, clearing his throat. "I haven't done enough yet. It appears as if I may be of some assistance to you in the last stretch of the journey."

Nodding, Connie walked over and called her two large Dobermans into the house. "We were off on our last guess. We didn't get in-depth enough to see that Nemesis takes away something the *arrogant* one really cherishes." Sighing and letting two teardrops roll down her cheeks, Connie plopped next to Megan and laid her face in her hands. "And he couldn't have taken anything more precious to me than Gina."

"We'll get her back," Megan said, eyeing Delta for some reassurance.

"And we have less than twenty-four hours to do it."

"Oh my," came the soft sounds of Dr. Rosenbaum. "I hadn't realized the situation was so dire."

Delta nodded. "You couldn't have come at a better time, Professor. If you hadn't been here . . ." Delta's voice trailed off, and she shook her head. The thought of Megan in Elson's grasp was too much even for her to comprehend. No wonder Connie was barely hanging on.

Suddenly, Connie was on her feet. "I assume Megan has filled you in thus far, Dr. Rosenbaum?"

Dr. Rosenbaum nodded. "Yes. My field of specialty is Greek mythology, and please, call me Mort." Mort Rosenbaum strode over to the sheets of butcher paper like a professor nearing the chalkboard. "And if I have the story correct, your little warrior faced Poseidon and retrieved the trident from him, yet you can't manage your way beyond him."

Connie nodded. "Getting the trident is one thing, Professor, but moving to the next level of the game is what the game is all about. I don't know how to do that."

"Right." Dr. Rosenbaum studied the paper and scratched his chin. "Well, I may not be of any help where the game is concerned, but if it's mythological answers you need, I may be of some use to you. What is happening in the game as we speak?"

Delta studied Connie as she turned the computer on. Her movements were quick and jerky, like someone who had too much caffeine in their system. Delta was well aware of how close Connie was to the edge, and it frightened her. "We're counting on that help, sir."

"Mort."

Delta smiled. She liked this man with graying temples and steel blue eyes. He reminded her of her grandfather when he was much younger. "Okay, Mort." Handing the tape from the racetrack to him, Delta explained what happened there before he listened to the entire tape.

When the tape finished, Mort Rosenbaum nodded to himself, wrote down a few notes and examined the sheets taped to the fireplace. "Your culprit sounds most insane."

"He is. And he'll make good his threat if we fail this time."

Dr. Rosenbaum nodded as he studied the many pieces of butcher paper taped across the room. "I am assuming, of course, that you are aware that Poseidon is immortal and cannot be killed."

Everyone in the room nodded.

"Then the clue he gives you on the tape leads me to believe only one thing."

Connie turned completely around in her seat to hear him. "What clue was that?"

"Why the Laestrygonians, of course. He mentioned you would face them after defeating Poseidon."

"But you just said—"

"I said he couldn't be killed. I said nothing about defeating him."

Connie and Delta looked at each other but said nothing.

"The Laestrygonians," the professor explained in his most professorial tone, "were cannibals who lived on the islands around Sicily. They lived in a city called Telepylus, which was founded by Poseidon's son. Odysseus and his men faced the Laestrygonians in *The Odyssey*, and it was a slice of luck that Odysseus was able to escape unharmed and uneaten."

Delta cringed. "Uneaten?"

"They're cannibals. Giant cannibals."

"So, what's the clue in all of that? That we have to eat Poseidon?" Delta asked, feeling somewhat stupid for even suggesting it.

Mort nodded. "Precisely."

"What?"

Dr. Rosenbaum was in full lecture mode now. "You see, as the myth goes, Poseidon's father, Cronus, devoured him, his four siblings, and a rock when they were born. Only Poseidon's brother, Zeus, hadn't been swallowed by Cronus."

"How'd he luck out?"

"Cronus ate them so fast, he didn't know he was swallowing a rock instead of Zeus. Anyway, years later, Zeus came back and made Cronus vomit his children back to life."

Delta rubbed her aching temples. "Damn, those Greeks had some kind of imagination. How in the hell did they dream these stories up?"

"For many years, the Hellenes, which is what Greeks were called then, didn't believe these were just stories. They regarded the existence of all the gods as real and capable of changing mortal lives. It's pretty much the same thing as our Bible is: stories that are too far-fetched to be believed, but we believe them nonetheless."

Delta nodded. "Like the parting of the Red Sea."

"Precisely. The Hellenes prayed to these gods and even sacrificed to them."

"Really. But aren't Cronus and Zeus immortal as well?"

Connie rose from the computer and nodded. "Right. It took another immortal to defeat Poseidon. Cronus ate them, and it still didn't kill Poseidon. Dori is just a little warrior. She doesn't have the capabilities."

Mort nodded. "Of course she doesn't. And that would lead you to believe that at this point, there is nothing you can do, correct?"

Connie nodded.

"Then, may I be bold as to suggest," Dr. Rosenbaum offered, stepping away from the paper, "that you do nothing."

"What?" came three voices in unison.

"You must be joking," Delta said, joining Connie.

Dr. Rosenbaum smiled patiently, like a man used to having his students not understand him.

"You must admit, Professor," Megan added, "it sounds like a preposterous thing to do."

"Exactly. But hear me out. Since Cronus was the only force strong enough to apparently destroy his five children, why don't we stick with that vein for a moment and wait for Cronus to destroy Poseidon."

"But there isn't a Cronus in the game. I've been everywhere on this level, and all there is is me and Poseidon. No Cronus, no Zeus, nothing."

Again, a warm smile spread across the professor's face. "Ah—nothing that you can see. That is key. It appears as if we are searching for an agent to destroy Poseidon; is that correct?"

All three nodded.

"And, if the gamesmaster ascribes to Greek mythology as we know it, then he has supplied that agent."

"We're hoping so."

"Then, it's there. You simply cannot, as you stated, see it."

Connie's eyebrows knitted together to form a frown, but she did not move out from under the gaze of Dr. Rosenbaum's blue eyes.

"You know the answer, Connie, but you're too close to the game and, I would imagine, too scared to slow down long enough to see it."

"You mean it's invisible."

The smile deepened. "Tell me, ladies, what exactly does Cronus mean?"

The frown instantly disappeared from Connie's face and was replaced by a wash of brilliance in her eyes. For the first time in days, Connie's face lit up.

"That's it! Time! Cronus means time!"

Dr. Rosenbaum smiled proudly. "It is where we get words like chronological."

"Of course, Doctor, that's it. What a dope I've been."

Megan and Delta shrugged at each other. "What? What does that have to do with anything?" Delta asked. Time was something they had little of, and Connie was cheering as if she'd solved the puzzle.

Sitting back down at Eddie, Connie released the pause button and maneuvered Dori directly in front of Poseidon. "Stop me if I'm wrong, Professor, but that son-of-a-bitch knew that I would try everything to get past Poseidon. He knew I would exhaust every possibility we could think of."

"Which we have."

"Right. We've done everything except the one thing that he never thought I'd try."

"And what's that?" Megan asked, standing behind Connie at the computer.

"Nothing," came Connie's short response.

For a moment, no one in the room moved as unspoken questions whirled around in the air.

Delta was the first to speak. "Nothing?"

Connie nodded. "Exactly. See, we know that Cronus was the only immortal ever to contain Poseidon, and he did this by eating him when he was a baby."

"Right. I followed all of that."

"That means we need a Cronus in this damn game so we can kill or get rid of Poseidon, right?"

Everyone nodded.

"But there doesn't appear to be one does there?"

Again, Megan and Delta shook their heads. "I sure as hell haven't seen him."

"Exactly. And we might not have ever seen him had the good professor not reminded us that Cronus means time. Elson anticipated that I would stop at nothing to find a solution, when the solution is actually to do nothing."

Now, Megan and Delta stood behind Connie at the computer.

"Do nothing." Megan echoed.

Connie nodded "Right. Absolutely nothing. Elson understands that we're doers. We'd do anything to find Gina; anything, except the hardest thing, which is to do nothing."

Delta inhaled slowly. Doing nothing would be far harder than trying everything again. Watching the screen, Delta saw Dori standing quietly before the looming Poseidon. "That's got to be the hardest thing we could ever do. I mean, we could be wasting valuable time on a strategy that might not work."

Dr. Rosenbaum completed the circle by joining them at the computer. "Precisely. If this man is as deranged as he sounds, then he most certainly would enjoy putting you in a position to do what does not come naturally for you."

Connie leaned back and just let Dori sit in front of Poseidon. "Doing nothing goes against everything Delta and I are about. He's gambling that time will run out on us because we will keep trying and trying until the buzzer sounds and the game is over. It makes sense if you see it through his distorted eyes."

"How long should we wait?"

Connie shrugged. "I'd say two, maybe even three hours."

"And if nothing happens?"

Connie rubbed the back of her neck. "Then, we will have wasted three hours of Gina's life."

"And if something does happen in that time?"

"We'll face the Laestrygonians and take it from there. Dr. Rosenbaum—"

"Mort."

"Mort, can you give us as much information as we'll need to defeat the Laestrygonians?"

Dr. Rosenbaum nodded. "You'll have everything you'll need to know to face them, I assure you."

"Speaking of eating," Delta said, hearing her stomach growl at her. "Would anyone else care for some dinner?"

Dr. Rosenbaum patted his stomach. "I would."

Turning to the professor, Megan took his hand in hers. "I can't thank you enough, Dr. Rosenbaum—"

Mort waved her off. "Think nothing of it. A young woman's life hangs in the balance. Besides, when's the last time an old codger like me had the chance to tell his colleagues that he spent the evening with three beautiful women?"

At that, Megan took his arm and headed toward the kitchen. "Dr. Rosenbaum and I will make dinner. You two just keep your peepers on Dori and let us know if anything happens."

As soon as they were out of the room, Delta pulled a chair over and sat next to Connie, whose eyes didn't move from the screen.

"He may have just saved her life."

"Don't count your chickens, Del. We have as much now as we did before the professor got here. Only time will tell. Literally."

"You okay?"

Connie shrugged. "Coming apart at the seams. You know that or you wouldn't have asked."

Delta rubbed Connie's neck. There were golf ball-size knots on either side, and Delta winced as she gently rubbed them out. "Be strong. She needs your level head now more than she ever has."

"I know." Connie hesitated, as if searching for the right words. "Del, do you think people can sense when their loved one dies?"

Delta thought back to the instant Miles was shot. She had felt something spiritual being ripped from her soul in the darkness that surrounded her that night. She remembered the fist of death reaching through her chest and grabbing her heart, tearing from her someone she loved more than life itself. Yes, she knew he was dead even before his body hit the pavement. She knew, because her heart felt it.

"Yes, Con, I do."

"Then Gina's still alive."

"It's important that you remember that."

Connie turned from the monitor and looked closely at Delta. "The fear of losing her would consume me, Del, if I wasn't running on deep-seated anger. I don't think I have ever loathed anyone as much as I do Elson Zuckerman. And to be honest, I'm a little afraid of what might happen if I catch him before you do."

Delta stopped rubbing her neck and held her hand. It was uncharacteristically cold. "Cross that one when you get there, babe. Right now, keep the focus on finding Gina and the rest will follow."

"I know. But this fear threatens to incapacitate me, Del. Only the anger and determination to see him dead move me forward."

"I understand."

"Do you? Do you understand that it feels like the hate and anger are controlling the rest of me, like a boa squeezing the life out of its victim."

Now, for the first time, Delta picked up on a different sort of fear in Connie's voice. It was a fear that said she knew how much Elson had poisoned her spirit and eroded her gentle nature. It was a fear that admitted he had won on an emotional level because Consuela Rivera would never truly be the same. It was a fear shared by both women in the room.

"I won't let that happen to you, Con. I promise, I won't."

Connie nodded, but her gaze was miles away. "That's good to know because once in awhile I feel like I've moved away from me and gone deep inside the fiery heart of this anger. I don't trust what I would do or how I would act if I ever see him again."

A cool chill ran up Delta's arms. "Hey, we're going to bring Gina home, and we're going to catch this crazy bastard and get our lives back."

Slowly, Connie looked up and blinked two large tears down her cheeks. "That's what I'm afraid of, Del. That he's tainted us for good, that we'll never be what we once were. I'm scared to death that no matter how this turns out, he will have destroyed a part of me and my life anyway."

Holding Connie as tightly as she could, Delta rocked her.

"Del, I didn't get the chance to tell you before all of this insanity broke loose, but—Gina and I were talking about having a baby."

Delta's stomach dropped. "No kidding? I'm going to be an aunt?"

Connie pulled away and tried to grin. "A baby, Delta. We had just started talking about Gina getting pregnant and moving to a bigger house . . . and now . . . God, I don't know what I'll do if I lose her."

"You won't lose her." Delta's voice was commanding and hard. "And you've got to stop thinking that way. Damn it, Connie, you're going to get Gina back and have a baby, and our lives are going to move forward after this."

"I hope so," Connie said quietly. "Because if they don't, I'm going to jail for murder."

43

"Odysseus and his men were successful at defeating the Laestrygonians, and I'm quite sure we will as well." Dr. Rosenbaum spent the last two hours expounding on portions of the *Odyssey* and other interesting tales. He seemed very aware of the need to pass time and did his best to keep the three women occupied. In the middle of the third hour, Connie jumped up.

"There's movement on the screen!"

In a second, the other three were at the computer.

"Look!"

Delta stared at the monitor and saw that, ever so slowly, Poseidon was disappearing from the screen. "It worked! Mort, you were right!" Watching the screen, Delta thought about the Cheshire cat and how he faded away and left his smile. Poseidon faded and left only his shadow.

"He's leaving!"

Cheers and hugs all the way around, as Poseidon disappeared completely from the screen. Dr. Rosenbaum's smile went from ear to ear.

"Okay, Professor, now what?" Connie asked excitedly, grabbing the joystick and moving Dori.

Delta glanced over at Dr. Rosenbaum and saw elation on his face. He really relished his success. He enjoyed it even more when Dori used the trident to part the water and was whisked to the next level.

"Here we go." Connie announced. "You might as well relax for a few hours while I fight my way through the next level."

"And then what?" asked Dr. Rosenbaum, stretching.

"Then we meet and kill the Laestrygonians, right, Mort?"

Dr. Rosenbaum nodded. "Just let me know when you need me. I am curious about the notes you made and would wish to peruse them further."

"Peruse away, Mort." Turning to Delta, Connie grinned. "Two outs, bottom of the seventh, and we're still alive. Put a pot of java on, would you?"

Walking into the kitchen, Delta peered back into the living room and watched Connie move Dori through the next level. "Con?"

"Yeah?" Connie did not look up.

"When we find him, I mean, when we meet up with him, we have to bring him in. We have to find out where Gina is. You know that, don't you?"

Connie did not reply.

"I mean, I know what you would like to do to him, and frankly so would I."

"But?"

"But you don't need that hanging over your life. I know what it feels like to kill a man. Trust me. You don't want to feel that forever."

Connie shrugged. "We'll see. Right now, let's just worry about finding him."

Right now, Delta thought to herself, let's just worry about not losing you.

44

Five hours later, Connie had just finished killing off a little Fury when she entered what was known to computer adventure enthusiasts as the "Dragon Room." It was the final destination of each level, and this one held the notorious Laestrygonians.

Depressing the pause button, Connie turned to find Delta with her head on the table, Megan asleep on the couch, and Dr. Rosenbaum quietly reading one of the two large volumes of mythology that Megan checked out from school.

"Well, Mort, we're here."

Delta slowly raised her head from the table and glanced up at the large watch hanging in the kitchen.

"Seven-thirty? Shit." Rising gingerly, Delta rubbed her bad leg. It was stiff and sore and itched like crazy. "Whatcha got, Con?"

"We're there. I've got the trident, and the Laestrygonians are advancing toward Dori licking their lips."

Dr. Rosenbaum laid his volume down and took his reading glasses off. "Do they appear as giants?" he asked, rising from the recliner.

Connie nodded.

Dr. Rosenbaum clearly suppressed a grin. "The Laestrygonians were known to spear men in the same fashion as we would spear fish. Then, they would pick them up and eat them whole. I would imagine—"

"Wait!" Connie interrupted, pointing to the screen, which was turning white. "It's him. He's leaving us another message."

Connie read the message out loud. " 'Congratulations, Consuela. I am indeed impressed. Perhaps you are brighter than I gave you credit for. We'll soon see. Thus far, you have been allowed to use the old trial-and-error technique that got you through college. But no longer. From here on out, once Dori gets killed, your part in the game is over. That's o-v-e-r. That means if she dies, so does your lover. Surprised? Don't be. By now, you know that I am playing for keeps.

"'And make no mistake about it, I am. So, try all you want, but when Dori is eliminated from the game, that's the end. And how will I know? The game has a microchip which will signal me when Dori dies. Don't bother wasting precious moments trying to remove the chip. Removing or tampering of any sort will emit the same signal. In both cases, I'll carve your little sweety up like Helen Keller trying to slice the Thanksgiving turkey. So, be careful—one wrong move and . . .'"

For a moment, all eyes were on Connie, who closed her eyes and did not move. As the screen appeared, and Dori and the Laestrygonians faded back into the picture, Delta lightly touched Connie's shoulder.

"Con?" Delta said, barely above a whisper.

"I'm all right."

Dr. Rosenbaum shook his head. "I'm afraid I wasn't prepared for the enormity of this situation."

For two silent, unmoving minutes, the red-eyed group stood staring at the screen, as if waiting for the characters to move themselves. Finally, Connie reached down and took the controls in her hand. Turning to Megan, Connie's glare was icy, almost maniacal. "Okay, here's what we need to do. Megan, you watch Dori's backside for me to make sure we don't get snuck up on. Put your finger on the pause button in case we get into any trouble; we can pause before anything terrible happens."

"You're really going to play this out?" Dr. Rosenbaum asked.

"We have no choice. I'm not going to waste time trying to remove the chip."

Delta agreed. "We've gotten this far."

"What can I do?"

"Mort, you can hang out until we need some answers. Do you mind?"

"Of course not. It's just . . ."

"Scary?" Megan finished for him.

Mort Rosenbaum nodded. "It's frightening."

"Well, hang on, Mort, because we're going for broke."

For three hours, Connie worked to both kill the Laestrygonians and keep Dori alive. Nothing she tried worked; no data Dr. Rosenbaum gave her seemed to make a difference. She tried harpooning them with the trident, but it only bounced off. She tried throwing things, giving them poison, setting them on fire, bargaining, poking them in the eyes, and even bribery, but nothing worked. Her only consolation after three grueling hours was that Dori was still alive.

"Eight hours, Connie. We have a little over eight hours left."

Connie nodded to Megan, who pressed the pause. "Unless we missed something back at the ranch, we've done everything we can, and still no results."

Dr. Rosenbaum approached the computer and rubbed his chin. "At the risk of sounding chancy, there is one more thing we might try."

"And that is?"

"Well, to be quite frank, it would put Dori in a great deal of danger."

"Go for it, Mort. We're running out of time."

Mort Rosenbaum nodded wearily. "I've been thinking. Poseidon was also called the 'Earth Shaker' because striking the ground with the trident caused earthquakes. There is, of course, the uncertainty that if you cause one, little Dori might be in as much danger as the Laestrygonians. There are no guarantees she'll survive the falling rocks and opened craters."

Delta glanced over at Connie and shrugged. "It's your call."

Turning back to the computer, Connie rubbed her eyes and fiddled with the joystick. "I think we're out of choices. We have to take a shot." Cracking her knuckles, Connie inhaled deeply and slowly. "Okay, Mort, how do we start this earthquake?"

"Strike the trident on the ground."

Delta reached out and took Connie's hand. "Wait!"

"What is it?"

"Do we still have the winged sandals?"

Connie nodded.

"That's it, Con. Strike the trident on the ground—"

"And get the hell off of the earth!" Connie finished for her.

"Yes!" Dr. Rosenbaum added for emphasis. "That's perfect! What a wonderful idea."

"Get as high as possible, Connie," Megan said, her finger still on the pause button.

Connie nodded vigorously. "Got it." Taking the joystick in her right hand, Connie rolled her head from side to side until her neck cracked. Then, she wiped her left hand on her pants. Tiny beads of perspiration dotted her forehead and upper lip. "Okay, baby, here we go."

As Megan released the pause button, Connie moved Dori around to avoid the spears being thrown at her. Twice, she was almost stepped on before reaching the clearing between the forest and Olympus.

"Okay, everyone, here she goes."

Striking the ground and immediately taking to the air, Dori hovered inches above the large rocks tumbling off Mount Olympus and crashing to the earth below, smashing into the huge Laestrygonians. One by one, they fell prey to the falling boulders, until finally, there were no Laestrygonians standing.

"We did it! We did it! We did it!" Delta cried, hugging Megan tightly. "We killed them! We killed those damn things!"

"Look!" Dr. Rosenbaum said, pointing to the screen. At the foot of the forest was a box.

"What in the hell is that?"

"Don't open it," Mort stated calmly. "I'll bet a year's salary that that's Pandora's box."

"So?" Delta's nose was inches from the screen. She had heard the phrase about opening a Pandora's box, but she wasn't sure of the origin.

"Pandora was the first woman created by Zeus and Athena and the other deities. They named her Pandora, which means 'all gifts,' because everyone living on Olympus at the time gave her a gift. What they didn't know at the time was that Zeus had made her as a trap to ensnare mortal men." Dr. Rosenbaum paused, as if lecturing at the university.

"So, what happened?"

"Epimetheus, one of Pandora's lovers, warned her to stay away from the chest."

Megan pulled away from Delta and nodded. "I remember. Pandora was told not to open it, but she did, and out flew lust, old age, sickness, et cetera."

Mort smiled proudly at Megan. "Quite right. But when Pandora was finally able to close the box, she sealed in one gift. That gift was hope. Thus, no matter how futile things may seem, man always has hope. It's a rather uplifting myth, if you ask me."

"What do we do with the chest?" came Megan's logical question.

"The box is Elson's idea of a final trap."

"Or a clue."

"Or both."

Connie looked at the clock on the wall. "We don't have time to sit around, wondering. Any suggestions?"

"I vote we open the box." This from Megan.

"Ditto." Delta agreed.

Connie turned fully around. "Professor?"

Scratching the top of his head, Dr. Rosenbaum exhaled loudly. "I must concur. But before you do, examine it carefully. Perhaps, the clue is without."

"Try picking it up and taking it with us," Delta offered, remembering the last box they came across.

"Pick it up?" Connie mused. "Why not?"

"It's as good an idea as opening it. I believe a desperate person would open it. We are not quite there yet."

"Agreed. Well, bottom's up." Maneuvering Dori toward the box, Connie had her bend down and pick it up. When she did, a secret opening lay beneath it. "Bingo. Thank God, we didn't open it yet."

Dr. Rosenbaum studied the screen carefully. "Oh, dear."

"What?"

"It would appear that you have uncovered a portal to the underworld."

Connie rubbed her eyes. "A portal to the underworld? You mean hell?"

"In a manner of speaking. Hades is Poseidon's brother. He is the ruler of the underworld."

Delta checked her watch. "We don't have time for too many more levels."

"Well, we can't sit around here doing nothing. We either take the plunge, or we don't."

Tension filled the room. Gina's life hung by their every decision, by every move they made. Time didn't move, the screen didn't blink, and four hearts barely beat, awaiting Connie's decision.

"Storm, I need you to close your eyes and think for a moment."

Delta cocked her head in question. "About what?"

"What do you feel? I mean, what do you think Elson would do? Can you get a bead on where he's going with this?"

Delta understood what Connie was after and closed her eyes. She saw a lot of images flirting with danger, but nothing stood out. Opening her eyes, she looked back at the dark eyes drilling into her. She went with what she would do if Megan's life were in danger. "I think we should take our box, our trident, and our courage and jump down the blasted hole."

Megan and Dr. Rosenbaum agreed.

Connie hesitated for just a moment before moving Dori to the edge of the hole. The tense seconds that chugged by were weighted like cement shoes, as Connie stared at the black-haired warrior who personified both her and Delta.

"Okay, Dori," Connie whispered, "Come on, baby, and stay alive." Barely moving the joystick, Connie sent Dori plunging into the dark hole.

Down, down, down she fell, head over heels, trident in one hand, box in the other. Minutes elapsed as Dori tumbled helplessly through the dark shaft.

"She's doomed," Connie muttered, holding her head with her hands. "Doomed."

"The shoes!" Megan cried. "Use the shoes!"

Connie tried the joystick. "I'm trying, but it doesn't work. Lord help her, she's on her own."

Down, down, down Dori fell, until at last, with the bottom rapidly approaching, she landed on her back with a sickening and all-too-realistic thud.

No one in the room moved.

No one breathed.

All eyes were focused on the monitor and the tiny warrior lying still atop the red dirt. For an eternity she lay, unresponsive to the joystick's movements or Connie's heartbreaking pleas.

"Get up, goddamnit! Get up!" Delta yelled. "You can't be dead. You can't!"

Fires licked at Dori's feet, and harsh winds blew tumbleweeds by her, but still no movement.

"Please, God, please don't let this be happening," Connie said, rising. "If he comes on this screen, you better sedate me, Delta. I swear to God, I'll go ballistic."

Three more minutes plodded by without any movement from Dori. She just lay there, on her back, as the fire lapped at her feet and more tumbleweeds blew carelessly across the screen.

"Do something!" Megan cried.

"I'm trying," Connie said, moving the joystick every direction.

And then, quite suddenly, Dori raised to her elbows and looked around.

"She's up!" Connie cried, patting the computer.

"Oh my," sighed Dr. Rosenbaum, wiping his head with a handkerchief. "I've never seen anything like this."

"I thought we were goners," Megan added, hugging Connie and Delta.

Wiping her palms on her pant legs, Connie inhaled deeply. "Tell me about the underworld, Mort. What are we looking for down here?"

"There's your answer," he said, pointing to the screen, which now displayed a canoe being guided to shore by a skeleton dressed in a black robe.

"That's Charon, the ferryman of the river Styx."

Connie turned and stared at Dr. Rosenbaum. "Styx? As in the river of Hell?"

"That's the one. You'll need to pay him to get across the river."

Connie smirked. "Another ploy to get me to open the box for money we don't have. I'd rather try the shoes first."

Trying the shoes, Dori was immediately lifted off the ground and glided over Charon's canoe to the other side of the river. Once there, a large vulture swooped down and picked her up in his talons.

"Damn. What now?" Connie muttered to herself, as the vulture glided through the air carrying Dori.

Dr. Rosenbaum peered over Connie's shoulder. "We've moved from the side we were on because we're . . . well . . . she's not dead. Only the dead cross the river Styx, and only if they pay the proper fee."

Silently, they all watched as the vulture dropped her down to a group of islands.

"We've landed on the island of the Blessed Elysian Fields," Dr. Rosenbaum continued. "That's where the heroes go instead of to Hades. Elysium is the dwelling place of mortals made immortal through the favor of the gods."

"Then we're here?" Connie asked. "Have we reached the end?"

Before Dr. Rosenbaum could answer, the screen faded and was replaced by a lighter screen that resembled an ancient scroll.

"This is it," Connie announced, as the screen came into full view.

" 'Congratulations, Consuela and Company. Or is it? Have you left yourself enough time? Did you build for yourself a margin of error? Do you still believe this is all there is to it? I would assume not. For if you do, then you have made a grave error.

" 'This will be your greatest challenge yet. To stop me, the Dark Lord, you must find me. To find me, you must first solve the following riddle. I do remember how you and "the boys" loved riddles and crass jokes. Let's see how you enjoy the riddle of your life.' "

As the scroll faded, Connie glared at the screen. "You'll get yours, you bastard."

"Here it comes." Suddenly, the screen came to life, and music accompanied the riddle, which Connie read aloud.

" 'One is a falling star, one comes from afar—

One is body, one is brains, neither cares about man's pains—

One breaks laws the other makes, both are clearly just big fakes—

The origin of one is the destiny of the other,
Which will die, the sister or the brother?
From this your quest will come to end—
Upon your choice does her life depend.' "

Megan jotted down the riddle and handed it to Dr. Rosenbaum, who studied it before giving it back to Delta.

"There's more," Connie said, pointing to the ever-changing screen. " 'Should you thus be able to discern the exact whereabouts of my latest victim (and that is a tall order), there is one last bit you should know. Up to now, I've allowed you aid. No longer is that true. If I am to be challenged in this final arena, it must be you and you alone, Consuela. To ensure that, I have already rigged up a major building on Officer Stevens' beat with dynamite. The controls of that little explosive package are on my person. Should anyone else interfere—the cops, a by-stander, anyone—I will detonate the building, sending all of those innocent beings to their deaths. Of course, should you accost me on your own, their lives and the life of your loved one will be spared. *As long as you defeat me.* So—while I have enjoyed matching wits with you and Officer Stevens, she is out of the game for good. Don't try calling my bluff because you will have to live with being responsible for hundreds, if not thousands, of unneces-sary deaths. Think about it. Good luck, Consuela, and may the best person win.' "

Delta rested her hand on Connie's shoulder, as the screen went blank. "That S.O.B. didn't miss an angle, did he?"

Rising, Connie took the notepad from Megan and read the riddle again.

"You know I'm not going to let you go after him alone," Delta stated flatly.

Connie returned her penetrating gaze and nodded. "I didn't expect you would."

"We can do this. We can nail him before he gets to her."

Bowing her head, Connie drew in a jerky breath. "We have to, Delta."

"We will. Like Pandora's box, you gotta have hope. You have to believe we can." Pulling Connie to her, Delta felt her finally give way and cry uncontrollably into her chest. The pressure of playing the game was off, only to be replaced by a pressure of far greater magnitude.

"We'll find her, Con."

Pulling away and wiping her eyes, Connie nodded. "And when we do, don't get in my way, Delta. Promise me you won't get in my way."

Gazing down into the eyes of a woman who was at the very end of her rope, Delta nodded solemnly.

"I promise."

45

Dr. Rosenbaum stepped up to the huddle of women and cleared his throat. "Excuse me, ladies, but it would seem that time is of the essence."

Connie shook her head as if coming out of a daze. "The riddle. God, we bust our asses just keeping Dori alive through that madman's maze, and that bastard lays a damn riddle on us."

Megan took the pad and read the riddle out loud again. "God, he's a nutcase. Anyone have any ideas? Where do we go from here?"

"I'd say we're looking for persons or people who advertise their schedules," Delta offered. "In order for him to make this all come together this far in advance, he'd have to know when and where these two people would be."

"Wait a minute," Connie said, taking the notepad. "First off, he mentions a brother and a sister. He's comparing two potential victims. Agreed?" Everyone nodded. "Then, we do this systematically. Split that butcher paper down the middle, and we'll do a compare and contrast."

Dr. Rosenbaum was the first to pick up a pen. "Let's start with the falling star. Can we agree that he's talking about someone who used to be great but is no longer?"

"I like that." Megan stated.

"It could be a movie star or an athlete or some kind of entertainer. Someone who has a touring schedule of some sort."

"Unless," Dr. Rosenbaum continued, "He means it literally. Does anyone know what a falling star is called?"

No one knew.

"I'll look it up," Megan said, moving toward the stacks of books on the floor.

"Okay, how about the next line: 'One is body, one is brains'?"

"I'd say the body is a woman, and the brains is a man. As chauvinistic as Elson is, it's a sure bet it isn't the other way around." Connie watched as Dr. Rosenbaum scribbled on the paper.

Megan looked over Connie's shoulder. "The line I find curious is 'One breaks laws the other makes.' Who makes laws?"

"Politicians do," Connie said, as all eyes turned on her. "Elson always thought politicians were the phoniest people on earth. He used to say they were all phony and more interested in lining their pockets than with taking care of the people who voted them into office."

"Oh my God," Megan said, cupping her hand to her mouth. "You don't think he's going after a politician?"

Connie picked up one of the many newspapers lying on the floor and thumbed through it. "It's beginning to makes sense. A politician would pack the house in any hotel or auditorium." Delta picked up the pink sheet and studied the front page. "Right. And a politician's schedule of speaking engagements is often available in advance. I'll make some calls and see if anyone special is scheduled to speak." Taking her portion of the paper with her, Connie went into the kitchen to use the phone.

"Good. We'll keep working on the other end." Turning back to Dr. Rosenbaum, Delta frowned. "So far, we're making a quantum leap in our guess that it's a male politician we're after. What else do we have?"

"Not much here on the other side," Dr. Rosenbaum offered. "It's a woman, of course, but only if we're correct in our thinking that the other is the male. If she's a woman . . ."

"I think he's talking about a prostitute," Megan added quietly.

"You do?" Delta asked, smiling warmly at Megan, who returned the gesture. "Why?"

"She's all body, she doesn't care about man's pains, she's not real. Or, at least, the love men think they get from her isn't real. She also breaks the laws. I've been there. It fits."

Nodding, Delta watched Dr. Rosenbaum jot this possibility down on paper. "It works."

Dr. Rosenbaum rubbed his chin. "And a politician and a prostitute are diametrically opposed. I concur with Megan. If it isn't a prostitute, I think we're pretty damn close."

Megan smiled at him. "The problem we run into, however, is that practically every hotel in the city has prostitutes. We couldn't begin to narrow down the places unless we have a specific name to look for."

"I agree," Delta said, nodding. "We have to be looking for a certain woman. One who fits the Greek theme."

Suddenly, Connie came running back into the room. "Okay, here it is: Congressman Antony Stiropoulos is in town, and he's speaking to poli-sci students at the Hyatt tonight."

Delta clapped her hands together. "Look at his last name. That's Greek if ever I saw it!"

"Bingo!" Connie cried out, as Dr. Rosenbaum wrote 'Stiropoulos' in big capital letters on one side of the butcher paper. "He fits the riddle. I'll bet he's our man."

"Now we can use it to figure out the woman," Megan said. "We have a male politician whose family name is Greek."

"The origin of one?" Connie said. "That must be it."

"Right. So let's go with a woman who breaks the laws, who doesn't care about man's needs, and whose destination is Greece."

Megan grinned and shook her head. "I'm telling you, it sounds like a prostitute to me."

For a moment, the room quieted while everyone mulled over their own ideas and opinions.

"But what about the falling star line?" Connie asked. "Megan might have a point, but I think an average prostitute would be impossible to find and even harder to obtain a schedule from."

Delta eyed Connie and could see her mind spinning. "So?"

Connie reached down for the newspaper. "So, let's take it one step further. Let's look for a porn star."

"An aging porn queen." Megan uttered, and without hesitating, she snatched a different pink sheet of the newspaper from the floor and tore it open. "How could I have forgotten? A friend of mine from the streets, JoJo, used to love watching her perform. And her name . . . God, what was it?" Turning the pages so quickly, they ripped, Megan nodded. "I'll know it when I see it. It's right there on the tip of my tongue."

Dr. Rosenbaum cleared his throat. "I . . . uh . . . I believe the woman you're speaking of is . . . ahem . . . Rana Agnost." A fine red blush erupted over the professor's face. "Otherwise known as—"

"The Love Goddess!" Megan shouted, tossing the open pink sheet on the table. "Aphrodite!"

All three women turned to stare at the now completely embarrassed Dr. Rosenbaum.

"I, uh, well, we're not computers, you know. Bachelor parties rent those kinds of movies and, well . . ."

Connie jumped up and hugged him. "No excuses necessary, Mort. We've got that S.O.B., and that's all that matters." Releasing him, Connie swiped up the pink sheet and read what Megan had seen. "She's hosting a big bash at the Carlton tonight—the Aphrodite Ball."

Delta paced across the floor. "Damn it. The Carlton and the Hyatt are at opposite ends of the city. He isn't going to make this easy."

Megan whipped the phone off the hook and dialed a few numbers, spoke quietly into the receiver, and hung up before anyone could ask what she was up to.

"We've got tickets to the Aphrodite Ball for tonight." She smiled and shrugged. "Connections. What more can I say?"

"Now what?" Connie asked.

"Now, we need to get some men over to hear Stiropoulos speak."

"I can be of some assistance there," the Professor said. "I'll call the head of the political science department and see if he can get us tickets."

"Good. We'll want men inside as well as out," Delta said, going into the kitchen and returning with the phone. "We have a lot of bases to cover before this thing is over."

Connie stopped Delta before she could dial. "You're not calling Leonard, are you?"

Delta stared into Connie's eyes. "Con, I have to."

"Delta, you heard what Elson said. No cops, not even you." Connie shook her head as she reached to take the phone from Delta.

"I know what he said, Con, but we have two places to cover. We can't be at both. We need his help on this one."

Connie's eyes narrowed. "No way. I won't let you do this."

Delta gently pulled the phone away from Connie's grasp. "We have to. Leonard and his men can help."

"Or hurt. I won't put Gina in danger, Delta. I mean it. Find some other way."

"Connie, right now, this is a crap shoot. We can't cover both hotels. We have to take one and hope it's the right one. In the mean time, we might be able to skirt a disaster by having the second choice covered as well. We have no other choice."

Megan nodded. "Delta's right, Connie, it's a fifty-fifty shot at this point. All we can—"

"Maybe it isn't," Mort interrupted.

"What?" All eyes turned to the man reading the riddle again. "The final line reads 'upon your choice does *her* life depend.' "

"So?"

"So, it's a play on words. Don't you see? Is the 'her' Gina, or the woman in the riddle?"

Connie was over to him in one long stride. Taking the riddle, she read it again to herself. "God, Mort, you may have just found the edge we need." Looking up from the paper, Connie grinned. "He's right. Elson has given us an obvious clue; just like they do in the damn computer games. Mort, you're a genius!" Throwing her arms around him, Connie held him in a bear hug.

"Then we go to the Carlton." Delta stared at the paper and ran her hand through her hair. "The Carlton is the last hotel in the string of hotels in the city."

"The party is on the tenth floor," Megan added. "I'll bet that's the last floor. Del, call and find out."

One minute later, Delta depressed the receiver and nodded. "Aphrodite's suite is at the top."

"The last floor of the hotel."

"That makes it two omega's—two lasts. I say we go with that one."

Connie folded her arms across her chest and stared hard at Delta. " 'We,' meaning who?"

Delta looked into the face of a woman hanging on the edge of desperation. She was afraid of what Connie might do if Delta didn't play it her way. Delta was also scared of what Connie might do if left to her own devices.

"All right, Con, how about this? We can send Leonard and his men to the Hyatt. Just to be safe, we'll have him clear out the whole damn building. We can lead him to believe that Elson might show up there. While he's doing that, we'll go to the Carlton."

Connie frowned. "We? You keep saying that."

"Well, you're not facing him alone, Con."

Megan nodded and stood next to Delta. "Del's right. We need to stick together. He wants to face you alone, Con. Don't play into his hands."

Sighing, Connie nodded. "Fine. We don't have time to argue about it."

Delta sighed as well. She didn't want to have to wrestle Connie on the matter, and was relieved she gave in. "We'll take him out at Aphrodite's party."

Megan raised her hand as if she was in school. "How do we find out where he's keeping Gina?"

Delta quickly answered. "Take him alive. Right, Con?"

Connie's dark brown eyes narrowed. "Right."

Connie walked over to the refrigerator and pulled a picture of her and Gina at Disneyland out from under a magnet. She held it in her hand a long time before dropping it in her chest pocket. "We'll give this to Leonard, just in case Elson is holding her in the Hyatt." Turning to Dr. Rosenbaum, Connie reached out and shook his hand. "Mort, I can't thank you enough for all you've done for us. You've been a tremendous help."

"It's been my pleasure, really. You three ladies are quite a team. I certainly wouldn't ever wish to cross any of you." Dr. Rosenbaum's eyes sparkled as he spoke.

Connie smiled as she opened the front door. "How can we thank you?"

"Thank me over dinner. But for now, Godspeed to you all."

Starting down the driveway, Connie took the picture out of her pocket and looked at it one last time.

"I'm coming, baby," she said, stuffing it back in her pocket. "I'm coming."

46

When Delta pulled into the dark parking lot, she saw Detective Leonard's beat-up Oldsmobile sitting next to a maroon Porsche. At the other end of the lot sat five other unmarked vehicles, waiting like poised cobras.

"Who's the Porsche?" Megan asked, as they parked.

"It's Alexandria's." Delta peered through the dark and noticed the auburn hair flowing out the window. "Wait here."

"Stevie!" Leonard announced, jumping out of his car. "What's the poop?"

Delta hobbled over to the Porsche and opened the door for Alexandria.

"Alex, what are you doing here?" Delta asked.

"I gave Detective Leonard instructions to notify me the moment either of you had a lead. My butt is on the line here, too, Delta. I need a suspect."

Delta nodded. She understood, all too well, the politics involved with catching a killer. With a conviction, Alexandria would have little trouble defeating Wainwright for re-election. Without one, her time behind the big desk was about to run out.

"I would imagine, Delta, that you have a game plan of sorts?"

Leonard chewed his cigar. "We gotta take him out before he gets to the Hyatt."

Delta nodded. "But we can't intercept him until we find out where Gina is. If you do, he'll blow that hotel sky high and take Gina's life as well. Those aren't chances we're willing to take. Connie gets to face him alone. Understand?"

Alexandria's eyes grew wide. "What?"

"He wants a showdown with Connie," Delta explained. "If he doesn't get one, he'll detonate and somewhere along the line, slit Gina's throat. End of story."

"I don't like this, Delta. I don't like it at all. We have to evacuate an entire hotel building, which is no small feat, mind you, and then give this killer the opportunity to kill or seriously injure Rivera?"

Delta nodded, feeling only slightly guilty that she wasn't being completely straight with them. "That's precisely what I'm telling you. This is his ball game, Alex. We play by his rules. If you can't, get out of my way, because I'll shoot anyone who puts Gina or Connie's life at risk."

Alexandria held up a hand to silence Leonard before he could issue a response. "Delta, you should know better than to talk like that around me."

Delta shrugged. "I mean it, Alex. We've come too far and worked too hard to settle for a field goal. It's our way, or it isn't."

Alexandria looked down at the rows of cars waiting to move. "There's something else, isn't there?"

Delta turned away. "I'm just a little scared, that's all."

"Then, let's get going, Stevie. Time's a-wasting." Leonard hiked up his pants and motioned for his men to get started. "We'll have those people out of there and the hotel surrounded in no time. He won't get through us this time."

Delta smiled weakly. "Thanks, Leonard."

"We'll bring this prick in tonight, Stevie. Just tell Rivera not to press. She's got plenty of help now."

"Just remember what I said. You keep the civilians safe, but leave Elson to Connie."

"I got it, Stevie. We won't move without your okay. Trust me."

As Delta watched Leonard hop in his car, she could feel Alexandria staring hard at her.

"What?" Delta asked, shrugging innocently.

"This was too easy. You're keeping something from us, aren't you?"

Delta returned Alexandria's penetrating gaze. "And if I am?"

"Then, I don't want to know. I just want him stopped."

"Even if I have to bend the rules a little?"

This made Alexandria smile. "I wouldn't expect anything less. Just be careful. Do it right. I don't want him off on some technicality."

"Roger."

"Oh, and Delta—be careful."

Delta nodded. "Careful is my middle name."

Lowering herself into her Porsche, Alexandria shook her head. "Somehow, I don't quite believe that."

Watching Alexandria drive away, Delta ambled back to the van.

"Well?" Connie asked.

"They bit. Leonard and his men will evacuate the Hyatt. While he's covering that end, we're taking Elson on at the other."

"Did Pendleton suspect anything?"

Delta grinned. "I think she knew."

"And?"

Shrugging, Delta carefully pulled herself into the van. "And if we catch her a serial murderer, I'll bet a month's salary that whatever suspicions she has go unspoken."

Starting the engine, Connie nodded. "Then let's do it."

47

As soon as Delta walked into the lobby of the Carlton, she knew they had made the right choice. The electricity in the air told her all she needed to know. In an odd, mystical sort of way, it hung in the air like the gaudy candelabra looming over the center of the red and gold carpeted interior. She had felt his insidious presence enough to know she was feeling it now. Self-consciously, she tugged at the grey wig scratching at the back of her neck. They had barely made it to the costume shop before it closed, and Delta had had to settle for the old lady look. Since her leg prevented her from walking normal, it was the perfect cover.

On the way over, she and Connie worked out a plan which included disguises, tape-recording devices on Connie, and various codes, should their first plan fail. They were as ready as time allowed them to be.

It was the two-second warning, and they were on their own ten-yard line.

Checking the front desk, Delta sat in the bar across from the lobby watching many brightly dressed individuals flow through the lobby and wade over to the private elevator leading to the top-floor suite. Delta's eyes did not leave the elevator, as scores of people waited for the polished brass doors to open. While she watched, she checked to make sure that the wire in her earplug was out of sight. She left nothing to chance. With Connie wired, Delta would be able to hear everything that was going on if she confronted Elson anywhere in the building.

Wiping beads of sweat off her top lip, Delta realized how exhausted she was. Her leg was pounding and burned, and her stitches itched like mad. It felt like days since she'd gotten any sleep, yet here she was, just about at the end of the play. When this night was over, they would either rejoice wildly or be in deep despair. But then, that was how police work really was—feast or famine, win or lose, black or white. Maybe Megan was right. Maybe the right and wrong of the job was simply too rigid—too diametrically opposed for anyone to really see through.

Suddenly, Delta watched a short, red-headed woman approach the elevator and slide in between two people just as it closed. Connie had just joined the party.

Glancing at her watch, Delta realized that Connie had gone up ten minutes sooner than planned. Gingerly stepping off her bar stool, Delta joined the crowd waiting at the elevator. As the seconds turned into minutes, beads of sweat formed underneath her wig, as she tried to ignore the stitches pulling on her leg. Being jostled by the growing crowd at the elevator wasn't helping matters, either.

"What's going on?" someone asked, when it appeared as if the elevator was not coming back down.

Delta glanced up at the elevator lights and saw it was still on the top floor. "Shit." Stuffing the newspaper into her borrowed Gucci bag, Delta hobbled like an old woman to the reception desk. "What in the hell is taking that elevator so long?"

"I'm not sure," the young receptionist answered. "I think it's stuck."

"Stuck? What do you mean, stuck?"

"Well, more like jammed. There's a delay button on the elevator, and sometimes, especially when people are partying, someone leans up against it, and it stops. No big deal."

"Can't you un-delay it?" Delta's voice rose.

"I'm afraid not."

Delta's heart jumped into her throat. "How long before it can be reset?"

"I've called the union guys, and someone should be here to fix it within the hour. We've notified Ms. Agnost, and she requested that we open the bar up to her guests and put it on her tab. She wasn't very happy about this, I can assure you."

"Neither am I." Reaching into her bag, Delta pulled out her badge. "Listen, it's very important that I get to that suite within the next few minutes. I don't have an hour. I don't even have five minutes. Can you get those doors opened without the union?"

The wide-eyed clerk nodded slowly as she picked up the phone. "Well, I would have to ask my supervisor, and he's—"

Delta reached across the desk and grabbed the telephone out of her hands. "Look, someone's life is at stake here. I don't have time to mess around with procedures and protocol. You call up to Ms. Agnost's suite and ask—"

"I've tried to, but the line has been busy ever since I made my first call to her."

"Damn it!" Delta smashed her fist on the desk. "Get me two of your strongest bellboys down here now." Moving toward the elevator and pushing through the crowd, Delta announced that free drinks were being served at the bar. In an instant, the crowd dispersed and happily headed into the bar.

"Come on, come on," Delta muttered under her breath. She cursed herself for not having seen this coming. How could she have been so blind? She knew, beyond any doubts, that Connie had jammed the elevator. She should have known that Connie would try to take him down alone, that Connie was too scared that he would see Delta and make good his horrific threat. She should have watched Connie more carefully—been more aware of the pressure, the guilt, the gruesome responsibility she must be feeling about the lives already taken as well as those he'd threatened to take. He had succeeded in pushing Connie to the edge. And in that one final, irrevocably desperate move, Connie made the decision to take Elson on herself.

Alone.

And there was nothing Delta could do about it now.

No sooner were the doors pried apart than Delta reached for the rung of the iron ladder attached to the side for emergency repairs.

"Ten flights up is a long way to climb, Officer. Are you sure . . ."

But Delta had stopped listening. She didn't have time for suggestions. Under normal circumstances, they might have been fine suggestions, but they all involved the one thing Delta did not have.

Time.

Swinging her legs onto the ladder, a sharp, jagged pain grabbed her leg like a hot fire. Wiping the sweat from her brow, Delta ignored the searing ache and started climbing.

As she climbed, so did her rage. She didn't know who she was angrier with—Connie, for pulling such a foolish stunt, or herself, for not seeing this coming. Wasn't it obvious that Connie would choose to go after Elson herself? Hadn't she seen the sorrow on Connie's face when they spoke about Helen's broken neck? Hadn't Delta witnessed the stoic jaw set when Connie realized Gina had been abducted?

Of course, she had. Only she didn't listen. Delta didn't want to believe that Connie would go off half-cocked. She didn't want to believe that Connie would react precisely as Delta would act if the roles were reversed. Not Connie. Not level-headed, slow-to-react Connie. Connie was the reasonable one. She was the logical one. But now, she was the desperate one, and Delta hadn't seen it coming. Delta could only imagine the fear Connie must feel knowing that her lover was tied up somewhere, alone, afraid, and praying for Connie to save her.

But who would save Connie?

Grabbing another rung, Delta shook her head. If the situation were reversed, she would have done the same thing. It all amounted to not being able to imagine her life without Megan.

Her life.

Connie's life.

That was what Elson was trying to destroy—Connie's life. For surely, if he killed Gina, Connie's life would be ruined—she would never be the same. She might never truly recover from a blow, a pain that devastating.

Maybe it was too late. Maybe the rigid exterior and angry eyes Connie now wore had replaced the gentle soul Delta so loved. Maybe, in the end, Elson had accomplished what he had set out to do.

And then again, maybe Delta wouldn't let that happen.

As she slowly pulled herself over each rung, ignoring the burn in her leg, Delta pushed her earplug deeper into her ear when she heard noises coming from it.

"Come on, damn it. Say something." Pulling up to the next floor, Delta turned the volume up. "Anything." When the next floor came and went, Delta stopped, threw the wig off her head, and readjusted the earplug. Had she heard something? Holding her breath, Delta released the rung and wiped the perspiration from her forehead.

"Del?"

Delta waited. She *had* heard something. Holding the earplug in her ear, Delta listened.

"I know you're probably really pissed off right now, but don't follow me. I have to do this myself, and you know it. There's been enough carnage. I know what he wants, now, Del. He doesn't want to hurt me physically, he wants to hurt me by destroying those I love. If you came up here, as he suspected you would, we'd only be playing into his hands. We'd be giving him what he wants. Well, he already has my Gina. He sure as hell isn't getting you, too. He won't kill me, Del. That's not what he wants. He wants me to suffer. And he knows that killing you and Gina will make the rest of my life unbearable. He was counting on you to follow me. Please, Delta. If you're following me, don't. Let me do this my way."

Delta wanted to curse and bang her fist on the side of the shaft. She should have known. Connie was going to kill him.

"Haven't we met someplace before, doll?" came a new voice.

"I doubt it."

"Sure we have. Maybe it was at Leslie's party a few months ago?"

"Maybe."

"Can I get you a drink?"

"You can if you can tell me who that man is over there in the black beard and eyepatch."

"Shit," Delta uttered. She had a bead on him already.

"Never seen him. How 'bout that drink?"

"Later. I have to use the ladies' room."

Delta started climbing faster.

"Del? I think that was him. He's been stalking Aphrodite since I got here. But I don't think he's going to hit now. He's every bit as trapped as she is. With the elevator jammed, it's just the two of us. Ironic, huh? Me and Elson to the bitter end."

Delta shook her head. "Not if I can help it," she mumbled, catching her breath as a shard of pain poked through her leg. Gritting her teeth through the pain, Delta pressed on.

"Champagne?"

"Yes, thank you. Mmm. Pretty good champagne, Del. I think . . ."

Delta stopped climbing and waited. "What? You think what?"

Nothing. It was as if the tape had gone dead.

"Come on, Connie! Talk to me!"

Silence.

More silence.

"Oh my God, Del. I think . . ."

"What?"

"I think he's poisoning her champagne. Don't you see? The circle would be complete then, wouldn't it? He started at the drugstore for a poison, and that's how he's going to end it. He and I started as adversaries, and that's the finale of his script. I've got to stop him."

"Connie, no!" Delta screamed, quickly pulling herself higher.

"Delta, if anything should happen to me up here, just know that I love you more than you could ever know. But this began because of me and it's going to end because of me. Right now."

49

As a new tray of champagne headed toward Aphrodite, so did Connie. She had to stop her from drinking anymore, and even then, it was possible she'd already consumed enough to kill her.

"Delta, call the paramedics. Have them waiting," Connie said tersely.

As Aphrodite's long arm reached for another glass, Connie knocked into her, spilling champagne down the front of her dress.

"Look what you've done, you clumsy bitch!"

Seeing the man with the eyepatch disappear out of the room, Connie bolted past the cursing porn queen. He had recognized her even with the red wig and glasses on.

As Elson pushed past the barrier intended to keep partying people from wandering out to the veranda, Connie followed. One glance over her shoulder told her that the crowd was more concerned with the champagne on their hostess' dress than with her pursuit of Elson.

"The veranda, Del. He's heading for the veranda."

As she reached the double glass doors, Connie knocked them open with her forearm and took one step out before closing them behind her. Looking around, she reached for a length of metal pipe lying in the drain gutter and yanked it loose. Once in her hands, she stuck it between the handles of the doors, locking them shut from the outside.

"I've locked us outside, Del. Now it's just me and that fucking lunatic."

Slowly turning around, Connie stared across the veranda at Elson, who stood about twenty-five feet away.

"I am impressed," he said coolly, folding his arms across his chest.

"Don't be, you bastard. Where's Gina?"

"All in good time, my dear. You don't really believe that you've won, now do you?"

"Aphrodite is still alive, isn't she?" Connie took a step closer, but Elson didn't move.

"For the moment. I must say that I never imagined you would figure out the riddle. The game, well, it was easy enough, but the riddle? I suppose I thought it would stump you. What made you choose Aphrodite over our Congressman?"

"Don't fuck with me, Elson. Where is Gina?" Connie stepped closer.

"Alive and well, I assure you. I am a man of my word. I must say," he continued, taking a step back, "that it was clever of you to deduce the poison. I'm afraid, however, that our Goddess of Love and Beauty has already consumed a great deal. You may be too late."

Connie watched Elson's hands as she took a step closer. "Look, all I want is Gina back. I couldn't give a shit if Aphrodite dies and you blow up the entire city. I'm nobody's hero, Elson. I just want Gina. Tell me where she is."

Elson shook his head. "Still the same selfish bitch you were back then. You never really care about anyone but yourself."

"I want her back. The rest is moot for me."

"Not until we ascertain—that's a police word, is it not? Not until we ascertain whether or not our little porn goddess meets her maker. I wonder if there is a goddess Maybelline or Mary Kay. What do you think?" Elson chuckled at his small piece of humor.

"What have you done with her?"

"Consuela, you must remember that, for once, you are not in charge. I'm calling the shots here, so you might as well relax. I am the conductor here, and I intend on orchestrating everything to the quintessential finale."

Connie's eyes shot from Elson's hands to a bundle on the railing of the veranda. It looked like a pile of ropes, and Connie knew it must be a rope ladder.

"I will say that I am surprised and a little impressed that you have the courage to come after me alone. I anticipated your Officer Stevens to have found some way of interfering. She's like a bad cold one can't get rid of. Leaving her behind takes guts I didn't think you possessed. It's nice to know you can still surprise me."

"You gave me no choice." Connie edged closer, keeping her eyes on his hands. She was not about to let him embed one of those stars into her body. "You may have Gina, but you're through hurting Storm. One of my loved ones is all you get, you arrogant asshole."

"Indeed. I would have derived great pleasure from killing your precious friend. That, I imagine, would have been a pain you would never recover from."

"You've inflicted enough pain, Elson. It's me you want to hurt, and this is your chance. It's just you and me, now, you sick piece of shit."

Elson sighed. "You've gotten a trash mouth since becoming a pig. I suppose the two go hand-in-hand."

"It's not trash, Elson. It's pure, unadulterated hatred." Connie stepped forward. "And it's time we finished this."

Elson didn't move. "It was ingenious of you to jam the elevator. That was my thought exactly. Ironic, don't you think, that you are actually aiding Aphrodite's death? I wonder what it will do to you knowing that your inability to out-think me has ended the lives of all those people I killed. How will you feel when you are totally alone, dear Consuela?"

"You make me sick."

"Do I?" A twisted grin flitted across his face. "The only thing left to take from you is Officer Stevens. You have thrown a wrench into my plans by not bringing her along, but she's an easy enough target. I'll deal with her on my way out of town."

"You must really despise me," Connie said, hoping to delay him long enough so she could rush him before he got to the railing.

"Despise you? Why, Consuela, you have it all wrong. I have always loved you. Never in my life have I held such devotion as I have for you. Don't you see?" Elson stepped away from the railing and removed his eyepatch. "You were the only woman I've ever met who is my equal. I was mad about you until I saw the immense cruelty you were capable of. And oh, how you disappointed me."

"Oh, you're mad all right, but not about me."

Elson shook his head. "That's where you're wrong. I'm quite sane. Do you honestly think a madman could have planned all of this?" Elson held his arms out to the side.

"And what have you done? Destroy, murder, and ruin innocent lives?" Connie inched closer and was now within ten feet of Elson. Two more steps, and she would be in striking distance.

"Don't be so limited in your vision, Consuela. It's so much more than that. You see, I have avenged the private and public humiliation by the woman I loved. I have sought retribution and found it. Have you any idea of the emotional scars you inflicted on me?"

"I apologized for all of that years ago. I was young. I made mistakes."

"Yes, yes, you did. But an apology didn't make the scars go away. You robbed me of everything that should have been mine. Not only did you take my number one spot in the class, but you rejected the love I had to give and ruined my life in the process. You, my dear Consuela, did what no one else ever could."

"What's that? Beat you at your own game?"

A cruel smile played across Elson's lips. "Perhaps you beat me then, but not now. Then, you took from me the only things that ever really mattered. You stripped from me the one accolade that meant anything to me or my parents. The things you robbed me of were irreplaceable, Consuela, and so, I have done the same to you. I have taken away things from you that you will never get over: the boys, your lover, your self-confidence, and soon, your dearest friend. I have ruined you, Consuela, as you ruined me all those years ago. I am leaving you what you are in real life: an empty, hollow shell. Justice, my dear, has been served. I can take my leave now, knowing that you will be miserable for the rest of your pathetic life. *Adieu*, dear Consuela." Elson grinned at her and turned to the railing.

"Wait!"

Elson turned back, one hand poised on the railing.

"Is this it then? Are you done with the killing?"

"After I torture Gina and murder Delta Stevens?"

Connie swallowed the great ball of fear and anger in her throat and nodded.

"Then, yes. I've done all I've set out to do. It's over. After this evening, you won't hear from me again. I can go in peace, knowing that retribution has been paid and revenge exacted. You need not worry about me coming back. I have a life somewhere else." Elson turned back to the ladder. As his left hand reached down to secure the hooks, Connie saw the large black wristwatch attached to his arm. Even at that distance, she knew what it was.

"Elson, what makes you think I won't kill you now?"

Looking impatient, he turned around and sighed. "Because you know I'll take half a city block and your lover with me, if you try. As long as you know she's still alive, and she is, you won't do anything to jeopardize her safety. You see, Consuela, the reason you lost is because you are so damned predictable. You always were. It's one of your major character flaws."

As Elson turned once more to go down the rope, Connie made one final desperate lunge at him.

50

Pushing the lid open, Delta eased herself into the elevator. Searing pain ripped through her leg and toppled her to the floor of the elevator. Grabbing her thigh, Delta felt her whole leg throb as a warm sensation spread down her leg.

"Shit," Delta cursed, seeing the blood oozing through her pants. "Not now," she argued with herself, as she pulled herself to her feet and tore off the tape that was holding the pause button down. Dropping her pants to her ankles, Delta saw that all of her stitches had torn loose, and the gash was open and bleeding again. Pressing the tape firmly to her wound, Delta steadied her shaking hands before pulling her blood-soaked pants back up.

Having heard Connie's half of the conversation with Elson, Delta knew that Connie was stalling. But why? Was he trying to escape even from the top floor of the hotel? Delta wondered if this was his second escape by helicopter. Grabbing the phone in the elevator, Delta called for a paramedic unit before the elevator doors opened at the suite.

"Your name, madam?" the butler asked with a slightly British accent.

Delta pulled her badge out and showed it to him. "Don't serve any more champagne. We believe it's been . . . uh . . . well, it was a bad year. We're waiting for the Dom to arrive."

The butler stepped back with a perplexed look on his face, and nodded. "Yes, ma'am."

"Where's the veranda?"

"Over there, ma'am, but I don't thi—"

Heading in the direction he pointed, Delta limped around the corner just as Connie said, "Is this it, then? Are you done with the killing?"

Running as fast as her bleeding leg would let her, Delta came to the double glass doors and watched in fear as Connie charged Elson. Seeing the two of them hurtle toward the railing, Delta tried unsuccessfully to open the doors. For a frozen moment, Delta was caught between doing what was right and what was best. And as this pregnant pause of life slowed down, she watched helplessly as the two black-belts violently separated and then maneuvered around each other like two wild dogs checking each other out.

"Come on, you son-of-a-bitch," Delta heard Connie say. "Finish it! If you think I'm going to let you out of here alive, you really are crazy! Crazy and stupid!"

"The game's over, Consuela. Don't make me hurt you, too." With that, Elson levelled a kick that propelled Connie backwards against the railing. As Elson moved in, Connie regrouped and sent her foot flying toward his face.

It was now that Delta made her decision. Right, wrong, or indifferent, she wasn't going to stand by and watch him kill her best friend.

Picking up a chair, Delta heaved it against the glass doors, shattering them into large and small pieces, some of which clung desperately to the metal frames. The noise reverberated through the building, catching both Connie's and Elson's attention. As he turned toward the noise, Connie clipped him full in the face with her left heel, sending him reeling backwards.

"Stay out of this, Storm!" Connie yelled, twirling in a jump-kick that Elson warded off with a forearm.

Pulling her nine-millimeter from her purse, Delta tried to draw a bead on Elson, but he and Connie were too close together for her to get off a clean shot.

"Listen to her, Stevens. I'm warning you. I can and will do as I said."

Keeping her eyes on him, Delta watched in horror as they danced the ancient art of self-defense and battered each other with a series of smashes and blows that would have downed anyone else. Elson seemed to instinctively know how to place himself so that Connie was between him and Delta.

Suddenly, the fight took a turn for Elson's side. He had smashed a hard kick to Connie's stomach, sending her reeling against the railing once more. In one swift step, he was upon her, hands around her throat, bending half her body over the railing.

Delta caught her breath. Raising her gun, Delta aimed at his shoulders. She couldn't afford to hit him square off for fear that the impact would send them both over the edge. In a second which lasted a lifetime, Delta weighed her options.

Before she could squeeze the trigger, Connie had broken free from his grip and locked her fingers with his high above her head. For a moment, they looked like mirror images dancing together with their arms over their heads, their hands gripped together like death's embrace. In the silence of the moment, nothing could be heard except the rustling of the wind.

And then, Delta heard it.

Ever so softly, she heard Connie struggle to grunt out, "The watch, Delta. It's the detonator."

Spying the watch on his left wrist, Delta did not hesitate. She inhaled, held her breath, and gently stroked the trigger.

The ensuing scream from Elson was followed shortly by the sound of a second bullet shattering his left shoulder blade and sending him over the railing.

"NO!" Connie cried, as the force of the bullet sent him flying over the edge.

In one desperate grasp, Connie grabbed his right wrist as he hurled over the railing.

Gripping him tightly as he dangled off the side of the building, Connie braced herself against the railing.

"Hold on, Elson!" she cried, reaching for his right arm with her other hand.

"Don't drop me, Consuela," he pleaded weakly. His white shirt was quickly turning red, and his left hand hung by a single tendon from the shattered wrist. The watch was nowhere to be seen.

"I won't drop you, Elson," Connie grunted from the strain. "Tell me where Gina is."

Elson closed his eyes and inhaled. "You'll let me go if I tell you."

Connie shook her head. "No, I won't. I'm trying to save you, aren't I?"

Elson nodded slowly, the blood gone from his pasty-looking face. "You won't drop me?"

"It's me, Consuela, remember? Always predictable. I'm a cop, too. Sworn to protect lives. You know I won't let you go. Just tell me where she is, and I'll pull you up."

Delta appeared at her side and looked down at the bleeding man dangling like a broken set of wind chimes. His left hand looked like it would fall off any moment.

"Pandora's box, remember?" he said quietly.

Connie nodded and tightened her grip.

"Let me help," Delta said, bending over the railing.

Connie shook her head. "Don't." It was a voice Delta had never heard Connie use.

Delta raised up and eyed Connie, who had not taken her eyes off Elson. "You know what you're doing?"

Connie nodded. "What about Pandora's box, Elson?"

Licking his lips, Elson whimpered. "Pandora's box is the name of the abandoned box factory next to the Hyatt. She's there. In the basement."

"You swear?"

"Check, check computer if you don't believe. Answer was in the box, if you opened it."

Connie stared at Elson a second before turning to Delta, who shrugged.

"Come on, Con, let me help you pull him up."

"No." Turning back to Elson, whose shirt was now completely red, Connie grimaced. "You're lying, you little fuck. I opened the box and there was nothing. Where is she?"

"All right, all right. She's at . . . 1439 Plato Way. It's a green apartment building . . . number 7 . . . I swear."

Connie glared hard at the little man hanging on to her. "Is she okay?"

"I didn't touch her, I swear. Come on, Consuela, I can't hold on very much longer."

Connie nodded. "And where did you say she was?"

Elson repeated the address.

"The game is really over now, you motherfucking psycho bastard."

"S-Stevens," Elson whined. "Please, help pull me up." A bit of blood dripped from the side of his mouth.

Delta did not move.

"You've destroyed enough, you sick puke. What makes you think anyone here is going to save your sorry ass?" Connie yelled.

A slow grin spread across Elson's face. Sweat made the Indian gum on the beard pull off, and it dangled from his face like he dangled from the building. "Because you really are predictable, Consuela. You'd never let me die. You could never live with yourself if you did. You've sworn to save people. Even people like me."

Delta looked at Connie, who was wearing a grin the mirror image of Elson's. In that moment, Delta wondered who had truly won.

"You think so?" Connie mocked, sneering viciously at him. "You really think I'd save you after all you've done?"

Elson coughed and nodded. "You're not a murderer, Consuela, and that's what you'll be if you drop me."

"You're right there, Elson. I'm not a murderer. But we're done playing by your rules now, little man. Now, we're playing by mine and my rules say that you messed with the wrong woman. You're through hurting people, Elson, and I intend to see that you pay for your crimes."

And before Delta could move, before she could even blink, Connie released a screaming Elson. Delta watched in horror as he clawed the air and rolled over once before landing face first on the cement below.

For a second, the two women stared in silence at the broken figure below, neither noticing the sounds of the paramedics as they drove right up to the body. Neither of them noticed or heard people now scrambling through the broken glass doors. Neither of them saw the crowd gathering around the lifeless figure oozing blood onto the pavement. And neither of them noticed as a uniformed officer bent down to study the small black object lying next to Elson's body. For a moment, all Delta could hear was the rush of the wind and the pounding of her heart in her temples.

Finally, Delta laid a bloody hand on Connie's shoulder. Connie did not look away from the corpse lying beneath the swelling pool of blood. Only a gentle tug from Delta turned Connie away from the gruesome scene.

Looking into Connie's eyes, Delta realized they were small, dark blanks. There was no anger, no fear, and no remorse. Only the blank eyes of a woman who had stared into the face of death and survived.

"Del . . ."

Delta held up a hand. "Shh. It's okay. It's over," Delta whispered, taking Connie in her arms.

Connie shook her head. "But I . . ."

Holding her tightly, Delta pressed closer. "You tried to save him, Connie. Period. End of story. I don't want to know what you meant to do or didn't mean to do. What I saw was you trying to save him, and that's how it goes down."

Connie slowly pulled away and looked up into Delta's eyes. A flash of understanding passed between them. "Is it really over?"

Delta nodded. "It's really over. Let's go get your gal."

51

The summer sun pierced through the spotting clouds that looked more like cotton balls than cumuli. Delta had been sitting on the bench for fifteen minutes, enjoying the sunlight as it stroked her hair and the back of her neck. Looking down at the scar on her leg, Delta pulled her shorts down to keep it covered from the sun.

"Hello, Delta," came the low, scratchy voice of Alexandria.

Delta turned around to see Alexandria smooth her skirt before joining Delta on the bench.

"Well? How did it go?" Delta tossed the last of her breadcrumbs to the pigeons.

"Looks like a suspension for you, Connie, and Leonard."

Delta's eyebrows flew up. "Leonard, too?"

Alexandria nodded. "For allowing you to pretty much take over a homicide case and keeping so much of this under wraps. Internal Affairs went pretty hard on him, but his suspension isn't that bad."

Delta nodded. "I see. And ours is?"

Alexandria nodded. "I wish there was something more I could have done."

"You did enough, Alex, by keeping Leonard off our backs long enough for us to solve this thing. A suspension is a small price to pay to have Gina back."

Alexandria smiled. "I had a feeling you'd say that. Do you have any idea what your vigilanteism has done to this department? Half the guys think you're some kind of hero, and the other half think you should turn in your badge. My God, Delta, your file is eight inches thick. You'll never make detective."

This made Delta smile. "Maybe not. Maybe that's not what I'm supposed to be. I'm really good at what I do, and I just want to be able to keep on doing it."

Alexandria looked away. "I wish it was that easy, Del. Internal Affairs is having a field day with you."

"I know."

Alexandria turned back, her green eyes hard. "No, you don't. They may want more than a suspension. They may ask for your badge."

Delta locked eyes with Alexandria and inhaled slowly through her nose. "Look, my best friend is alive, her lover uninjured, hell, even Aphrodite pulled through. I'd say we won this round against the bad guys, wouldn't you? If we're scolded and reprimanded for saving lives but not following the rules to do so, then it's not worth it."

Alexandria reached out and laid her hand on top of Delta's. "Is that honesty or bravado speaking?"

Delta grinned. "A little of both."

"You know my hands are tied or I'd help you if I could."

"Look, Alex, I don't expect you to come riding up on your white charger every time I need saving from myself. I broke the rules. Now I have to pay the price. It's simple math."

Alexandria shook her head. "It's just so damned frustrating that you're being penalized for a job well done. The lives you two saved—"

"But don't you see? That's the bit that I.A. can't take away from me. They can't dismiss the fact that Helen's parents sent a letter thanking me and the department that justice had been done. They can finally rest now that their daughter's killer is dead. Those are the people I work for. That's what this job is all about."

"I wish our system could see it that way."

"But they don't, and I have to live with that fact if I'm not going to follow all of the rules." Delta sighed with disgust. "Alex, I've never been one to walk the paved road. I deviate, test, explore, and venture into uncharted paths. Sometimes that gets me into trouble. But that's who I am. I find a problem, and I create a way to fix it. If I have to bend some silly rule to do it, then so be it. And you know what else? I like that part of me. It's who I am. It's what makes me so good."

Alexandria smiled and squeezed Delta's hand. "So do I. I admire your courage and determination, Delta Stevens, even if it does seem to cause you more heartache than good. I just wish there was something more I could do to help. I, I feel in part responsible for this."

"Don't be silly. You know I would have done this with or without you. Sometimes, the needs of the many outweigh the needs of the few. You just made that easier by giving us some time, that's all. Stop kicking yourself, Alex. What's done is done."

For a minute or two, the two women sat quietly watching the pigeons waddle among a group of young children.

"Delta, I have to ask you this one last question before I go. Call it a guilty conscience if you will, but I need to know."

Delta cocked her head in question. "Shoot."

"It's something I just need to know, and I want it to be between me and you. I swear it won't go any further."

Delta's expression did not change. She knew what it was Alexandria was after. "No, Alex, Connie didn't drop him on purpose. She did everything in her power to hold onto him. In the end, he just let go."

Alexandria nodded and stood. "I knew that. I just needed to hear it from you."

"Did you doubt it?"

"Well, I wondered. I mean, if I were in her position . . . well, let's just say, I thought about what I might have done."

"Rest assured, Alex, Connie hung on for as long as she could."

Alex nodded. "With Internal Affairs, the Chief of Police, and the Mayor all pressing to find out whether or not one of their cops killed a man, you see why I needed to hear it from you."

Delta grinned. "That's politics for you. Forget the fact that the asshole got what he deserved, we just don't want to look bad in the public eye. That kills me."

"I'm sorry."

"Me, too."

"How's your leg doing?"

Delta shrugged. "Hurts like hell still, but I manage." Delta squinted in the sunlight and wondered what it was Alexandria was struggling with so much. "Alex, are you okay?"

"Me? I'm fine. I just wish things could be different, that's all."

"You and me both. But you won't hear me complaining. I've got my lover, my best friend, and her lover all safely tucked away. I'll take whatever consequence comes my way, knowing that I'd do it all again if I had to."

A warm smile spread across Alexandria's face. "The world could use a few more women like you. I'm glad we're on the same side."

Delta's smile equalled Alexandria's. "Me, too." Watching Alexandria climb into her maroon Porsche, Delta smiled to herself.

A few more Delta's?

What a scary thought.

52

"You two sure you have everything?" Delta asked, peering under the huge blue tarp covering their camping gear.

Connie checked her list and then looked over at Gina. Gina had lost weight over the past week and had a few nightmares, but other than that, she bounced back from her ordeal quite well.

"Ask my co-pilot. She's the one who packed."

Gina gave Delta the thumbs up. "Yosemite, here we come!"

Connie hugged Megan before turning to Delta. "I wish you'd change your mind about coming. We'd have so much fun."

Delta shook her head, as she gingerly patted her thigh. "This bad wheel would only hold you back. El Capitan will just have to wait until next year."

Reaching out, Connie held Delta for a long, long time. "I can never repay you, you know."

"Don't have to." Delta stepped back and smoothed her hand through Connie's hair. "You'd have been there for me, and that's what we're all about. Now get out of here before we both start bawling."

Smiling into Delta's eyes, Connie opened the car door and got in. "You two take care of each other."

Megan threaded her arm through Delta's. "We will. As a matter of fact, that's the first order of business."

"Good. We expect you two to be on firm ground when we return."

Waving goodbye to the campers, Delta slid her arms around Megan's waist and pulled her closer. "A vacation is just what they need."

Megan turned in Delta's embrace and peered into her eyes. "And what do we need, my love?"

Delta gazed into the electric eyes that held her like a magnet. "I don't really know. I understand that love isn't enough. I love you, and I know you love me, but—"

"But you love your job, too." Megan opened the screen door and watched Delta walk through. "You're right. Love isn't enough."

"But it's a start."

Megan nodded as she sat on the couch. "It's where we've been since we met. But if we're going to make it, there's more we have to build."

Delta held her breath, as she sat next to Megan. "I hate that word 'if'."

"So do I, but honey, we have to be realistic. Lesbian relationships fail because we hang our hats on love, and love alone. I wish it were enough, but it's not."

Delta stared at her hands folded in her lap. How could she be so good at reading people on the streets and so poor at analyzing her own relationships?

"Megan, I love you more than anyone I've ever loved. I don't care what it takes to make this work, as long as it does work. Tell me what I need to do."

"I know you love me. I don't ever question that. What I do wonder is, if you had to choose between dinner with me and busting a major case, which one would it be?"

Delta didn't answer the rhetorical question.

"See? In all honesty, you don't think twice about jumping into danger. Well, I need you to think twice. I need you to care about getting hurt, to care about coming home safely. I need you to care about our relationship first."

"And you don't think I do?"

Megan looked at her but said nothing.

"Suppose I can't? I mean, suppose I try to put us first, and we discover that I can't?"

"Then, I'll have to make some decisions for myself, won't I?"

"You'd leave?" Delta asked, grabbing Megan's hand.

"I don't know what I would do."

Delta thought about this a minute and then measured her words carefully. "Megan, I know that I'm a good cop, and I know that I'm an excellent partner to Jan. Something in me tells me that I can be a good partner to you, too, if you'll just show me. Help me learn what it takes to make a relationship work."

Taking Delta's face in her hands, Megan lightly kissed her mouth. "The first step is over. See how easy that was?"

"What step?"

Megan smiled. "Communication, my love. The first step is telling me that you want to learn, that you want to grow."

"I do. I've just never wanted to before."

Pulling Delta to her, Megan kissed the top of her head. "Well, I'm glad you want to with me. I love you, Delta Stevens, and I know how deeply you love me. If you're willing to try, we're going to be just fine." Holding Delta to her, Megan gently rocked back and forth, stroking Delta's curly hair.

Closing her eyes, Delta nestled against Megan's chest and listened to her heartbeat. There she was, Officer Delta "Storm" Stevens, saver of lives, pursuer of evil, hero of the young and old, and she didn't even know how to make a relationship work. How could she be so good at one thing and so incredibly lousy at another? What had she said the other day to Alexandria about the needs of the many outweighing the needs of the few? It was ironic that the needs of the many should affect her life so much. Maybe that was what Megan meant. Maybe that was the problem. Maybe it was time to pay more attention to the needs of the few; the needs of the one.

"Megan?"

"Yes, babe?"

"I love you with all my heart."

"I know."

Linda Kay Silva, an ex-cop and ex-teacher, now manages a children's fitness center in northern California. She has completed the third and fourth novels of the *Storm* Series, as well as a medieval romance, and is currently working on the fifth *Storm* novel. When she isn't writing (which isn't often), Linda Kay can be found playing with her new dog, Shasta, or travelling to the Costa Rican rainforest to see how she can help preserve it.

Paradigm Publishing Company, a women owned press, was founded to publish works created within communities of diversity. These communities are empowering themselves and society by the creation of new paradigms which are inclusive of diversity. We are here to raise their voices.

Books Published by Paradigm Publishing:

Taken By Storm by Linda Kay Silva
(Lesbian Fiction/Mystery)
A Delta Stevens police action novel, intertwining mystery, love, and personal insight. The first in a series. ISBN 0-9628595-1-6 $8.95
". . . not to be missed!" — *East Bay Alternative*

Expenses by Penny S. Lorio (Lesbian Fiction/Romance)
A novel that deals with the cost of living and the price of loving. ISBN 0-9628595-0-8 $8.95
"I laughed, I cried, I wanted more!" — Marie Kuda, *Gay Chicago Magazine*

Tory's Tuesday by Linda Kay Silva (Lesbian Fiction)
Linda Kay Silva's second novel is set in Bialystok, Poland during 1939 Nazi occupation. Marissa, a Pole, and Elsa, a Jew, are two lovers who struggle not only to stay together, but to stay alive in Auschwitz concentration camp during the horrors of World War II. ISBN 0-9628595-3-2 $8.95
"Obviously knowledgeable about the period, Silva builds a historical framework around her various characters, drawing in the reader with her steady prose and effective dialogue." — Terri de la Pena, *Lambda Book Report*

"*Tory's Tuesday* is a book that should be widely read — with tissues close at hand — and long remembered." — Andrea L.T. Peterson, *The Washington Blade*

Practicing Eternity by Carol Givens and L. Diane Fortier
(Nonfiction/Healing/Lesbian and Women's Studies)
The powerful, moving testament of partners in a long-term lesbian relationship in the face of Carol's diagnosis with cervical cancer. It is about women living, loving, dying together. It is about trans-formation of the self, relationships, and life. **Finalist** for the ***Lambda Literary Awards***! ISBN 0-9628595-2-4 $10.95

"*Practicing Eternity* is one of the most personal and moving stories I have read in years." —Margaret Wheat, *We The People*

"That they . . . recorded every deed and every thought of this harrowing period of their life together is the richness and reward of this book, the essence that makes the reading of it a matter of conscious decision for all of us." — Barbara Grier, *Lambda Book Report*

"I more than recommend it . . . it should be required reading." — Shelly Roberts, *Arts, Entertainment and Travel*

Seasons of Erotic Love by Barbara Herrera
(Lesbian Erotica)
A soft and sensual collection of lesbian erotica with a social conscience. By taking us through the loving of an incest survivor, lesbian safe sex, loving a large woman, and more, Herrera leaves us empowered with the diversity in the lesbian community. ISBN 0-9628595-4-0 $8.95

". . . the sex is juicy and in full supply." —Nedhara Landers, *Lambda Book Report*

Evidence of the Outer World by Janet Bohac
(Women's Short Stories)
Janet Bohac, whose writing has appeared in various literary publications, brings us a powerful collection of feminist and women centered fiction. By examining relationships in this symmetry of short stories, the author introduces us to Dory and a cast of characters who observe interaction with family, parent and child, men and women, and women and women. ISBN 0-9628595-5-9 $8.95

". . . an insightful collection of stories . . . enjoyable and easy to read." —Andrea L.T. Peterson, *Baltimore Alternative*

The Dyke Detector
(How to Tell the Real Lesbians from Ordinary People)
by Shelly Roberts/Illustrated by Yani Batteau
(Lesbian Humor)

The Dyke Detector is lesbian humor at its finest: poking fun at our most intimate patterns and outrageous stereotypes with a little bit of laughter for everybody, single or coupled. This is side-splitting fun from syndicated columnist Shelly Roberts, and every dyke, lesbian, gay woman, and anyone else who has ever been curious will thoroughly enjoy it. ISBN 0-9628595-6-7 $7.95

"What a riot! A must read for all lesbians. Brilliant!" — JoAnn Loulan

"To say that *The Dyke Detector* is a funny book would be like saying that Somalia is a poor country." —Jesse Monteagudo, *TWN*

"A humorous guide to identifying women with that sexual orientation." —*Chicago Tribune*

Storm Shelter by Linda Kay Silva (Lesbian Mystery)

Officer Delta Stevens is back in the long awaited sequel to *Taken By Storm*. And Delta will have to use every bit of her courage and determination to capture a killer who is terrorizing people on her beat and murdering them with bizarre and ancient weapons. Delta and her best friend, Connie Rivera, again join together in a deadly race against time. Only now, they must enter the complex world of computer games in order to solve the mystery before the murderer can strike again. *Taken By Storm*, the first of the series, received rave reviews. In the sequel, Silva has done it again!
ISBN 0-9628595-8-3 $10.95

EMPATH by Michael Holloway (Gay Fiction/Sci-fi)

In an era when making love can kill you, *EMPATH* views that horror from a variety of different angles—some of which may shock and surprise you. This is a story of industrial politics, and how one man with supernatural abilities is thrust into this vortex to single-handedly eliminate the AIDS epidemic. This is a book about AIDS that has a **happy** ending and it will keep you on the edge of your seat!
ISBN 0-9628595-7-5 $10.95

<u>Ordering Information</u>

California residents add appropriate sales tax.

Postage and Handling—Domestic Orders: $2 for the first book/$.50 for each additional book. Foreign Orders: $2.50 for the first book/$1 for each additional book (surface mail).

Make check or money order, in U.S. currency, payable to: Paradigm Publishing Company, P.O. Box 3877, San Diego, CA 92163.